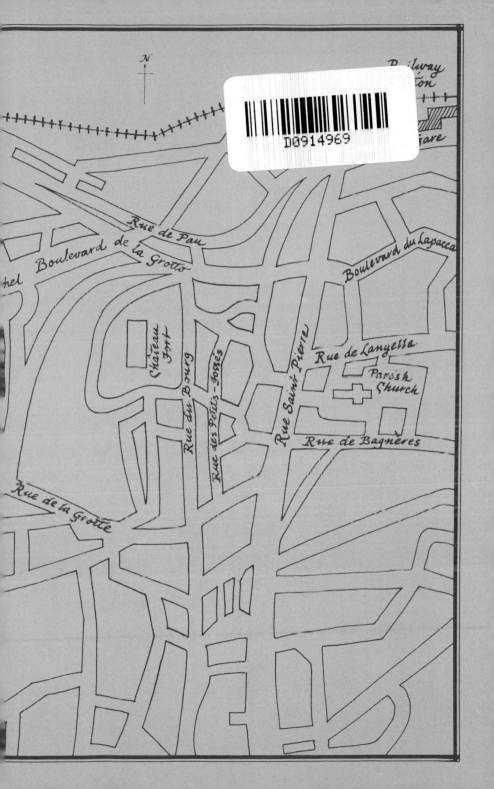

The Miracle

The Miracle

A NOVEL

Irving Wallace

E. P. DUTTON, INC.

NEW YORK

Published in the United States by
E. P. Dutton, Inc., 2 Park Avenue, New York, N.Y. 10016

Published simultaneously in Canada
by Fitzhenry & Whiteside Limited, Toronto

For

Elijah

"They say miracles are past."
—SHAKESPEARE, c.1602

"The age of Miracles past?
The Age of Miracles is forever here!"
—THOMAS CARLYLE, 1841

"For those who believe in God,
no explanation is necessary;
for those who do not believe in God,
no explanation is possible."
—REV. JOHN LA FARGE, S.J.

The Miracle

1

The Third Secret

It had been a dark night, gradually graying, the darkness before the dawn, and it was six o'clock in the morning when the small, pretty peasant girl, Bernadette Soubirous, came down from the hill to the cave gouged out of rock, the grotto of Massabielle. There were already 150 people waiting for her, watching her, waiting for what would happen next.

Bernadette, wearing a white capulet, a patched second-hand dress, and wooden clogs, put a light to her candle, took the rosary from her pocket, and with a smile, bowed toward the vision that she expected to see.

Twelve days earlier, while standing near this spot, she had seen the apparition in the grotto, "a Lady dressed in white" as Bernadette would later recall, a mysterious young Lady wearing "a white dress, a white veil, a blue sash, and a yellow rose on each foot." There had been seven visits by Bernadette to the grotto in those twelve days, and the Lady had appeared before her on six of these occasions, the Lady who would eventually, after fifteen appearances, identify herself as the Immaculate Conception, the Virgin Mary.

This dark Tuesday morning of February 23, 1858, was Bernadette's eighth visit to the grotto. At the grotto, with a smile, she awaited the return of the Lady who would soon identify herself as the Virgin.

Among the 150 persons present, there was at least one cynic, Jean-Baptiste Estrade, a tax official and an important man in the nearby market town of Lourdes.

Estrade had brought his sister, Emmanuélite, and several of her curious women friends to witness the much discussed spectacle. On the way to the grotto he had joked about this superstitious nonsense. "Have you brought your opera glasses?" he had asked his companions. Now, joined with the spectators, he watched the peasant girl on her knees fingering her rosary. Afterward, he would record what he witnessed:

"Whilst she was passing the beads between her fingers she looked up toward the rock as though waiting for something. Suddenly, as in a flash of lightning, an expression of wonder illuminated her face and she seemed to be born into another life. A light shone in her eyes; wonderful smiles played upon her lips; an unutterable grace transfigured her whole being . . . Bernadette was no longer Bernadette; she was one of the privileged beings, the face all glorious with the glory of heaven. . . .

"The ecstasy lasted for an hour; at the end of that time the seer went on her knees from the place where she was praying to just below the wild rose tree hanging from the rock. There, concentrating all her energies as for an act of worship, she kissed the earth and returned still upon her knees to the place which she had just left. A last glow of light lit up her face, then gradually, almost imperceptibly, the transfiguring glory of the ecstasy grew fainter and finally disappeared. The seer continued praying for a few moments longer but it was only the face of the little peasant child which I saw. At last Bernadette got up, went to her mother, and was lost in the crowd."

Climbing the hill toward home with her mother, Bernadette repeated a portion of the conversation that she had just had with the mysterious Lady. During the apparitions, the Lady had confided three secrets to her, and this morning she had revealed the third and last of them.

Shortly after, when the converted cynic, Estrade, had become Bernadette's friend, he had asked her "what the Lady had said to her during the seventh Appearance," and he learned "that three secrets had been entrusted to her but that they concerned nobody but herself. The seer added that she could not reveal these secrets to anyone, not even to her confessor. Inquisitive people have often tried by insinuations, by trickery, or by promises, to get these revelations of the Virgin out of the child. But all attempts failed and Bernadette carried her secrets with her to the grave."

On another occasion, a young lawyer from a nearby town, Charles Madon, dared to bring up the subject once more.

"And your secrets? What are they about?"

"They concern only me."

"If the Pope were to ask you for them, would you tell them to him?"

"No."

Years later, when Bernadette had become a nun in the convent of Saint Gildard—in Nevers, in central France—her harsh and distrusting superior, Mother Marie Thérèse Vauzou, the Mistress of Novices, had posed the question about the secrets once more. Bernadette had again refused to reveal the secrets.

"Suppose the Pope required you tell under obedience," Mother Vauzou had demanded.

"I can't see how it could be any concern of his," Bernadette had replied.

After reading this historical report from the Lourdes Commission, Pope John Paul III, Vicar of Jesus Christ, Supreme Pontiff of the Universal Church, lowered the pages and chuckled. "But now, suddenly, almost 130 years later, those secrets *are* the concern of a pope."

"Yes, Your Holiness," said his secretary of state. "Especially the final secret given to Saint Bernadette during the seventh apparition."

They were in the Pope's spacious and ornate private office on the top floor of the Vatican. From his high-backed white satin chair, behind the neat papal desk, Pope John Paul III stared past the gold damask drapes framing the clear recessed windows that overlooked St. Peter's Square. He turned back to the cardinal, his secretary of state, who sat in one of the red satin armchairs across from him.

"And now," said the Pope, "we know all three of Bernadette's secrets. Of that you are certain?"

"No question," said the cardinal. "The full documentation, from the Commission of Lourdes, is in your hands."

"This is absolutely authentic?"

"As you will see, Your Holiness. The first two secrets are minor, and have come to pass, and are of no interest to us. The third secret, the last, as you have agreed, could be momentous. All that remains is for Your Holiness to decide if we should disclose the third secret to the world."

The Pope was thoughtful. "When must I give my decision?"

"By week's end, it is hoped, Your Holiness. The Commission of Lourdes will remain in session until you inform them of the course to take. The Great French National Pilgrimage is to begin in three weeks."

"The commission—" said the Pope. "Does the commission have a recommendation?"

"They have put it entirely in your hands, Your Holiness," said the cardinal. He hesitated. "I happen to have heard from Father Ruland in Lourdes that a few of the clergy and all of the local merchants on the commission favor disclosure. They insist that any announcement will heighten interest in the holy shrine, and that the entire community, in fact the entire world, will benefit from this. The other members of the commission, all clerics, are either against disclosure, or reluctant to have it made, lest Bernadette's secret rebounds and fails to serve the best interests of the Mother Church. But Bishop Peyragne, who heads the commission, told me quite correctly that the final word must be your own."

The Pope nodded, considering the documents before him. "I will study what is here. I will meditate upon this discovery. I will pray for wisdom. Certainly you shall have my decision by week's end, by Friday."

The secretary of state came briskly to his feet. "Very well." Before turning away, he gazed intently at the Holy Father. "If I may inject a comment of my own—"

"Please."

"There is grave risk in this, Your Holiness."

The Pope smiled. A worldly man, he replied cheerfully, "God will know the odds."

When the discovery had been made, and purchased secretly by the church, Bishop Peyragne of Tarbes and Lourdes had seen fit to appoint a commission of inquiry—the Lourdes Commission, the weekly local newspaper *L'Essor Bigourdan* called it, and reminded readers that this was the second time in the city's modern history that there had been such a board of notables. The editors and readers wondered about the reason for the appointment of such a commission, having been told only that the members were to discuss "a historical discovery of great significance." Speculation ran rampant, but no one outside the commission had even the faintest idea of what was going on.

The first commission of inquiry, appointed by an earlier bishop of Tarbes and Lourdes, Bertrand-Sévère Laurence, in November of 1858, had been constituted with a clear purpose. Its nine members had been selected to investigate the young Bernadette's experience and determine if, indeed, she had received a vision from God. After four years of study, a decision had been arrived at, and the bishop of Tarbes and Lourdes had announced it to the world: "We judge that Mary the Immaculate Mother of God, did really appear to Bernadette Soubirous on the 11th February, 1858, and on certain subsequent days, eighteen times in all, in the grotto of Massabielle near the town of Lourdes; that this apparition bears every mark of truth; and that the belief of the faithful is well grounded. . . . We authorize the cult of Our Lady of the Grotto of Lourdes in our diocese."

That had been the verdict of the first Lourdes commission of inquiry in 1862.

Now, so long after, the sixteen members of the second Lourdes commission of inquiry were gathering in a conference room of the Town Hall not to make a decision but to hear the decision made by the Supreme Pontiff of the Universal Church in Vatican City. After six fruitless weeks of debate, the members had been unable to reach a decision of their own.

Unable to get a majority on one side or the other, the bishop of Tarbes and Lourdes had forwarded the findings, and the authentication, to the archbishop in Toulouse, who had advised that in a matter so divisive and controversial, the final decision must be left to His Holiness, the Pope, in Rome.

And now, having been alerted that the Pope would have word for them this very morning, the members of the commission had assembled. While the members were largely religion-minded, the setting—the conference room of the Town Hall—was secular, a delicate arrangement made by the bishop at the suggestion of Father Ruland, the Lourdes historian, who himself professed to be neutral in the matter to be decided.

Even though their arguments were no longer meaningful, members of the commission were still embattled when the telephone had rung in Mayor Jourdain's next-door office. Father Emery, one of the ten parish priests in Lourdes, was saying, "To make such an announcement presents a danger to the church, to the faithful, to the town. Any failure can invite disillusionment and mockery, and discredit what we stand for. I say let things be as they are." His opposing number across the long table, Jean-Claude Jamet, owner of an important tourist restaurant in Lourdes, was responding as before, "We must make this announcement, and thereby create a revival of interest in religion and also encourage in pilgrims a desire to come here in great number. By making this announcement we can halt the falling away in faith."

The telephone call in the adjacent office had put a restraint of silence on any further debate. Mayor Jourdain had left the conference room to take the call, then momentarily returned to summon the bishop and Father Ruland.

For the members, the wait had seemed interminable, but in fact it had lasted no longer than two minutes.

Again, the tall, rangy bishop was at the head of the table. In his stark black cassock, he resembled an austere authoritarian figure who had stepped out of an El Greco canvas.

His voice was low and strong, his words clipped and firm.

"The Pope wishes us to arrange to have Bernadette's secret announced to the world—yes, announced to the world—at once. Not to do so, His Holiness remarked, would be a profession of lack of faith. His Holiness added, one assumes jocularly, that he, for one, remains a true believer."

The bishop paused, and glanced about the room. With the decision, disagreement had evaporated. They were all in this together, and excitement was evident.

"That settles it," resumed the bishop. "I shall notify the archbishop in Toulouse to proceed immediately with arrangements for a public announcement by Cardinal Brunet in Paris." He offered a frosty smile. "The crucial eight days, beginning three weeks from now, will be the most momentous and critical in Lourdes' history since that afternoon when Bernadette heard the sound of a gust of wind and saw the Lady in white materialize in the grotto. And, I am certain, the announcement will be momentous and critical for the many people on earth who will hear it and make their way to our beloved Lourdes."

Usually, when Liz Finch drove her second-hand Citroën from the Place de la Concorde up the Champs Élysées in the mad and unruly Parisian traffic, she remained keenly aware of the magnificent structure of the Arc de Triomphe far ahead. The noble Arc was for her the symbol of everything that Paris offered—classical beauty, wonder, excitement, and support and promise for the life she wanted to live here.

The Arc translated her dreams and ambitions into reality. It helped her see herself in tomorrow's Paris: a highly paid and renowned yet literary foreign correspondent such as the admirable Janet Flanner had been; a sophisticated hostess with an exquisite apartment on the Île St.-Louis, the envied wife of a mature, wealthy, and handsome French business executive (of worldly intellect and devoted sexuality, who possessed admiration for America and who had brought to the marriage an incredible collection of French primitive art); the mother of two brilliant children, who played in the Luxembourg Gardens under the supervision of a warm and intelligent British nanny. When Liz Finch saw the Arc ahead, she saw beneath its soaring curve this life for herself, and even the leisure to absorb and charm friends of the international set, each a "Name" in his or her field, during her weekly Sunday salons.

But this morning, possibly for the first time in her three years in Paris, Liz Finch's second self was not fixed on the Arc de Triomphe. Instead, when not concentrating on the insane traffic, she was studying the reflection of herself in the Citroën's not-too-flattering rearview mirror.

What Liz Finch could see of herself did little to kindle dreams. What she could see of herself dampened any hope of fulfilling her ambitions, of even remaining in Paris very much longer.

Because when Liz Finch had sneaked a look at the memorandum on Bill Trask's desk at Amalgamated Press International this morning, and then received her day's assignment from Trask and learned the assignment that her rival, Marguerite Lamarche, had been given, Liz realized that she had lost, or was losing. She was entered, she felt, in a beauty contest, not a talent contest, and when it came to beauty she had no chance.

The private memorandum on his desk had come from New York. It had stated that New York demanded a retrenchment in the Paris Bureau of API to take effect in one month. The French force in the office, mostly clerical, would be cut in half. As for the editorial staff, instead of two feature correspondents there was room for only one. Since the two feature correspondents were Marguerite Lamarche and herself, one of them would remain, with greater responsibility and a more solid job, and the other would be cast out, in Liz's case to oblivion. While Trask had mentioned the necessity of a cutback, he had been vague as to details. But Liz knew the truth and it was threatening.

When Liz had come off that Wisconsin newspaper for a better position in API's Manhattan office, and then been assigned to the prestigious Paris Bureau three years ago, her life had dramatically changed and had become thrilling and full of hope. She had, lately, even met a young business executive, Parisian and attractive, who found her interesting and even complimented her on her French. It was a relationship that might develop slowly, given a year or two. But a month? If she was fired, in a month she would be forced to leave France and there would be no chance with Charles. And there would be no opportunity to develop her byline. She would be lucky to wind up doing routine work in Cedar Rapids or Cheyenne, and lucky to marry an insurance salesman, and have two cretins for children.

The whole thing, then, came down to beating Marguerite out for the single feature-writer job that would exist at API in a month. And that's where it came down to a beauty contest, and Liz didn't like her prospects. Liz knew that she was a more gifted reporter and writer than Marguerite, but less attractive. Liz was the office workhorse, covering drab bread-and-butter assignments, everything from the French economy to the auto shows. Inevitably, Marguerite had been awarded the more glamorous assignments, the fashion shows, interviews with famous politicians, authors, movie stars.

This morning's latest assignments had proved it.

There had been a plum of a story waiting to be assigned, and Liz had prayed to get it and prove herself as the basic whiz reporter the bureau must keep, but instead Trask had offered the plum to Marguerite Lamarche. It was way over Marguerite's frivolous head.

Bill Trask had got himself a lead—oh, he was good at those hot tips—that the charismatic minister of the interior, André Viron, heading for the seat of prime minister, was teetering on the brink of disaster, a potential national scandal, having had some questionable dealings with a shady underground character named Weidman. Weidman, owner of a sleazy movie production company that fronted for his small-time cocaine ring, had managed to make a tie-in to float some fraudulent bonds for big money, and had obtained Minister of the Interior Viron's endorsement. The money poured in, but the value of the bonds was undependable. The question was whether Viron had trusted Weidman and had acted as an innocent or whether he was in secret association with Weidman to line his already-gold-lined pockets. To Bill Trask, this smelled like another Stavisky Affair, which had so enlivened and disrupted France in the 1930s.

Really, it had been a perfect assignment for Liz Finch to sink her teeth into. But an hour ago, it had gone to Marguerite Lamarche. And Liz, instead, had been given this unpromising religion assignment, a press conference by Cardinal Brunet of Paris to be held in the Hôtel Plaza Athénée. Some dopey nitpicking religious announcement to be covered. As if anyone who counted in the New York office would pay the slightest attention to it.

Marguerite had got the plum because she might seduce Viron into confiding the truth. Liz had been thrown a bone because nature had prepared her to seduce no one.

It was all reflected in her rearview mirror.

She saw the mop of red hair, become orange in the last rinse-and-color job. She saw the predator's beak of a nose that couldn't even be called Roman. The lips were two thin tight lines, the jaw undershot. Despite the fair, unblemished complexion, she was dismayed. She knew that what could not be seen in the mirror was even worse. Her breasts were unfashionably large and they sagged. There was too much hip and she was slightly bowlegged. In sum, her five-foot-three frame added up to disaster. The best part of her—and this was the real cruelty of nature —could not be seen: her mind. She was brainy, inventive, tenacious.

But this mind was also unsparing. Relentlessly, it conjured up Marguerite Lamarche floating through the city room. Marguerite, twenty-eight and four years her junior, had been made to be a model, and had indeed once been a model briefly. She was tall, slender, graceful, with glossy dark hair, the small perfect features of a pretty geisha, full pouting ruby lips, enviable small firm French breasts, long legs. And a banal brain. But who cared? It was just goddam unfair.

Then the thought came to Liz, as she turned her car into the Avenue Montaigne, that Bill Trask had awarded Marguerite the plum assignment not because he wanted her to seduce Interior Minister Viron but because he wanted to seduce her himself. Maybe already had.

Liz Finch groaned inwardly. If her assessment was correct, and it probably was, her chances of winning the single API post in the next month were nil. Marguerite would have a big scandal, a beat, to showcase herself to the top brass. Liz would have dregs, such as she was going to now.

She pulled up before the Plaza Athénée, and braked to a stop. The uniformed doorman opened her door, greeting her with a courteous but not, unhappily, a flirtatious smile. Liz snatched up her work purse, the bulging scuffed brown one, and hurried into the hotel. There were several fat and swarthy Mideastern types lolling about in the spacious lobby, and not one gave her so much as a glance.

Heading for the elevator in the second smaller lobby, the gallery in which guests had afternoon tea, Liz tried to remember where in the hell she was going. She had intended to go to the Montaigne Room downstairs, but before reaching the elevator she remembered her destination and halted. When Trask had given her the assignment, he had also handed her the telegram announcing that Maurice Cardinal Brunet, archbishop of Paris, would have an important announcement to make at a press conference in the Salon Régence of the Plaza Athénée hotel at ten o'clock this morning. So it was the Salon Régence, the most important of the hotel's public rooms. Liz spun about and started up the gallery toward the doorway of the salon. She tried to think what the Catholic Church could have to announce that was so important. It would likely be some minor canonical reform. Boring. Dead weight on the API wire.

Passing through the open glass doors, Liz was mildly surprised at the large turnout this ecclesiastical press conference had attracted. The long, narrow, stately room, with its three grand chandeliers and carved brown paneled walls, was packed with reporters. Edging her way to the rear, to the table beneath the huge oil of Louis XV where coffee was being dispensed, Liz realized that there was a general stir in the room, that the conference was about to begin, and that those reporters still standing were taking seats.

Going for the nearest empty padded chair, Liz recognized Brian Evans, the cherubic Paris correspondent for the London *Observer*, whom she knew from countless cocktail parties. "Brian," she called out, "whatever is going on here? Look at the crowd."

Evans came to her side, and said in an undertone, "I have it that the church is going to spring a super big story from Lourdes. No idea what, but since Lourdes doesn't do this often, it could amount to something. That's all I know."

"We'll see," said Liz doubtfully, and she sat herself down on the empty chair, snapped her purse open, and removed her pad and pencil.

She was just about organized, when she heard the tall glass entrance doors being shut and became aware that at the far end of the room someone on the small temporary platform positioned before the marble fireplace, someone in a clerical collar and surplice, was concluding a brief introduction. She heard, "Maurice Cardinal Brunet," and saw a bespectacled stout older man, also attired in clerical dress, come to the podium. He was carrying two sheets of paper and he placed them carefully on the lectern. He adjusted his horn-rimmed glasses.

"I have a brief statement to read," he said in French, in a loud, hoarse voice. "After the statement, I will entertain ten minutes of questions from the floor."

At once, he began to read his statement:

"Everyone in this room surely knows the story of Saint Bernadette of Lourdes, the story of the blessed Bernadette Soubirous and her visions of the Virgin Mary at the grotto of Massabielle in Lourdes during 1858. In response to prayers at the grotto and the use of water from the spring found by Bernadette, cures of the disabled and ailing began almost immediately. In time, there have been nearly seventy sudden cures that the church has declared to be of miraculous origin. As a result, Lourdes is recognized as the leading miracle shrine in the world.

"In addition to the matters of faith which the Virgin Mary discussed with Bernadette, there were three secrets that were conveyed to her, and, indeed, Bernadette kept these three secrets to herself up to her very death. However, as it has recently been learned, Bernadette confided her secrets to a journal that she kept after she departed Lourdes to become a nun at the Convent of Saint Gildard in Nevers, and which she left in the safekeeping of a family relative in Bartrès.

"Bernadette's journal has now been found. Its holograph contents have been scientifically authenticated.

"We now know that, in this journal, in her own hand, Bernadette recorded the three secrets told her by the Virgin Mary. Two of the secrets, minor ones, personal ones, have already come true. The third secret, the one imparted to Bernadette during the seventh apparition of the Virgin Mary on February 23, 1858, has not yet come true."

The cardinal paused and then resumed. "Bernadette recorded a date and time when she was told it would come true, and that time is three weeks from this day in this very year. At the instigation of His Holiness, Pope John Paul III, and with the approval of the Holy Father, that third secret conveyed to Bernadette by the Virgin Mary is being revealed to the world today.

"The Mother of Heaven's secret was this—

"That She, the Virgin Mary, would reappear at the grotto of Massabielle in Lourdes in the twentieth century. 'She told me,' wrote Bernadette, 'that She would reappear as I had seen Her, would make Herself known to another and effect a miracle cure. She told me not to reveal this secret to anyone while I was on earth, but before I ascended to heaven, I could leave word of Her visitation in writing if I wished. Therefore, I make this record in my private journal so that one day it will be read by others.' Then Bernadette noted the year and date of the Virgin Mary's reappearance. The year is this year, and the date is three weeks from now, and during the period of eight days that follow, between August 14 and 22, henceforth to be known as The Reappearance Time.

"This is the Holy Father's news for the world.

"The Blessed Virgin Mary is returning to Lourdes."

Liz Finch sat, her pencil in a hand which had frozen over her notepad. She sat unmoving, her mind utterly boggled.

Behind her desk, on the third floor of the API building on the Rue des Italiens, Liz Finch finished writing the weird news story, ran it off on the printer beside her word processor, then gathered up the pages and took them over to Bill Trask's glassed-in office.

Trask, in rolled-up shirt sleeves, his bulk solid in a wooden swivel chair, was marking possible leads in a copy of the latest edition of *Le Figaro.* As ever, Liz could not take her eyes off Trask's hair. He affected to comb his hair the way his journalistic idol, H. L. Mencken, had combed his in Baltimore in the 1920s. It was unbecoming. She wondered what his probable paramour Marguerite thought of it.

Stiffly, Liz handed the story to Trask. "All done. Have a look."

Trask read the lead and lifted his eyebrows. "No kidding," he muttered. He read on and raised his eyebrows again. "This'll bring half the world pouring into Lourdes."

Trask was deep in the story once more. He read the second page and the third. He handed it back to Liz. "Good, very good. I like it. No changes. Put it through."

Liz hesitated. "You think it deserves this much space?"

"Sure. Why not? It's big news."

Liz was feeling defiant. "It's crap, Bill, and you know it. Surely you don't believe a bit of this nonsense, do you?"

With effort, Trask sat up in his chair. "Honey," he said, "I'm not here to believe or not to believe. Most of the 740,000,000 Catholics in the world believe it. Most of the five million persons of every faith who go to Lourdes every year believe it. The five thousand who claim they've enjoyed cures at the grotto believe it. The almost-seventy lucky ones whose miracle cures have been confirmed believe it. That's good enough to make the encore appearance of the Virgin Mary news, and that's all I'm interested in."

"Well, I still say bullshit," said Liz, "and I'm glad to be through with it."

She had turned to leave the office when Trask stopped her. "Hold on, honey." He waited for her to face him. "You're not through with it, Liz. You're just starting with it. I'm sending you to Lourdes for a play-by-play account. That's your next major assignment."

It was a body blow and Liz winced. "How do you want me to warm up for this, Bill? By doing a profile story on Cinderella or Goldilocks and the Three Bears? Please don't waste me on this, Bill. Some stringer can do it, for all that will happen. There's just no story. Why don't you give me something I can get my teeth into—like—well, like the Viron scandal."

Trask's countenance was expressionless. "I'm sure Marguerite is competent enough to handle Viron. She has Viron. You have the Virgin. Don't try to rewrite me, Liz. Just get me an eyewitness piece on the return of the Virgin, and you'll have a big one, big enough to make everyone happy."

She was tempted to go to the mat with Trask, tell him he was only insuring her dismissal by sending her to that holier-than-thou hick town in the Pyrenees. Whereas he had given Marguerite a sure thing, and it wasn't fair, wasn't fair at all.

But she could see only the top of his head now, the formidable Mencken hairstyle, and she knew that he was done with her and bent to his work. She saw that it was no use fighting further.

Sensing her presence, he growled without looking up, "Get going, young lady. File it. There are plenty of poor souls out there waiting to be saved."

"Fuck them all," she said under her breath, and turned to leave, and deliver the news, wondering who on earth could possibly believe it.

2

Chicago and Biarritz

It was a half-block's walk from the parking lot to Dr. Whitney's twenty-third floor suite of offices in the high rise in Chicago's Loop, just across from the elevated, and although the drizzle was light this morning, it had been enough to saturate Amanda Spenser's jaunty blue rain hat and blue raincoat. In the hall, going toward Dr. Whitney's suite, Amanda removed her soggy rain gear, and paused briefly in the ladies' room to see if the hat had messed her neat bobbed brown hair. It had, indeed. She patted her hair into place, took off her tinted blue-rimmed prescription glasses which she used for driving, wiped them dry, tucked them into her purse, and headed for her appointment with Ken Clayton's physician.

Once inside the tasteful reception room, the fabrics on the furniture all a restful pale green, Amanda hung her hat and coat on the wooden coatrack and went directly to the gray-haired receptionist behind the counter.

The woman was expecting her. "Miss Spenser?"

"Right on time, I hope."

"Oh, yes. But I'm afraid the doctor is running a few minutes behind. He'll be with you shortly. I know he's eager to see you. If you don't mind taking a seat—"

"Not at all."

"By the way, how is Mr. Clayton?"

"Still somewhat weak, but well enough to go to the office every morning and work a half day."

"I'm glad to hear that. He's such a wonderful young man. One of the most charming I've ever met. We all wish him the best, Miss Spenser."

"Thank you," said Amanda, taking a magazine from the wall rack, any magazine, in this case a medical magazine. Sitting, settling back, she thumbed through it. Pharmaceutical ads on every page. Then an article with color pictures and charts on diabetes. Amanda had no patience for it. She kept the periodical open on her lap, but blankly stared through it.

Yes, Amanda thought, the receptionist was right, Ken was extremely charming. Amanda had been charmed an hour after meeting him two summers ago. There had been a barbecue on the patio of the palatial residence of the elder Claytons', Ken's parents, on Chicago's North Shore. An informal outdoor dinner mostly for the members of Bernard B. Clayton's prestigious law firm, in which his son, Ken, was a partner specializing in estate planning. One of the firm's juniors had brought Amanda along.

After that, Amanda and Ken began seeing each other regularly, and within a year were living together in Amanda's five-room apartment off Michigan Boulevard. Everyone said they made a perfect couple. Ken, at thirty-three, was five foot eleven, with a shock of unruly black hair, collar-ad masculine features, brawny and athletic (a champion at handball). Amanda at thirty was equally trim (tennis her game), actually comely and fair, brown eyes wide set, a broad tip-tilted nose, a generous rosy mouth, a svelte figure, abundant bosom, shapely legs. And a brain, a brain as fine as Ken's.

Strangers were always surprised to learn that Amanda was a well-paid, full-time clinical psychologist, dividing her crowded days between a carefully limited private practice and an associate professor's post in the department of behavioral sciences at the University of Chicago. Her interest in psychology had been inspired by reading Alfred Adler at an early age. Her role model had been the psychoanalyst, Karen Horney, for Amanda the greatest woman in the field. The fact that the famed John B. Watson had got his Ph.D. at the University of Chicago helped direct her to that school, and learning that Carl Rogers had once been director of the University of Chicago Counseling Center encouraged her to serve there for a period, which in turn led to her current private practice.

She was busy, and so was Ken, and they had time for each other only late evenings and weekends. They spent more than half of their togetherness in bed. They were sexually compatible, and made love at least four times a week, and it was divine because Ken was thoughtful and experienced.

A year ago, secure in their relationship and their need for one another, they had decided to get married. Bernard and Helen Clayton, both devout Catholics, had wanted a formal church wedding, and Ken didn't care one way or the other, and neither did Amanda, whose Minnesota father had been a nonpracticing Catholic and her mother of no remembered religion at all.

The marriage had been planned for August of this year.

But then, one early evening, in the midst of a handball game, Ken collapsed. His right leg had given way, and he had folded up. His leg, actually his thigh, was causing him unremitting pain. This had been less than six weeks ago. Dr. Whitney, the Clayton family physician, had dispatched Ken on a round of specialists, examinations, tests, X rays.

Finally, the verdict was in. A sarcoma, a bone cancer. Deterioration of the bone tissue involving the head of the right femur, or thigh. Gradually, the disease would worsen. Ken would lose mobility, require crutches, eventually a wheelchair. Most likely, the cancer would be fatal. The options for a possible cure were threefold: surgery, radiation, chemotherapy. Was the condition operable? It was. Dr. Whitney began to investigate the chances of successful surgery. The prognosis was gloomy, the odds weighted against success, but still there were odds, and there was no alternative.

So surgery was settled upon. It was to be performed almost immediately. The Clayton wedding date, the marriage of Ken and Amanda, was indefinitely postponed.

Amanda considered her feelings. She felt like a widow, and she was not yet a bride.

But still there was the surgery. That was the hope.

"Miss Spenser," she heard the receptionist say. "Dr. Whitney can see you now."

The receptionist was holding the hall door open. Amanda, clutching her purse, was on her feet and through the door. She went down the short corridor, and turned into the doctor's private office, shutting the door behind her and wondering for what reason he had summoned her. It seemed a portent of some unhappiness.

Dr. Whitney half rose from his desk chair. "Miss Spenser," he said, and gestured her to a chair across from his desk. Dr. Whitney was one of those physicians whose very aspect inspired confidence. He had a square, nicely aging face, a few good wrinkles, a furrowed brow and hair whiting at the temples, not unlike those pseudomedicos in television commercials whose presence bespeak experience, wisdom, and authority.

As Amanda sat, Dr. Whitney lowered himself onto his leather chair, closed the manila folder on his desk, and went right to it. "Miss Spenser, I thought it best if we could talk face-to-face. I wanted to discuss Ken's surgery. I hope this sudden call didn't inconvenience you?"

"Nothing is more important than Ken's surgery."

"I know he told you about it, that it is the primary option we have."

"He told me a little. Just that there were no guarantees, but that there was a fair chance, and that he was going to go through with it. I was glad he was going ahead. I encouraged it." She hesitated. "What *are* his chances?"

Dr. Whitney measured his words. "With surgery, some. Without surgery, none. There is some advance work being done in this field, but I'm afraid it hasn't come to fruition yet. About a year ago, I read a paper by a Dr. Maurice Duval in Paris who had evolved a new technique, surgery and implants coupled with genetic engineering. But his experiments at that point, although fully successful, had involved mammals other than man. I discussed this with several highly accredited local surgeons, who had also heard of Duval's progress, but they felt that it was not ready to be applied to human beings as yet. So, since time is of the essence, we are left with the only surgery we know and can depend upon, standard bone surgery with replacement of the malignant portion of the femur. Sometimes it works successfully."

"Sometimes," Amanda echoed dully.

"Let me be more precise," said Dr. Whitney, "based on case histories of these surgeries. If undertaken right away, before there is more deterioration, Ken may have a 30 percent chance of getting rid of his cancer and being restored to normal life. But the fact remains, statistically, that there would also be a 70 percent chance of failure. Nevertheless, I repeat, there is no other choice but to go right ahead."

"Well, when do we go ahead?"

Dr. Whitney frowned. "We don't," he said simply. "I had the surgery scheduled for this week, but now the operation has been cancelled."

Amanda was on the edge of her chair. "For heaven's sake, why?"

"That's the reason I called you in today, as the one closest to Ken, to discuss the problem with you." Dr. Whitney cleared his throat and looked away. "I saw Ken late yesterday, and outlined one final time what had to be done. He approved, approved of the surgery. This morning, first thing, he telephoned me. He had changed his mind, was turning down the operation."

Amanda was shocked. "He what? He won't go through with it? I didn't talk to him this morning—he was still asleep—so I haven't heard about this. But it makes no sense. Are you sure? We had agreed surgery was his only chance."

"Apparently Ken doesn't think so. He now thinks there's a better course. Have you seen this morning's paper?"

"Not yet."

"Have a look." Dr. Whitney took the Chicago *Tribune* off the corner of his desk and held it out for Amanda. She surveyed the front page and was more bewildered than ever. "There's just some headline about Lourdes."

"Turn to page three. Read the full story."

Amanda opened the paper, and the headline hit her. VIRGIN MARY TO RETURN TO LOURDES. The story that followed was bylined by someone named Liz Finch, and it was datelined Paris.

Amanda hastily read the news story. When she was through, she let the paper drop to the floor, and met Dr. Whitney's eyes. She was aghast as the full import of what was happening struck her. "The Virgin Mary returning to Lourdes to perform a miracle? The hallucinating of an adolescent peasant girl over a century ago? Are you telling me Ken has read and believes in this?"

"Yes."

"Ken depending on a miracle to save him instead of surgery? Dr. Whitney, that's not like Ken, you know it isn't. He doesn't believe in miracles. He's hardly a churchgoer. You *know* him. He's reasonable, logical, intelligent—"

"Not anymore, he's not," said the physician. "Not when he's so desperate."

"But I'm telling you it's not like Ken."

"You know his mother fairly well, don't you? You know Helen Clayton is a fervent believer. Can you imagine how this story affected her? She was all over Ken at once. Since she doesn't like the surgeon's odds, she's decided that Lourdes will offer her son a better chance for complete recovery. She's already sent Ken to see their priest, Father Hearn, and it was after seeing Father Hearn that Ken phoned me and cancelled the surgery. He told me that he's going to Lourdes. He's been brainwashed into thinking he may have a good chance for a miracle cure. It was no use arguing with him. One can't argue with blind faith. Even when it's out of character."

Amanda sat there, worrying her purse, deeply shaken. "Dr. Whitney, I try to deal with realities in my work. You know I'm a psychologist."

"I know."

"Perhaps this is a momentary aberration of Ken's that will pass. Let me ask you a question. What if we let him go to Lourdes, let him pray for a miracle, let him believe in the fairy tale until he sees for himself that it hasn't cured him? Couldn't he return here then, having come to his senses, and undergo the surgery?"

"Miss Spenser, I must be absolutely candid with you. I will say again what I said earlier. In this kind of disease, time is of the essence. The loss of a full month may make Ken almost inoperable, at least reduce his chances for a successful surgery from thirty percent to fifteen percent. His chances for survival are low enough. To cut them in half again reduces his chances drastically. Such are the facts. Unless he is saved by a miracle, he won't be saved at all. I'm sorry. But I had to apprise you of the turn of events, and the current situation, and hope you could influence Ken's thinking. I'm hoping somehow you can do something about it."

Amanda gathered up her purse and resolutely stood up. "I am going to do something about it. Immediately."

Dr. Whitney was on his feet. "Are you going to speak to Ken or his mother?"

"To neither. They'd be impossible to talk to in their present state. I'm going to talk to Father Hearn. Right now. He's our only hope."

It was not until late afternoon that Amanda Spenser was able to get an appointment to see Father Hearn. Even that had been difficult to arrange on such short notice, but she had invoked her friendship with Bernard and Helen Clayton and explained her relationship with Ken Clayton.

In a way, however, the delay had been a good thing.

After making her appointment, Amanda had realized that she was poorly prepared to debate with an educated Catholic priest about Lourdes and miraculous cures. While she knew vaguely about Bernadette and her visions, probably from having once seen the film *The Song of Bernadette* revived on television when she was in college, she knew nothing about the miracle shrine itself.

Since Father Hearn could not meet her until four-thirty in the afternoon, Amanda had five hours to brief herself for the visit. More than an hour of it she had devoted to calling her secretary and arranging to have all her sessions with her patients cancelled for this after-

noon, and then having a salad and two cups of coffee in a crowded cafe in the Loop.

After that, she had spent four hours in the reading room of the Chicago Public Library skimming through the few volumes available that were devoted to Bernadette and Lourdes. She had gone through *Bernadette of Lourdes* by Frances Parkinson Keyes, which was pro, and *The Happening at Lourdes* by Alan Neame, which was evenhanded, and *Eleven Lourdes Miracles* by Dr. D. J. West, which was con, jotted a few notes, and by the time the appointment with Father Hearn neared, she felt sufficiently briefed to hold her own in a discussion on the subject.

The Church of the Good Shepherd was near Lincoln Park, and it had its own parking lot. The place of worship, from its size and well-maintained exterior, was obviously attended and supported by a wealthy congregation. Certainly, Amanda realized, her future in-laws would have belonged to no other.

Refusing to be intimidated by such splendor, Amanda went directly inside, where she was met and shown to the chancery office occupied by Father Hearn. The priest proved to be full-faced, potbellied, and amiable. By contrast with the church itself, his office seemed unprepossessing. Plain gray drapes framed the windows. There was a fireplace, and above it a large bronze crucifix depicting an elongated Giacometti-like Saviour on the Cross. Father Hearn offered Amanda a velour-covered chair beside his table desk, then took his place in the straight chair at the desk.

On the wall behind him was a framed photograph of Pope John Paul III.

Father Hearn was disarmingly apologetic. "Normally, I am not this difficult to see. I enjoy meeting people, and rarely constrict their visits. But this has been an unusually busy day. I'm sorry to limit your visit, Miss Spenser, but only through a bit of sleight of hand have I managed to squeeze you in, and I can give you just twenty minutes. Perhaps another time we can—"

"No," said Amanda. "Twenty minutes will do." She realized that she could not squander a second. She must get to the subject of potential contention as quickly as possible. "As I told you on the phone, I'm Ken Clayton's fiancée."

"I'm delighted to meet you, at last. Yes, I've known about you. I was to officiate at your wedding. I still expect to do so at a later date."

"Then you know about Ken's illness, his cancer?"

"I've heard about it from his parents. And now from Mr. Clayton himself. I assume you know he was in to see me this morning. We discussed his condition at some length."

"That's why I'm here," said Amanda, "to discuss it with you further."

"I'm glad to have this opportunity to talk to you," Father Hearn assured her earnestly.

The smooth moon face before her was phlegmatic, revealed no pretense of knowing what Amanda's visit was about, but Amanda was certain that it masked shrewd understanding of her motive in wishing this appointment.

"I have no idea if you know anything about me," said Amanda. "Do you know I'm a clinical psychologist?"

Father Hearn's mouth puckered. A faint suggestion of surprise. "No," he said. "No, I don't think I'd been told that."

"I have a private practice," said Amanda. "I teach part-time at the University of Chicago. I teach clinical psychology, abnormal psychology, theory of personality. I speak of this only because I want you to understand that while my concern for Ken is that of a woman who loves him, it is also that of a person who can view his illness objectively. Father, you *do* know how serious his illness is, don't you?"

"Yes, I do, Miss Spenser. I'm sorry for his ordeal, and your own. I shall be offering prayers for his speedy and complete recovery "

"That's kind of you, Father Hearn, and I appreciate it." She tried to control herself, keep any tinge of sarcasm out of her voice. "Helpful as prayer may be, I'm afraid Ken will need more than that. His only real hope, his one hope, lies in immediate surgery. He was prepared to undergo this surgery until he saw you this morning. Now he has cancelled it, and is off to find a miracle. For me, Father, his decision is suicidal and deeply distressing. Only by having an operation—"

Father Hearn interrupted her. "Miss Spenser, I have in no way tried to dissuade Mr. Clayton from undergoing an operation. It is not in my province to sit in judgment on a parishioner's desire to seek help from the medical profession. This was a decision Mr. Clayton had to come to himself. When we talked this morning, he had great misgivings about the surgery's being a success. He said that if he underwent an operation now, he'd sacrifice a God-given opportunity to be in Lourdes at the time of the Virgin Mary's visitation. He realized that after his surgery he'd be convalescing, bedridden, and would therefore be unable to pray directly to the Blessed Virgin for a miraculous cure of his possibly fatal illness. Mr. Clayton made his choice on his own. He decided to put his life in the hands of Our Lord and of the Mother of Heaven at a Christian shrine that has provided—constantly provided—miraculous cures to afflicted pilgrims from all over the earth."

Amanda felt a rush of anger and impatience that transcended her control. There was a life at stake, a human life, and this pious poop was trying to disregard it with banalities. "Father Hearn, you don't believe all that, do you?"

Momentarily, the priest was taken aback. "What are you saying—don't believe what?"

"That this illiterate shepherdess really, in reality, saw the Virgin Mary? Wait, let me finish, let me make myself clear, without being disrespectful in any way. Even assuming that there was a corporeal Virgin Mary, Bernadette would have been a poor choice to see her or report her message. From my reading, the evidence available, what is obvious to me is that Bernadette fits perfectly into the mold of the hysteric. There she was, in this backwater village, a half-starved, always ailing, semi-ignorant peasant girl, a little adolescent hungry for attention and love. She was the ideal type to have hallucinations, to wish for and hence conjure up a beautiful friend like the Virgin Mary, and be convinced that she had actually seen the Holy Mother and conversed with her. Bernadette deluded herself into thinking that she had seen what she claimed to see, and others then and since have been eager to be deluded also, to believe in this, to fulfill their own personal needs."

Amanda caught her breath. "Father, do you expect me to put the life of the one person I love more than any other on earth in the hands of an unstable adolescent who lived briefly 130 years ago? Can you actually expect me to believe that Ken, or anyone with a medically determined serious disease, possibly incurable, can be cured by kneeling and praying at some French cave because a simple-minded peasant girl, her head filled with dreams, claimed that she had seen and talked with the Mother of Jesus eighteen times at this spot?"

Drained, Amanda sat back, hoping that she had resistance enough to weather the storm that she was sure would follow. But, to her surprise, Father Hearn displayed no anger. He appeared calm, the figure of reasonableness.

The tone of his response was quiet and steady. "If the Virgin had not appeared at the grotto, to be seen and heard by a pure and innocent believer, and had not endowed the grotto with special powers, how do you account for the scientific, the medical, facts that have been produced in the decades since? How do you account for the nearly seventy persons who have experienced a miraculous cure of what had been diagnosed by the leading physicians of many nations as an incurable disease? How do you account for the fact that in every one of these terminal cases, the best doctors in the world certified the patient as totally cured, not by medicine but by the power of the miraculous? How do you account for five thousand other cases of crippled or dying persons being reported as fully cured because of the grotto in Lourdes?"

Amanda had already brought her library notes out of her purse. Glancing at them, she said, "I read a study made by a doctor of eleven of the so-called miracle cures at Lourdes. He posed the question, 'Was there a real physical change or was it all psychological?' He decided that all or most of the so-called cures were of diseases or illnesses induced by hysteria, bodily effects of emotional disturbances such as depression, anxiety, or tension that affect the heart, blood vessels, kidneys, and so forth. 'Under hypnosis,' he wrote, 'and given appropriate suggestions, subjects have been known to produce blisters corresponding to imaginary burns and even to develop bruising and oozing of blood from the skin.' In the same way, under the hypnotic influence of Lourdes, ailments aggravated by the imagination can be improved and healed by the imagination. Not usually, but often enough to make believers think that they are sudden miracles."

"I gather," said Father Hearn wryly, "you don't believe in miracles at all."

"Father, in my profession I've seen many cases—and read many case histories—in which the mental has had an effect on the physical. But mental healing can't be depended upon, certainly not in Ken's case where he is suffering from a very real bone cancer. I'm ready to trust his life to a surgeon's scalpel. I can't trust it to an imaginative fable. No, Father, I don't believe in miracles."

"But surely you have not come here to debate with me?"

"I have come here because I assumed that, whatever your profession, you are a rational and logical man. I hoped that you would disenchant Ken with the idea of leaving his life to a mystical cure at Lourdes, and that you would convince him to go into surgery at once. I hoped that you would understand me, and I hoped that you would help me."

Father Hearn sat in silence for many seconds, and finally he spoke. "Miss Spenser, I can't help you because I can't understand you, just as you can't understand me. We speak different languages. My language speaks only in the words of faith, unreserved faith and belief in God, in the Lord, in the Virgin Mary, and the wonders, the miracles, they choose to perform. If you do not understand my language, there is nothing more we can say to each other."

Amanda felt sickened. "Then you are saying there is no chance you'll try to dissuade Ken from making the pilgrimage to Lourdes and waiting for the Virgin and her miracle?"

"No chance. I've already succeeded in getting Mr. Clayton on an official British pilgrimage to Lourdes being led by an old colleague and friend, Father Woodcourt of London. I will pray that Mr. Clayton's pilgrimage proves successful."

Amanda sighed, and stood up. "You've made his reservation, you say?"

"On a pilgrimage train from London to Paris to Lourdes. Yes, the reservation for Mr. Clayton is secure."

Amanda went to the door of the chancery, then turned. "I'd appreciate it if you'd make it two," she said.

"Two?"

"Reservations. One for Ken. The other for me. I can't let that damn fool take this horrible risk by himself. Thank you, Father. I hope that the next time we meet it will not be at a funeral."

Sitting in the Cadillac limousine taking him from the United Nations to the Soviet consular building on East 67th Street in New York City, Sergei Tikhanov still enjoyed a sense of elation at the excellent reception given his speech at the UN, especially by delegates of the Third World bloc. While the Soviet ambassador to the United Nations, the good-natured Alexei Izakov, delivered the routine speeches, it was Tikhanov, as veteran foreign minister of the USSR, who was always sent to New York to make the more crucial public statements.

This morning's address, on the continuing nuclear weapons confrontation with the United States, had been a crucial speech, and it had gone down well. If Tikhanov had any one reservation about his speech, it was that Premier Skryabin had placed limitations on its contents and the invective that might be used. This was the one thing that irked Tikhanov, his superior's conciliatory and soft policy toward the Americans. Tikhanov knew the Americans better than anyone else in the Kremlin hierarchy, and he knew they were like children who responded only to sternness and threats. But nevertheless, within its limitations, the major policy address had been effective, he was sure.

The only other thing that had bothered Tikhanov about the speech had been the rude way in which it had been treated by the leading member of his own delegation. Midway through Tikhanov's ringing address, Ambassador Izakov had abruptly risen from his seat and left the hall. Tikhanov had been momentarily embarrassed by this boorish behavior.

He intended to tell Izakov so, and expected an apology, unless the ambassador had some acceptable excuse to offer.

Perhaps there was an acceptable excuse. Because the moment that Tikhanov himself had left the UN auditorium, and the applause, he had been intercepted by a member of his delegation with a message that Ambassador Izakov wanted to see him at the consulate at once. Maybe, Tikhanov speculated, there had been some emergency that had called the ambassador away from his speech.

Now, hardly aware of the KGB security guard beside him, eager to learn what Izakov had on his mind, Tikhanov leaned forward in the back seat, peering between the driver and the second KGB guard to make out the Soviet consular building up ahead.

Inside the consulate reception room, Tikhanov had unexpectedly found an impatient Izakov waiting for him. Hastily, the ambassador led the way to his safe office, electronically secured against eavesdropping, and hastily shut the door behind them.

Without bothering to sit down or wait for Tikhanov to be seated, Ambassador Izakov, appearing strained, began to speak. "Sergei, my apologies for having to walk out during your magnificent speech, but I was called away by an urgent emergency phone call from Moscow, from Kossoff, none other."

General Kossoff was chairman of the KGB, and now Tikhanov was listening attentively.

"It's Premier Skryubin," the ambassador went on "He's suffered a stroke. He's in a coma."

"A stroke," repeated Tikhanov. "I'm used to his little heart attacks. But a stroke? How bad?"

"Massive. Whatever happens, the old man is through. If he comes out of the coma, recovers, he will be a vegetable, incapacitated. Or he may linger on in his present state. At best the doctors give him no more than a month."

"A month," said Tikhanov, trying to think.

"His successor has to be alerted and placed on standby. That's why General Kossoff called. He wanted you to be informed that an informal secret vote of the Politburo overwhelmingly favors you as the next premier of the Soviet Union. Congratulations, Sergei!"

He stuck out his hand, and awkwardly Tikhanov took it, nodding.

Tikhanov felt dizzy. "I-I'd better sit down," he said. "Let me sit down."

As if suffering an imbalance, Tikhanov made his way to the sofa, groped for an arm of it, and lowered himself onto a cushion.

"Let me get you a drink," Izakov said in a celebrating mood. "One for each of us." He started for the bar. "Let's drink to it." From the bar he called back, "Vodka? I have Stolichnaya."

"Yes, vodka, a stiff one."

As he poured the drinks, Izakov went on talking. "What are your plans now, Sergei? Kossoff wanted to know. But I had no idea what your reaction would be."

"No changes. Still two days in Paris. Two days in Lisbon. Then I've told my wife to meet me at the dacha in Yalta. I thought I'd take my four-week summer vacation now. The Black Sea is at its best in these months."

Izakov approached with the drink. "Maybe you should go straight back to Moscow."

Tikhanov considered this. "No, I don't think it would be wise to appear to be hovering. Also, I don't wish to get mixed up in any of the Politburo's internal politics, certainly not this time. I'll stick to my plans. I'll just go to Yalta and wait. Kossoff can find me there if he wants me."

"He'll want you," said Izakov. "Soon as the old man dies, they'll be installing you as premier."

"Gratifying," said Tikhanov modestly. He was beginning to feel a thrill of excitement. He had worked so hard, hoped so long for this achievement. He didn't give a damn about the old man dying. He'd never respected nor cared for Skryabin anyway. It was only Skryabin's high seat and authority that he had respected, and hoped for. Now, overnight, it was all his.

Sipping his vodka, he realized that Izakov was speaking to him again, something about having to settle some matter in another office, but that he'd be right back.

Tikhanov was pleased to be alone for a brief interval. He had a compulsive need to retrace the road that had brought him to this high moment. He had been born on an isolated farm, today only an hour outside Minsk by car. His stolid father, owner of the farm, had been a decent man, uninterested in politics, a tiller of the soil and a primitive. His mother had been a bookish person who taught primary school in a nearby village. From the earliest age that Tikhanov had been able to read, and comprehend, he had read newspapers and biographies of Soviet heroes. His first and most enduring hero had been Russia's legendary Foreign Minister Andrei Gromyko.

Tikhanov had vowed that he would follow in Gromyko's footsteps, and this he had done from the very start, and all along the way, as best he could. Like Gromyko, he had joined the Communist Party, attended the Minsk Institute of Agriculture, sought and won a post-graduate degree from Moscow's Lenin Institute of Economics. Like Gromyko, he had wanted to specialize in American affairs, and eventually had been appointed to the American division of the National Council of Foreign Affairs. Next, he had been transferred to the Soviet Embassy in

Washington, and had displayed such shrewd understanding of the Americans that he had finally been appointed Soviet ambassador to the United States. As a statesman, he had been quiet but articulate, and effective. Like his idol he had come to be known, as one American newspaper put it, for "the granite solemnity of his face." After a few years he had been recalled to Moscow and made the head of the Ministry of Foreign Affairs at 32–34 Smolenskaya-Sennaya Ploshchad. In the decade since, he had become the Soviet Union's greatest foreign minister, and the one most admired by the majority of the members of the Politburo. If he had wanted to go upward any further, there had been only one place to go, and he had dreamed of just such power.

Now it was within his grasp. Drinking his vodka, he realized that now he would have the power to put into effect his own ideas on how to treat Russia's greatest rival and foe, the United States. He would bring a new toughness to the Kremlin. He would bring the United States to its knees, neutralize it, without war, because he had observed the Americans closely and knew better than any other Soviet official that at heart the Americans were selfish and weak, lacking guts or patriotism, no longer willing to die for their country, as decadent as ancient Romans had been. This ascendency of the Soviet Union over America would bring lasting peace to the world, and Premier Tikhanov would be not only the most lionized hero in the USSR, but the world's master as well.

He came out of his reverie as he finished his drink aware that Ambassador Izakov was standing over him once more.

"Well, Sergei," Izakov was saying, "have you reconsidered your plans? Is it still Yalta?"

"Definitely Yalta. And I think I'll keep to my schedule of visits to Paris and Lisbon first. Can your people get me on a plane to Paris tonight?"

"No problem. I presume you'll want to speak with General Kossoff in Moscow before you leave, just so that he knows you've been informed and where you can be reached."

"Absolutely."

"Oh yes," said Izakov, "I almost forgot. My secretary took one other call for you. A Dr. Ivan Karp wants you to stop by and see him today."

"I'll give him a call," said Tikhanov.

Izakov had gone to his desk to find the memorandum slip, and he reread the message on it as he returned to Tikhanov. "He seems to have been most emphatic about wanting to see you in person." He handed the slip over to the frowning Tikhanov. "Of course, you'll know whether it's important enough to bother about."

"It's not important," said Tikhanov quickly. "Just a report on the results of a routine checkup. All right, I'll arrange to look in on him." But he knew that this explanation might not be enough. He was certain that Izakov filed regular reports on everyone's activities to the KGB. Plainly, Izakov had never heard of Dr. Karp and might be curious. In this case it was nonsense, but Tikhanov liked to be orderly. "My physician in Moscow was out of the city when I left, and I knew my annual physical was long overdue. Someone mentioned that, since I was going to New York, this Dr. Karp, a Russian by birth, was reliable. So I saw him briefly the day I came in. He's a bit fussy and pedantic. I guess that's why he wants to see me. But it'll be the usual. More exercise. Diet. Less drinking."

"They always say less drinking," Izakov agreed.

"I'll arrange to see him after five—still a lot to do today—and I want to leave time for our dinner." He set down his empty glass. "Let me get hold of Dr. Karp, and then I'll call Moscow."

Tikhanov sat at the small dining table in the alcove off Dr. Ivan Karp's office, on the fourth floor of an old building around the corner from Park Avenue, impatiently waiting for the physician to finish his ritual of pouring a strong brew of tea from the china pot sitting on top of his antique brass samovar.

Tikhanov had decided upon a routine physical checkup, because one was long overdue and because he had been troubled by mild anxiety over the unevenness of his gait. He had not wanted to bother with a strange physician abroad, had intended to see his regular doctor in Moscow, but the doctor had been away on a vacation and the trip to New York had been ordered almost overnight. Tikhanov had planned to look in on the staff doctor for the Soviet UN Mission, but on second thought had decided against it because the Mission physician would certainly be a KGB agent. Tikhanov had determined to find an American who was dependable and who would not report any of his bad habits to the KGB. A chess companion in Moscow, a merchant who often visited New York and was a longtime friend of Tikhanov, had recommended that he see Dr. Ivan Karp. This Karp, a Jewish emigré of many years, now an American citizen, was intellectually sympathetic to the Marxist philosophy.

Upon his arrival in Manhattan, Tikhanov had contacted Dr. Karp, who had agreed to give him his general checkup at a modern midtown medical facility. Leaving his security guards in the doctor's reception room, Tikhanov had submitted to a thorough examination. At its completion, Karp had said that he wanted to take his patient upstairs for some further tests by a colleague who was a neurologist. "We don't have to drag along all your KGB guards, do we?" Karp had inquired. "We can slip out the private door to my suite." Tikhanov had been more than agreeable.

Now, brought to Dr. Karp's private office for the test results, Tikhanov was becoming irritated by the deliberate movements of the doctor. Tikhanov wanted to get down to business, be done with it in time for dinner, and then be off to Paris and Lisbon and Yalta to await his summons to power.

He watched Dr. Karp, a gnomish man with a tiny pointed beard, setting out the teacup and a plate of *kvhorost* biscuits.

"Thank you," said Tikhanov. "I don't have much time, doctor. We might as well get right down to it. Since there is always something, what is it this time? High blood pressure? Heart murmur? An indication of diabetes?"

Sitting across from him, Dr. Karp finished sipping his tea, and said gently, "I wish it were that simple."

"Meaning what, doctor? There's something else wrong?"

Dr. Karp was thoughtful a moment. He looked up. "Yes. I must be forthright with you. There is something of serious concern. The sooner you know, the better. Let me add, it is not of immediate concern, but in the long run—"

Tikhanov's impatience had turned into a grip of anxiety. He tried to disguise his fear with levity. "Well, as someone once said—in the long run, we'll all be dead."

Dr. Karp offered him an uneasy smile. "True. I'm glad you make it easier for me."

"So—what is it?"

"The examination, tests, indicate without question you are suffering from muscular dystrophy."

Tikanov felt a shortness of breath, his anxiety at its peak. "Muscular—what?" he asked, almost inaudibly. He had heard of the disorder, of course, but was only dimly aware of what it was all about. Now it sounded ominous, terrible.

Dr. Karp was speaking more rapidly, more professionally. "The majority of cases of muscular dystrophy fall into one of four categories, and your category is known as the mixed type. This is a disease involving the progressive symmetric wasting of skeletal muscles, in your legs, in your arms."

Tikhanov refused to accept the diagnosis. "You must be mistaken, Dr. Karp. Have you felt my muscles, arms, legs? They are strong, stronger than ever."

"A typical symptom, and deceptive," said the physician. "Connective tissue and fat deposits make the muscles seem larger and stronger, but in fact this is not so and they are wasting away."

Tikhanov would not surrender. "How can you be sure?"

"I know this must be a blow to you, Mr. Tikhanov, but the results of the tests cannot be disputed. We cannot deny the findings of the electromyography, which substantiate the positive muscle biopsy. You can expect progressive muscular deterioration, and in this kind of dystrophy the voluntary muscles would be the most affected."

Tikhanov came jerkily to his feet, in despair, and ransacked his jacket pockets for his pack of cigarettes. With trembling hand, he put his lighter to a cigarette. Remaining on his feet, he said, "All right. What can I do about it?"

"Not too much, I'm afraid. There is no known means to stop the impairment. However, there are things that might be done to, well, ease the symptoms. A regime of physical therapy, exercise, possibly some surgery. Of course, one more thing on the positive side. If you do what should be done, you might enjoy ten or twelve more years of good living before you are fully incapacitated."

"That's all the time I want, Dr. Karp."

"You can have it, if you retire."

"Retire? You know very well who I am—"

"I know who you are. You've had many years of success. But this can no longer be. You must resign from your present post, retire and enjoy a leisurely life, and undergo all the therapy possible."

"If I refuse to resign? Or if I take an even more active job?"

Dr. Karp absently fiddled with his pointed beard, his eyes cast downward. "The deterioration will intensify, Mr. Tikhanov. You will not survive more than two or three years."

Tikhanov felt almost suffocated with rage at the unfairness of what was happening to him. He sat down next to Dr. Karp, grasped his arm and shook it. "I won't accept this, I can't. There must be some way to arrest this disease."

"I know of no physician on earth who can tell you anything other than what I've told you. However, if you want to seek a second opinion—"

"That would seem to be pointless, from what you say."

"Of course, there are a few doctors in the world who claim they can sometimes do something about this. I've twice sent patients of mine, at their insistence, to a well-known rejuvenation specialist in Geneva, Switzerland, who believes that he has upon occasion eradicated the disease. It didn't work for my two patients, so such therapy remains in question, a long shot—"

"I suggest this is the time to try a long shot. You know this rejuvenation specialist?"

"I've spoken to him on the phone several times, some years ago. Yes, you might say I know Dr. Motta."

"Then do me a favor," said Tikhanov. "Call him in Geneva and make an appointment for me."

"Well, I could . . ." Dr. Karp looked at his watch. "Of course, at this hour he would be asleep."

"Wake him."

Dr. Karp appeared doubtful. "You insist? Really, tomorrow would be—"

"I insist," said Tikhanov forcefully. "Wake him tonight and make an appointment for me. Nothing can be more important."

Dr. Karp had resigned himself to the uncomfortable assignment. "Very well. It may take a little while. If you don't mind waiting."

"I assure you, I have nothing more vital to do."

Tikhanov watched Dr. Karp leave the dining alcove, go through his office, and disappear into another room.

Tikhanov gulped his tepid tea, filled the cup again with hot tea, drank it, brooding over his imminent mortality and the possible loss of his great opportunity. He had not yet recovered from the initial shock of the diagnosis. He pondered the choice that lay immediately ahead. To accept an active role of power, and its excitement, which could promise him no more than two or three years, or to resign himself to an inactive life that would give him ten or twelve years. Unlike many Russians, Tikhanov was not a fatalist. True, life was sweet, and there would be pleasure in added years, but he wondered how much pleasure could be derived in days without work and decision and authority.

Pushing his teacup aside, he found his lighter and a fresh cigarette. The smoking seemed to calm him, and with calm came more hope. Certainly his future could not rest on two impossible choices. Certainly somewhere in the world there must be someone with the means, especially for a person of his stature, to arrest and subdue the fatal disease. Perhaps there was some scientist in the Soviet Union, with all its medical advances, who could help him. Yet, he instinctively knew that if he sought help in his homeland, even found a treatment to prolong his life, the word of his uncertain health would be out and his career and political advancement doomed. The old men of the Politburo would not want to bet on a premier who already had a blemish on his being. Secrecy overrode everything else. He would have to find help outside his homeland, among strangers with no tie to his government, and be treated swiftly and soon. At the moment, the Swiss healer, this Dr. Motta, offered the only hope of salvaging his future.

Nearly twenty minutes had passed, and Tikhanov was wondering how Dr. Karp had made out with his call to Geneva, when Dr. Karp reappeared in the dining alcove. He sat down next to Tikhanov, a piece of scratch-pad paper in hand. Tikhanov was immediately alert.

"I reached Geneva," said Dr. Karp, "and woke Mrs. Motta and spoke with her at length. Dr. Motta left Geneva yesterday and will be gone for three weeks."

"Where?" asked Tikhanov sharply. "Can he be reached?"

"He's gone to Biarritz—you know, the beach resort in France—to treat a wealthy Indian patient from Calcutta with his cellular-therapy injections. Dr. Motta is combining this visit with a much-needed vacation. He expects to be at the Hôtel du Palais in Biarritz for three weeks."

"But will he see me?" Tikhanov inquired anxiously.

"No problem. His wife arranges his schedule. She has written you in for a noon appointment in her husband's suite three days from now. She speaks to her husband daily and will report this. Is the time suitable?"

"Any time is suitable," said Tikhanov quickly. He felt a surge of relief, instantly followed by a stab of apprehension. "You didn't tell her who I was, did you?"

"No, no, of course not. I just made up whatever came to mind. I said you were a well-known American language professor who taught Russian, and I gave your name as Samuel Talley."

"Samuel Talley?"

"I just made it up on the spur of the moment, a name with your real initials in case you have any monograms on your luggage or clothes."

"Clever of you."

"It comes of reading espionage and detective novels," said Dr. Karp with a tinge of embarrassment. "I passed on to Mrs. Motta the nature of your illness. She will, in turn, relay it to Dr. Motta in their next conversation. He will be prepared for you. Now, if you will give me fifteen minutes more, I will type up a summary of my diagnosis for Dr. Motta, and you can present this, along with the results of your tests, to him in Biarritz." Dr. Karp stood up. "I repeat, it is a long shot. But it will give you a second opinion, and, if you are lucky, a possible chance. Maybe you will be lucky. Who knows? You can only try."

For a man of Tikhanov's renown and high station, it had not been easy to get to Biarritz in complete secrecy.

He had flown to Paris, settled into the Soviet Embassy briefly, and played his first day there by the rules. He had put a call through to General Kossoff in Moscow, and realized that the KGB director's tone was tinged with a special respect, as befitted conversation with the next premier. Tikhanov had learned that Premier Skryabin was still in a coma, and on a life-support system, but that his end was no more than a few weeks off at the most. With the new value placed on him, Tikhanov had found it easier to double-talk about his forthcoming schedule, his flexible plans, a secret mission and meeting with a subversive group gathering from the Middle East, a more prolonged stay in Portugal. He had promised to be in constant touch with Moscow along the way and to check in when he reached Yalta.

Then Tikhanov had used his remaining time in Paris to develop the identity that he would take to Biarritz. There had been no trouble contacting French Communist elements who could lead him to nonpolitical persons able to supply him with an American passport bearing the name Samuel Talley, along with the American social security and credit cards that should be possessed by Talley.

The last day in Paris, with Kossoff's reluctant approval, Tikhanov had rid himself of his KGB security guards by telling them that the Middle East subversives he was to meet with in private would supply their own protection for him.

By himself, using no one else, Tikhanov had booked the Air-Inter flight from Orly Field in Paris to Biarritz, and once safely in the sunny, windy southwestern French resort, he had taken an ordinary taxi to the spectacular old Hôtel du Palais, at one time the summer residence of Emperor Napoleon III and Empress Eugénie.

As Samuel Talley, American citizen, Tikhanov had registered in the hotel and been shown to a spacious ornately furnished double bedroom much too luxurious for his taste.

An hour later, carrying the packet that Dr. Karp had sent along, and wearing as a disguise not only thick clear nonprescription glasses but a bushy false mustache obtained in Paris to cover the well-known wart above his upper lip, he rang the doorbell to suite 310–311. He was surprised when one of the double doors opened to reveal a petite, serious young nurse garbed in white. But then, Tikhanov reminded himself, Dr. Motta was here in Biarritz to give injections to a wealthy Indian and would naturally have brought along his Swiss nurse, although Tikhanov decided that she was much too young and pretty to serve her employer merely as a nurse.

Tikhanov followed her up a stretch of interior hallway that opened into the largest sitting room Tikhanov had ever seen in a Western hotel.

"Mr. Talley," the nurse said, "if you will be seated, Dr. Motta will join you in a few seconds."

Tikhanov walked slowly, unsteadily—reminding himself of his ailment—beneath the ornate chandelier to an antique desk that stood in front of a window. From the window, he could see that this was a corner room overlooking both an outdoor swimming pool and a restaurant, perched above a sandy beach that was dotted with umbrellas, lounges, and cabañas. And beyond that was the wavy Atlantic running out to the pure blue horizon.

Turning his back on the view, Tikhanov inspected the sitting room's furnishings, a three-cushion gold sofa, two deep gold armchairs around a glass-topped coffee table, two silver satin-covered pull-up chairs. Obviously, Dr. Motta was rich and successful, which Tikhanov equated with being in the best hands, and therefore offering the promise of hope.

As he considered where to sit, Tikhanov was startled by a booming Germanic voice. "Mr. Talley. Glad to have you. Let's sit on the sofa."

The speaker entering from the bedroom was an ebullient, heavyset older man wrapped in a purple silk bathrobe that revealed the lower portion of his hairy naked legs. His auburn hair was combed in a pompadour, the eyes small and narrow, the nose prominent, the freshly shaved face florid. "I'm Dr. Motta. Forgive my attire. Just came straight up from the Grande Plage. Wonderful place. You been here before?"

"No, sir."

"You'll like it. Give yourself a few extra days. Yes, you'll like it." Dr. Motta sank down into the sofa with a wheeze, summoning Tikhanov to sit beside him, and Tikhanov complied.

"I knew you'd be here at lunch time," Dr. Motta continued, "and I expect you're ravenously hungry. I hope you don't mind, but I took the liberty of ordering a light lunch for each of us before we settle down to business. Give us an opportunity to become acquainted."

"Very kind of you," said Tikhanov stiffly. He wanted only to get to what mattered, the consultation, his life, but he also wished to show his appreciation of the physician's hospitality, wanting to be in his good graces, wanting the other's goodwill and best mood.

Dr. Motta was packing tobacco into his straight-stemmed briar pipe. "You don't mind if I smoke, do you? I don't allow my patients to smoke during therapy, but we're not in the clinic and we can relax a bit."

"I'll have a cigarette," said Tikhanov, finding and lighting one.

The doorbell rang, and then the room-service waiter appeared, rolling in the cart carrying their lunch. As the waiter laid out the dishes on the coffee table, Dr. Motta eyed them greedily. Puffing his pipe, he identified each dish. "To start with, *Salade à l'Oiseau.* Then, for the two of us, *Carré d'Agneau Rôti.* Toast, as you can see, and French coffee. I did not order a dessert, but if you wish one, I would recommend their *Crème du Chocolat.*"

"No, thank you, there's quite enough already."

The waiter had finished. "If anything is not to your wishes, please ring room service. When you are through, let us know and I'll remove the service pieces and cart."

After the waiter had gone, Dr. Motta knocked the ashes out of his pipe and sat up. "Let's dine now, and we can talk."

"Very well," said Tikhanov, stubbing out his cigarette and starting to pick at the salad.

"I have only a clue as to your ailment, the reason you are here," said Dr. Motta, eating. "I know the problem is muscular dystrophy. But that need not be a death sentence. Some cases have been treated successfully. It all depends. We shall see, we shall see."

Tikhanov enjoyed a wave of relief, and began to look upon the Swiss doctor as a savior.

"Are you going to examine me?" inquired Tikhanov.

"If necessary," said Dr. Motta, absorbed in his food.

Tikhanov touched the package on the sofa beside him "Dr. Karp sent along the results of all his tests for you to see."

"Very good. I shall study them with care. Then we will know what can be done." He raised his head. "You know, I have had several successes with this disease."

Tikhanov nodded. "That is why Dr. Karp sent me to see you. He told me of your successes, and mentioned two failures."

"Failures, of course. It depends on the stage of the disease, the degree of deterioration." He wiped his mouth with a linen napkin. "Treating dystrophy is not my specialty, but it is often an inevitable adjunct of my main work. Do you know anything about my work?"

"Very little, I'm ashamed to say," said Tikhanov apologetically. "I had no time to learn. I know only what Dr. Karp told me, no more. Basically, that you treat the aging, apply regenerative therapy to your patients."

"Ah, so you do have an idea," said Dr. Motta, pleased. "Yes, I was one of several protégés of the celebrated Dr. Paul Niehans at his chalet in Clarens on Lake Geneva. Dr. Niehans pioneered cellular therapy—a simple therapy. He prepared solutions from freshly ground-up organs of a fetal lamb, one taken from the womb of a black sheep by Caesarian section, and injected them into the buttocks of his patient. If the patient suffered from an underactive thyroid, he was injected with thyroid cells. In menopausal disturbances, the patient was injected with ovarian cells. And so forth. The basic thrust of cellular therapy is to hold off old age, extend life by rejuvenation or revitalizing despite the illnesses of aging. Naturally, this meant treating many diseases ranging from anemia to serious ulcers. When I took over from Dr. Niehans, dystrophy was just one of the many diseases I had to contend with."

Tikhanov was intrigued. "And Dr. Niehans had successes?"

"I am certain. He treated Pope Pius XII. He treated King Ibn Said, the Duke of Windsor, German Chancellor Konrad Adenauer, the British author W. Somerset Maugham, the actress Gloria Swanson, even your former American Vice-President Henry A. Wallace. On the other hand, when he was given the opportunity to treat Igor Stravinsky, he refused, because the composer was ill with polycythemia, a chronically high red-blood-cell count, and Dr. Niehans felt that he could not cure him. I, too, have had many well-known patients, and I have treated them if I believed I could help them. Others I resisted treating because I felt that they would not respond to the injections. They were, in my view, incurable. But in most cases there are favorable opportunities."

Dr. Motta had completed his lunch, and was wiping his mouth once more.

"Now, Mr. Talley," he resumed, "let us see what can be done for you. Let me review your tests." He reached out, and Tikhanov quickly handed him Dr. Karp's package. "You finish your meal," Dr. Motta said. "I will retire to the desk in the bedroom where I can concentrate. I don't expect to be too long."

He rose, and briskly left the sitting room, tearing open the package as he went into the adjacent bedroom.

Alone, Tikhanov puttered with the rest of the food, but his stomach was in his throat and he had no appetite. He attempted to occupy himself with the bitter coffee, but finally gave up. He forced himself to sit back, smoking incessantly, and tried not to think.

After almost a half hour, Dr. Motta reappeared, stuffing the test findings back into the manila envelope. This time he took his place in an armchair, facing Tikhanov. His broad face was grave.

"I am sorry, Mr. Talley, but I am afraid I cannot help you," intoned Dr. Motta. "You suffer the mixed type of dystrophy, affecting the voluntary muscles, and the deterioration is advanced. The muscle biopsy reports are conclusive. I can do no more than confirm Dr. Karp's opinion and his timetable, and support his suggestions. I am truly sorry."

"You mean—you mean there is nothing that can be done?"

"Nothing short of a miracle," said Dr. Motta.

An hour later, Sergei Tikhanov finally left his own room.

Depressed, certain of his death sentence, he had tried to make up his mind which course to take. To announce his illness and enforced retirement dramatically, and gain ten or twelve years of miserable life, sitting by in the shadows while a more vigorous and healthy colleague took over the reins of the Soviet Union. Or to keep his illness a secret, and plunge into the top level of Soviet rule, and have the satisfaction of two or three years of power and activity before an early extinction. Since he could come to no decision, not yet, he had decided to continue with his schedule and proceed to Lisbon, and from there return to Yalta.

Pale and dizzy, Tikhanov reached the concierge's desk in the ground floor lobby of the Hôtel du Palais, prepared to book a seat on the earliest plane to Lisbon. The bald concierge was busy with another tourist, arranging a dinner reservation for four at the Rôtisserie du Coq Hardi in Biarritz. Waiting his turn restlessly, Tikhanov glanced at the rack beside the second counter with its lineup of international newspapers for sale. One word in every bold headline, and recognizable in every language, assaulted him. The word was MIRACLE . . . MILAGRO . . . MIRACOLO.

Curious, Tikhanov moved around the corner of the concierge's counter to the newsrack. The headlines all seemed to be shouting about the same thing. Obviously, a big event of some kind. Tikhanov tugged free a copy of *France Soir*, left some change on the counter, and scanned the headline, the bank of headlines. MIRACLE EXPECTED AT LOURDES. BERNADETTE'S LEGACY. Her lost journal reveals the secret Virgin Mary entrusted to her long ago. The Virgin will reappear at the grotto in Lourdes in three weeks, sometime during the week and day following August 14. Some fortunate pilgrim will see the Virgin. Some ailing pilgrim will enjoy a miraculous cure.

Normally, at another time when he was in full control of his senses, Sergei Tikhanov would have cast this typical Western nonsense, this fable for gullible readers, into the nearest waste basket.

But a phrase that Dr. Motta had used in concluding their conversation still rang in his ears. What could be done to save Tikhanov? Dr. Motta had replied: *Nothing short of a miracle.*

Thinking about the coincidence, newspaper held open before him, Tikhanov shambled across the brown carpet, with its imperial design, spread on the marble floor of the lobby. There was a narrow red couch resting near two towering marble pillars. Tikhanov lowered himself into it and carefully read the story in French from Paris, the cardinal's announcement at a press conference that the Pope had authorized word to go out to the world that the Virgin Mary, during the seventh of her eighteen appearances before Bernadette, had promised to reappear at the grotto in Lourdes and provide a miraculous cure for an ailing pilgrim.

Religion and its miracles, the opium of the people, as Lenin had stated. Actually, Karl Marx had stated it first. "Religion is the soul of soulless conditions, the heart of a heartless world, the opium of the people." And Marx's collaborator, Friedrich Engels, had echoed, "Get rid of the Church, which permits working people to suffer silently in this world while awaiting their reward in the next." Lenin had preached this, Stalin had supported it, and the Communist Party had demanded that every member shed his belief in religion. And Tikhanov had become, was still, a loyal Party member, an unswerving atheist since adolescence. As a veteran Communist, Tikhanov knew that not for a minute could he take this ignorant rubbish about the Virgin Mary seriously.

No matter how deep his depression, no matter what weakness had afflicted his brain, no matter how desperate his need for hope, this Lourdes story was impossible. About to throw the newspaper aside, Tikhanov's eyes fell upon a second story from Lourdes. This was a feature about the almost seventy miracle cures that had already been attributed to the grotto or the water from its spring. His gaze fastened on the list of incurables and their potentially fatal illnesses, persons from France, Germany, Italy, Switzerland who had been saved by miracles. Sarcoma of the pelvis—cured. Multiple sclerosis—cured. Addison's disease—cured. Cancer of the uterine cervix—cured. And other diseases miraculously cured, several diseases that seemed to resemble muscular dystrophy.

Following this story was an interview with a Dr. Berryer, head of the Lourdes Medical Bureau. The cures, certified by priests, were first thoroughly investigated and attested to by the best medical men in the world. Tikhanov's eye held on another statement that Dr. Berryer had made: Even non-Catholics and nonreligious visitors had been blessed by cures.

Impressive.

Tikhanov sat still. Very impressive. He thought back to his childhood in the farmhouse outside Minsk. His worn mother had been an orthodox Catholic, a cheerful one, and his father had paid lip service to this faith. Tikhanov remembered the small wooden church—the candles, the priest, the Mass, the rosaries, Communion, holy water, the confessional. Growing up, he had grown away from the sweet, comforting mysticism, and as a mature intellectual had found a more acceptable faith in the preachings and writings of Marx, Lenin, Stalin, much to his mother's distress.

But once, in innocence, he had been a believer. Maybe it was not necessary to remind himself of this now, but it was a kind of credential.

Only a miracle, Dr. Motta had said.

It was a dangerous enterprise, a key Soviet official going to a Catholic shrine to abandon momentarily Marx for Mary. But it could be done in secrecy. He could work it out.

He *would* work it out.

My God, his life was on the line, and there were no other options. Only this one. Besides—

What was there to lose?

3
Venice, London, and Madrid

The last time she had taken a private motorboat from a wharf outside the Marco Polo Airport to the Hotel Danieli Royal Excelsior in Venice, it had been a dazzling sunny morning three years ago. Natale Rinaldi remembered that morning vividly. The wondrous ride in the motorboat past fields and swamps, mounds of islands, the turning into a canal, the moist dirty-gray buildings on either side, the emergence into the shimmering main lagoon, the rich umber of the Hotel Danieli with its array of miniature white balconies jutting out on every floor.

It had been strange coming back to Venice this morning in total darkness, although her Aunt Elsa had reassured her that the morning was as sunny as it had been during their last visit.

Darkness had permanently enveloped Natale's world one week after she had returned to her parents' apartment in Rome following the vacation in Venice three years ago. She had rehearsed all that afternoon and into the early evening at the Teatro Goldini for her role as the Stepdaughter in Pirandello's *Six Characters in Search of an Author,* part of the fall repertory and her first real opportunity, and she had come back to the apartment and her bedroom tired but stimulated by the director's predictions of what the future held in store for her. Going to bed, she had been comforted by the cozy beige print wallpaper surrounding her—she had known it since childhood—and then she had blinked out the bed lamp and closed her eyes. When her alarm had gone off at nine o'clock in the morning, and she had opened her eyes, she was lost in darkness. At first, confused, she had been unable to understand, and then she had realized that she had lost her sight. Somehow, somewhere in the night she had become totally blind. And then she had screamed. It would be the first and last time that she would ever panic.

Her frenzied parents had rushed her to a hospital. Rome's leading eye specialist had been called in. There had been a slit-lamp examination. There had been the ophthalmoscopy. There had been weeks of examinations to determine the cause of her blindness. There had been discussion of an occlusion in the central retinal artery. There had, finally, been a verdict: optic atrophy, abrupt, with no possibility of restored vision.

Three years ago, it had happened. Natale had been frightened and deeply shaken, but not shattered. At twenty-one, before the sudden darkness had come, she had been a gay, cheerful, optimistic young woman, and like her Catholic parents she believed unquestioningly in God, His Son, and in the Holy Ghost. The Lord knew what was best and He would look after her.

From the onset of her blindness, Natale had refused to buckle under or wallow in despair and self-pity. She had resolutely determined to be as independent and cheerful as possible. Although forced to give up her budding stage career, she had tried to maintain the life that she had known. Rejecting a Seeing Eye dog, refusing a white cane, she had encouraged her Aunt Elsa to guide her and teach her to get around on her own, in the apartment, in the street, in the antique shop her parents had on the Via Veneto. Aunt Elsa, her mother's younger sister, had been a perfect companion for her, a realistic and practical spinster in her late forties. Natale loved her parents, but their emotions had been hard to cope with, and she adored Aunt Elsa, who was solid and stable. Natale had continued to visit with her friends, and to go to the movies for the dialogue. Superficial changes had included wearing dark glasses at all times, learning Braille, and subscribing to a Talking Books service. As for church, she had gone to Mass more often and, when by herself, prayed more frequently. Her major sacrifice had been to deny herself dating or being with young men alone. There had always been so many, because of her beauty, she supposed, but with her handicap she had not wanted to become involved, become someone's burden.

This summer, for the first time since her blindness, she had wanted a vacation, to go back to Venice for three weeks, to the last city outside Rome that she had seen and loved before her loss of sight. Understanding and indulgent as her parents were, neither had been able to accompany her to Venice, not during Rome's tourist season, their busiest time of the year. But they had agreed that Aunt Elsa, who was the manager of their shop, could take Natale.

Now, in the familiar third floor bedroom of the two-room suite at the Hotel Danieli, Aunt Elsa was unpacking their bags, and Natale stood before the twin beds, singing as she changed her clothes for their first foray into the streets.

Natale had already zipped up her blue jeans, pulled on the tight T-shirt (knowing, by feeling the raised initial sewn inside, that it was the becoming yellow one that contrasted so well with her loose shiny brunette hair), and with sure fingers she had patted down her hair and tied it at the nape of her neck with a ribbon. She fumbled on the bed for the dark glasses and adjusted them on the ridge of her small but perfect nose. She pirouetted in the direction of the unpacking and asked, "Aunt Elsa, am I together? Do I look all right?"

"Neat and beautiful as ever."

"You wouldn't be prejudiced, would you?"

"I've always told you, you could win any beauty contest. Why not? You take after me."

Natale laughed, remembering that her dumpy Aunt Elsa, with her straggly black hair and faint outline of a mustache, always believed that everyone else was beautiful.

Natale heard her aunt approaching, enjoyed her companion's warm hug, her aunt's forehead pressed against her cheek. Aunt Elsa was five feet two inches, and Natale was five feet six, thin and graceful as a reed.

She took Aunt Elsa's arm. "Let's go outside. You can finish unpacking later. I want to see Venice again." She felt Aunt Elsa unconsciously wince at the use of the word "see," and Natale said with determination, "Yes, Auntie, I will see it if you point things out. I'll remember exactly."

"Very well," said Aunt Elsa. "I'm about ready, too."

"We'll go to the Piazza," said Natale, taking her purse from her aunt. "I want some fruit juice at Quadri's, a little walk on the Mercerie, and then lunch at Harry's Bar."

Leaving the two-room suite, Natale would not let her aunt guide her. Starting from a familiar fixed point, the familiar suite, she felt sure of herself. She had been to Venice and the Danieli many times with her parents, when she had been growing up. The last visit, three years ago, was still fresh in her mind. Touching the railings, she descended a few steps ahead of Aunt Elsa, recalling that the second flight of stairs down into the lobby was marble. In the lobby, she slowed to let Aunt Elsa catch up with her, then smilingly acknowledged the greetings of several of the older concierges who had known her through the years and now had been informed of her condition.

Outside, on the Riva degli Schiavoni, Natale asked, "What kind of day is it? I know it's warm and a little sticky."

"The sun's out, but hazy. It'll be hot by noon."

"Is it crowded?"

"Swarms of tourists. Lots of Germans, British, a group of Japanese. You'll know it when we get to the bridge."

The bridge formed an arch over a canal, the Ponte della Paglia, upon which visitors always jammed to photograph the Bridge of Sighs, the high passageway on their right that led from the Doges' Palace to the ducal dungeons, from which Casanova had once escaped. As an adolescent, Natale had read the forbidden parts of Casanova's *Mémoires* and wondered what had made him such a legendary lover, or if it had all been self-promotion. She had fantasized having Casanova make love to her, and supposed that it was the variety he had offered and his endurance that had excited so many women from every social class.

They were walking, and there was a constant babble of voices in numerous languages, and she felt the pressure of Aunt Elsa's hand on her arm. "There are three young men, locals I think," said Aunt Elsa, "who have stopped and are staring at you, stupefied."

"Because they pity me?"

"I said stupefied, stupid," said Aunt Elsa. "They don't know there's anything to pity. They see only a gorgeous young girl with an inadequate brassiere beneath a flesh-tight T-shirt, and they're awed."

"Oh, sure," said Natale, but she was pleased.

"Here's the bridge, step up."

The Ponte della Paglia *was* crowded, as it had always been, and this time Natale took pleasure in the bumping, pushing, elbowing as they reached the top. It was easier coming down and crossing the pavement toward the two granite columns of the Piazzetta. Natale could picture the colonnaded side of the Doges' Palace to her right, and to her left, across the bobbing moored black gondolas, the magnificent San Giorgio Maggiore rising up out of the glistening lagoon.

"There are all kinds of bookstalls and vendors along the ducal palace," said Aunt Elsa.

"Yes," said Natale remembering. It was poking through these stalls that she had first found Byron, Stendhal, Ruskin in Italian paperbacks and devoured them.

"Caffè Chioggia isn't too filled right now," said Aunt Elsa. Natale pictured the long outdoor café across from the Doges' Palace where she had once flirted with a timid American boy, who had been afraid to approach her.

"Are we in the Piazza San Marco yet?" inquired Natale.

"Just about. Nothing's changed. There's the Campanile, tall as ever. The four bronze horses are still over the front of the Basilica. The Piazza is—well, you know—hectic as usual, the pigeons waddling about for their maize, and fluttering off when the children chase them. It's the same, Natale. It never changes in Venice."

"Thank God," said Natale.

"You want to sit down?"

"I'm thirsty," said Natale.

"Is it still Quadri's? The music has just begun there."

"Yes, let's sit in Quadri's." Unaccountably, Quadri's with its small circular gray tables and yellow wicker chairs and the bandstand to the rear had always been her favorite outdoor café. Caffè Lavena, beside it, seemed to have less character, and Florian's on the opposite side, although the oldest of the Piazza cafés, built in 1720, often occupied by Lord Byron in his day, always seemed to take too much sun. But Quadri's, on her last visit, had been most restful.

They were going across the Piazza San Marco, and Natale could hear the shrieks of youngsters and the flapping rise of pigeons, and she hoped that she wouldn't step on one, although nobody ever did.

Apparently, they had reached Quadri's café, because Aunt Elsa was saying, "There's a free table in the shade." Natale allowed Aunt Elsa to take her hand, and lead her up an aisle.

Stopping, Natale groped for a chair, sat down, and listened to the music as Aunt Elsa ordered grapefruit juice for Natale and a Coca-Cola with a slice of lemon for herself.

They had been sipping their drinks in silence, Natale content to be in Venice, refusing to permit herself a moment's unhappiness at being unable to see it again, thinking it was just good to be alive (really only half-alive, but she put down the thought), when the metallic clanging from a nearby bell made her sit up. That would be the mechanical Moors above their heads, at the summit of the Clock Tower, hitting the big bell.

"What time is it?" asked Natale.

"Exactly one o'clock. Too late to shop on the Mercerie. Most of the stores will be closed until three. Although a few may be open."

"No," said Natale. "I want to go to Harry's Bar. I'm hungry, and it's cooler there."

While she waited for her aunt to pay the check, she heard heavy

footsteps approach her and she sensed a presence just above her. In-
stinctively, she looked up, as she heard a rich male baritone voice say,
"Forgive me, but I thought I recognized you. You're Miss Rinaldi from
Rome, aren't you?"

Bewildered, Natale nodded.

"I'm Signore Vianello," the voice was saying. "Again, forgive me,
but I couldn't resist being sure and saying hello."

"Vianello," Natale repeated blankly.

"I'm a play producer from Rome, on vacation. I first saw you—I
was sure you were the same actress—at a rehearsal of a Pirandello play
at the Teatro Goldini several years ago. A friend had brought me along.
I don't remember whom. But I could not forget you." He hesitated. "I
don't want to interrupt you two—"

Quickly, Natale introduced her Aunt Elsa, then added, "Thank
you."

"I expected to see you at the opening night, but you weren't in the
cast," the producer went on. "I learned only that you had retired." He
chuckled. "Retired? For one so young? Anyway, I was reminded, spot-
ting you here in the Piazza." Natale meant to stop him, but this Vianello was going on "I have a new play of my own I am planning to
produce. I'll be casting in a month. There is a perfect role for you if
you're interested."

Natale couldn't let this continue anymore. "Signore Vianello," she
blurted. "Can't you tell? I'm blind."

"You're—?" She heard the quick suck of his breath, and knew that
he was taken aback and utterly embarrassed.

"I'm sorry," she said.

"Oh, I had no idea," he said. He stammered the rest. "You look—
you look—well, better than ever. Uh, many of these things are temporary. I'm sure you will regain your—your full vision. If you do, I would
certainly want you to call on me. Uh, let me leave my card. Here."

Natale held up her hand for the card, but apparently the producer
had given his card to Aunt Elsa. "Thank you, Signore Vianello," said
Aunt Elsa. "Perhaps things will change. If they do, I'll remind Miss
Rinaldi."

"Do that, do that," said Signore Vianello. "I hope to meet you
both again. Have a good vacation."

Silence followed. Apparently, Signore Vianello had fled.

Natale felt her aunt's hand on her forearm. "Let's go to Harry's
Bar."

Still unnerved, Natale said, "I'm not sure I'm hungry."

"Then have something to drink there," said Aunt Elsa, forcing Natale to her feet. "Let's go."

Natale allowed Aunt Elsa to guide her into the Piazza. She could hear the goddam pigeons.

She felt Aunt Elsa release her arm. "Wait. There's a man with *Il Gazzettino.* Let me buy a paper."

When her aunt was at her side again with the Venetian newspaper, and starting to lead her away, Natale said, "Where are we exactly?"

"In front of the Basilica, on the way to the Piazzetta, and there we'll turn right for Harry's Bar."

"The Basilica," Natale repeated dully. "Is it open?"

"Of course."

"I want to go inside."

"You're sure?"

"For—for a minute," said Natale. "I want to pray."

Aunt Elsa, who had no affection for churches, said in a resigned voice, "All right, if it'll help you forget that idiot."

"He did nothing wrong, Aunt Elsa. Poor man, he didn't know. Actually, I should feel good that he was still attracted by me. But, well, I just had a momentary ache at—at what I'm missing. Can we go inside the church?"

Natale stumbled along with her Aunt Elsa in darkness, feeling the wooden planks beneath her feet, listening to the shuffling, and the hushed voices.

After genuflecting, she entered a pew and slowly knelt. Then, to herself, she prayed to the God that she could not believe ever abandoned anyone. The brief rapport with her Maker settled her nerves, made her feel peaceful once more. She pushed herself upright. "Aunt Elsa?" she whispered.

"Right here."

"Let's eat."

She accompanied Aunt Elsa out into the black daylight.

She held Aunt Elsa's hand as they strolled across the Piazzetta and swung off. Natale tried desperately to revive the scene along the canal. She spoke only once, as they passed the Giardinetti, wondering aloud, "Is the old lady with all the cats still there?"

"She's there feeding them all."

"There are nice people in this world."

As they walked on to the air terminal, around it, and over the small bridge, jostling past people hurrying from the San Marco vaporetto station, Natale kept thinking that if God could find someone to take care of stray cats, why couldn't He show mercy to her by giving some doctor a newly discovered means of curing her? It was a rare wave of self-pity and discouragement, and by the time they had arrived at the swinging doors that led into Harry's Bar, she was ashamed and regretful of her lapse, and determined to make the best of simply being alive.

Inside, she was relieved to find that it was definitely cooler, and that there were no crowding bodies or jarring voices.

"Very few here for lunch today," whispered Aunt Elsa. "We have it almost to ourselves."

Natale heard the bartender from the left call out, "Good to see you again, Miss Rinaldi."

"Good to be here, Aldo," replied Natale.

Aunt Elsa was speaking to someone, probably a waiter, saying, "We'll take that table in the corner, against the back wall."

Holding her aunt's hand, Natale went between the chairs and tables, bumping into a few. She felt a pang, remembering the little round lacquered tables and the undersized chairs, and the fascinating people she had met here, and the meals she had enjoyed.

As they were settling into the corner, the waiter said, "This is Luigi, remember me?"

She smiled a real smile, remembering the handsome, dimpled waiter who had always been wonderfully funny and friendly.

"Luigi, I'm so glad. It's been too long."

"We heard of your illness, Miss Rinaldi," he said in a gentle undertone. "You will be better one day, believe me. We all pray for you."

"You're a dear, Luigi, and I'm grateful for your prayers."

Aunt Elsa's voice came on firmly. "I think two Bellinis are in order, Luigi."

"Immediately," promised the waiter, fading away.

Natale sat waiting for her drink of peach juice and champagne, which she needed, heard her aunt scratch a match to light a cigarette, inhaled the smoke that wafted toward her, then listened as Aunt Elsa described the few persons in the restaurant.

Natale heard Luigi return and set down the drinks. "Two Bellinis," he said. "Enjoy."

Taking up her glass, Natale drank and found the Bellini cool and refreshing. She heard her aunt unfold the newspaper. "Good old *Gazzettino,*" her aunt said. "Let me read you the latest."

Normally, daily, someone, her father or Aunt Elsa read to her from a newspaper, to keep her alive, involved, part of the distracting world. Today she wasn't in the mood at all. "Not now. I'm not interested now."

"Natale, you've got to keep up," Aunt Elsa said in a mildly scolding voice. "You've . . ." Suddenly, her aunt's voice trailed off. She was obviously reading something in the newspaper. "Sa-ay, imagine this."

"What?" said Natale with disinterest.

"The Virgin Mary. This story from Lourdes in France. The Virgin Mary is supposed to be coming back to Lourdes."

At first, Natale did not grasp it. "Whatever are you talking about?"

"Let me read it to you as it is printed." Clearing her throat, Aunt Elsa read aloud from the paper. " 'According to a secret journal kept by Bernadette Soubirous, now Saint Bernadette, late in 1878, recording the eighteen apparitions of the Virgin Mary that she had seen and conversed with at the grotto called Massabielle in Lourdes, France, the Virgin Mary had confided to the young peasant girl that she would return to the grotto in the eight days following August 14 of this year. The Virgin Mary had promised Bernadette that she would not only return to be seen by someone at the grotto but that she would also cure someone who was afflicted. This account in Bernadette's recently discovered private journal has been fully authenticated by a newly appointed Commission of Lourdes. The announcement, which was made at a press conference yesterday by Cardinal Brunet of Paris as authorized by Pope John Paul III, electrified a huge gathering of the world press, and as soon as the announcement was made public, it caused a rush of pilgrims everywhere seeking transportation and accommodations for Lourdes for the thrilling Reappearance Time.' "

Natale had listened with a rising excitement that at first nearly suffocated her, made her heart palpitate harder, until gradually a flush came to her cheeks. "The Holy Mother coming to Lourdes again to be seen, to cure," she whispered.

"Well—"

"I believe it," Natale whispered passionately. "If the Virgin Mary promised Bernadette, it will happen."

"This may be one of those sensational newspaper exaggerations," said Aunt Elsa, trying to calm her niece.

"Read me the rest of it, all of it," Natale urged.

"It's a long article, Natale."

"Read me every word of it. Start from the beginning again. I want to hear every word."

"Well, if you insist."

"Please, Aunt Elsa."

"Very well."

In a low monotone, not wishing to disturb anyone else in Harry's Bar, Aunt Elsa read the entire newspaper account from start to finish. Natale absorbed it as if in a trance. When her aunt had completed her reading, Natale spoke up. "I'm going to Lourdes," she said without equivocation. "I've got to be there."

"Really, Natale—"

"I mean it, Aunt Elsa. I want to be close to the Virgin Mary, pray to Her right at the grotto. It's the chance of a lifetime. She might decide to cure me. You've just read about those thousands of cures."

"Natale, be sensible. I know your faith, and I don't contest it. But considering the number of people who have been visiting Lourdes year after year, only a minute percentage, the tiniest percentage, are ever cured, if it really is a cure. You know about my father—your grandfather. When I was your age, I accompanied him to Lourdes for a few days. His arthritic condition was crippling, and he, too, hoped for a cure. I remember him praying and praying at that grotto, but nothing happened. When we came home to Naples, he got worse. There's little chance that a so-called miracle can help you. You'll just have to be patient and wait for medical advances that will come along and one day restore your sight."

"No, you don't understand, Aunt Elsa. I've got to go to Lourdes. I believe in it."

"So does everyone else in half the world—but most of the believers won't bother to go."

"I'm going," said Natale. "We'll have our three weeks here in Venice and then we'll fly to Lourdes for the beginning of the holy eight days."

"We'll not be flying to Lourdes," said Aunt Elsa. "I can't. You must be practical. Your parents let me take this trip with you. But I had to swear I'd be back in the shop the day after the vacation ended. Your parents need me, Natale. I can't let them down."

"Then I'll go to Lourdes alone. You put me on the plane and we can arrange for one of those volunteer helpers or whatever—the ones mentioned in the paper—"

"*Brancardiers,*" interjected Aunt Elsa. "Men who go to Lourdes every summer to assist the pilgrims. But women go also, like my friend Rosa Zennaro. You've met her several times. She's been going to Lourdes for the last half dozen years, to help, out of the goodness of her heart."

"All right, Rosa then. Surely she'd help me. Fix it so I can be enrolled in a tour group that has accommodations, and can help me get around. That won't get in your way. Please, Aunt Elsa, give me my chance."

Natale waited for a reply, heard her aunt emit a long drawn-out sigh, and finally surrender. "Okay, little one, no use arguing with faith.

You win. Let's have our lunch and go back to the hotel. I'll phone Rosa's family in Rome and find out how we can contact her in Lourdes. Hail Mary, you're on your way. Now let's get practical. What'll it be? A toasted prosciutto sandwich or *tagliatelle verdi?*"

From her second-floor office window Edith Moore could see that the day was grayer than it had been earlier, and a mist and drizzle were beginning to cover London. Consulting the clock on her secretarial desk, she could see that it was time to leave, not for lunch but for something more unusual, an appointment made with her by Archbishop Henning. The great man himself—she had met him only once before—had telephoned her yesterday and asked if it would be convenient for her to call upon him today. He would be waiting for her in the chancery of the Westminster Roman Catholic Cathedral in Ashley Place. The meeting would be brief, but it was of some importance.

Brimming with curiosity this entire morning, Edith Moore had found it difficult to concentrate on her heavy work load. Fortunately, her employer, a movie agent, had been out of the office throughout the morning, and there had been no dictation to take.

But her clock told her that it was time to leave. If she departed immediately, was lucky enough to catch a taxi right away, she could make the appointment in time and the mystery would be solved. Coming off her chair, she took her khaki-colored raincoat from the hanger, and pulled it on. Momentarily, she surveyed herself in the narrow wall mirror. The fitted raincoat made her look a bit slimmer than she really was. Edith had no illusions about herself. Her short hair, her flat face as bland as brussels sprouts, her square, thickset, middle-aged figure, had never been anything to crow about. She considered it the luck of her life that she had been able to capture someone as dashing and brilliant as Reggie Moore for a husband. Nor, in their eight years together, had he ever shown himself to be tired of her. Nor, to her knowledge, had he ever strayed.

She hastened out of the office suite, ran down the two flights of stairs, delighted with her agility, and rushed into Wardour Street, jammed as always with vehicular traffic. Among the crush of cars she could make out an empty taxi. She quickly stepped into the wet street to claim it and once she was safely in the back seat, and had given her destination to the driver, she was able to unbutton her raincoat and sit back and relax.

She wondered what Archbishop Henning wanted with her, and in memory she tried to fix the occasion when she had met the regal primate of the Church that one time. It had been because of Lourdes, of course, her success at Lourdes. As the taxi rumbled and edged ahead, Edith's mind went backward in memory.

It had happened just after she had been married three years, which would have been five years ago. Edith, who had been working for the movie agency, was suddenly promoted to the position of her employer's personal secretary, and given a raise. Reggie had been making progress with his wonderful scheme to introduce American baseball into Britain (eventually spoiled, a failure, because of the boycott by those wretched cricket diehards). But things had been going wonderfully well for both of them, when the illness began. It had begun with a simultaneous loss of appetite, and Edith's difficulties and pain in her left hip and leg. Worried, she had gone to her family doctor, who had sent her to a specialist, who, in turn, had put her in the hospital. She had undergone extensive radiography, microscopic biopsies of muscle cells and bone marrow of the left hip, and numerous other tests and examinations which she preferred not to recall. She had resumed her job, fearfully awaiting a final verdict until the verdict had come. She was afflicted by a sarcoma, a malignant tumor of the conjunctive tissue at the base of the iliac bone, and there was no effective means of treatment known. Despite orthopedic surgery, and megavitamins and drugs, the diseased area degenerated, the tumor enlarging, and the femur was soon attached to the pelvis by "a few sheaves of bone marrow." Edith was never misled as to her fate. She would become crippled, immobilized, and the malignancy would bring early death.

Forced to quit her job, knowing that she was doomed, she had sought any means of cure. Four years ago, when her parish priest, Father Woodcourt, had heard of her failing condition and been kind enough to call upon her—kind enough, because she had not seen him often since her marriage, had ceased attending Mass or going to confession and, like Reggie, had paid only mild attention to their Catholic faith—she was ready for anything. Father Woodcourt had reminded her that he had begun to lead an annual pilgrimage from London to Lourdes, and if she wished to accompany his Pilgrims of the Holy Spirit this summer, there would certainly be room for her. He could not guarantee any favorable results. Still, he had been impressed during the two pilgrimages he had previously led by the inexplicable cures that he had observed at the shrine.

Edith had been uncertain, but had realized that there was no place else to turn. After talking it over with Reggie, and finding that she could borrow the money from her widowed father, she had enlisted in Woodcourt's Pilgrims of the Holy Spirit. During the first three-day visit to Lourdes and the grotto, barely able to get around with the use of a crutch, she had enjoyed no cure but did experience some sense of well-being and hope. The winter and spring following had been one of continuous pain and lessened mobility. Although it had been a financial strain, without a job and Reggie's promotional scheme having failed, she had insisted upon a second visit to Lourdes with Father Woodcourt's next pilgrimage.

On the last day in Lourdes, after prayer at the grotto, drinking water from the spring, taking a bath, she was suddenly able to discard her crutch and walk on her own. There had been remission, then regression, the disappearance of pain, and ultimately self-reconstruction of the iliac bone and the acetabular cavity. Spontaneously, her good health had returned. Between London, and the Medical Bureau in Lourdes, after three more visits there, sixteen doctors had scientifically attested to the wonder of her cure.

Over a year ago, she had resumed full-time employment with the movie agency. Meanwhile, Reggie had been more prolific in his promotional speculations, always on the verge of success and of striking it rich, with his introduction of the all-black soccer team, the all-star private detective agency that used experts in every field of criminology, his clever introduction of a rock group composed of midgets—but always success had eluded his genius. Meanwhile, too, after having the opportunity to witness his daughter's cure, Edith's father had died and in his will had left her 50,000 pounds. It had been a mighty sum, and while Edith and Reggie had deposited it in their joint savings account, she had made it clear to him that this money must never be used for speculation but should be kept as a nest egg to support them if she ever lost her job, or until the medical profession positively reiterated that she would be well for the remainder of her days.

Entirely lost in memories of the recent past, Edith realized that the taxi had arrived in Ashley Place, was slowing and halting before the main entrance to the Byzantine-style Westminster Roman Catholic Cathedral.

"Here we are, ma'am," the taxi driver said.

She paid him the sum on the meter, added a generous tip because she was in high spirits, opened the taxi door, and walked in an even step to the cathedral.

Inside, directed to Archbishop Henning's quarters, she was surprised to find three men in the tastefully decorated study waiting for her. All three came to their feet as she entered. The dour large-boned archbishop she recognized, but the other two she knew better. One was Father Woodcourt, young and pink as ever, her devoted parish priest, and the other the full-bearded, amusing Dr. Macintosh, who had been the physician in attendance on her last pilgrimage to Lourdes.

They all greeted Edith warmly, as the archbishop pointed her to the most comfortable chair opposite his desk. While they were being seated, Father Woodcourt inquired about her health and her husband's health, and Dr. Macintosh made some funny reference to the grim weather. Archbishop Henning, alone, seated at his desk, seemed to have no taste for small talk.

"Mrs. Moore," the archbishop said, riffling a handful of papers, "I promised you this visit would be a short one—I want to be sure you have time for lunch—and so it will be. A short and happy one. Before I begin, may I offer you some coffee?"

"No, thank you, Your Excellency," said Edith nervously, even though relieved to know that this was going to be a happy visit. He *had* said "happy," hadn't he? She was sure he had.

"I've summoned you here today," said the archbishop, "and have invited two persons who have been closer to you in the matter of your health than I have, to discuss with you the merits of your cure."

Edith sat puzzled. The merits of her cure? What could that possibly mean?

"As you may know, Mrs. Moore," Archbishop Henning went on, "it was Pope Benedict XIV who set down the criteria for each Canonical Commission to apply when trying to determine if a cure at Lourdes is miraculous or not. To decide that a cure is supernatural, the Canonical Commission must be satisfied beyond any doubt . . . that the malady was a grave one, and impossible or at least difficult to cure . . . that the cured malady was not in a state of decline to such an extent that it could have declined soon afterward . . . that no medication had been used, or if there had been, that its inefficacy was certain . . . that the cure was sudden—instantaneous . . . that the cure was perfect . . . that there had not been beforehand a crisis produced by some cause and at its natural hour; in this case, one cannot say that the cure was miraculous but natural, wholly or in part . . . finally, that after the cure there had been no recurrence of the illness."

The archbishop raised his eyes to Edith. "This is clear to you?"

"Perfectly, Your Excellency," said Edith, her heart thumping.

The archbishop was turning over the papers in his hand, reading to himself. He fixed his attention on Edith once more. "At the end of your third year and last examination by the physicians at the Medical Bureau in Lourdes, the participating doctors were asked five key questions. I will read you four of them. 'Did Mrs. Moore's illness described by the medical record exist at the moment of the patient's pilgrimage to

Lourdes? Was the malady suddenly stopped in its course at a time when there was no tendency toward improvement—and did all symptoms disappear at this time? Is there a cure—can you prove it with certainty —and did the cure take place without medical treatment?' Then the most important question, in two parts. 'Is there any possible medical explanation of this cure? In the present state of science, can any natural or scientific explanation be given?' "

Feeling more reassured, Edith dared speak up. "Of course, the answer to all those questions is Yes, except the final one in two parts, which is No."

"And, indeed, so the doctors of the Medical Bureau have found," said Archbishop Henning. "I can tell you they were looking for the following characteristics in your cure—that no outside treatments or drugs made it possible, that your cure was instantaneous and did not require convalescence, and that your natural functions were immediately restored. The Medical Bureau members were satisfied that these characteristics were evident in your cure. They noted, 'We find no natural or scientific explanation of this cure.' "

Archbishop Henning gathered up his papers, and sat back, his eyes on Edith once more.

"The Medical Bureau sent on its recommendation to the bishop of your diocese here in London. He appointed a Canonical Commission of five to study the findings and evaluate them. Then the Canonical Commission sent its own recommendation on to me.

"Mrs. Moore, I am prepared to state that your cure is definite and durable and ends an extremely serious pathological state. I am prepared to state that your cure has received no valid medical explanation. I am prepared to state that only your pilgrimage to Lourdes can be related to the disappearance of a terminal illness and that your cure was entirely unforeseeable. I am prepared to state that your cure can be regarded as extraordinary owing to the fact that you not only have normal use of the limb and hip joint, but also have experienced bone regeneration in the affected areas. I am prepared to make the final statement affirming the veracity of your cure—except for one minor technicality—a minor question remains unanswered among the five that the Medical Bureau undertook to answer. The question: 'Is it necessary to delay a decision?' My answer: 'Yes, but only briefly.' It seems that the Medical Bureau would like to have a final routine examination made by one of the two leading medical experts in the field encompassing your onetime illness. They have requested that Dr. Paul Kleinberg, of Paris, come to Lourdes and give you one last examination. This must be done at the Lourdes Medical Bureau. I repeat, it is a mere routine examination.

Once Dr. Kleinberg has confirmed what the Medical Bureau has found, I will be able to announce officially in a few weeks that there are sufficient elements in your cure to recognize special intervention of the power of God, the Father Almighty, Creator of heaven and earth." He paused. "Mrs. Moore, are you ready to go to Lourdes one more time, to undergo this final examination?"

Edith was breathless. "Of course, I'll go. I'd like to be there during the week in which the Virgin Mary will reappear. I—I might see her and be able to thank her."

For the first time, the archbishop displayed the semblance of a smile. "You might, you might at that. In any case, except for the short delay, you may consider yourself one of the miraculously cured of Lourdes, an authentic one of the handful of Lourdes miracle cures. With my entire soul I wish to convey to you my happiness and congratulations."

Her heart had gone wild. Edith Moore, a miracle woman. She would be world famous, immortal. But now she only wanted to get to a telephone and tell Reggie, tell Reggie he was married to a miracle woman.

Reggie Moore was never one to get discouraged. No matter how many of his daring schemes evaporated into thin air, no matter how many setbacks he suffered, he somehow always believed that there was a silver lining up there and a pot of gold (marked *Reginald Moore)* at the end of the rainbow.

But this morning, he suspected, he had badly overslept, not from lack of sleep but for lack of a reason to get up. He was always awake by eight o'clock, and on the move by nine, with some new promotional venture to research, investigate, organize, sell. But this morning, uncharacteristically, perhaps because he had no special new venture in mind, he had half awakened, turned over in bed, and slept on until ten minutes to noon.

When he had seen the time, he had worried about it, pushed himself out of bed, reluctantly done his sitting-up exercises (which gains would be lost to ale consumed in several pubs throughout the day), shaved, showered, dressed, and waddled into the combination kitchen-dinette of their Chelsea ground-floor flat for breakfast. While eating his breakfast—two eggs, black coffee, a scone—he had opened the book he had recently found in the outdoor bin of a secondhand bookstore. It was a thick old reprint of an autobiography by a onetime famous American who'd also sought success in Great Britain. The book was *Struggles and Triumphs; or, Forty Years' Recollection* by P. T. Barnum. Although

Reggie Moore rarely read books, in fact never read them, he considered himself well-read and knowledgeable due to the fact that he religiously perused both the London *Mirror* and *News of the World* from first page to last every day. His purchase of the Barnum autobiography had been motivated by a desire to seek creative stimulation, maybe come on one of Barnum's old schemes that might lend itself to conversion into some modern exhibit and promotion.

He had started to read the Barnum book in the middle—the early years would be a waste and unprofitable—at the time the old humbug had been at the peak of his powers with his Tom Thumb and Feejee Mermaid enterprises, when Reggie had been interrupted by the unexpected phone call from Edith.

The old girl had sounded crazy at first, words tumbling one over the other in a rush that made them almost incomprehensible. He had finally realized that she had just finished her visit with Archbishop Henning, and then it came back to Reggie that Edith had told him last night about the mysterious appointment.

She was trying to explain what had happened at the meeting, and in order to understand her, Reggie had finally broken in on the torrent of words to say, "Edith, slow down, it's hard to make out what you're saying, slow down. You seem very excited. What's this all about?"

After that, she had gone on a bit more slowly, articulately, but still very excited.

After a minute or two he had understood, grasped it all, and somehow had realized that this was not only of great importance to Edith, but might be of importance to both of them.

"Edith," he said, before hanging up, "don't bother to shop for dinner tonight. This deserves a celebration at a proper restaurant. Let's say Le Caprice."

"Oh, Reggie, but that's so expensive." Edith was beginning to come down.

But then Reggie was high. "Nothing is too good for a miracle woman."

He had trouble finishing his breakfast. His mind was dancing. He shut the boring Barnum book and shoved it aside. He gulped down his coffee, and gave his mind the freedom to wheel and deal.

Miracle woman!

My God, there must be a thousand ways to convert this into cash, gold, coin of the realm. Immediately, it came to him—it always came to him fast and whole when he was at his best—what could be done.

The initial inspiration had come on a previous visit with Edith to Lourdes three years ago. They had taken to having dinner in a small, comfortable restaurant in Lourdes, Café Massabielle, on the Avenue Bernadette Soubirous. Despite the wretched and colorless replica of the Virgin Mary in a niche above the red awning, the little restaurant was attractive, homelike, with a first-rate cuisine and chef, and a wonderful location. But what appealed to Reggie most about the eatery had been its proprietor. Reggie had got to know the owner, Jean-Claude Jamet, whose father had been French, his mother English. Although Jamet had proved a bit aloof, reserved, his fish-faced countenance and pencil-thin mustache put-offs, there was something special about the man that appealed. Reggie could discern that Jamet, at heart, was also a promoter. Unfortunately, he did not use his gifts to make a good thing of his restaurant in Lourdes. He used the restaurant only for a small profit. His real devotion was to his lively and innovative travel agency, Full Circle, in London, which arranged numerous money-making pilgrimages to Lourdes during the season.

Yet, Reggie had felt, the restaurant could be more than a minor adjunct, could become a major adjunct, an equal in profitability. True, it needed expansion and modernization—but even more it needed a partner who believed in it. Reggie had gone to Jamet and offered himself as that partner, the right partner, one with get-up-and-go. For his investment Reggie had offered a modest sum of money and his own creativity. Jamet had flatly turned him down. The money offered was not enough and the creativity was not proved. Reggie had not brooded over the defeat. He was a veteran of rejection. He had turned to other things.

But today, his mind was back on Jamet and the restaurant. Because, today, Reggie had the money to invest and a stunning creative idea.

Reggie went quickly to the telephone to learn whether Jamet was still in London, and if in London but out to lunch, to learn when he would be back in the office and available. He was there, but not easily available. He was eating a sandwich at his desk. He was extremely busy trying to schedule additional pilgrimages to Lourdes because of the demand created by the news of the Virgin Mary's expected reappearance in three weeks, or soon after.

"Great turn, that Virgin Mary bit," said Reggie, "and I've got something super that will tie in with it. I have a wonderful piece of news that will help both of us."

"Like the last time?" said Jamet dryly.

"Jean-Claude, this is something special, a once-in-a-lifetime thing, manna from heaven. I thought of you right away. You've got to find a minute for me."

"Well, I'm still eating, haven't gone back to work yet. I suppose I could see you while I'm on the dessert, if you can come right over. Might as well get it done with or you'll keep nagging me. If you have to see me, do it now, right now."

"Be over in a flash," said Reggie, hanging up and grabbing for his sports jacket.

Outside, the sprinkles had stopped, the sun was doing its late act, and Reggie was whistling as he strode to the garage. There was trouble in starting his old Rover, but at last he had it going. He backed out of the garage, shifted into high, and raced off in the direction of Piccadilly Circus. Jamet's Full Circle Agency was three blocks north of the Circus.

Once at his destination, and snugly parked, Reggie straightened his tie and plaid jacket, pressed down a stray lock of hair, and moved confidently into the agency. It was busy, all right, as Jamet had said it was, and there were at least a dozen would-be tourists at the two counters vying for the attention of the three clerks. With a possessive air, Reggie barged in behind the long counter. When the nearest clerk made an effort to stop him, Reggie said airily, "Jamet's expecting me. We have an appointment."

Reggie moved on to Jamet's private cubbyhole of an office in the rear. Jamet, at his desk surrounded by walls decorated with scenic delights of the European Grand Tour and a square of color photos of Lourdes including the Café Massabielle, was shoving the last piece of his apple pie into his mouth.

He gave Reggie an uninviting sour look as his visitor entered breezily. When Reggie was up, nothing could put him down. He had a salesman's armadillo shell, thick and insensitive. Reggie tugged a straight wooden chair around to the front of the desk and quickly seated himself, ready to start.

"What's the big deal this time?" Jamet asked coldly.

"Your restaurant in Lourdes. I'm still interested in buying into it. I still think it can become an enormous winner."

"Do you now? Well, my friend, you'll have to do much better than you did last time."

"I'm prepared to, or I wouldn't be here," promised Reggie with verve. "This time I've got it all together, and you won't be able to resist. Jean-Claude, for a half ownership of the restaurant, I'm ready to put up fifty thousand pounds in cash toward expansion and improvement of your property. The money is my wife's inheritance that she's held on to in case she should ever become ill again. But now she knows she's not going to be ill anymore. She's cured, and she won't need her nest egg.

Yes, I'm ready to toss in the whole sum, the entire fifty thousand pounds—"

Jamet had been listening stonily. He interrupted. "Sorry, not enough." He dumped the remnants of his lunch into a wastebasket, prepared to terminate the meeting. "For you to come in, you'd have to have much more to offer."

"But I *have* much more," Reggie exclaimed. "I have something far more valuable than a mere fifty thousand pounds to invest. I have something unique, a surefire thing that'll make the Lourdes end of your business boom."

"Oh, yes?" said Jamet with unconcealed boredom, twisting to look in the desk mirror as he combed his hair.

"Listen to me. My wife, Edith, was called to a meeting by Archbishop Henning a few hours ago. It was to report something important to her about her cure at Lourdes over three years ago. The Medical Bureau of Lourdes and the Canonical Commission have decided that Edith's cure is of a miraculous nature, and she is being officially added to the 'Cures of Lourdes Recognized as Miraculous by the Church.' Since 1858 there have been only sixty-nine of these—only five since 1978—and now Edith Moore will be the seventieth."

For the first time, Reggie had Jamet's undivided attention. "Really? This is true?"

"You can confirm it. Call Archbishop Henning's office. Tell him I told you."

"I congratulate you," said Jamet, cautiously but interested. "This will be good for both of you."

"Good for both of us?" said Reggie, jumping up from his chair. "It'll be slam-bang sensational. Overnight, Edith will be famous, a living legend. Everyone will want to meet her, everyone. In fact, she's going to Lourdes again, the center of everything, to be honored. She's probably the one the Virgin Mary is coming to see. Now, as to the rest of my proposition, Jean-Claude. Besides the fifty thousand pounds, I'm ready to throw Edith in as well, Edith Moore the authentic miracle woman. Can't you see it? Edith to go along on your pilgrimages and give advice. Why, you could immediately raise your rates for the next pilgrimage groups. And at the restaurant—after you enlarge it, improve it—Edith could be the star, the special attraction, in effect the hostess. In order to meet her, see her, touch her, listen to her, even dine with her, the wealthier tourists and pilgrims would order from a Miracle Menu at our new Miracle Restaurant at double your present prices. I tell you, you'd triple your profit. Pilgrimages arranged at one end, restaurant waiting at the other—and Edith Moore, the latest miracle woman, your main attraction." Reggie gulped for air. "Now, what do you say to that?"

For the first time, Jamet's stony exterior displayed a fissure. It was a reluctant smile, but an actual smile. He stood up, hand extended. "Reggie, my friend, now you are talking my language. Let's shake on our partnership."

Grinning, Reggie pumped the other's hand. "We're celebrating tonight at Le Caprice. Join us, partner, and get to know the miracle woman."

Mikel Hurtado sat tensely at the wheel of the dusty blue Seat Panda parked in the Calle de Serrano across from the iron gate at the entrance to the massive Catholic church and kept an eye on the schoolchildren and Madrid matrons going inside for nine o'clock Mass. This was the tenth and last day of their scouting vigil. If their quarry arrived today, as he had the previous nine mornings, the pattern was set. They would place the dynamite in the tunnel beneath the street tonight. They would detonate the explosives and assassinate their hated enemy tomorrow morning.

Hurtado peered at his wristwatch. "You better go in now," he said quietly to the girl in the front seat beside him. "If our man is on schedule, he should be here in five minutes for Mass."

"Do I have to?" Julia Valdez protested. "What purpose? He'll never get to the church tomorrow morning."

"For positive identification," said Hurtado. "I want you to see him close up. We've got to be certain he is Luis Bueno, our deputy prime minister in charge of defense, and no other. Go ahead, Julia, it's the last time."

"Father knows best," she said with a shrug, and then laughed and they both laughed. It was a joke between them because she was nineteen and he, in her eyes, an elder at twenty-nine.

Hurtado watched her leave the car, cross over, and reach the landing below the massive church door. She fell in among other worshippers at the steps, climbing up and going inside the church.

A good girl, this one, Hurtado thought, and brave for one so young. They were lucky to have her enlisted in their cause. Julia had come down to Madrid from Bilbao two months ahead of the rest of them. She had enrolled at the University of Madrid for the fall term, and then spent her spare time acquainting herself with the big city and finding them a $200-a-month apartment, all in preparation for her comrades' arrival. Their leader, Augustin Lopez, had met her through family ties, had been satisfied with her loyalty to the nationalist cause, and had recruited her for the ETA—the underground Euskadi Ta Askatasuna, or Basque Homeland and Freedom Organization—two years ago. When Hurtado had begun to work with her, he was pleased by her intelligence. Although she had not been exactly his type of woman—too much nose and jaw, too short and sturdy (he had always preferred the more delicate, fragile feminine types in his writing days)—he had slept with her any number of times. Neither had been in love with the other, but they had respected and liked each other, and their sexual encounters had usually been for physical release and fun. If Julia could be faulted at all, it was for a hangover of religiosity which she had carried into the separatist revolutionary movement with her.

He consulted his wristwatch once more. Any minute now. His mind went to his two veteran Basque companions at the apartment, awaiting this last scouting expedition and eager to prepare for tomorrow's assassination.

Suddenly Hurtado became aware of a bustle among the spectators at the entrance across the street. Casually, from the corner of his eye, he observed the arrival of the three government cars, one, two, three. The middle one was the maroon Mercedes in which Minister Luis Bueno should be sitting. Sure enough, it appeared to be the devil himself who emerged from the Mercedes, as his bodyguards leaped out of the other two cars and flanked him. Oddly enough, Bueno was still reading a newspaper as he started for the entrance to the church.

Bueno was an ugly old man, small and strutting in his immaculate black suit. His mustached monkey face could be seen as he turned toward one of his guards. He was smiling cheerfully and handing the guard the newspaper. Since Bueno rarely smiled, Hurtado was curious. Bueno was a mean man, and even though he had been a friend of Franco, he had been retained by the King as minister in charge of defense. A rigid Catholic and conservative, Bueno had proved to be the ETA's main enemy in the cabinet and had been unswervingly opposed to Basque autonomy. Now, Hurtado thought, the little bastard will pay for it.

Watching Bueno disappear into the church, Hurtado thought—go and pray, you bastard, for the last time.

Tomorrow, Luis Bueno would be roasting in hell alongside Admiral Carrero Blanco.

It gave Hurtado much joy, picturing Bueno and Blanco and the devil in the deepest recess of Dante's flaming hell.

Hurtado could not deny that the assassination of Admiral Blanco, in 1973, a classical Basque assassination operation, had provided the blueprint for the current Operation Bueno and had made the preparation for it easier, almost too easy.

In the upheaval after Franco's death, the Basques' killing of Admiral Blanco had been half-forgotten, relegated to Spain's distant past. But no Basque had ever forgotten it, and the ETA's president, Augustin Lopez, and Mikel Hurtado least of all. The 1973 Basque commandos—there had been a dozen of them—had carefully spied on Admiral Blanco, and learned that every morning he attended Mass at this same church (a practice that Minister Bueno, a more fervent Catholic, happily emulated).

Having been reassured of Admiral Blanco's consistent route to the church every morning, the 1973 Basque commandos had rented a basement apartment on this route near the church. They had painstakingly dug an eighteen-inch-high tunnel beneath the street, removing the dirt in baskets, and planted seventy-five kilos of dynamite in three spots in the tunnel. Then they had run electrical wires from the detonating cord into a corner room in the apartment from which Admiral Blanco's approach could be seen.

On the fateful morning, Admiral Blanco had ridden to Mass in his black Dodge, and as the car passed over the tunnel, the dynamite had been detonated.

Admiral Blanco and his vehicle had been blown over a five-story building.

Fantastic.

Tomorrow morning, Minister Luis Bueno, enemy of the Basques, would be given the same free flight.

And this one act of terror, after a long period of passivity, would remind the government that the ETA was prepared to go to any length to unshackle the 2,500,000 Basques in northern Spain from their servitude.

Not that he was by nature a violent person, Hurtado told himself. He had been a writer from the time he had first been able to pick up a pencil, and writers by and large achieved action through fantasy. He had published three books—a collection of his poetry, a play about Lope de Vega, and a short novel based on the life and death of García Lorca—when Franco's terror had struck against his own family and convinced him to put down his pencil for a rifle. Words, he had realized, would never be enough to fight the oppressors. He had joined the ETA to take up arms.

He wondered what was delaying Julia this long, and then as he wondered about it, he saw her emerging from the church.

He started the car, waited for her to settle into the seat beside him, and began to drive the Seat Panda away from the curb and into Calle de Serrano.

Eyes on the traffic, concentrating, because this was no time for an accident, he asked Julia, "Identification confirmed?"

"Confirmed. Minister Luis Bueno himself right there."

Hurtado was jubilant. "We're on target. We blast him tomorrow. Good work, Julia. Thanks."

"You're welcome."

For a short while he drove in silence. "What took you so long?"

"I'll tell you—" But she did not tell him more until the Seat Panda had attained the Gran Via, and they were rolling along the sweeping boulevard. "Fascinating thing," she said. "I heard one of Bueno's bodyguards talking about it to some official, so I hung around to listen. It seems that Bueno had a call from a Spanish journalist in Paris yesterday. A French Catholic cardinal held a press conference. He had an announcement to make about Lourdes."

"Lourdes? What about it?"

"They just found Saint Bernadette's diary. The Virgin Mary told her that She would reappear in Lourdes this very year, in about three weeks, I think. Interesting, isn't it?"

"Not especially. What's more interesting is the news we'll give the world tomorrow."

"Maybe," said Julia uncertainly, feeling in her purse for a cigarette. "Anyway, this news made our friend Luis Bueno very happy. Even with the solemnity of Mass, he couldn't hold back his pleasure. I'd never seen him smile that broadly before. In fact, he was reading the Lourdes story when he went into church."

"Yeah, I saw him reading the paper," said Hurtado. He spun the wheel of the Seat Panda off the Gran Via and headed for their apartment. "Can't wait to tell the others it's on. They've probably got the dynamite by now. Tonight we'll place it, and tomorrow morning the big bang."

Ten minutes later, Hurtado led the way up the hall to their apartment. He felt good about the apartment, the building, the neighborhood. Despite the cost, it was worth every peseta because it was safe. This was an upper middle-class neighborhood, white collar, and therefore attracted fewer informers or grises, the Spanish security police.

At the door, Hurtado could hear the television playing inside. "They must have got the explosives," he whispered to Julia as he took out his key and let them in. The room was darkened, the curtains drawn, the lights off, obviously to make television viewing better. Hurtado turned on the overhead lights, and to his surprise he saw seated in the armchair not one of his commandos but the husky, rough-hewn figure of Augustin Lopez, their leader and the ETA president from San Sebastián. Lopez had straggly eyebrows and full mustache, a lined, leathery wide face with a jagged scar along one cheek. At first, devoting himself to the television program, he did not look up.

"Why, hello, Augustin, what brings you here? This is unexpected."

Even more surprising was Lopez's attire. He was actually wearing a suit and a tie. Hurtado could not remember when he had seen his leader dressed up before.

With a grunt and the movement of a big bear, Lopez pushed himself out of the armchair, acknowledging Hurtado and Julia, reaching down to turn off the television set. As their leader returned to the armchair, and busied himself lighting a cigar, Hurtado followed him.

"You've come at the right moment to hear good news," said Hurtado. "We've just finished our final check on Luis Bueno. We know he'll be going to Mass tomorrow morning at nine, following the same route and procedure he has followed for ten days. We're set to assassinate the pig in the morning." Hurtado glanced around the room. "Where are the others?"

Lopez drew on his cigar. "I sent them home to San Sebastián," said Lopez calmly, "one in the panel truck with the explosives, the other on the Talgo Express with the detonating device."

Hurtado blinked, uncertain that he had heard right. "You what?"

"I sent them both back to San Sebastián," said Lopez. "I'm sending you and Julia back today. That's what I came here to tell you."

"What the hell," said Hurtado, bewildered. "I don't understand. What about our operation tomorrow—?"

Lopez remained unperturbed. "There will be no operation tomorrow," he stated matter-of-factly. "It has been cancelled—or at least temporarily postponed."

Hurtado stepped closer to his leader. "Hey, what are you talking about? What's going on here?"

"Let me tell you," said Lopez, lighting his cigar again.

"There's nothing to tell," said Hurtado. "We're all set—"

Julia had gripped the sleeve of Hurtado's jacket. "Mikel, give Augustin a chance to explain."

"He'd better explain," snapped Hurtado.

Augustin Lopez straightened in his chair. He was not a man of many words, but now he mustered the words to relate what had happened. "Yesterday, in San Sebastián, I had a telephone call from Madrid, from the minister himself, Luis Bueno. He wanted to see me at once. He wanted to have a preliminary talk about Basque autonomy. He wanted to see me at his home this morning before he went to church."

Hurtado was astounded. "You saw Luis Bueno?"

"For the first time, yes. Until now we had always communicated through intermediaries. But this time he wanted to do so in person. So I met with him for an hour. It was the first time, also, I ever found him ready to discuss our nationalist cause and our autonomy."

To Hurtado this was beyond belief. It was something that he would never have been able to imagine. "He discussed our freedom with you?" said Hurtado. A dark suspicion crept in. "Or did he have word of our assassination plan?"

Lopez shook his head. "He had not even a suspicion of that. It was our freedom he wanted to talk about." Lopez placed his burning cigar on the edge of an ashtray. "It had to do with negotiating our freedom. Luis Bueno is, as you know, an extremely religious man. When he heard about the announcement in Paris yesterday, about the expected return of the Virgin Mary to the grotto in Lourdes—or have you heard about that?"

"Everyone's heard," said Hurtado irritably. "What's that got to do with us?"

"Shh, Mikel," said Julia tugging his sleeve once more. "Let Augustin speak."

"Apparently, it has very much to do with us and our future," continued Lopez. "Bueno was extremely and deeply moved by the announcement of the reappearance of the Virgin Mary. He believes it will happen, and if it does, he believes it will be a sign that Christ wants him, and all those in positions of power, to show more charity on earth. Therefore, with the coming of the Virgin Mary, Bueno will release all Basque political prisoners, proclaim a broad amnesty, and initiate a series of formal talks here and in Bilbao to resolve the Basque problem. These talks, he promised me, will lead to some form of autonomy for us, something satisfactory to both sides." Lopez took up his cigar, waved it. "So, in the light of this real possibility, this reasonableness—and there was every indication that Bueno was sincere—I decided that I should indefinitely postpone any further violent actions."

Hurtado had been fidgeting throughout the recital. He spoke at last. "Augustin, I have always had the greatest respect for your counsel, your judgment, but about this matter I must express my doubts. Surely, you don't trust Luis Bueno, do you?"

"I do. I must. This is the first time the government has offered to negotiate. If we can resolve this through negotiation, it would be the most satisfactory means to a happy end."

"That bastard is just buying time, trying to soften us up," insisted Hurtado. "Augustin, this Madrid operation was your plan. You had lost patience with them. Now, after weeks of planning, days of work, we have everything in order. The operation can be our greatest success. It will make the King see how strong we are, how determined, and that we must be dealt with as equals. Augustin, I implore you, recall the others and the equipment."

"No," said Lopez with finality. "If we can achieve autonomy without bloodshed, all the better. We are not killers. We are patriots. If the enemy wants to give us our freedom peacefully, we must allow him the opportunity."

Hurtado would not let go. "What you're saying is we may not be killers—and what I am saying is that they are. They are oppressors and ruthless murderers who cannot be trusted. I will not forget what they did to my family—that raid—killing my father, my uncle, my cousin in one night, simply because of their anti-Falangist pamphlets."

Lopez stood up, a giant presence. "That was under Franco. This may be a new day."

"New day?" said Hurtado loudly. "Bueno was a Franco puppet."

"Mikel," Julia interrupted, "maybe he's right. Give it a chance. For all the violence, you've never killed a man before. It's worth the risk to avoid that."

Mikel turned on her furiously. "Who asked you? What do you know about killing."

"I know it's a sin."

"I have already killed him in my heart, for what that's worth. I am not afraid to do what has to be done." He turned to Lopez. "Bueno is a murderer. The leopard does not change his spots. He is no different from before."

"I am guessing he is different, both mellowed and excited by the miracle he expects to happen at Lourdes. I am betting that the possibility of the miracle has wrought a change in him, and if it happens, the change will be permanent. To our benefit."

"What if the miracle doesn't happen?"

"Then we would have to reassess matters. And see how Bueno behaves toward us. Let's wait for the happening at Lourdes. Let's wait and see."

Lopez started across the room to the door, but Hurtado was at his heels, angrily mocking him. "Wait and see, wait and see," Hurtado shouted. "The Virgin Mary, that lousy cave, that's all bullshit. I was raised a Catholic like my father. Where did it get him, get any of us? Bueno's God is not my God. I won't recognize a God that allows oppression and genocide. Dammit, Augustin, come to your senses. Don't let us be handcuffed by their God. Nothing will happen in

Lourdes, and nothing will be changed for us. Their tactic is to pacify us, slow us down, splinter us, bring resistance to a halt. Bueno hasn't guaranteed you autonomy. He's guaranteed you only talks, more talks, more wind. I beg you not to fall for it. We must go ahead with our plan. The language of bombs is the only language they understand and respect."

Lopez stopped at the door. "Mikel, the answer is still No. As of now, for the time being, all plans of violence are suspended. We will listen for a different language, the language of the Virgin Mary. I will see you in San Sebastián."

The leader opened the door and left.

Hurtado swayed on his feet, almost apoplectic with rage and frustration.

After a few seconds, seething, he whirled about to the table next to the television set, uncapped the bottle of Scotch and slopped a glass full of the whisky. He drank it down in long gulps, glaring at a troubled Julia who had dropped into the armchair.

Julia began to plead with him, gesticulating with her arms. "Mikel, maybe Augustin is right. He has always been right before. Maybe there are better ways than bombs to settle things. Let's wait and see."

"You, too," said Hurtado, swallowing the last of his raw whisky, and filling the tumbler once more. "Another Catholic nut waiting to see what? Waiting for the Virgin Mary to show up in some damn grotto and give us the freedom we deserve? Is that what we're waiting to see—the damn Virgin in the goddam grotto—a miracle that will tell that bastard Bueno to free Euskadi? Is that what is holding us up, stopping us dead?" He was drinking steadily, almost done with the second glass of straight whisky.

He set the glass down with a clatter and turned on Julia. "No," he rasped, "now I'm the one saying No. I won't let that happen. I'm putting an end to this nonsense."

He wove his way toward the bedroom.

"Mikel," Julia called out, "where are you going?"

"To the telephone, and don't interrupt me. I'm calling San Sebastián, my mother, and telling her to get hold of her priest and have him put me on one of the Spanish pilgrimages to Lourdes as soon as he can."

Julia was filled with disbelief. "You—you're going to Lourdes?"

Hurtado held himself steady in the doorway. "I'm going to Lourdes," he said thickly. "That's where I'm going. You know what I'm going to do there? I'm going to blow up the goddam grotto, blast the whole shrine to smithereens—so the Virgin'll have no place to show up and Bueno'll have nothing to wait for—and there'll be no more reason to stop us from going ahead with our plans."

Julia had jumped to her feet, eyes filled with fright. "Mikel, you don't mean it!"

"Watch me. I'll blow that grotto into a million pieces."

"Mikel, you can't! It would be a terrible sacrilege."

"Comrade sister, there's only one sacrilege. Letting that fucking Bueno stall us, sidetrack us, and keep us in bondage. When I'm through there'll be no more grotto, no more miracles, and no more Basque slavery. No more, ever."

4

Lourdes

Liz Finch was walking slowly up the twisting Avenue Bernadette Soubirous, which she assumed was one of the main thoroughfares of Lourdes, and she was stunned by what met her eye. Walking, she tried to think of the tawdriest honky-tonk streets she had ever visited. Several came to mind right away:

Forty-second Street in New York, Hollywood Boulevard in Los Angeles, the streets leading to the birthplace of Jesus, in Bethlehem. They had been tawdry enough, but somehow for crass commercialism, cheap commercialism, sheer vulgarity, this street in Lourdes surpassed them all.

She recalled, from her preparatory homework done in Paris, what Joris Karl Huysmans, the French Catholic novelist, had written upon seeing Lourdes. She drew her notes out of her purse, and found the Huysmans quote: "The ugliness of everything one sees here ends by being unnatural, for it falls below the known low-water marks. . . . At Lourdes there is such a plethora, such a flux, of base and bad taste that one cannot get away from the idea of an intervention of the Most Base."

Amen, brother, she thought, as she continued to walk along in a daze.

Liz Finch had purposely arrived in Lourdes a day early, on this hot Saturday afternoon, August 13, before additional crowds of pilgrims began to descend on the town the following day, the beginning of the much-publicized Holy Reappearance Time. For her assignments in unfamiliar cities, Liz Finch always tried to arrive twenty-four hours before an occasion, to get the feel of the community, to get some leads, to map out a plan for what she was to do.

It had been an eleven-kilometer ride from the airport to Lourdes, and not scenic at all except for the vineyards and cornfields, the usual outcropping of flamboyant French billboards, and some roadside cafés with unexpected religious names.

Her immediate impression of Lourdes itself was the meanness of it, the countless shops, cafés, hotels crammed together on a narrow street that twisted downhill toward a river. She had to remind herself that it was really a small town of 20,000 inhabitants, yet it accommodated 5,000,000 tourists annually in its 402 hotels and numerous outlying campsites.

Suddenly, she found herself being discharged before her own hotel, something identified on a marble overhang as the HÔTEL GALLIA & LONDRES, its front jutting out to the sidewalk of a busy thoroughfare. Liz had followed her taxi driver, who was carrying her two bags, between columns through a dark entry flanked by souvenir shops, and found herself inside a broad, bright, rather sizable reception lobby. After paying the driver, she had gone to the plump young blond lady waiting behind the wide reception counter, paneled in wood with inlaid marble squares, and registered.

Liz had not bothered to accompany her bags up to her room, or to inspect the room itself—whatever it was would have to do, because in the coming eight days Lourdes would be entertaining one of the largest mobs of pilgrims and tourists in its history.

As soon as possible, Liz had wanted to take a stroll along the gaudy street she had seen from the taxi. She was told that to obtain an overview of the town, upon leaving the hotel lobby she should turn left, walk the length of the Avenue Bernadette Soubirous, and then proceed up the Rue de la Grotte. That was it, the main street.

And now, for ten minutes, she had been doggedly walking uphill, and it was a horror. Maybe, for people of piety, people seeking remembrances of Lourdes to take home, it was promising and attractive. But for anyone with a cold, unblinking, and sophisticated eye, like Liz Finch, it was a horror.

Side by side, unrelentingly, without break, both sides of the narrow street were lined with hotel entrances, cafés, small restaurants, and souvenir shops. The hotels, some advertising garages, ranged from the Grand Hôtel de la Grotte to the Hôtel du Louvre. The outdoor cafés, with their inevitable whitewashed statues of the Virgin Mary set in niches above the entries and their bright wicker chairs on the sidewalk, bore such names as Café Jeanne d'Arc, Café au Roi Albert, Café le Carrefour and featured, in four or five languages, quick meals of hot dogs, pizza, steaks, French fried potatoes, *croque-monsieurs*, sweet cakes, ices, Cokes, beer. The restaurants, usually located beneath hotels, displayed their prix-fixe menus prominently outside.

But what made Liz Finch's head swim were the endless open-fronted souvenir shops with glass cases abutting the sidewalks, with even more cases in their dim interiors. Liz stopped at several—Confrérie de la Grotte, À la Croix du Pardon, Saint-Francis, Magasin de la Chapelle—and browsed through their wares. Almost everything was exploitive of the historic happenings at Lourdes—mostly there were plastic bottles in all sizes, many shaped like a statue of the Virgin Mary, to contain the curative water; thin square cardboard shields to slip over long candles; copper frying pans decorated with portraits of Bernadette; tiny imitation grottoes lit by butterics; countless rosaries and crucifixes; ceramic dishes emblazoned with the word "Lourdes"; plaques bearing religious homilies; posters and leather purses and wallets, all reproducing the figure of either Bernadette or the Virgin Mary; and worst of all, white pieces of candy (called "Pastilles Malespine") with tiny engravings of the Virgin in the center and guaranteed to be made with water from the grotto.

Really, it was shocking, the vulgarity of it, Liz Finch told herself, and no wondrous event could redeem this low-grade cheapness.

With determination, Liz hiked on. The only relief from the souvenir shops and outdoor eateries was an occasional perfume store, a Catholic bookstore, the wax museum with its taped recording blaring out that replicas of scenes from the life of not only Bernadette but Jesus could be viewed inside.

Liz walked a short distance more, tiring of the repetitious scene, her brain growing weary, finally telling herself that all of this must be the mere by-product of the miracle area, and that she had better get to the essential area that had made Lourdes become world famous.

She went inside one shop, cornered a sleek but surly young man, who seemed Italian, and inquired how she could get to the Lourdes press office.

He pretended not to understand, and then did and said in French, "Bureau de Presse des Sanctuaires?" He pointed off in the direction from which she had come and said in English, "Go back down this hill to the Boulevard de la Grotte and turn to the right. You will find it in a modern building with much glass, which sits back from the boulevard."

Dulled, Liz retraced her steps to the end of the street. To her left, she could see the upper portion of a mammoth church that appeared to rise over an area covered with huge trees.

Ignoring the church, she made her way through crowds becoming more dense by the minute. What surprised her were how few invalids seemed to be in evidence. There were a few, of course, older persons propped up in miniature buggies with rollback tops and a long handle in front like rickshaws. These were either pulled by nurse's aides, or pushed while the more alert invalids steered. Mostly the visitors seemed healthy and curious, not only French but of every nationality and color, largely pilgrims, some tourists, and quite a few of them athletic and young, wearing T-shirts and white shorts. The invalid invasion, Liz decided, would increase tomorrow for the start of the big week.

With the help of a blue-shirted Lourdes gendarme, who had been directing traffic, Liz discovered where she must go.

It had taken almost fifteen minutes, but she had finally reached her destination. There was the modern glass-fronted building set below the street level, and separated from the area beyond by the boulevard and an iron fence. On the ground floor, a man at a desk pointed Liz up to the press office on the first floor. When Liz reached it, and entered, she was surprised by the limited dimension of the reception room, no more than ten-feet square, and by its sparse furnishings. There was a modest desk behind which an older woman was sitting. The woman quickly ushered Liz into one of the two offices that opened off the reception room. Here she found at a small desk a younger woman speaking to two persons, presumably journalists, seated in plain chairs, one being addressed in French, the other in German.

Patiently, Liz waited her turn, and when a chair was vacated, she took the seat. The tall dark blonde with angular features, behind the desk, was in her thirties and plainly French and eager to be of help.

"I'm Elizabeth Finch from the Paris Bureau of the American national syndicate, Amalgamated Press International, API," said Liz formally. "I've been assigned to cover the Lourdes story for the next week, and I've just checked in."

The blonde put out her hand. "I am Michelle Demalliot, the first press officer," she said. "Welcome. Let me see if you have been accredited."

"You may have me down as Liz, Liz Finch, my byline."

Michelle was thumbing through a sheaf of papers. Her forefinger poked at a page. *"Voilà,* here you are. Yes, Liz Finch of API. You are here, fully accredited. You are staying at the Hôtel Gallia & Londres?"

"Correct."

Michelle stood up and walked to a bookcase that covered one wall of her crowded office. "Let me get you your credentials, a packet of background material, a map to help you get around. Or have you been here before?"

"Never. This is the first time. I'm eager to get going before it becomes any more crowded. I want to see the Bernadette landmarks, and the grotto, and spring, and all that. I'm no good with maps. Do you have a guide available for the press?"

From the bookcase, where she was filling a manila envelope with pamphlets, Michelle said, "As a matter of fact we do. We will have five or six tours for the press, with excellent guides, starting out from here every morning at ten o'clock. I can schedule you for one tomorrow morning."

"No, I'd prefer to avoid any group tours, seeing everything that everyone else sees. And I'd prefer not to wait until morning. I'd like to start on a sightseeing tour as soon as possible, right now, if it can be done while it's still light. I really would like my own individual guide. Of course, I'll pay."

Closing the envelope, Michelle shook her head. "I don't think that's possible on such short notice. Most guides are booked at least a day in advance. Also, they prefer to take several sightseers at once. I suppose because they can make more money."

"Well, I'd gladly pay for the equivalent of several people, even though there'll only be me to show around."

Michelle shrugged. "I'm still afraid it would be impossible on such short notice. I can phone the agencies for you, but I don't predict you'll have any luck." She had started back for her desk when abruptly she stopped, and faced Liz. "I just thought of someone, a close friend of mine. She's about the best tour guide in Lourdes, in my opinion. She told me that she was going to wind up her last large tour this afternoon—" The press officer squinted at her wristwatch. "—about now. She wanted to go home early, to rest for the busy week ahead. She lives out to town, nearby, in Tarbes, where she stays with her parents. Maybe, for the money, she would take you around by yourself for an hour. You would have to pay a little more. Even then I cannot be sure."

"How much is a little more?" asked Liz.

"I would guess at least one hundred francs an hour."

A paltry sum, Liz thought, for someone on an expense account. She could be generous just to be sure. "Tell her I'll pay her one hundred fifty francs an hour."

Michelle was impressed and immediately reached for the telephone and dialed. After a brief wait, someone on the other end answered.

"Gabrielle?" said the press officer. "This is Michelle Demalliot at the Bureau de Presse des Sanctuaires. I'm looking for Gisele—Gisele Dupree. She told me she'd be returning from her last tour for today about . . . What? She's just walked in? Perfect. Can you put her on?" Michelle cupped the phone. "So far, so good. Now we shall see."

Liz leaned forward. "Be sure to tell her I'll pay one hundred fifty francs an hour, and that I probably won't need her for more than an hour today."

Michelle nodded and was back on the phone. "Gisele? How are you? This is Michelle again. . . . Tired, you say? Ah, we are all tired. But listen, this is something special. I have with me a prominent American journalist, a lady from Paris named Liz Finch. She has just arrived in Lourdes. She does not wish to take our routine guided press tours. She would much prefer to have her own escort to show her around the city, to visit the historic sites, the domain, the grotto. It could be worth your while." A pause. "One hundred fifty francs an hour." A pause. "Thank you, Gisele, I'll tell her."

Michelle hung up and swiveled to face Liz. "You are in luck, Miss Finch. Gisele asked that you wait for her right here. She'll pick you up in fifteen minutes."

"Great."

"Pleased to be of help. While waiting, you might want to acquaint yourself with our latest accommodation, a press tent outside, especially put up to handle the influx of journalists starting tomorrow. There are counters and desks with electric typewriters, a battery of telephones for long-distance calls, supplies, refreshments. You can use anything you wish, at any time, when there is free space."

"Thanks. I'll have a peek at it tomorrow. I want to concentrate on one thing at a time. I want to learn all about Bernadette and Lourdes before I do anything else. I hope this friend of yours, this guide—"

"Mademoiselle Gisele Dupree."

"Yes, I hope she can help me."

The press officer smiled reassuringly. "I promise you, Miss Finch, she'll tell you more than you'll ever need to know."

They were on the first lap of their walking tour, in the footsteps of Bernadette, on the way to see the *cachot,* or cell—the Gaol as Gisele called it—where the Soubirous family had dwelt in poverty when Bernadette was fourteen and had seen the first apparition of the Virgin Mary at the grotto.

They were striding in step, and Liz kept her gaze fixed on the young tour guide, pretending to be attentively listening to her, but actually studying her. When they had been introduced in the press office twenty minutes ago, Liz had taken an instant dislike to her guide because at first impression the girl had reminded her of Marguerite Lamarche, her API rival. Gisele Dupree was beautiful and sexy in that special French way, possessing the overall beauty and sensuality that Marguerite had always flaunted. The guide had made Liz immediately feel ugly and uncomfortable, and once more aware of her own kinky carroty hair, beak of a nose, thin lips, undershot jaw, sagging breasts, flaring hips, bowlegs. In the world of femininity, Gisele was one more of the enemy.

But now, since meeting, walking with her, studying her more closely, Liz could see that except for her overall perfection Gisele was not like Marguerite at all. Marguerite was willowy and aloof. Gisele, striding beside her, was completely different. She was not your typical high-fashion French model. She was your typical French gamine. Gisele was small, maybe five foot three, with pale corn-silk hair pulled back in a ponytail. Her face was frank, open, serious. A pair of white-rimmed heart-shaped sunglasses sat low on her petite nose. Above were large green-gray eyes, and below, moist full lips, especially the lower lip. Beneath her sheer white blouse, her skintone bra hardly hid her straight firm breasts and prominent nipples. In her pleated white skirt, she resembled a healthy, tanned, outdoor child-woman. Liz guessed her to be about twenty-five years old.

Marching along, Gisele recited her piece with gravity, trying to make it interesting, with certain emphasis here, certain pauses there, even though she was only repeating what she declaimed during her tours every day. For a French girl, her colloquial English, Americanese really, was right off the streets of Manhattan. When she was greeted by passersby who knew her, she replied not only in French, but in acceptable Spanish and German upon occasion. A remarkable young one to be trapped in a remote provincial town like Lourdes. Liz was beginning to warm up to her companion. Liz decided to be more attentive and tuned in.

"So, as you can gather," Gisele was saying, "Bernadette's father, François Soubirous, was always a loser. He was a strong, silent, maybe hard-drinking man, and inept at business. At thirty-five, he had married a nice gentle woman of seventeen named Louise, and a year later the couple had their first child, and this was Bernadette. They were living at the Boly mill, where François ground his neighbors' grain, but he eventually lost the mill. He was too extravagant with money, and had a poor head for business. Then he worked as a day laborer, later was loaned some money which he invested in another mill, and within a year he had lost that mill, too. Of the eight children that followed Bernadette, only four survived infancy—Toinette, Jean-Marie, Justin, Bernard-Pierre—and the family sank deeper into poverty, until a relative installed them in an abandoned prison cell, the Gaol, which an official at the time described as 'a foul, somber hovel.' It was four meters forty by four meters, damp, malodorous, smelling of manure. It was awful. You shall see for yourself in a few minutes."

"That's where Bernadette lived?" Liz inquired. "How did she get along?"

"Not too well, I'm afraid," said Gisele. "She was a tiny, rather attractive, girl, only four foot six, gay and basically bright, but she was uneducated, unable to read, spoke no French, only the local Bigourdan dialect, and she was frail, suffering from asthma and undernourishment. To help her family, she worked as a waitress in her aunt's bar. She also often went to the nearby river, the Gave de Pau, to pick up bones, driftwood, pieces of scrap iron to sell to dealers for a few sous."

They had turned into a narrow street, many of its old buildings with flaking plaster and in general disrepair, when Gisele said, "Here we are. The Rue des Petits-Fossés, and that's the Gaol straight ahead on the left. Number fifteen. Let's go in."

Passing through the entrance into the building, Liz heard Gisele explain that the room that had sheltered six members of the Soubirous family was at the back, at the end of a long hall, from which a litany of subdued voices could be heard. They walked along the hall to a low doorway in the rear. Inside, Liz saw a group of perhaps a dozen English pilgrims, gathered in a semi-circle, heads bowed as they chanted in unison, "Hail Mary, full of Grace, the Lord is with Thee . . ."

Moments later, their devotions completed, the group filed out, and Gisele motioned for Liz to enter. Except for two crudely made wooden benches, and a few logs stacked on the fireplace hearth, the room was devoid of furnishings. A large crucifix, brownish wood, hung above the mantel.

Liz shook her head. "Six people?" she asked. "In this hole?"

"Yes," agreed Gisele. "But remember, it was from here that Bernadette went on February 11 in 1858, to gather the firewood that would—well, in a sense—light Lourdes up for the whole world." Gisele gestured toward the room. "Well, what do you think of it?"

Liz was studying the plaster that had fallen away from the walls exposing the dirty embedded rocks.

"What I think," said Liz, "is that the city fathers and the Church have done a lousy job of preserving the room in which the girl lived, the girl who would make the town so famous and prosperous. I don't understand the neglect."

Gisele apparently had never thought of this, had seen the historic site too often to realize how poorly it had been kept up. She looked around it with fresh eyes. "Maybe you're right, Miss Finch," she murmured.

"Okay, let's go on from here," said Liz.

Emerging into the street once more, Gisele announced professionally, "Now we will go to the Lacadé mill, then the Boly mill where Bernadette was born, after that the Hospice of the Sisters of Christian Instruction and Charity of Nevers where Bernadette finally received some education—"

Liz held up her hand. "No," she said. "No, we're not bothering with all that nit-picking. I'm a journalist, and there's no story in any of that. I want to go straight to the main dish."

"The main dish?"

"The grotto. I want a taste of the grotto of Massabielle."

Momentarily off-balance by this change in her routine, Gisele recovered quickly. "All right. Off we go. But we might just as well walk past the Boly mill on our way. It's just a few meters from here, Number Two on the Rue Bernadette Soubirous—and from there we can walk downhill and head for the grotto."

"Is it far?"

"Not far at all. You will see."

They resumed their walk and within a few minutes were standing in front of the stone dwelling that bore one-foot-high block letters that read: MAISON où est-née Ste BERNADETTE/MOULIN DE BOLY.

"So what's this?" Liz wanted to know, gazing up at the three-story house in the corner of an alley. "Is this where her parents lived?"

"Yes, when Bernadette was born."

"Let's give it a quickie," said Liz, as she went inside followed by Gisele.

From the entry hall, Liz saw an open doorway and a wooden staircase. Through the doorway, Liz looked into a souvenir shop. Gisele hastily explained, "What is now a shop used to be, in Bernadette's time, a kitchen and downstairs bedroom. Let me take you upstairs to see Bernadette's own bed." As they began to ascend the staircase, Gisele added, "These are the original stairs." They feel like it, Liz thought, uneven and creaky.

The pair arrived in a bedroom. It was not large, but it was not cramped, either. "Not too bad," said Liz.

"Not too good," said Gisele.

"But it's not exactly one of your hovel hovels," said Liz. "I've seen worse family rooms in parts of Washington, D.C., and in Paris."

"Do not be fooled. This was remodeled and cleaned for tourists."

Liz examined the furnishings of the room. Bernadette's own double bed, covered with a blue checkered bedspread, was enclosed in a glass showcase, which was cracked. On the wall, amid a mess of graffiti, were hung three framed timeworn photographs of Bernadette, her mother, her father. At the far end, an aged grandfather clock and a bureau upon which stood several cheap statuettes of the Virgin Mary were protected from tourists by ordinary wire meshing.

Liz sniffed. "What is it? A room, another shabby room, that's all. No story. I want to get to the story."

Descending into the street, they were on the Boulevard de la Grotte once more. They began walking again, then halted. "There," Gisele said, pointing toward a gray, wrought-iron gate on the far side of the bridge across the river, "that's the beginning of the *Domaine de la Grotte,* also called the Domain of the Sanctuaries. Forty-seven acres. To give you a better picture, we really should approach the grotto from this far end."

Peering off, Liz saw a vast expanse that might be regarded as a football field, except that it was somewhat oval. She shrugged amiably. "Whatever you say."

They came off the bridge, advanced toward the gate, and entered through it onto what Liz realized resembled a vast parade ground.

"We've just come through the Saint-Michel gate into the actual domain area," explained Gisele, "and this esplanade leads all the way up to the three churches at the far end—the tallest on top with the two bell-turrets and the octagonal spire is the Basilica of the Immaculate Conception or the Upper Basilica, below it the Crypt, and at the bottom the Basilica of the Rosary. The Crypt with its chapel was built first, followed by the Upper Basilica, but when the clergy realized that these couldn't hold the daily influx of pilgrims, the planners added the Basilica of the Rosary at ground level, with its fifteen chapels, to seat two thousand more people. The holy grotto is off on the right side of the Upper Basilica. It cannot be seen from here."

Liz Finch was hobbling to a metal bench. "I've got to get off my feet a minute." She sat down with a sigh of relief and kicked off her flat-soled brown shoes. She waved her hand at her surroundings. "What in the hell is all this? You called it the domain. What does that mean?"

Gisele came over briskly to join her. "Well, it—but first, before you can understand what this means, you've got to understand what the grotto means. Because the grotto made this possible." She eyed Liz squarely. "Do you know why the grotto is so important?"

"Well, sure, that's where Bernadette claimed that she saw the Virgin Mary a number of times, and the Virgin Mary told her a secret. Isn't that right?"

"Yes, but to understand fully, Miss Finch, you'd better know exactly what happened here if you intend to write about it. The Virgin Mary appeared before Bernadette eighteen times between February 11 and July 16 of 1858."

"That's right," said Liz. "I remember their mentioning that at the press conference in Paris, and later I researched those apparitions."

"Well, you should know as much as possible about the visitations, because that's what this is all about."

Liz sighed again, suffering in the heat. "If you insist. But don't describe all eighteen. I couldn't endure that in this weather."

"Oh, no, no, you don't need every detail. Just allow me to tell you of the first apparition completely. After that, a few highlights of the other visits. Surely, that will be enough."

Liz found a handkerchief and mopped her brow. "The first one," she said. "Then a few highlights. Okay, I'm listening."

At once, comfortably, Gisele Dupree sat down and fell into her tour-guide patter. "At daybreak, a Thursday morning, February 11, 1858, Bernadette, her younger sister, Toinette, and one of her sister's schoolfriends, Jeanne, decided to go to the banks of the Gave de Pau, the river at the edge of town, and gather driftwood and scraps of bone to help Bernadette's family. Because the morning was chilly, and Bernadette's health was poor, her mother insisted that she wear her capulet— a sort of hood—and stockings besides her dress and sabots. Remember, Bernadette was fourteen years old at the time, unschooled but intelligent. The three girls went past the Savy mill and along the canal toward the Gave which joined the canal near a large cave, or grotto, known as Massabielle. The other two girls quickly waded through the cold water of the canal, and after urging Bernadette to follow them, searched along the bank for bits of driftwood. Bernadette planned to wade across the canal, but held back to take off her shoes and stockings. As she leaned against a boulder to do so, something curious happened, something that would affect the entire world." Gisele paused dramatically. "It was very curious."

"Go on," said Liz, patiently.

"I will relate the occurrence in Bernadette's own words," continued Gisele. "I have memorized them. Here is how Bernadette spoke of it afterward. 'Hardly had I taken off the first stocking when I heard a noise something like a gust of wind. I turned toward the meadow and saw that the trees were not moving at all. I had half noticed, but without paying any particular attention, that the branches and brambles were waving beside the grotto.

" 'I was putting one foot into the water when I heard the same sound in front of me. Then I was frightened and stood straight up. I lost all power of speech. I looked up and saw a cluster of branches and brambles underneath the highest opening of the grotto tossing and swinging to and fro—although nothing else stirred.

" 'Almost at the same time there came out of the grotto a golden-colored cloud, and soon after a Lady in white, young and beautiful, exceedingly beautiful, no bigger than myself, who greeted me with a slight bow of Her head. At the same time She stretched out Her arms slightly away from Her body, opening Her hands as in a picture or statue of Our Lady—over Her right arm hung a rosary.

" 'I was afraid and drew back. I wanted to call the two girls but did not have the courage to do so.

" 'I rubbed my eyes again and again. I thought I must be mistaken.

" 'Looking up, I saw the Lady smiling at me most graciously and seeming to invite me to come nearer. But I was still afraid. It was not a fear such as I have felt at other times, however, for I would have stayed there forever looking at her, whereas when you are afraid you run away quickly.

" 'Then I thought of saying my prayers. I put my hand in my pocket and took out the rosary I always have with me. I knelt down and tried to make the Sign of the Cross but I could not lift my hand to my forehead: It fell back.

" 'The Lady meantime stepped to one side and turned toward me. This time she was holding the large beads in Her hand. She crossed Herself as though to pray. My hand was trembling. I tried again to make the Sign of the Cross and this time I could—I was not afraid anymore.

" 'I said my rosary. The Lady passed the beads through Her fingers but did not move Her lips. While I was saying my rosary I was watching as hard as I could.

" 'She was wearing a white dress right down to Her feet, and only the tips of Her toes were showing. The dress was gathered high at the neck from which there hung a white cord. A white veil covered Her head and came down over Her shoulders and arms almost to the bottom of Her dress.

" 'On each foot I saw a yellow rose. The sash of the dress was blue and hung down below the knees. The chain of the rosary was yellow, the beads white and big, and widely spaced.

" 'The Lady was alive, very young, and surrounded with light.

" 'When I had finished my rosary, the Lady bowed to me smilingly. She retired to the interior of the rock—and suddenly the golden cloud disappeared with Her.' That was Bernadette's first vision. That was the beginning."

Gisele fell silent. Liz remained silent.

At last, Liz spoke. "You mean everybody believed in that hallucination?"

"Nobody believed it at the start," said Gisele simply. "In fact, Bernadette wanted to keep the story to herself. But her sister repeated it to their mother, and the mother slapped Bernadette for speaking such nonsense. After that, after subsequent visions at the grotto, the parish priest, Father Peyramale, mocked her and the normally good-natured Commissioner of Police Jacomet accused her of being a liar."

"But she kept going back to the grotto and saw the Virgin Mary seventeen more times?"

Gisele nodded seriously. "Eighteen times in all. You wish to hear the highlights?"

"All right. The highlights only."

"Three days later, Bernadette was drawn back to the grotto, fell into a pale ecstatic trance, and saw the Virgin Mary again. Four days after that, Bernadette saw the Virgin a third time, and the Virgin spoke and requested Bernadette to come to the grotto regularly for the next two weeks. She said, 'I do not promise to make you happy in this world, but in the next.'

"Despite much opposition, Bernadette obeyed the Virgin's instructions and continued to pray at the grotto. Impressed by Bernadette's sincerity and demeanor, the townsfolk began to follow her to the grotto and watch her."

"And Bernadette kept seeing the Virgin Mary?"

"Yes. The seventh time was when the Virgin told Bernadette the last of her secrets, that she would make a reappearance at the grotto this year. The thirteenth time the Virgin appeared before Bernadette, she told the girl two things. 'Go and tell the priests to build a chapel here . . . I want people to come here in procession.' It was recorded that there were 1,650 persons gathered as spectators at the grotto on that morning."

"Did they see and hear what Bernadette saw and heard?"

"No, of course not," said Gisele. "The Virgin Mary was visible only to Bernadette and could be heard only by Bernadette."

"Umm. Well—"

Ignoring Liz's obvious skepticism, Gisele hurried on with her story. "Bernadette's most important sighting of the Virgin was the sixteenth one. It happened at five in the morning. The Virgin was waiting for her at the grotto and, according to Bernadette, 'She put Her hands together again at the level of Her breast, lifted up Her eyes to Heaven and then told me that She was the Immaculate Conception.' Since presumably Bernadette did not know, at that time, what the Immaculate Conception was, her repeating of what she had heard gave her report greater veracity. In fact, when she reported that to Father Peyramale, the parish priest, up till then a skeptic, he did a turnaround. He became convinced that Bernadette's visions of the Celestial Lady were true wonders. Bernadette saw the Virgin again on April 7, and then there was a long lapse until July 16, when Bernadette had an inner call, hastened to the grotto, and saw the Virgin Mary for the last time."

"You're telling me it was when the Virgin called herself the Immaculate Conception," said Liz, "that everyone turned into true believers?"

"There was more that did it," said Gisele. "There was the fact that the seventeenth apparition was attended by a skeptical scientific person, a Dr. Pierre-Romain Dozous, who watched as the flame of the lighted candle Bernadette was holding licked at her fingers, yet afterward she showed no burns from the flame. And then real miracle cures began. Above all, there was Bernadette's unquenchable belief and sincerity. The police chief tried to trap her, to prove she was reporting the whole event to make money. But she never accepted a single sou. And she could not be tricked into making a contradictory statement. She was simple, straightforward, and wanted no public attention. Actually, she retired from the public eye, became a recluse, and then a nun eight years later. Anyway, five days after her last vision, the bishop of Tarbes and Lourdes formed his commission of inquiry. And less than four years later, he announced, 'The Apparition which calls itself Immaculate Conception, what Bernadette saw and heard, is the Very Holy Virgin.'"

"It didn't stay simple," said Liz. "How did we go from sweet, simple Bernadette to—to *this?*"

The guide's face was creased in thought.

"Look, it would take too long to explain it all, but let me tell you the main things that happened after Bernadette's visions were proclaimed authentic. Father Peyramale, following the Virgin's request, began to build a church above the shrine. But the diocesan authorities decided that the happening was too momentous to be left to a local priest, who was small-time, had no good head for finance. So they turned the area over to a nearby group of Catholic fathers, the Garaison fathers, later called the Fathers of the Immaculate Conception, known for their aggressiveness and promotional skills. These priests, under Father Pierre-Rémy Sempé, the bishop's former secretary, went to work. For processions, they purchased land and built this esplanade, a kind of super park, as part of the Domain of Our Lady. Then they finished the Upper Basilica. Then they raised money to build the Rosary Basilica. Finally, two years after the first large organized pilgrimage of eight thousand people came here to the grotto, the railway company—which had been lobbied—diverted its trains to pass through Lourdes. Within seven years, the first foreign pilgrimages arrived from Canada and Belgium. After that, Lourdes belonged to the entire world, and today over five million pilgrims and tourists come here annually."

Gisele Dupree stood up. "Now I think you are ready to see the grotto."

Liz mopped her brow once more and rose to her feet. "Okay, the grotto."

As they strode along the seemingly endless grounds of the domain, Gisele pointed off to a series of offices under a sloping walk that led to the Upper Basilica. "There you see The Hospitality, which is in charge of the comfort of visitors, mainly pilgrims. Further down is the center for the brancardiers, the volunteers who come from everywhere to push the three thousand bath chairs, the several thousand wheelchairs, and to carry the most serious invalids in one hundred fifty stretcher trolleys. The Medical Bureau, where miracle cures are reported and studied by doctors of every religious faith or no faith at all, is also under that rising walkway on our right. Nearby is a hospital—there is a second one on the far side of the river." Gisele saw Liz take out her pack of cigarettes, and admonished her firmly. "Sorry, Miss Finch, smoking is not permitted in the domain."

"Wouldn't you know," said Liz in an undertone.

"Now we are at the Upper Basilica, quite a sight," said Gisele. "We can climb up either of those twin walkways and staircases to the entrance and go inside."

"Thanks, but no thanks," Liz said grumpily.

"Are you sure? The interior is so immense and overwhelming—the nave, the silver-gilt hearts around the nave bearing some of the words that the Virgin spoke to Bernadette, like, 'Penitence . . . You must pray for the conversion of sinners! . . . Go and drink at the fountain and wash in it! . . . I am the Immaculate Conception!' You'll appreciate the nineteen stained-glass windows."

Liz shook her perspiring face and head vigorously. "Gisele, no more guide-book stuff. Just show me the grotto."

Gisele emitted an unhappy sigh. "The grotto. Very well. It is around the corner of the Basilica, through that archway."

On aching feet, Liz trailed after her guide to the far side of the obscenely mammoth churches. They went past a rack of candles for sale, and came upon a sizable group of people standing, sitting on benches, kneeling in prayer. Some were in wheelchairs. They were all focused on one object to the left.

Liz turned slightly, and there it was. The grotto. The grotto of Massabielle. A plain old dark-gray cave burrowed into the hillside by nature, with shrubbery and trees high above it. Liz had not known what to expect, but she was disappointed. For a wonder of the world, it was not much.

She studied it more carefully. In a niche above the opening, there stood a statue of the Virgin Mary. A traditional one, no different from any other that Liz had ever seen. Below the statue was a circular eight-tier rack with a hundred or more votive candles burning. Gisele was speaking. "A sculptor in Lyon made the statue and presented it in 1864. Bernadette did not like it."

"No kidding?"

"Bernadette was always very forthright. Now, all around you can see crutches hanging, crutches discarded by crippled pilgrims who have been cured here." She indicated a line of visitors inching into the interior of the grotto. "Would you like to see the grotto closer?"

"Why not?"

Gisele and Liz got into line. As they moved forward, between the marble slab of an altar and the grotto wall, Liz could see that many people in the line were leaning over to kiss the wall. "There are actually three openings into the grotto," Gisele was saying, "although there seems to be only one." As they passed by the altar, Gisele pointed down at a locked grill through which Liz saw a glass-covered stream of water. "The curative holy spring," said Gisele. "In 1858, that was merely dirt. During the ninth apparition, Bernadette reported that the Lady 'told me to go and drink and cleanse myself in the spring. I saw none and went toward the Gave. She replied that it wasn't there, and pointed at a spot below the precipice. I found a bit of water which looked more like mud, but there was so little I could hardly get any into my hand. I started digging and so I got more.' That night the water continued to trickle, and eventually became the miraculous spring."

They moved out of the grotto into the sunlight. Gisele pointed to a rustic wall behind them that Liz had overlooked approaching the grotto. At the wall, pilgrims were lined up at a row of spigots to fill containers with holy water. "The underground spring the Virgin directed Bernadette to discover now is piped to these spigots. Also, farther on, there are the fourteen baths in which pilgrims can bathe in these waters from the grotto. The bath waters are drained and refilled freshly twice a day. Drinking the water, bathing in it, as well as prayer at the grotto, seems to be responsible for most of the miracle cures that have taken place. Want to have a closer look at the spigots and baths?"

Liz Finch grunted. "I want only one thing. To sit down. My feet are killing me. Is there a café anywhere around here?"

"Why, yes, there's a ramp just the other side of the church that takes you straight up to the Boulevard de la Grotte. Right across the street there's a nice café, Le Royale. You can sit down there and have something."

"Let's go," said Liz. "Hey, if you've got a few minutes, why don't you join me? Have some ice cream or coffee. What do you say?"

Gisele was pleased. "I say that's a good invitation. I accept."

With effort, breathing like a beached porpoise, Liz followed the girl guide up the steep ramp to the Boulevard de la Grotte. They waited for a break in the traffic and hurried across the street, swerving toward the corner where the outdoor café could be seen.

Liz stumbled toward the first vacant square table and almost fell into the black naugahyde chair. A slender male waiter wearing a black vest over his white shirt materialized almost at once.

"Evian water and ice cream, any flavor," gasped Liz in English, too impatient to use her French.

"*Glace vanille pour deux,*" said Gisele. Switching to English, she added, "Also, a small bottle of Evian."

After the waiter had left, Liz restlessly surveyed the café and its scattering of occupants. She clawed into her purse for her pack of cigarettes. "Am I still in the domain?" she wanted to know. "Or can I smoke now?"

"You may smoke," said Gisele.

Lighting up, blowing out a cloud of smoke, Liz gave her full attention to her guide once more. "Gisele, I'm curious about something. All that stuff you've been telling me about Bernadette and the Virgin Mary, you don't actually believe it, do you? You were just giving me the routine tourist pitch, weren't you?"

Gisele hesitated before replying. "I *was* brought up a good Catholic."

"You haven't answered my question."

"What can I say? I don't think we know everything that goes on in the world. Maybe there are miracles."

"Maybe there are things like propaganda and publicity, too."

"Maybe so," admitted Gisele. "But you are not a Catholic, obviously, so you would see things differently."

"It's not that," said Liz impatiently. "Hell, I know there are inexplicable events in the world out there. I read Charles Fort."

Gisele looked blank. "Who?"

"Never mind. He was a fellow who wrote about happenings that science couldn't explain. But this Bernadette stuff is a bit much. The kid must have been a loon. Do you truly believe that the Virgin told her she will be reappearing this next week?"

Gisele hesitated again. "I—I can't say. It all seemed more acceptable in 1858, I suppose. The world is so rational and realistic today. Mysticism and religious wonders have a lesser place."

"Well, I don't for a moment think there will be a Second Coming by the Virgin. I think that's a Church hype. Things must have been falling off in the pew department, and the Church decided on a hype."

"A hype?" Gisele puzzled momentarily over the word. "Oh, yes, you mean something that has been built up through publicity." She smiled. "Still, it brought you here. Why *are* you here?"

"Because it's my job. I have to make a living. So I have to do what my boss tells me to do. And whether this event is nonsense or not, he still thinks it is news for millions of gullible dummies out there. Yes, I'm here. But so are you. Why are *you* here?"

Before Liz could have an answer, the waiter came with a tray holding two dishes of ice cream and a small bottle of Evian water. He set the ice cream, spoons, napkins before them, put down two glasses, opened the bottle and poured the pure water.

The second the waiter had left, Liz snatched her glass of water and drank deeply. Then she began to spoon her ice cream.

"I repeat," said Liz, "why are you here?"

"Because I was born here," replied Gisele simply. "Because I make my living here. But I am also interested in Lourdes. I do not need—as you put it—any hype to be interested."

"Well, I'm asking only because I think you're too classy for this dumb town. Besides, your English, it's right on the ball. Like the word hype. Where did you pick up on a word like that? Or on colloquial English at all? Not just by hanging around a provincial town like this, or by attending some hick school. How come?"

"I haven't been here always, I've been in New York," Gisele said proudly. "I worked at the United Nations."

Liz did not hide her surprise. "You did? No kidding?"

"That's right."

"The UN? What were you doing there?"

At first, Liz detected, Gisele seemed reluctant to reply, but then she did boldly. "I was hired by Charles Sarrat to be his secretary when he was appointed as the French ambassador to the United Nations."

"Sarrat," said Liz. "You mean the former minister of culture? Why should he hire a—well, let me say a provincial girl for a sophisticated job like that?"

"I wasn't his only secretary, you understand. He had several. But I was the one who worked closely on his personal matters."

"Still—"

"I'll tell you how it happened," Gisele went on quickly. "Sarrat and his wife are devout Catholics, at least she is, so naturally they came to Lourdes for a visit three years ago. I happened to be their guide, the one to show them around. Sarrat was quite impressed by me—my quickness, knowledge of English even then, which I'd picked up from American and British tourists. So when he was appointed to represent France at the UN, and began assembling a staff, he remembered me and sent for me. I was thrilled."

"I bet," said Liz.

"After a few weeks of training in Paris, I accompanied Ambassador Sarrat and some other new staff members to New York." Gisele's eyes shone as she wagged her ponytail in a gesture of enthusiasm. "It was exciting beyond belief. The job gave me new horizons, a real picture of the world. I could have worked there forever, but after a year, Sarrat cut back his staff and I was dismissed."

Liz appraised the beautiful girl shrewdly. "Was Madame Sarrat along during that first year in New York?"

"No. She was tied up in Paris. She came to New York after the first year."

"And that's when you were dismissed."

"Well—" said Gisele helplessly.

"You don't have to explain," said Liz. "Yes, I can understand why you might have been dismissed, looking at you and having met Sarrat's wife at several functions. I assume you were sleeping with the boss, or Madame was afraid you might. I imagine anyone under thirty, and pretty, was dismissed. You don't have to answer. Not important. Anyway, that was that, so you came back here."

"Not right away. I returned to Paris and stayed there for several weeks. I had a new ambition. I wanted to get back to the UN as an interpreter and translator. That's a marvelous job, and well paid. I'd heard at the UN that there was a special translator's school in Paris, the ISIT—in English, The Superior Institute of Interpretership and Translation. I investigated it. There is a four-year course I could do in three years, concentrating on English, German, and Russian. A very good school, but very expensive. Entrance fee is ten thousand francs a year—thirty thousand for three years—plus much more for room and board. I was qualified in every way except financially. So I decided to come back to Lourdes, work hard, save every franc possible—I even save on my room and board by living with my parents, who have an apartment not far from Lourdes, commuting distance. I go home for dinner every evening, and come back to Lourdes early in the morning. I'm determined to save up for that translator's school. Once I study there, and get a diploma, I'll be able to get a top-level job at the United Nations. Ambassador Sarrat promised to help me. That is all I want."

Liz Finch had been listening attentively. Having finished her ice cream, she drank her water, eyeing the girl guide over the rim of the glass. "So it's money, saving money, that's where you're at?"

"Yes. I'm trying to save, but this job doesn't pay much. It'll take me forever."

Liz plucked a fresh cigarette from her pack, and applied the flame of her lighter. "Maybe it need not take you forever," she said casually.

Gisele's smooth brow knitted. "What do you mean?"

"There are many ways to make a fair sum of money, the amount you might need."

"How?"

"Take me, for instance, as a possible source for money," said Liz. "I'm not rich. Anything but. Yet, I work for a rich American newsgathering organization. API has been known to put up substantial sums to get their hands on an exclusive big story. It would be worth a fat hunk of cash if I found someone who could help me dig up a big story on Lourdes. It would help me, help API, and certainly help the person who led me to it."

Gisele was alert and fascinated, but confused. "A big story? What does that mean? You mean, like if the Virgin Mary reappears at the grotto?"

"Certainly that would be a big story, but it wouldn't be exclusive and so would not invite any special payment. But anyway, that's not practical, not what I'm talking about. The Virgin won't reappear, so forget about that angle."

"If there is a miracle, a sudden unexplained cure, is that a big story?"

"It might be, but only if Liz Finch got it first, learned about it before anyone else did. But even that's second best, and unlikely."

"What is first best?" Gisele wanted to know.

"To get some clue to the truth about Lourdes, and to be able to put the blast on it," said Liz. "To get hard evidence that Bernadette was a mixed-up kid or a phony and that there were no apparitions at all, ever. To prove that the shrine, the grotto here in Lourdes, the miracle cures, are all myths and make-believe perpetuated by certain vested interests. To get indisputable evidence that Bernadette never saw what she had claimed to have seen. Put on the wires before the week is out, that would be the perfect big story."

Gisele was taken aback. "But that would be a sacrilege. Bernadette is a saint."

"She wouldn't be once we got the goods on her. If we exposed her, good-bye Bernadette, good-bye Lourdes. But it would take real hard evidence to put an end to Bernadette."

Gisele was shaking her head. "It would be impossible to prove anything against—against her."

Liz offered a crooked smile. "Gisele, as your church people say, nothing on earth is impossible if you have faith—in this case reverse faith—in what you believe. And I believe, without equivocation, that the whole Lourdes story is basically phony. But to be realistic, we need to prove it. You want money for that translator's school in Paris? You want a lot of money, and right away? Okay. You know this town, you know the people like nobody else does. Snoop around. Find me one shred of evidence, one lead, something, anything to give me the big story and you're on your way to translator's school in Paris and a good job at the UN in New York."

"And that—that's the only big story worth money?" asked Gisele weakly.

"I'm not saying that it's the only one. I'm saying an exposé is the main one. Look, failing that, there might be something else that could qualify. Thousands of people from all over the world have been pouring into Lourdes, and more will come tomorrow for the Virgin's encore. Maybe some of them will be newsworthy, and crazy things will happen to them. There could be a story there, too, that would be worth considerable money. Mind you, it would have to be a big story. But since I don't know who'll be here, what's coming up, I can only say at this point that the one sure-fire big story would be one that exposes Bernadette. I think evidence could exist. I think that's worth going after. What do you think? It's worth a try, isn't it?"

Gisele nodded. "Yes, it is worth a try." Her voice was barely audible. "I will try to find it for you."

5

Sunday, August 14

By midafternoon of Sunday, the first day of what the travel agencies were calling The Reappearance Time, thousands of pilgrims and tourists had begun to converge on Lourdes from every point on the compass, from the cities of Europe, from countries as distant as India and Japan, Canada and the United States.

"Lourdes radiates like an appeal," one of the tourist booklets stated. "A unique meeting place, it is for the Christian the revival of his faith, for the invalid a hope of recovery, for the heart a reason to hope."

Despite the haze of heat that hung over the little French town, the winding streets were jammed thick with newcomers. A normal year brought 5,000,000 visitors to Lourdes. But this year, predictions were that the influx of tourists would set a new record. There would be 3,000,000 private automobiles, 30,000 buses, 4,000 air flights, 1,100 special trains disgorging visitors by the hour.

One and all, they swarmed toward the grotto of Massabielle. For some it was curiosity. For others fascination.

For most it was—a reason to hope.

Through the dusty window of her Wagon-Lits carriage, Amanda Spenser could see the front and rear cars of the long train as it snaked around a sharp curve in the rocky valley. Soon, in an hour and a half, a voice on the loudspeaker told her, they would be arriving in Lourdes. Once again, a recording on the loudspeaker was playing the Lourdes hymn.

Of the four of them in the train compartment, Amanda was the only one not catnapping, although she ached from the discomfort of the tiresome journey. Ken, rocking in the seat beside her, was blissfully dozing, still blanketed by the sedative taken the night before. To her eyes, he had in recent days begun to look macerated. Next to him, Dr. Macintosh, senior physician on the pilgrimage, mouth open, eyes closed, was snoring lightly. Squeezed into a chair across from them, Father Woodcourt, the veteran leader of the tour, was stirring as the rays of the midafternoon sun touched his face, and he would soon be awake. Like Ken, the priest and the doctor had found the journey pleasant. Of the four of them, Amanda alone, a child of the air age, had found the twenty-four-hour trek tiresome.

The annual pilgrimage by the Pilgrims of the Holy Spirit, led by Father Woodcourt, had begun from London's Victoria Station. They had left the boat train at Dover, on the channel, milled about the departure terminal, and boarded the chartered P & O Ferry for the bumpy crossing to Boulogne. There they had found their reserved places on the French train, and the delay had been interminable because there had been 650 of them—largely British, a few Americans—for the coaches. About 100 of these passengers had been invalids in stretchers and collapsible wheelchairs and they were loaded into the three custom-built ambulance cars.

One of the longest stops had been Paris last night, when Amanda had made her final effort to get Ken to transfer to a plane and make the rest of the journey by air, but once more he had stubbornly refused, insisting on going all the way by train with his fellow pilgrims. And then after the monotonous night, there was the long stop in Bordeaux this morning. Then followed lush forests and meadows with cows chewing their cuds, which was better. While lunch had also improved Amanda's mood, she had wanted only to be off this rattling old train and to be relaxing in the comfort of a luxurious hotel, even if it was in Lourdes.

As the train ran along the river, everyone else in the compartment seemed to sense that they were nearing their destination and began to awaken.

Ken Clayton, straightening, rubbing his eyes, addressed Amanda, "Well, that was quite a snooze. Are we almost there?"

"Almost," said Amanda.

Dr. Macintosh leaned forward, eyeing Ken. "How are you feeling, young man? Are you all right?"

"I'm fine, thank you."

Father Woodcourt was squinting out the window at the sun-drenched hills. "Yes, it won't be long," he said. He rose, stretching. "I think I'll take a walk through the train, see how everyone is doing. What about you, Mr. Clayton? Would you and your wife like to come along? You might find it interesting."

"No, thanks," said Amanda. "I'm not up to it."

"I am," said Ken, wobbling to his feet. "I'd like to have a look before we get off."

"Ken, you should rest," said Amanda.

"I said I'm okay," Ken assured her.

Dr. Macintosh was also standing. "I'll join both of you. There are a few people I want to say hello to, actually see how they are."

"Come along then," said Father Woodcourt.

He left the compartment, with Ken and Dr. Macintosh right behind him.

As they disappeared from sight, Amanda was relieved. She had wanted a short interval to herself, so that she could finish the book that she had been reading at every opportunity since they had left Chicago. Actually, in the three weeks preceding this trip, Amanda had voraciously gone through every book about Bernadette and Lourdes that she had been able to lay her hands on. She had read the one standard novel, *The Song of Bernadette* by Franz Werfel, an inaccurate piece of historical fiction written to show the author's gratefulness for being given refuge in Lourdes during the Nazi occupation of France. The other books had been factual stuff. The first she had reread. A sticky, religious book by Frances Parkinson Keyes, a converted Catholic, who was inspired by her visits to Lourdes in 1939 and 1952. A book by Robert Hugh Benson—the son of the Protestant archbishop of Canterbury but himself a strict Catholic—which was a rather snobbish defense of the shrine drawn from his stay in Lourdes in 1914. A biography of Bernadette in one volume, a condensation of the seven volumes that the bishop of Tarbes and Lourdes had directed Father René Laurentin to write to celebrate the centenary of Bernadette's visions; obviously a pro-Bernadette book but surprisingly fair and balanced.

Throughout her reading, Amanda had constantly come across mention of the book that had intrigued her the most, and she had sought it through a rare book store. It was a scandalous novel called *Lourdes* by Emile Zola, the anticlerical skeptic and realist who had visited Lourdes in 1892. The novel had been published in English in

1897, and no longer was easy to come by. It was a novel that many Catholics and Lourdes lovers had considered scurrilous. It was intended to debunk the Bernadette story and Lourdes completely. It was just what Amanda had needed as ammunition to bring Ken to his senses, especially since Ken the lawyer had always idolized Zola for defending Alfred Dreyfus, and his daring letter "J'accuse," which exposed the anti-Semitic frame-up arranged by the French general staff.

If Zola had attacked Lourdes, Ken would certainly have to listen.

Luckily, the rare-book dealer had obtained a copy of the novel, which had proven to be an old-fashioned double-decker, the first volume 377 pages, the second volume 400 pages, and small type at that. Cumbersome though it was, Amanda had determined to pack it in her luggage. Obtaining it on the eve of her departure, she had dipped into it steadily since, and now she had only a handful of pages left.

She had found it rather good, the story of a priest named Pierre Froment, a disillusioned clergyman who had lost his faith, accompanying a childhood friend, an incurable invalid named Marie de Guersaint, to Lourdes. After praying at the grotto, Marie would be cured by a miracle, although Pierre would always suspect that she had actually been invalided by hysteria rather than an organic illness. Throughout her reading, Amanda had marked those passages that questioned the validity of Bernadette's vision and the so-called miracle cures at the grotto.

Alone, at last, Amanda reached into her canvas tote bag for the second of Zola's two volumes, and resumed her reading. In fifteen minutes, she had finished the novel. Quickly, before Ken's return, she went back to the first volume to find the pages in which she had inserted slips, pages with marked passages that she would read to Ken as soon as it could be done. This would counteract the brainwashing that Ken had received from his mother and her priest. This would clear his head, bring him back to his senses, make him turn away from Lourdes.

As if to reinforce her argument, Amanda began to pick through the first volume, seeking out more narrative passages that she had marked, especially the ones about Bernadette.

At last, she found one she liked.

"As a doctor had roughly expressed it, this girl of fourteen, at a critical period of her life, already ravaged, too, by asthma, was, after all, already an exceptional victim of hysteria, afflicted with a degenerate heredity and lapsing into infancy. . . . How many shepherdesses there had been before Bernadette who had seen the Virgin in a similar way, amidst all the same childish nonsense! Was it not always the same story, the Lady clad in light, the secret confided, the spring bursting forth, the mission which had to be fulfilled, the miracles whose enchantments would convert the masses?"

Perfect to read to Ken.

Amanda put the first volume down on the seat and opened the second one. Bernadette had been sent away from Lourdes, to Nevers, there to become a nun. Zola had met a physician, whom he called Doctor Chassaigne in his book, who had seen the nun Bernadette six years after the apparitions. "The doctor had been particularly struck by her beautiful eyes, pure, candid, and frank, like those of a child. The rest of her face, said he, had become somewhat spoilt; her complexion was losing its clearness, her features had grown less delicate, and her general appearance was that of an ordinary servant-girl, short, puny, and unobtrusive. Her piety was still keen, but she had not seemed to him to be the ecstatical, excitable creature that many might have supposed; indeed, she appeared to have a rather positive mind which did not indulge in flights of fancy."

Amanda weighed repeating these words to Ken. They might represent overkill. Amanda decided that she might best overlook this passage. She paused before more of her markings and reread the words to herself. Zola's doctor was speaking. "And if Bernadette was only hallucinated, only an idiot, would not the outcome be more astonishing, more inexplicable still? What! An idiot's dream could have sufficed to stir up nations like this! No! No! The Divine breath which alone can explain prodigies passed here." Listening, Father Pierre agreed. "It was true, a breath had passed there, the sob of sorrow, the inextinguishable yearning toward the Infinite of hope. If the dream of a suffering child had sufficed to attract multitudes, to bring about a rain of millions and raise a new city from the soil, was it not because the dream in a measure appeased the hunger of poor mankind, its insatiable need of being deceived and consoled?"

Yes, better, Amanda told herself, that would do nicely to bring Ken back to the realistic world. Zola's was a mind that Ken could not ignore or fail to respect. And, somewhere, Zola had referred to the infallible Bernadette as "a mere imbecile." Yes, Zola might do the trick.

But then, sitting back, she felt a moment of uncertainty. She knew that already Ken's chances with surgery were far less than they had been three weeks ago. Still, clinging to the thought of Zola, she told herself that there was time enough, that every minute counted. Also, she realized that she needed passionately for her own sake to bring Ken back to her reality, the realm of science. She had to fight this her way. She had to believe Zola counted.

As Amanda sat with the book in her lap, she heard Ken's voice in the corridor, and saw him outside the compartment with Father Wood-court.

The priest was saying, "Well, I'll leave you here, Mr. Clayton. You'll need a few moments rest before we pull into Lourdes. I'll just go on to the last few cars. I'm sorry if I tired you."

"Oh, I'll be all right," Ken said. "It was worth anything. Thanks for the tour, and thanks especially for introducing me to Mrs. Moore. That was really a thrill."

Ken watched the priest start off, and finally turned in to the compartment. As he dropped into the seat near Amanda, he tried to smile, but it was a wan smile. His once healthy features were pale, almost ghostly, and Amanda suffered a grip of fear again about his condition.

"Are you feeling all right?" Amanda asked worriedly. "You shouldn't have taken the tour."

"Wouldn't have missed it for anything," said Ken.

He seemed so plainly exhausted that Amanda could not stand it. She took his hand briefly. "Ken, let me give you something. You can use a little relief." She meant a sedative or pain-killer.

He shook his head. "No. I want my mind perfectly alert when we pull into Lourdes. That should be very soon." With effort, he sat up and suddenly his eyes brightened. "Amanda, something truly exciting happened on the train tour. I was introduced to Edith Moore. I spoke to her."

Momentarily, Amanda was bewildered. "Edith Moore?"

"You remember, the miracle woman we heard about in London. She's on this pilgrimage, a few cars down. You should see her. Robust and strong as an Olympic athlete. Five years ago she had the same—or a similar—degenerative bone cancer of the pelvis, very much like mine. The doctors gave her up, she was telling me, and then she made a trip, two trips, to Lourdes, and the second time, after praying at the grotto, drinking the water, taking a bath, she was instantly cured, totally cured, able to walk without a crutch, able to go back to work in London. The destroyed bone area was spontaneously regenerated. Doctors in London and Lourdes have examined her time and again, and they've now agreed that she has been miraculously healed. The official announcement will be made at Lourdes this week. Her cure will be declared a miracle." Ken Clayton sank back in his seat, life returning to his face, his smile broader. "I keep telling myself, if it could happen to her, to Mrs. Moore, it can happen to me. I'm really so happy we came here. I've never been more optimistic."

"I'm glad," said Amanda woodenly. "I'm glad you met Mrs. Moore."

"I'm sure you'll have an opportunity to meet her, too, after we arrive, and you'll feel as reassured as I feel." He glanced at Amanda. "What have you been doing while I've been going through the train?"

She dropped her hand over the title of the Zola novel in her lap. "Oh, just reading—a book."

Hastily, she stuffed the two volumes into her tote bag. She knew that the timing was wrong. She couldn't undermine her darling's optimism with Zola's harsh realities, not at this moment, not when Ken was so hopeful and happy after his encounter with Mrs. Moore.

Turning away from him, Amanda could see out the window that they were still running alongside the river. That would be the Gave de Pau. *Gave* meant a river from the mountains in this region, she had read. They were passing woods, and the outlying buildings of a town, and in the distance was the spire of what she presumed was the famous Upper Basilica, with an eighth-century castle perched high on a hill beyond it, and farther off, the jagged green Pyrenees. They were definitely approaching the city of their destination, a city circled by nine other venerable French shrine sites.

She had intended to point it out to Ken, but she saw that his eyes were closed and that he might be dozing.

Then the sweet and simple rockaby sound came drifting through the loudspeaker again. The Lourdes hymn, first sung in 1873. She listened to the lyrics:

> *"Immaculate Mary!*
> *Our hearts are on fire*
> *That title so wonderous*
> *Fills all our desire!*
> *Ave, Ave, Ave Maria."*

They must be in Lourdes.

Father Woodcourt, followed by Dr. Macintosh, bustled into the compartment to confirm it, and take up their bags.

Amanda started to awaken Ken Clayton, but his eyes, heavy, were open. "We're in Lourdes, my darling," she said.

For an instant his eyes brightened once more, and he made a clumsy effort to rise. She took his arm firmly, and helped him to his feet.

"Lourdes," he murmured as she reached down for her tote bag.

Assisting Ken, Amanda pushed into the crowded train aisle, oppressive and smelling of sweat, trying to stay behind Father Woodcourt. "Follow me," the priest called back several times.

They stepped down from the Wagon-Lits onto a station platform crammed with arriving members of their London pilgrimage. Father Woodcourt signaled Amanda and Ken, and some others near them. "We're on Quai Two, the main-line platform," he announced. "We'll cross the tracks and go into the station. Those three cars you see being uncoupled will be taken to the Gare des Malades, the adjoining station for invalids who'll need wheelchairs to go to their own special buses. Now, just stay with me."

They crossed over the tracks to a doorway above which was mounted a sign, ACCUEIL DES PÈLERINS.

"Means Pilgrims Welcome," said Father Woodcourt. The interior of the main hall of the train depot was no different from many others that Amanda had seen in her travels. Modern brown wood benches sat in rows on black rubberized flooring. The single cheerful sight in the hall was an ordinary mural of a Pyrenees mountain landscape.

The group moved outdoors, past a taxi stand, toward a parking lot lined with buses. "Our bus is straight ahead," said Father Woodcourt. "Can you see the ones with the poles and placards beside them carrying the names of the hotels?" He pointed off. "There we are between the ALBION and CHAPELLE." He headed directly toward the pole with the sign HÔTEL GALLIA & LONDRES.

In twenty minutes they had drawn up before the Hôtel Gallia & Londres, and were filing off the bus to trudge after Father Woodcourt into the airy lobby. The priest efficiently herded them together in the middle of the lobby, told them to have patience while he obtained their room assignments.

Amanda kept worrying about Ken, who had recovered sufficiently to speak up for the first time since leaving the train. "We're here," he whispered, "we're in Lourdes. We made it." Amanda nodded. "Yes, darling, we made it."

Father Woodcourt had returned with a packet of envelopes clutched in his hands. He called for attention, and there was an immediate silence. "I have the room assignments," he announced, "and will call out your names in alphabetical order. In these envelopes you'll find a map of Lourdes, several information sheets, the number of your room, and your key." He began reading off the names.

When he got to the "C's," he called out, "Mr. and Mrs. Kenneth Clayton." With a twinge, Amanda accepted their envelope and the lie of their union, which they had agreed in Chicago would be the best way to travel.

When Father Woodcourt had finished with his handouts, he asked for attention once more. "Each of you has all the information you require on your information sheets—your room number, the hours for breakfast and dinner, which are included in your demi-pension rate, and other hotel instructions." He cleared his throat. "Those who wish to can go directly to their rooms to rest, have a wash, unpack—if your baggage is not already in your room, it will be there shortly. We will dine downstairs, the floor below the lobby, and after that, for those who are up to it, we will observe the nightly candlelight procession in the domain, and tomorrow we will participate in it as a group. Meanwhile —" He paused, and resumed. "For those of you who would prefer enjoying a visit to the grotto before going to your rooms or dinner, I am prepared to lead the way. How many would like to go to the grotto before doing anything else? Hold up your hands."

Amanda observed that two-thirds of the group had lifted their hands high. And among these was Ken, standing beside her.

"Ken, no, you're not up to it, I won't let you," Amanda whispered fiercely. "You've got to rest. You can do the grotto tomorrow. It won't go away."

Ken gave her an indulgent smile. "Honey, I've got to see it now, do my prayers there right now. The very thought of it makes me feel better. I'll see you before dinner."

Dismayed, Amanda watched him hobble off with the majority who had chosen to accompany their priest to the grotto. Almost alone in the lobby, except for a cluster of pilgrims waiting for the elevator to return, and discussing their plans to attend Mass tomorrow on Assumption Day, Amanda opened the envelope in her hand. Mr. and Mrs. Clayton had bedroom 503 on the fifth floor. Gripping her tote bag, Amanda joined the cluster at the elevator. She simply couldn't understand this Ken Clayton, weary to the bone yet plunging forth to hike to a cave in a hill and fervently devote himself to prayer there, exhausting himself to seek salvation, expecting to be saved as that Mrs. Moore had been saved. The sensible Ken she had known in Chicago, the smart and sharp lawyer, would have seen through the Mrs. Moores and all the other miracle cures at once. That Ken would not have expected miracles, would have understood that sudden cures were not miracles but psychosomatic in origin. Such cures could not happen to everyone, especially to those like Ken who were truly and most seriously ill.

The elevator had come, and Amanda, with difficulty, had squeezed in it with the others. The ascent was slow, starting and stopping, and she and an aged and hunched male pilgrim were the last to get off on the fifth floor. There was only one direction to go, and Amanda went up the corridor until she found room 503. She inserted her key and opened the door. At least now she could rest and luxuriate until Ken's return.

What met her eyes as she took a few steps into the double bedroom made her blink, because it was so unexpected. The Gallia & Londres hotel had been advertised as a deluxe three-star hostelry, but what lay before her eyes was an abomination. The room was as confining for two persons as a room could possibly be. It was hardly a room. It was a drab cell. Twin beds, covered with vomitus green bedspreads, filled, or seemed to fill, the entire space. To the left, at the foot of the beds, there was a small table, a side chair, and next to it a bureau. There were simply no other furnishings in the room, and no adornments except a niche on either side of the headboards holding statuettes of Jesus and the Virgin Mary. Across the room there were tired drapes on either side of a window. To get to the window and open it for air, Amanda had to press sideways between the table and foot of the beds. Raising the window, she could see a long procession of people marching in the afternoon sun on the other side of a park. They were singing now, and what assaulted her ears once again was the refrain of the Lourdes hymn.

Amanda worked her way to a door leading into a closet of a bathroom containing a short tub, toilet, bidet, sink. The paint on the medicine cabinet was chipped, and the light over it flickered eerily on and off.

Sitting on the edge of the nearest bed, Amanda wanted to cry. This was no place for them, certainly not for Ken, who needed comfort and rest and quiet. This cell, pretending to be a room, would never do, never.

She tried to think out what could be done. There were no better accommodations in this "superior" hotel. All other accommodations in the town had been spoken for days ago. There was nowhere to move to, unless something could be found outside the town, something more— more acceptable.

That instant she remembered. The luxury hotel that she had stayed in for two days and one night the summer she had been given a trip to France after graduation. The place had been magnificent, memorable, and she had heard during her visit there that it was not too far from the shrine at Lourdes.

That would be the place to stay, perfect for poor Ken, perfect for both of them. It would make their few days here—and it would be no more than a few days, at most—it would make that miserable time endurable.

What in the devil was the place called?

Eugénie-les-Bains, that was it.

She would telephone the hotel there at once, immediately, for a reservation this very evening, and make the change the moment Ken came back from the grotto.

Sergei Tikhanov came to Lourdes late in the afternoon by way of Lisbon, Geneva, Paris—all short flights.

As he sat in the taxi that had brought him from the airport into Lourdes, he was conscious of the two changes in his person. One was the small blue counterfeit passport in his suit jacket's inner pocket that identified him as Samuel Talley of New York, a citizen of the United States of America. The other was the shaggy false mustache that covered the tell-tale brown wart on his left upper lip, and hung down the sides of his cheeks and masked a portion of his mouth. The mustache, he had decided, was more than sufficient disguise. Without it, his face with the trademark wart, so widely publicized throughout the world for so many years, might have made him recognizable to someone.

The airport taxi was slowing, and the French driver, catching his eye in the rear-view mirror, addressed him. "Here we are, monsieur."

Tikhanov looked out the window to his right, saw that they were on a street called Avenue du Paradis, and there was a parking lot and a wide muddy river flowing beyond it. He turned to his left to see that they had come to a halt in front of the entrance of the six-story brick-red hotel with the name emblazoned above the top story: NOUVEL HÔTEL ST.-LOUIS DE FRANCE.

Since newspaper accounts had made it clear that Lourdes would be overcrowded during this dramatic week, and that all accommodations had been booked by official pilgrimages within a few days of the announcement of the Virgin Mary's reappearance, Tikhanov had worried about finding a place to stay. Fortunately, the concierge at Geneva's Hôtel Intercontinental, a longtime acquaintance named Henri whom he had always generously overtipped, had been someone who might lend a hand. Tikhanov had told Henri that a close friend, an American in New York named Talley, a religious gentleman, was planning to visit Lourdes during the Reappearance festivities. The only problem was that his friend Talley had been too late to sign on with a pilgrimage and had been unable to obtain a hotel reservation on his own. Knowing that Tikhanov was well traveled, Talley had wondered whether he had any contacts who might discover a hotel room in Lourdes for a week or two. Tikhanov had said that he had not been able to promise his friend anything, since he himself had never visited Lourdes nor did he intend to do so. But he had assured his friend that he would ask around, and upon arriving in Geneva, it had occurred to Tikhanov to see whether Henri could make any suggestions.

It turned out that Henri had been ready to cooperate with one suggestion. Henri had, a few years earlier, accompanied his grandfather to Lourdes and they had stayed at the Hôtel St.-Louis de France and formed a friendship with Robert, the head concierge. In fact, even as Tikhanov waited, Henri had telephoned Robert in Lourdes, to put in a word for Tikhanov's friend—what was his name again? Talley? Ah yes, Mr. Talley from New York—but then Henri had learned that Robert was off on a vacation and would not be back at his desk until the first day of The Reappearance Time. "No matter," Henri had reassured Tikhanov. "Just have your friend present himself in person the day Robert is back, have him invoke my name, and Robert will remember and give Mr. Talley a room. There is always an extra room, believe me."

Believing him, Tikhanov had felt relieved. But now, stepping out of his taxi before the hotel, he was less certain. In life, as in diplomacy, Tikhanov was always cautious, always leaving back doors open, even in the most minute matters. Right now, he decided to keep his taxi on hold. As the driver stepped down from the front seat to remove the suitcase from the trunk, Tikhanov told him, "Not yet. Just wait a few minutes. I must be sure I have a room. They might send me somewhere else."

His condition, as he had come to think of his muscular dystrophy, nagged him today, and Tikhanov went up the outer dark-gray steps slowly. The ground floor lobby was modest and modern, an elevator and staircase directly ahead. Behind the counter, musing over a ledger, was a bespectacled, uniformed concierge.

Tikhanov approached him confidently, and addressed him in French. "Monsieur, I am looking for the chief concierge Robert."

The concierge peered up at him through bifocal lenses. "I am Robert, at your service."

"Ah, good, good. I am here on the advice of a friend of yours, who sends his best regards. I refer to our mutual friend, Henri, the head concierge at the Intercontinental in Geneva."

Without hesitation, Robert said, "Henri, yes. How is he? A fine fellow. Is he well?"

"Never better. Henri advised me to see you about a room for this week. He said you would know better than the hotel receptionist. He realized how crowded it would be, but thought you might be able to accommodate me as a favor to him. Anything will do."

Robert's face fell. "Henri is right. Usually there is something. But today, and for every day of this week, there is nothing, absolutely nothing. I am embarrassed, desolate, not to be able to do something for my friend. But truly, there is nothing, not even a vacant closet."

Tikhanov reached for his wallet. "You are certain?"

"It is no use. I am positive. The hotel is occupied to the rafters. This has never happened before. But this is an extraordinary time. After all, the Virgin has not appeared in Lourdes since 1858. Everyone wants to see her. Next week, I can probably help arrange an accommodation."

"I have only this week."

"Then I am sorry."

"What can I do? Might there be another hotel, someone you know, who would have a room?"

"None. The hotels are filled to overflow." A thought occurred to him, and the concierge held up a finger. "One possibility. In other times when Lourdes has been crowded, there have been some room rentals outside the city. There are many small towns near us, all within commuting distance, and often families decide to let their spare rooms to earn a few francs. Yes, I am sure that is happening now to take care of the overflow. That would be the best thing for you, Mr.—Mr.—"

"Talley, Samuel Talley."

"Yes, that would be best, Mr. Talley. Learn what private housing is available outside the city."

"Where would I find out about that? I've never been to Lourdes before."

Robert offered immediate help. "I can tell you exactly where to go to find out. We have what we call the Syndicat des Hôteliers de Lourdes on the Place de l'Église in the Old Town. Here, let me show you." He sought and found an orange-covered map with the heading, *Lourdes, lieu de pèlerinage,* and unfolded it. He traced the route to the Place for Tikhanov, then refolded the map and handed it to the Russian.

"This should lead you to a roof over your head. I am sorry I could not accommodate you here. Good luck."

Leaving the hotel, descending the stairs, Tikhanov opened the map and handed it to the waiting driver. "There is no room here," he explained. "I must go to the Syndicat des Hôteliers. You see, the concierge drew a line to it on the map."

The driver consulted the map, nodding, and gestured Tikhanov into the back seat once more.

During the fifteen minute ride, Tikhanov was completely inattentive to his surroundings. His mind was turned inward, assessing his foolishness in coming here, weighing the risk involved in visiting a "holy land" of which his government and party disapproved against the growing incapacity of his body.

By the time he had been discharged at the Place de l'Église, he had made up his mind that his health and its reward was worth any risk. Moreover, he felt safe behind the camouflage of his new mustache. Paying off the driver, following his directions, he gripped his bag and proceeded toward the nearby building.

Tikhanov found the office unoccupied except for two middle-aged women at their desks. The nearest one, dark bangs, wire-rimmed spectacles, greeted him pleasantly. He introduced himself as Samuel Talley, American, recently arrived in Lourdes on a pilgrimage, but not an official one, and therefore without a place to stay for the week. A friend at the Hôtel St.-Louis de France had suggested that he come here to obtain a spare room in some private household outside the city.

The lady with the bangs looked sad. "Yes, we had a long list of accommodations earlier in the week, but those are all spoken for. I'm afraid—" She had begun to read her listings, but then halted to study a note paperclipped to the top page. "Wait, monsieur, there may be something here. You may be in luck. This note was left by one of the tour-agency guides, a local girl who lives with her parents in Tarbes. She says here that her parents have a bedroom that can be rented for the week. They would want 225 francs a day for the room and demi-pension. Are you interested? If you are, I'll check to see if the room is still available."

"Please," said Tikhanov. "Where did you say it was?"

"Tarbes. A mere twenty minutes from Lourdes by taxi. Lovely town." She took the receiver off the hook and dialed. "Let me see." She waited as the phone rang. A voice had finally come on. The lady in bangs spoke in French. "This is the Syndicat des Hôteliers. Is Mademoiselle Dupree still there?" The lady in bangs waited a moment then spoke into the phone again. "Gisele? About the note you left this morning. The room your parents were willing to rent out, is it still free?" She listened, then said, "Good. I have a client, a Mr. Samuel Talley from America. I will tell him." She put down the receiver and beamed at Tikhanov. "Good news. You have a room. I will give you the address in Tarbes. It is the home of the family Dupree. Respectable people. I have never met them, but their daughter Gisele is a lovely one, which always reflects on the parents. Here, let me write it out for you, Mr. Talley."

Tikhanov did not get to Tarbes until early evening.

He had lingered in Lourdes, actually in the domain area, until night was beginning to fall. The lady with bangs in the Syndicat had proved to be talkative, and she had told him what he should see in the immediate area. He had walked unsteadily on the Esplanade des Processions, covering much of its distance until he realized that he was going in the wrong direction, toward an exit gate. Reversing his path, he had gone slowly toward the Upper Basilica, even climbed the stairs to the entrance and observed the ornate interior. After that he had descended to seek the legendary grotto, and had seen all the worshippers standing, sitting, kneeling before a cave, but he had not joined them and had made up his mind to have a closer look tomorrow.

What really held him back, he knew, was his feeling of being apart from this scene, a foreign stranger, not belonging to all these ecstatic superstitious people. He had to remind himself that he belonged here as much as anyone, remembering his childhood with a religious mother. What kept him at a distance, too, was that he had never liked crowds, indeed had never been a face in a crowd. From his earliest successes to his rise as the Soviet Union's foreign minister and a world figure, he had addressed crowds, as one above them, lecturing them. Or he had counseled with other world figures, premiers and presidents and kings, as one-to-one equals. Such contacts and situations were acceptable, but for him to be a nobody lost in a throng was unthinkable.

Finally, leaving, he knew the truth of why he had not walked closer to the crowd around the grotto. The truth was that he suddenly ached to the marrow of his bones, felt weak, terribly weakened by his fatal illness, and unable to remain erect much longer.

Somehow, he managed to attain the top of the nearby exit ramp, knowing that he had in some mysterious way been reduced to the low status of all those worshipping pilgrims because he was like each and every one of them. Illness had subtracted from his individuality. He was the same as every person there. He, too, wanted hope, to pray for a cure.

The street above was illuminated by yellow lights, and traffic was humming. He must get to where he was going, and settle in his room, and rest for tomorrow and his first effort to have himself healed.

He hoped it would not take long to find a taxi, and immediately he saw a vacant one, hailed it, and soon, with his suitcase, was on his way to the family Dupree.

The ride on the highway to Tarbes was, indeed, a short one, and to his relief, Tarbes was not one of those dreary, primitive, crumbling French villages but a modern city of pleasant aspect. The driver, noting Tikhanov's interest, was pleased to point out the sights. The wide thoroughfare they were driving on led to a square called the Place de Verdun. Tikhanov could see that most of the shopping streets emerged from this square like spokes on a wheel.

"Is the place I'm going to very far from here?" Tikhanov inquired.

"Five, six blocks, on a side street," said the driver. "Be there in a minute." He pointed off. "First monsieur, observe the little house on our right—France's greatest war hero, Maréchal Foch, was born there." Then the driver announced, "The cathedral of Tarbes, where some cures have been reported this week."

The driver was moving his taxi through a series of one-way streets, and slowing. "The next block," he called back.

Tikhanov's destination proved to be a cheap, four-story apartment building near the Jardin Massey, an extensive public park with unidentifiable outdoor sculpture half-hidden in the darkness. The family Dupree had five rooms on the ground floor, this written out on Tikhanov's Syndicat slip as Apartment 1.

Tikhanov was admitted by Madame Dupree, a thin small-boned woman with loose graying blond hair and faded, delicate features, who might have been young once, and possibly attractive.

"Monsieur Samuel Talley, l'américain?" she asked.

"Yes," he said, also using French. "The Syndicat in Lourdes notified you, then."

"My daughter, Gisele, telephoned that you were taking the bedroom and would be here for dinner. Please, come in."

The living room was dim, lighted by only two bulbs, but Tikhanov could make out that it was a heavily draped room with old-fashioned overstuffed French furniture. The television set was on, and then off, as someone rose from beside it and loomed before him. This was Monsieur Dupree, a squat, powerful man with rumpled hair, a cast in one eye, a square stubbled jaw. Having muttered a "Bon soir," he took Tikhanov's suitcase. "I will show you the room," he said in French. "My daughter's room. She will sleep on the couch for the week."

The daughter's room was another thing. It was bright, recently redone and fresh, and it was feminine. A pastel spread covered the single bed. Instead of a headboard, there was a shelf of books, all French, of course, but no, not all French, several with English titles about New York specifically and the United States in general. There was a bedstand with a lamp wearing a ruffled shade. Tikhanov wondered about the daughter of this lowly French family who owned books in English about the United States.

Dupree had set down Tikhanov's bag. "We will be prepared to have supper in about a half hour, Mr. Talley."

"I'll be ready for it. But in case I doze off, do you mind letting me know again?"

"I'll rap on your door."

After his host had gone, Tikhanov had meant to unpack for the week ahead. But the ache persisted in his arms and one leg, and finally he gave in to it, wishing only to get off his feet and have some relief. He lowered himself to the bed, lifted his legs, rolled over on his side and was at once fast asleep. The sharp knocking on the door awakened him, and he raised his head, momentarily confused, and then he remembered.

"Thank you, Mr. Dupree," he called out. "Be right with you."

A few minutes later, he wandered into the dining room, another dimly lit room, where Dupree was already stolidly seated. Madame Dupree, wearing an apron, hurried from the kitchen to show Tikhanov to his place. She indicated the empty chair beside him. "We won't wait for Gisele. She phoned to say she was still at work and will be late."

Madame Dupree paused at the kitchen door. "We eat modestly," she apologized. "Tonight I have consommé and for the main course an omelette with smoked salmon." Tikhanov held back a smile at the formality of her announcement.

He took in the hideous dining room. Soiled striped wallpaper. A yellowing sketch of Jesus cut from a newspaper and framed. A metal crucifix. On another wall a framed photograph of a marble statue of the Virgin Mary. Serving the soup, Madame Dupree saw Tikhanov studying the hangings. She said, defensively, "We are a religious family, Mr. Talley."

"Yes, I see."

"But you would not have come to Lourdes unless you are a believer."

"That's right."

Once they were served, and Madame Dupree was seated, Tikhanov was about to dip his spoon into the soup when he heard a brief rumble. Startled, he looked up to see his host and hostess with their eyes shut, heads bowed, as monsieur muttered grace under his breath. Embarrassed by this public display, and what he was expected to do, Tikhanov laid down his spoon and bowed his head, also.

After that, they ate. At first the Duprees were silent, but eventually there was some halting conversation. Tikhanov politely wanted to know about them, but the most he could find out was that monsieur was a garage mechanic and madame was a maid at the Hôtel Président on the edge of town. As to recreation and social activity, these were confined to watching the state television programs, attending Mass at the nearby cathedral, and appearing at various church affairs. Did they know anything about Lourdes? A little, what everyone knew, but mainly what their daughter told them.

"Gisele should be here any minute," Madame said. "She can tell you anything you want to know about Lourdes."

"That will be most helpful," said Tikhanov.

As the plates from the main course were removed, the basket of bread taken away, and the crumbs swept off the tablecloth, Tikhanov's mind went to his Mother Russia. What would members of the Politburo think if they could see their great international diplomat, and future premier, the renowned and respected intellectual Sergei Tikhanov sitting here consorting with two morons, oafs, drones.

About to cut into his *tarte aux fruits,* he felt the room suddenly come alive. A breathtakingly beautiful young woman, more a girl, with honey-colored hair caught in a ponytail, and incredible green-gray eyes, had burst into the room, was pecking kisses at her parents. Tikhanov watched her round the table, full of vitality and the outdoors, trim and energetic.

She held out her hand to Tikhanov. "And you must be our boarder, Mr. Talley."

"I am Sam Talley," said Tikhanov awkwardly. "And you are Mademoiselle Gisele Dupree."

"None other," she said, switching to English, sitting beside Tikhanov. "Welcome to the house of Dupree and welcome to the town next door to all those miracles."

"Thank you," said Tikhanov. "I hope so. The miracles, I mean."

Madame Dupree had gone into the kitchen to retrieve her daughter's warmed-over soup and make her an omelette.

Gisele babbled on, to her father in French, to Tikhanov in English, recounting her adventures this first day of The Reappearance Time in Lourdes.

Tikhanov listened to her closely, and observed her with fascination, wishing fleetingly not only for health but for youth. No doubt about it, a real beauty, perhaps from the mother's side. But more. Unlike her parents, Gisele was apparently well-educated, knowledgeable, with a perfect grasp of the American English. But still more, as she ate and talked, there was something about her, something that made Tikhanov feel uneasy. He tried to pin it down, this uneasy feeling. Her alertness, that was it, she was too alert, possibly clever, maybe perceptive. He wondered if she might give him trouble. He doubted it. She was too young, too limited, strictly a local who knew little beyond the life in Lourdes and her Catholicism. Still, his fake mustache itched and he told himself to be wary. The young ones were so smart these days, made worldly-wise by television.

He realized that she had finished her food and was speaking to him, curious about what had brought him to Lourdes.

"Why?" he found himself saying. "Well, why not? I haven't been feeling well for some time. An illness I do not like to discuss. Too boring for dinner conversation. I became impatient with my doctors, and a Catholic friend suggested I visit Lourdes, especially now. He knew I was a fallen-away Catholic, but one never falls far from that tree of life, does one? So I had a vacation, so I thought I would take it in Lourdes."

"You never can tell," said Gisele cheerfully. "There are lucky ones here every year. They are cured. I have seen it happen to them. You may be one of this year's lucky ones, Mr. Talley. Go to the grotto every day. Pray with the pilgrims, drink the water, take the baths. And have faith."

He met her eyes to see if she was teasing, but she was evidently serious. He decided to be serious, too. "I would like to have real faith, pure faith," he said earnestly. "But it is hard for one like me, a man of certain intelligence, to accept the fact that there are gravely ill persons who have been cured by faith and not science."

"Believe me, it happens. As I told you, I've seen it happen with my own eyes. You know, I'm a guide in Lourdes, and I get around, and I see them all, and now and then I see one lost soul who is totally healed, totally. Not by science, but by faith."

"I'm impressed," said Tikhanov.

"In fact, I know our latest miracle cure personally. I met her a number of years ago. She's been coming to Lourdes for five years. She is an Englishwoman, a Mrs. Edith Moore. She was given up as a terminal cancer case, but on her second visit to Lourdes she was blessed with a miraculous cure. Poof. Cancer gone. The blood cells a healthy red, the bones strong. Actually, she's in Lourdes for a last time, a last examination, before being declared a miracle cure. I ran into her before dinner. She's robust, the picture of well-being, and excited. Would you like to meet her? Would that prove something for you?"

"It certainly would," replied Tikhanov, feeling a surge of optimism. "I'd very much like to meet your Mrs. Moore."

"Then you shall. I'll try to arrange lunch with her. If you'll pay for it. And for my time, taking time off from a tour. The price for the meal and a hundred francs for your guide. Is that too much?"

Tikhanov felt the smile beneath his shaggy mustache. "A bargain, as we Americans say."

"Okay, we've got a date," said Gisele. "Since you are staying here, you can drive to Lourdes with me in the morning. You'll have time to take the baths, and after that have lunch with Edith Moore. Okay with you?"

"Okay by me," said Tikhanov trying to sound like Talley. "I'll be ready to go when you are."

6

. . . August 14

"What's it like?" Natale Rinaldi asked as she clung to Aunt Elsa's arm.

They were going into the hotel, she knew, but this was her first visit to Lourdes and unfamiliar territory.

"It says the Hôtel Gallia & Londres in two places out in front, and it looks like a very nice hotel," said Aunt Elsa. She described the entrance, the reception lobby, and the public rooms beyond, then asked, "How do you feel, my dear?"

"It was hot outside," said Natale. "I could feel the heat all the way from the airport." They had taken the train from Venice to catch their plane in Milan, an Aer Lingus jet chartered especially by a Roman pilgrimage for Lourdes which they were allowed to accompany on the flight, although they were not a part of the pilgrimage.

"There are some people checking in at the reception," said Aunt Elsa, "and I think—yes, it's Rosa Zennaro, probably inquiring if we've arrived yet. Wait here, Natale, let me make sure."

Natale stood in darkness, and tried to remember Rosa Zennaro, her aunt's friend from Rome who came each year to Lourdes to serve as a nurse's aide and who had agreed to be Natale's helper after her arrival. Natale remembered Rosa vaguely, a tall, spare woman, maybe fifty, with straight black hair. A taciturn, competent woman, a widow with enough to live on, and one not given to small talk. Natale felt safe in her keeping. Since Natale had come from darkness into darkness, she had to tell herself that early this morning she had been in Venice, later in Milan, and now she was in a hotel in Lourdes, a site of holy salvation that she had thought about unceasingly for the past three weeks. She felt safe in Lourdes, too. It was a good place chosen by the Lord and His Mother the Virgin to work wonders on deserving people.

She hoped that she was one of the deserving. She had never, in the last three black years, hoped for anything as much.

"Natale." It was Aunt Elsa's voice. "That was Rosa at the desk, and I have her here beside me. You met her a few times before your trouble."

"Oh, yes, I do remember." She put out her hand. "Hello, Rosa."

A strong smooth hand had gripped her own. "Welcome to Lourdes, Natale. I'm so happy you came." Natale felt the other's warm breath, and felt Rosa's dry lips touching her cheek, and she tried to return Rosa's kiss. She heard Rosa's voice again. "You've grown into a very pretty young woman, Natale."

"Thank you, Rosa."

Aunt Elsa broke in, taking Natale by the arm. "We mustn't lose any more time. I've checked you in and have your room key. It's number 205. I'd better see you up there, make sure your bag has been delivered, and then take off. I'll barely catch the flight back to Milan, and the last one to Rome. I did promise your parents I'd be at work tomorrow morning. But you'll be in good hands with Rosa." She tugged at Natale slightly. "We're going to the elevator now, Natale. It is to the left of the reception lobby when you come in, and beside it I'm told there is a staircase going down to the dining room. There will be a table reserved in your name, and three meals a day are prepaid."

Leaving the elevator, Natale felt Rosa take her hand. She could hear Aunt Elsa call back. "Here's the room, the fifth door on the left from the elevator."

Natale moved confidently up the corridor with Rosa, and allowed herself to be guided into the room.

"Is it a nice room?" Natale asked.

"Nice enough, and clean, thank God," responded Aunt Elsa. "From the doorway, there's a writing table and chair on the left against the wall. Just before the table, the bathroom. At the far end of the same wall, a bureau with five drawers, more than enough. The wall straight ahead has a good-sized window. On the right-hand wall, a closet with a clothes rack and hangers. There are two narrow beds pushed against that right-hand wall. I'll take the spread off the bed nearest the window, the one you'll probably use, Natale. There's a nightstand beside the bed, and I'll place your travel clock on it. I'll put your suitcase on top of the other bed for now. I have enough time to unpack you, and put your clothes in the bureau and closet. I'll tell you where everything is as I put your clothes away. But Rosa will be with you every day until she brings you back to Rome. She can refresh your memory on anything, should you forget."

"I won't forget," said Natale.

It was twenty minutes later, Natale learned, when Aunt Elsa finished her unpacking.

"I hate to leave you, Natale, but now I've got to run. I'll see you in a week or so."

"Maybe in a week I'll *see* you," said Natale.

"I hope so."

Natale thought that her aunt's voice sounded doubtful, but she felt and enjoyed her aunt's hearty hug and kiss, and hugged and kissed her back.

"Aunt Elsa, thank you for everything—for the wonderful time in Venice, for going to the trouble of bringing me here, for getting Rosa to help me."

"God bless you," said Aunt Elsa and she left the room.

Briefly, Natale felt terribly alone, until she heard Rosa's voice nearby. "Well, Natale, here we are. Would you like to rest or walk about the city?"

"I'd like to go straight to the grotto. I'd like to walk in the city another time. Right now, I want to spend as much time as possible at the grotto offering my prayers to the Virgin. You don't mind?"

"Whatever you wish, that's what I'm here for, Natale. I think the grotto is a good idea. It'll give you a real lift. It's just a few minutes distance from the hotel."

"There's where I want to go."

"It's still hot out. Do you want to change those jeans for something cooler?"

"I think so. There's a silk print dress in the closet."

"I'll find it."

Natale heard Rosa walk to the closet. She said, "Rosa, this need only be a short visit. I'd like to make a longer one to the grotto after dinner—"

Putting the dress in Natale's hands, Rosa was apologetic. "Tonight I cannot help you, Natale. I'm sorry but I'm committed to report to the Hospitality Center every evening for an assignment to push a wheelchair in the candlelight procession. But I'll be available to help you every morning and afternoon. Also, I'll skip eating with the other volunteers so that I can join you for dinner in the hotel. But right after dinner, I must leave you in your room and hurry back to the domain. You won't mind, will you? You'll have had a full day at the grotto, and after dinner you can rest, listen to your radio, get some sleep."

Natale hoped that her disappointment did not show. Putting down the silk dress, she unzipped her jeans and pulled them off. "Don't worry, Rosa. I understand. I'll manage." She *would* manage, she told herself, as she drew the light silk dress over her brassiere and abbreviated panties. She had learned to manage alone in Rome, and she would learn to find her way to the grotto and back alone every late evening. Difficult as it might be, she would not miss her nights of solitary prayer at the grotto. That was why she had come here. To be attentive to the Virgin. Yes, she would learn to do it alone. From the instant that they left this room, she would count the steps to the elevator, find the buttons to push for descent and ascent, learn the way out of the hotel, remember which direction to turn when she reached the street, and bear in mind each subsequent turning that would lead her to the grotto. She was adept at this, had done it before, and as an actress she excelled in memorizing.

"If my dress is on all right, I'm ready," she said. She felt Rosa's hand on her elbow. Rosa said, "We'll go now."

Leaving the room, Natale began counting the steps and storing them—so many steps to the elevator, so many steps after leaving the elevator and going through the reception lobby and the arcade to the Avenue Bernadette Soubirous. Turn right. Steps along the street to the corner. Stoplight. "There's usually a police station wagon, a red car with a white stripe around it, and a blue flashing light on top, standing at this corner until ten in the evening, or if not the station wagon, then one or two policemen on foot," Rosa was explaining. Policemen, Natale memorized, to help her across the street to the other corner. Steps past Le Royale café, steps past more shops to a souvenir shop, very busy, called Sainte-Thérèse/Little Flower. "Here we turn right and cross the avenue leading to a long ramp that will bring us down to the domain."

Natale continued counting and storing. Steps across the avenue to the ramp. Steps descending the ramp. "We are at the foot of the ramp now, Natale. To our left, a short distance, rises the Basilica of the Rosary, and around it to the right, on one side, is the grotto. Do you want to go into the basilica?"

"Not now, Rosa. I'll be attending Mass and confession tomorrow. Now I want to go to the grotto."

"Very well, to the grotto. We are passing the basilicas. Now through an archway beside the churches leading to the grotto area."

Natale walked surefooted beside her helper and friend, silently counting the distance to the grotto area.

"We are going past a bookstore that sells books and pamphlets on Bernadette. We are going past a series of spigots that issue water from the spring, then past a stand that sells candles. Next the grotto, and beyond it another trough with two more faucets, and then the baths with water from the spring."

"Stop me before the grotto," said Natale softly, as she started counting the steps again.

"Here, to our left—" Natale felt Rosa's sure hands turning her. "—is the grotto. There are many people before it on benches, chairs, kneeling on the ground, and some lined up further over to go inside."

"I want to go inside."

Natale counted as Rosa led her into line. With Rosa ahead, holding her hand and urging her forward, Natale walked hesitantly along, again counting.

Once, as they halted, Rosa whispered, "You are on the spot where I believe Bernadette knelt."

Natale nodded, and abruptly knelt, and prayed silently. Rising, she heard Rosa say, "You are inside the grotto. You can touch the inner wall of it with your right hand." Natale's hand groped for the wall, touched it, and realizing it was so close, she leaned over and kissed the smooth, cool surface. Feeling better for the act, Natale continued after her helper, allowing Rosa to guide her in what seemed a semicircle through the grotto and finally outside it once again.

"Do you want me to show you more of the domain?" Rosa asked.

"I want to remain here in front of the grotto and pray."

"There are free benches to the rear. In this heat it is better to sit when you pray."

Once seated, Natale found her rosary and gave herself over to intense prayer and contemplation.

She guessed that perhaps a half hour had passed when Rosa, who had left her alone, returned and said, "People are leaving for dinner. It is time to go. I'll take you back to the hotel exactly the same way we came here."

Natale rose to her feet and, her hand in Rosa's hand, tagged along after her companion to the foot of the ramp that led to the street above, counting, and climbed the ramp, counting again. At the top, pausing for breath, she was able to compare the steps made in her return to the steps counted upon her arrival, and found that they were almost the same, differing by only several short strides.

Presently, they were back inside the reception lobby of the hotel, waiting at the elevator.

Natale felt renewed and enriched. In the darkness of her mind's eye she tried to make out the Savior and His Mother, the Queen of Heaven.

She heard Rosa addressing her once more. "We'll go to your room. You can rest a bit and freshen up. I'd better do so, too. Then I'll take you down to the dining room, and we'll have a good meal. After that, I'll bring you back to your room, and leave you. I hope you won't be lonely."

"I'm never lonely," said Natale with a smile. "I'll have enough to do."

Across the lobby, facing the elevator, there were two of them behind the reception desk and one of them was staring at the women about to enter the elevator.

The plump middle-aged lady behind the reception desk, busy with her bookkeeping, was Yvonne, the regular daytime receptionist. The other was the recently hired night reception clerk named Anatole, a husky young man with heavy eyebrows, close-set gray eyes, a pugilist's nose, and thick lips. A native of Marseilles, Anatole had been hunting for work in Lourdes and had found this job a week ago. He had just arrived to replace Yvonne for the night shift.

And now Anatole was staring toward the two women entering the elevator.

"That's the first one I've seen in this hotel all week," said Anatole, "that I'd like to fuck good."

Yvonne, who quickly had become inured to her assistant's coarse language, looked up from her papers to follow his gaze toward the elevator. "You want that old lady?"

"No, stupid, the other one. Her back is to you, but watch when she turns around in the elevator. The gorgeous young girl. She looks Italian. Ever see such tits?"

His hungry eyes feasted on Natale as she turned around inside the elevator to face its door. Hypnotized, he studied the small, extremely shapely young girl with her wanton long black hair, provocative dark sunglasses, pert nose, scarlet lips, milky throat encircled by the chain of the gold cross dangling above the cleft of pointed breasts, and the summer dress that seemed to outline every contour of her body.

"Yup, she's for me," Anatole reaffirmed. "That's the one I want to fuck."

Yvonne, staring after him, was appalled. "Anatole, are you crazy? She's blind."

"Who says you have to see when you're fucking?"

"Anatole, you're gross and impossible. And what you're thinking is absolutely impossible."

"Maybe," said Anatole with a shrug. "But maybe the Virgin's on my side."

It was early evening when the dirt-streaked yellow bus, with a card propped against the windshield reading ESPAGNE, rumbled through the streets of Lourdes and came to a grinding halt in front of the Gallia & Londres hotel.

Eight passengers disembarked at this first stop before the bus continued on to other hotels where the remaining passengers of the San Sebastián Pilgrimage were to be billeted. The last of the eight to disembark at this hotel was Mikel Hurtado.

He stood on the sidewalk, stretching his cramped muscles, inhaling the cooling night air, relieved to be free of the claustrophobic bus and his babbling pious fellow countrymen. Actually, tiresome though it had been, the journey from San Sebastián across the Basque frontier into France and then through the countryside to Lourdes had not taken too long. The ride had been no more than six hours, but Hurtado had been eager to reach his destination, do what he had vowed to do, and get out of the town as quickly as possible.

Waiting with the others for the luggage to be unloaded, Hurtado scanned the vicinity around him. There were pedestrians of every nationality and age strolling along both sides of the thoroughfare, many of them browsing amid the displays of novelty and souvenir shops. Across the street, off to the left at the corner of an intersection, a massive gray granite building dominated the scene. A street light illuminated its name: HÔPITAL NOTRE-DAME DE DOULEURS.

Hurtado had no interest in Lourdes, except for the grotto. Having been raised in a Catholic family, he had always known something about the Lourdes shrine. He had no idea if the Bernadette story were true, and he did not give a damn. All he knew was that the grotto was Catholicism's major shrine, and that the Virgin Mary was expected to play a long-deferred encore here this week.

It had boggled Hurtado's mind that a revolutionary as hardheaded as Augustin Lopez, leader of the Basque underground movement, could actually have aborted the assassination of Minister Bueno because

Bueno had promised to negotiate Basque autonomy after the reappearance of the Virgin. Whether that peasant child Bernadette, in her day, had actually seen and conversed with the Virgin was of no importance. But to believe, in this day and age, that the Virgin would reappear in the damn grotto was too much to swallow. Even if Lopez believed in the possibility, Hurtado could not. His determination to end Bueno's stalling tactics had not wavered.

Although his young colleague and sometimes bed partner, Julia Valdez, had tried to dissuade him from his purpose, Hurtado had gone ahead with his plan. He had acted out a charade for his poor, nearly senile mother. He had been infected by a revived religious fervor after hearing the announcement of the return of the Virgin Mary to Lourdes, he told her. He wanted to be on hand in Lourdes to witness the remarkable event. But to obtain accommodations in Lourdes, he had to be a part of an official pilgrimage. There was a pilgrimage being organized in San Sebastián, and he hoped that his mother would intercede on his behalf. She had been thrilled, poor thing, by his revived passion for Catholicism, and she had seen her parish priest and succeeded in obtaining a place for him on the San Sebastián pilgrimage. He would have to use his own name—something against ETA rules—but he had never been listed by the police, and besides it was a small risk to take for so important a job.

Hurtado noted that his brown suitcase had been set on the sidewalk with the other luggage, and he quickly snatched it up and hurried into the hotel. He was ahead of the others in his party and went directly to the reception desk. Two clerks were conferring, a woman pulling on her sweater and giving some instructions to an openly bored young man.

Interrupting them, Hurtado said, "I was told to ask for Yvonne at the reception desk."

"I'm Yvonne," said the lady receptionist. "You caught me just in time. I was just taking off. What can I do for you?"

"I have a reservation for the week. I'm with the San Sebastián pilgrimage. My name is Mikel Hurtado."

She picked up a ledger, turned a page. "Hurtado, Hurtado," she repeated, running a finger down the page. "Yes. Here you are. We've been holding 206. It's ready. Let me jot it down for you. Anatole, get me the key."

Hurtado accepted the slip as Anatole went off to the key alcove at the entrance.

"Who gave you my name?" the lady asked.

"A friend of mine in Pau. He was to leave a package for me, and told me to see Yvonne about it."

"A package? Oh yes, I do remember. Someone delivered it this afternoon. I sent it up to your room. You'll find it there."

"Thanks, Yvonne," said Hurtado, placing ten francs on the counter. Anatole had returned with the key. Hurtado took it, picked up his bag, and headed for the elevator.

Upstairs, Hurtado found room 206. About to let himself in, he saw two people emerge from the next room, an older woman and a gorgeous young woman who appeared to be blind. He heard the older woman speak of being in time for dinner and start away.

Hurtado's mind was on the package that was supposed to be in his room. The package was all that mattered. It was the reason for his trip to Lourdes.

Setting down his suitcase, he shut the door, searching for the package. He saw it resting on the table near the foot of the bed.

He almost ran to the table, yanking up a chair, sitting, drawing the package to him, as he extracted the pocketknife from his corduroy jacket and pulled open a blade. The package was tightly wrapped in heavy gray paper, held firmly in place by a hard thin rope. Hurtado severed the rope, pulled it off, ripped away the gray wrapping. Inside, the contents were surrounded by stiff corrugated paper. Hurtado tore apart the cardboard.

At last, his treasure was revealed. He handled each piece lovingly: numerous sticks of dynamite bound together; the coiled green fuse; the plastic case; the clockwork egg timer he had requested; the battery. It was a powerful time bomb he had assembled many times in his recent nocturnal career. You set the clock. When the hand reached the appropriate number on the clockface, it touched a terminal connected to the battery, which completed the circuit and sent a charge of electricity through the detonator and wire, exploding the dynamite bomb and blowing the target into a million pieces. It had worked on targets of the Basques, on automobiles, on buildings; it would work on the grotto, blow the fucking shrine to smithereens. A dozen Virgin Marys would never be able to find it. The resultant explosion was guaranteed to bring Lopez back to his senses.

Hurtado came to his feet, lifted his suitcase onto the bed, and opened it. The suitcase was half empty, and there was plenty of room. Carefully, Hurtado carted the contents of the package to the bed, and laid the parts inside the suitcase. Closing and locking it, he gave silent thanks to his French Basque colleague in Pau, an ETA sympathizer he had once entertained in San Sebastián and whom he had telephoned a week ago to request these materials.

He had no patience for dinner now. Reaching into his jacket pocket, he took out the half of a sausage sandwich he had not finished on the bus, and he munched it as he found in his other pocket the map of Lourdes he had received on the bus. Taking the map to the table, he unfolded it, laid it out flat, and sought the location of the grotto. When he found the spot, he realized that it was not far from the X he had made on the map during the ride to show the site of his hotel. Chewing the remnants of the sandwich, he decided to waste no more time. He wanted to see the grotto, study it, determine what problems, if any, were involved. He was sure, from photographs he had seen in a picture book, that it was an easy setup. It would not be half as difficult as the preparations to blow up Minister Luis Bueno. The only problem here might be wiring the whole thing unobserved. People would be all over the place. But most had to sleep. There had to be a time, at night, in the early morning, when the grotto was largely unattended. He had to see for himself.

Before leaving, he went to the bathroom. After cleaning up, he considered himself in the mirror, and wondered if he should affect some kind of disguise. Then he realized that a disguise was pointless, since no one in this remote town had ever seen him before or knew who he was. In fact, his very calling had made him a nonentity, both at home and in Lourdes. The single subterfuge might be to use the stone in his shoe. He'd tucked a small smooth stone—a pebble really—in a pocket of his suitcase for his visit here. He went to the suitcase, opened it again, found the stone. After locking the bag, he kicked off his left shoe and dropped the pebble inside it. Putting his foot inside the shoe, lacing it, he knew that the pebble would definitely force him to limp. Perfect for Lourdes. He would walk with a limp because he had a rheumatic or severe arthritic condition in the knee joint. He had come here to pray for a cure.

Hurtado limped out of the room and was on his way.

Fifteen minutes later, after asking directions, and then following the crowd streaming down a sloping walk, he reached the area referred to on his map as the Esplanade des Processions. Indifferent to the three churches to his left, he jerkily made his way around them toward the grotto.

Minutes later he stood at the far edge of a vast mob that seemed to be coming apart, wheeling away, and he heard someone cry out, "Time for the Candlelight Procession!" As the mob dissolved, then reassembled into some kind of order—thousands of pilgrims lurching, swaying, tottering, striding away, many in wheelchairs, using crutches, wearing splints and braces, accompanied by priests, nuns, nurses, laymen with armbands and banners—Hurtado found the area emptying of humanity and he was able to make out his surroundings.

He was at the fringe of rows of chairs and benches, a handful occupied by pilgrims who were telling their beads, or murmuring personal prayers, but whose individual shapes were lost in darkness. What was illuminated in a yellowish hue was the grotto itself, well lighted by eighteen tiers of tall waxen candles. Higher up, he could make out a weatherbeaten, unappealing statue of the Virgin Mary, her marble hands touching as if in supplication.

The grotto itself was a surprise. When he had learned of The Reappearance Time, studied photographs of Lourdes, the grotto had loomed large in his mind. But it was smaller, much more ordinary, than he had imagined. It was hardly worth obliteration and the risk involved. Still, it was big in the eyes of Luis Bueno and Lopez, and as such must be dealt with and brought down.

He examined the grotto as best he could. A sheer stone cliff rose above it, and a wall of the Upper Basilica crowned the top of the hill. He peered to the right of the cave and immediately saw what could be done. Pilgrims and tourists were lined up, going through the grotto in a steady stream, and every nook and cranny inside was under constant observation. The dynamite could not be hidden there. But off to the right side of the grotto, just above it, there was the sizable niche that held the standing marble statue of the Virgin Mary. And around the niche grew an outburst of green shrubbery, while a small forest of trees and bushes covered an incline that offered solid footing and made the statue accessible.

At an advantageous time, when most of Lourdes slept, he would return and pretend to pray—and disappear into all that foliage. He could make his way to the niche above, plant the dynamite behind the base of the Virgin's statue, then run the green wiring—camouflaged by foliage—uphill to the detonator hidden among the trees. He could set the timer, scramble down and away, and in ten or fifteen minutes leave the area far behind. When the explosion came, he would be in a car he had arranged to rent tomorrow heading out of the city and well on his way to Biarritz and St.-Jean-de-Luz and the frontier at Hendaye before anyone realized what had happened. He smacked his lips at what would happen: The giant blast would turn the grotto into five grottos, bring down half the hillside, destroy the altar inside and artifacts everywhere, and probably release the underground spring and cause it to erupt and flood the area.

The shrine would be a mass of rubble and debris and granite boulders. Not even the Virgin Mary, if she decided to reappear, would ever find it. The site would be beyond recognition. Hurtado's grin broadened. The obliteration of the grotto was not only possible, but relatively easy.

Satisfied with his first survey, about to turn away, he felt the pressure of a hand on his left arm and heard a woman's whisper in the night. "Hi, Ken, I've been looking everywhere for you."

Hurtado whirled around to find an attractive young woman looking up at him. "I'm not Ken," he blurted. "You must be mistaken."

"Oh, dammit," the lady said, and was instantly apologetic. "Forgive me. I was searching everywhere for my husband—his name is Ken —Ken Clayton—and in the dark here, I was sure you were Ken. You're the same height. And he was wearing a corduroy jacket, too. Do forgive me."

Hurtado was amused. "My pleasure, I assure you. Your Ken is a lucky man."

She dimpled and put out her hand. "Thank you. I'm Amanda Spenser Clayton from Chicago."

"Pleased to meet you," he said, not introducing himself.

"Well," she said awkwardly, "I'd better have another look around and then go back to the hotel."

"Maybe I can help you," he said, falling in step beside her.

Amanda noticed his limp. "Are you here because of your leg?"

"An arthritic problem," he said offhandedly.

"Well, it's not fatal I'm sure—"

"Not at all fatal. Merely painful and difficult."

"But Ken's problem *is* fatal," she said. "It's a form of hip cancer. And it is operable, and in some cases there have been successes. Ken cancelled surgery in Chicago because of this Virgin Mary reappearance. He suddenly got religion and insisted that his best bet of finding a cure was in Lourdes."

They had emerged onto the broad Esplanade of the Rosary, her eyes seeking Ken, when Hurtado took her arm and pointed ahead. "Jesus, look at that. What's that bearing down on us?"

Amanda peered ahead with him. Coming toward them, like a massive army, enthusiastically, devoutly, were marchers as far as the eye could see.

"There must be thousands," said Hurtado, blinking.

"Over thirty thousand," said Amanda. "I heard about it, and read about it, too. The Candlelight Procession. The Virgin Mary told Bernadette—let people come in procession—and they came, and have never stopped coming since. There are two processions daily. One in the late afternoon, and this torchlight procession in the evening. This one begins with recital of the rosary at the grotto, then—"

"Yes, I saw them start off tonight," Hurtado said.

"—then they march down the left side of the esplanade and parade ground to the other end, and swing back toward the steps of the Rosary Basilica here."

Hurtado tugged at Amanda, and pulled her off the esplanade to one side to join the hundreds of other spectators who were respectfully watching the awesome torchlight procession.

As Hurtado observed the procession approach, splitting in two columns to march up opposite sides of the park, he could see that it was efficiently organized. The lines snaking along were made up of an incredible variety of people, some in exotic garb—group leaders carrying diocesan banners, bishops dressed in purple, priests in black, girls belonging to the Children of Mary and choir boys in white, countless believers wearing civilian dress of every color, everyone but everyone hoisting aloft flickering candles shielded by what seemed to Hurtado to be inverted cardboard hats.

"Those shields around the candles," Amanda was saying, "protect the flame from the wind. You buy them in the souvenir shops for two francs each. See, they are all raised in unison during the chorus of 'Ave, Ave Maria.' Quite a sight."

Even to Hurtado, the sight was breathtaking. At the head of each pilgrimage delegation a lay leader, or sometimes a priest, carried a placard identifying his group. The groups passing before Hurtado and Amanda now were lifting high placards imprinted BELGIUM . . . JAPAN . . . ALGIERS . . . METZ. Yes, there were thousands and thousands of torchbearers passing by, and their placards indicated that they had come from the far reaches of the earth.

Then, from somewhere behind him, from somewhere in the trees above, amplifiers were booming out the music and the lyrics of "The Hymn of Lourdes." Hurtado listened to the words:

> *"We pray for God's glory*
> *May His Kingdom come,*
> *We pray for His Vicar,*
> *Our Father, and Rome.*

> *We pray for our Mother,*
> *The church upon earth*

And bless, sweetest Lady,
The land of our birth.

We pray for all sinners
And souls that now stray
From Jesus and Mary
In heresy's way.

For poor, sick, afflicted,
Thy mercy we crave,
And comfort the dying,
Thou light of the grave.

Ave, Ave, Ave Maria,
Ave, Ave, Ave Maria!"

And from 30,000 throats in procession came the repeat of the chorus:

"A-ve, A-ve, A-ve Ma-ri-aa,
A-ve, A-ve, A-ve Ma-ri-aa!"

Involuntarily, Hurtado gulped, and turning away saw Amanda's face.

She sighed. "Yes, I know. Very moving."

"Very," Hurtado agreed.

"But it's ridiculous, when you think about it. Any one with any sense or intelligence knows there are no miracles. This is all a big religious circus, nothing more."

"You are obviously not a believer," said Hurtado.

"I'm a clinical psychologist," said Amanda. "I know the effects of hysteria, emotion, self-hypnosis on the human mind, and how the mind can temporarily paralyze the body and then unexpectedly cure it. If any of those invalids out there are cured, it won't be because of some so-called miraculous happening, I assure you. It'll be because they will themselves well, without knowing that was the real reason for their cure." She looked away from the procession at Hurtado. "And you?" she said.

"What about me?"

"Maybe I've been too outspoken. Are you a believer?"

Tempted as he was to agree with her dissent, he decided it would be wiser to play his chosen role. "I can only say that I was raised in the faith. That is why I am here."

"Each to his own," she said with a shrug, and turned away. "Ken's probably down in that army, marching with them. I'm going back to my hotel to wait for him."

They walked in silence up the hill, across the street, and around the corner.

"There's my hotel," she said. "Ken and I are staying at the Hôtel Gallia & Londres."

"That's where I'm staying, too," said Hurtado.

When they entered the reception lobby, and took the elevator, Hurtado got out at the second floor.

"Well, good-night, Mrs. Clayton. Pleased to have met you."

"I'm pleased, too. Be sure to get some rest."

"Going right to sleep," he said.

But when he reached his room, he knew that he would not sleep long. He would set his alarm for some time after midnight, early morning, and he would go back to the grotto. There was something important to find out as soon as possible.

In the rear seat of the taxi, Ken Clayton's head rested against Amanda Spenser's shoulder. Once more, she glanced down at his face. He was sound asleep, poor dear, and he had been asleep from the moment they had entered the taxi and left Lourdes. She tried to make out the dial on her wristwatch, and as far as she could tell in the semidarkness they had been on the road and speeding through the rolling Chalosse hills and fragrant pine forests for an hour and a half. She had been told the trip to the town of Eugénie-les-Bains should take no longer than this, and she peered out of the Mercedes window for sight of Les Prés d'Eugénie.

She had fond memories of the two days she had spent at this picturesque and chic country inn and spa on her last visit to France. She had enjoyed the baths, tennis, marvellous cuisine, and the magnificent wooded thirty-five acres of grounds surrounding it. Here Ken could find the rest he so sorely needed, and here, removed from that horrid hotel in Lourdes and those stupid pilgrims, in this seductive atmosphere, she could convince him that he must return to Chicago as soon as possible. If he stubbornly insisted upon another visit or two to that absurd grotto before leaving, she would drive him to Lourdes and back once or twice, no more.

There had been no difficulty in departing from the Lourdes hotel with him. She had moved their baggage down to the reception lobby— but had not checked out of the hovel of a room in case Ken wanted a place to rest should he insist upon seeing the grotto again—ordered a taxi to stand by, and waited for Ken's return from the procession.

He had returned with the pilgrims, sleepy-eyed, pale, stumbling, resembling the walking dead. She had drawn him away from the others. He was half somnambulant. Yes, he admitted, he had marched the full mile's distance in the nightly procession. Perhaps he had overdone it. Now all he wanted was to lie down and sleep. She told him that he could sleep in the taxi. She told him that she had found a better and roomier hotel, one that could provide more rest for him, but he had hardly heard her. He was drooping, and there was no awareness of, let alone resistance to, what she had been saying. She had ordered their bags to be taken to the taxi, and gently she had led Ken outside and into the rear of the vehicle, and he had fallen asleep at once.

"Les Prés d'Eugénie," the taxi driver announced.

Amanda squinted through the car window and could see the night illuminated by the lights from three stately buildings set back from the road.

They had parked before the tiled walk that stretched between low fountains to the outdoor terrace with its wicker chairs and hotel entrance. Amanda propped Ken up, and awakened him. His bleary eyes opened briefly as she tugged at him and got him out of the taxi.

"Where are we?" he mumbled, but sagged in a stupor, not interested in her answer.

The driver was at the trunk of the car, turning their bags over to a young bellhop. Amanda beckoned the driver and requested that he assist her in getting her husband inside. Together, they kept Ken upright, guiding him as he stumbled up the walk, past some white statue of a draped nude woman and along the rest of the path into the modest entry of the hotel. The driver held on to Ken, as Amanda went to register them.

"You have a lovely suite in the new building," the female receptionist assured her. "I hope you find it to your liking." She summoned the young bellhop. "Show Monsieur and Madame Clayton to suite Bois des Îles, and their their luggage."

Amanda paid off the driver, took charge of Ken, and guided him along behind the bellhop to the outdoor elevator. They rode up to the third floor, and not far from the elevator they were shown into their modern corner suite.

It was smart and airy, the sitting room a mix of contemporary and antique furniture, old clock, fresh flowers, carved wooden animals, television, and as attractive as she had remembered it, such a relief after the cramped hovel they had left.

Holding Ken, she tried to point out the lovely decor to him, the white sofa, wicker chairs, white fireplace.

"Let's order a drink from room service," she said, "and sit down and get you relaxed, and then if you're up to it we can go down to dinner."

"I want to sleep," he said. "Let me lie down."

He was so exhausted that Amanda didn't have the heart to press him further about the amenities of their new hotel. She led him into the open-beamed bedroom. The covers on the double bed were already turned back. She undressed him down to his boxer shorts, did not bother to unpack and find his pajamas, pushed him toward the bed, and lowered him onto the soft mattress. She maneuvered him into a comfortable position, and covered him. By the time she had finished, he was sound asleep.

She could not blame his exhaustion on their trip to the resort. The trip through the French countryside had been fast and smooth. She blamed his condition on the ordeal of the procession, the endless marching with those other fanatics. That had brought him down, that and his illness, of course.

She wandered around the bedroom, intending to unpack, until she realized how hungry she was. She had not had a bite to eat since lunch on the train. Going into the carpeted bathroom, with makeup from her purse, she washed, touched up her cheeks and lips, combed her hair, and then left the suite and headed downstairs.

In the modern lounge on the ground floor, she was alone on a beige sofa and had a martini. She was more pleased with herself than ever to have managed to bring Ken to this hotel. She tried to put her first-day impressions of Lourdes out of her mind. She felt more reasonable now, more generous, and could see how a shrine like that could be psychologically uplifting to ignorant visitors who possessed real faith. But then she shuddered. To her, with her professional background, it remained a spiritual horror.

Finishing the last of her martini, she rose and headed for the treat that awaited her in the dining room. Diners were still lingering over the last of their meals, but there were a number of tables available and the maître d' found one for Amanda in a quiet corner. She took the fancy menu, thinking how clever it was of the proprietor to furnish the dining area simply and depend on his lush menu for the real decor. Reviewing the choices on the menu—"La Carte Gourmande" or "Le Repas des Villes" or "Le Repas des Champs"—she decided to go all the way and order the full and most expensive dinner.

She made her selection from "Le Repas des Villes," the 235-franc dinner, plus 15 percent service *en sus,* and when the maître d' returned, she briskly ordered *La Salade à l'Oiseau* for openers, *La Fine Rouelle de Turbot Sauce Simple,* then a choice of two dishes and she selected *Les Piccatas de Foie de Canard en Vinaigrette d'Asperges,* and—what the hell, a dessert also—for a dessert *La Tourte Chaude au Chocolat Moelleux.*

Dinner took the better part of two hours, and when it was done Amanda could hardly move. She felt guilty that Ken had not been able to share this hedonistic indulgence, but felt better knowing that he would be at a table with her tomorrow night. She considered forcing herself to take a stroll on the vast lawn in back of the hotel, to walk off some of the meal, but finally decided to go up to their suite in case Ken was awake by now.

Arriving at the suite on the third floor, she went inside and directly to the bedroom. In the lamplight she could see that Ken was still asleep, head deep in the down pillow, and he had not so much as budged from his original position. Clearly, he needed the rest and would not be up until morning.

Quietly, she went about unpacking her bag and his, hanging up dresses and suits in the wardrobe, and when she was done, there remained only a half dozen books she had brought along in her tote bag and their suitcase. She unzipped the tote bag, extracted the two volumes of the Zola novel, and took them—along with the chocolate-covered mint that the hotel maid had left on her pillow—into the living room. She sat down, nibbling, and poked through both volumes of the Zola novel, once more going over the passages that she had marked. Through with the books, she placed them on the coffee table, then located a memo pad and a pencil beside the telephone. Should Ken awaken and rise for breakfast before she did, he might find it fascinating to have something to read with his orange juice. "Ken darling," she wrote, "hope you are feeling better. In case you are up before I am, here is something you'll want to read at breakfast. Don't try to go through the entire novel—just look at the passages in Zola I have marked off. I love you. Your own—Amanda."

She placed the note on top of the books, and realized that by now she, too, was tired. She would go right to bed, so that she could be up early and they could have a wonderful day outdoors tomorrow.

Stripped naked, going to the bathroom for her nightgown, passing mirrors, she was more conscious than ever of her nude body. She could recall with excitement how much Ken had enjoyed that body, how often and endlessly he liked to join it with his own in love. Well, the body was still here, mature, strong, but soft, and waiting for Ken's recovery and the love that he had given it when he was robust and athletic before the onset of his illness. Now the fatigued lump in bed was only a shell of that former self, but she was more than ever sure that surgery could repair and save him, revitalize him, enable him to make fantastic love with her for the rest of their lives, giving them not only children but an eternity of fleshly pleasures.

Having put on her nightgown and turned off the lights, she snuggled down on her side of the bed and was soon enveloped by sleep.

She had no idea how many hours she had slept. She only knew that it must be well into morning as she gradually opened her eyes to the sun's glare. She listened to the chirping of the birds in the plane and tulip trees outside the bedroom window, then yawning herself fully awake she rolled over toward Ken's side of the bed to speak to him. He was not in bed, his place empty, but she was not surprised. He'd had enough sleep and was probably in the living room having breakfast or lolling on the sofa perhaps reading through the Zola novel.

Throwing back her covers, Amanda sat up and swung off the bed. Stepping into her bedroom slippers, she decided to see Ken before brushing her teeth and showering.

She clumped into the next room, calling out, "Ken, how are you?" No answer. She looked around. He wasn't there. She turned toward the balcony where he might be having breakfast. He wasn't there either. Probably he had wanted a breath of air and she would find him outside.

She had started toward the bedroom when, out of the corner of her eye, she caught sight of a piece of paper Scotch-taped to the entrance door of the suite. She detoured to see what it was, and saw at once it was a piece of the cream-colored hotel stationery and she recognized Ken's scrawled handwriting on it. She tore the note free and read what Ken had written:

> *Amanda, dear meddling dear,*
> *Goddammit, don't you try anything like this again.*
> *You believe what you believe, and let me believe what I believe. But just don't try to obstruct my beliefs. I don't think you have the slightest notion of the depth of my faith. I believe in Bernadette's communications with the Holy Mother, I believe in the Immaculate Conception, I believe that the Virgin Mary will return, I believe in every one of the cures She has given to the blessed ones. I hope to be one of them—not only for my sake, but for us.*
> *On the day you can prove—prove—my faith is wrong, I might listen. But otherwise leave me be.*
> *As to this silly, shallow place, I don't belong here. I don't belong in a resort spa so far from where I want to be. I belong in my Lourdes hotel*

with the rest of my pilgrimage group, my friends, and I belong as close to the holy grotto as I can get.

I've taken a taxi back to Lourdes. If you wish, you can join me there. If not, I'll see you in Chicago once I am cured.

As much as you try me, Amanda, still I love you.

Ken

Amanda felt not anger but a wave of frustration that made her feel weak and helpless.

Ken, you fool, don't be an ass, don't commit suicide, she wanted to cry out.

She had crumpled his note and turned to the bedroom when she spotted the two volumes of the Zola novel and the note that she had left on top of it last night. She walked toward the books, wondering if he had scanned them.

Apparently he had, for she could see that he had scribbled something on the bottom of her note to him. She took it up and found two words in his hand:

"Fuck Zola."

She wanted to weep over Ken's pious craziness, his blind idiocy, his expecting to be rescued from the clutches of death by some ghostly apparition from outer space. But she did not weep. Instead, she went into the bedroom to get dressed and follow him back to Lourdes.

He needed someone more earthly to see that he survived. She was the one to do it. And she *would* do it, yet.

7

Monday, August 15

It was one minute after midnight in Lourdes, and the second day of The Reappearance Time had begun.

At precisely two o'clock in the morning, the alarm of Natale Rinaldi's travel clock on the stand beside her bed in the Hôtel Gallia & Londres had gone off shrilly. Immediately awakened, Natale had reached out, fumbled for it, and pressed her hand on it to still the persistent sound. She sat up fully aroused, coming out of a fuzzy dream-filled darkness into alert darkness, mind focusing and remembering that after dinner she had set the unique Braille clock for two in the morning and that she had gone to sleep without removing her dress, only kicking off her shoes which would be below the bed.

Since her helper, Rosa, had not been able to guide her back to the grotto a second time the evening before, Natale had resolved to go back alone when everyone else slept and she could enjoy the comfort of the shrine by herself. Swinging her feet off the bed, pushing them into her low-heeled shoes, she suffered a brief moment of panic. She wondered if she could possibly remember the direction, the count of the steps to each turning, once she departed her room and headed for the grotto alone. But the momentary void in her mind was instantly filled by the rows of numbers in order, the steps she must take to each turning, from her hotel room to the lobby to the Avenue Bernadette Soubirous to the ramp to the Rosary Basilica and the precious grotto itself. The numbers were there in her mind, as certain and vivid as if on a computer screen.

Relieved, she stood up, felt her way to the bathroom, doused her face with cold water, and combed her hair.

She stepped into the corridor, locked the door, and placed the key in an inside pocket of the purse she had slung over her shoulder.

She started to her right, seeking the elevator, and unerringly she reached it. She touched the rosary in her purse, thinking of her lone vigil at the grotto and the prayers she would offer to the invisible Virgin.

When she heard the elevator arrive, she was ready to go on. Nothing could keep her from the One she loved and would be able to speak to alone.

Slumped in a chair behind the reception desk, chin resting against the exposed mat of hair on his chest, Anatole was dozing. A sound of some kind, a familiar but unexpected noise, intruded upon his subconscious, awakening him. Opening his eyes, he could hear the elevator across the lobby descending. He listened as it rattled to a stop at ground level.

A quick check of the reception desk clock told him it was five minutes after two o'clock in the morning.

This was unheard of, someone using the elevator at this hour. Since arriving in Lourdes from Marseilles, and taking this boring job, Anatole had never seen anyone awake two hours after midnight in this dead-ass hotel. During the entire week of his employment here, the lobby had been like a morgue between one o'clock in the morning and five.

And now, at five minutes after two o'clock, someone was actually emerging from the elevator.

Anatole came to his feet, bending over the counter as he squinted across the lobby.

Of all people, the young woman, the great-looking girl, was emerging from the elevator. He recognized her at once. The absolutely dazzling blind girl.

There she was in person. And all alone. Crazy, crazy. What the hell was she up to at this hour?

She seemed to know what she was up to, because she was making her way, with some certainty, toward the hotel door and the street.

Anatole remembered that he had locked the hotel door, as he had been instructed to do, before taking his nap. The girl, the sexpot, would find it a secure barrier that would prevent her from going wherever she was headed. She deserved the courtesy of the hotel, he told himself, and he deserved a closer look. Immediately, he was moving, hastening along the reception counter and around it toward the door.

She had reached the door when he called out, "Mademoiselle."

She stopped in her tracks, startled, and turned her head.

"I am Anatole, the reception clerk on the night shift," he quickly explained. "You know it is after two in the morning?"

"Yes, I know," she said without hesitatiòn.

"You want to go into the street at this hour?"

"I have an appointment," she said.

"Well, the front door is locked. We always keep it locked after everyone goes to sleep. But I can unlock it for you."

"Please do," she said.

He was releasing the dead bolt. "If you expect to be back soon, I can leave it unlocked for you."

"I would appreciate that."

"Here, let me open the door," Anatole said.

He stepped in front of her, brushing against her, feeling the soft give of those fantastic young breasts against his arm. Easing the door back, he had a close look at her. A breathtaking pale face enlivened only by dark glasses. The pointed breasts. The soft short dress that clung to her hips and showed off the shapely legs.

"Is the door open?" she asked.

"Yes." He could hardly find his voice. "Can I help you in any way?"

"Thank you. I'm all right."

She went unhesitatingly past him into the street. The second her foot touched the sidewalk, she turned to the right. He stepped out to watch her. Her stride was measured, but sure, almost defiant. Anatole grinned. A gutsy little bitch. She'd be something in bed. He kept his eyes on her, the wonderful legs, the undulating hips, and he was inflamed with desire.

He'd had many women in Marseilles, mostly whores paid for out of his meager earnings from rotten jobs that required manual labor, those and a few beat-up drunken dames who would do anything with anyone, but he had never made it with a young lady, with a high-flying lady, certainly not with someone who looked like this one did.

He continued to keep his eyes on her receding figure in the patches of street lights that defied the darkness. In the distance, she had come to the corner, expertly stepped off the curb, crossed the street, and was going on past the café.

To an appointment? With whom?

And then he knew. The grotto. She was going to wait for the

Virgin at the grotto. Dumb kid. How could she hope to see the Virgin or anyone? When she realized that there was no Virgin there, she might want someone else, someone who could really keep her company.

Turning back to the hotel, he could barely walk, the erection between his legs was so enormous.

It was difficult to do in the flickering light of the candles far below, but Mikel Hurtado continued to crawl on hands and knees from the vegetation nearest the niche that held the statue of the Virgin Mary into the bushes and forest of trees.

Upon awakening from his nap in the hotel a half hour ago, he had at first planned to carry his dynamite and detonator to the grotto and either hide the equipment or set it up. Dressing, he'd had second thoughts. Yesterday, he had seen the grotto area in the evening, and it had been promising. Now he decided that he had better have another scouting exploration by night when there were no pilgrims around, but when there might be some guards on hand. His experiences in Spain had taught him it was essential to know the security situation at any target. So, without his equipment, he had gone down the stairs to the reception lobby, been let outside by the sleepy reception clerk, and gone along the empty street toward the domain.

From the shadows at the bottom of the street ramp, Hurtado had been able to make a preliminary survey of the area near his destination. There was not a soul in sight around the Rosary Esplanade, nor on the double walks rising to the Upper Basilica. There appeared to be no one in the entrance to the grotto. As for the Esplanade des Processions, as the map called it, not a human could be seen on its entire length.

Hurtado had started to move out of the shadows when, from nowhere it seemed, a figure appeared a short distance away—a man, an older blue-shirted night watchman wearing a shoulder holster. He was not exactly walking, really just shuffling along, coming up the Esplanade des Processions, probably from the gate at the far end, moving toward the Rosary Basilica. The watchman seemed to be sleepwalking, yawning, looking neither to right nor left, as he advanced toward the churches. Reaching the steps before the Rosary Basilica, he seated himself to have a smoke. This had taken five minutes. He had finally dropped the cigarette butt on the pavement and ground it out with his shoe. Then he stood up and resumed his circuit of the domain.

Eyeing the guard's retreat, Hurtado consulted his wristwatch and decided to time him. Crouching, finally sitting out of sight on one side of the ramp from the street, Hurtado patiently waited. Twenty-five minutes had gone by before the guard could be seen advancing from the far side of the domain toward the basilicas. Over thirty minutes, closer to thirty-five, before he reached the entrance to the Rosary Basilica, once more resting and enjoying his ritual smoke. Five more minutes and the guard was again on patrol.

Hurtado was satisfied with the timing. The guard came into this immediate area every thirty minutes, roughly on the hour and the half hour. Hurtado would wait until he was out of sight, and then make his way to the grotto. He would examine the shrubbery, bushes, trees beside and above the cave, and he would make sure to take his leave when he knew that the single guard was elsewhere in the domain.

No problem. None whatsoever.

When the guard was out of sight once more, Hurtado hurried down off the ramp, and silently as possible made his way around the corner of the church to the grotto. Again, there was not a human being in sight. The pilgrims slept in their beds through the night and early morning hours, and the grotto was abandoned.

Hastening past the benches and the tiers of burning waxen candles, Hurtado did not give the grotto a second look. He went to the grassy slope beside it, trying to find the best way to climb up the steep incline. He did not want to take the regular path, the one that led to the top of the hill much farther on. Fortunately, there was the semblance of a worn path, overgrown, that earlier adventurous visitors had trodden in making their way toward the basilicas for a view of the extent of the domain below. Having come to a midpoint in the hill, parallel to the statue of the Virgin in the niche overlooking the grotto, Hurtado cut to his left, going crabwise toward the niche so that he could examine it close-up and consider the practicality of planting the dynamite and running the wiring off.

Now that part of it was done, every aspect studied with care, and he was crawling upward again, into the more thickly wooded area, hunting for an obscure but perfect spot where he could set his detonator. In less than ten more minutes he had found the spot he wanted, a natural depression in the earth beside the broad base of a leafy oak tree. He marked it carefully in his mind. He would be ready tomorrow night.

He brought his wristwatch with its luminous dial up to his face in the darkness. The time was right to leave. The guard would already be departing the immediate area of the church and walking away on his circuit of the domain.

On his feet once more, a trifle uneasy about the slippery footing, Hurtado slowly made his way downward until the tops of the burning candles came in view. Cautiously, before crawling down the rest of the way, he bent forward to see if the area in front of the grotto was still devoid of life.

It was.

It wasn't! His heart skipped a beat. Someone was there.

Crouching at his high perch, holding onto the branch of a stunted tree, he tried to focus on the figure below. The figure, he could make out, was that of a young woman with dark hair, wearing black glasses, on her knees in a position of prayer. Her hands were clasped at her breast, and apparently she was silently praying before the grotto. There was something about her, the lack of movement, the stillness of her person, that indicated she was praying fervently, in a trancelike state. There was also something about her that Hurtado found vaguely familiar, as if he had seen her somewhere before. Then it came to him—the dark hair and black glasses—the girl he had seen leaving the room next to his own at the hotel during the dinner hour last night. But to be here alone, at this ungodly hour, holding communion with the Virgin Mary really exceeded religious fanaticism.

Also, her presence hampered his own plan to leave the area. The one thing he could not risk was being detected by anyone. He would have to remain in hiding until she had ceased petitioning the Virgin and departed.

He continued to stare down at the immobile, entranced young woman, when suddenly she began to move, or rather her body involuntarily moved. She seemed to be swaying, leaning sideways, and then she toppled over, collapsed on the ground and lay unconscious. Obviously, succumbing to religious ecstasy, she had fainted. Now she lay crumpled on the ground, as inert as if she were dead.

Instinctively, Hurtado wanted to scramble down the hill—or at least crawl down as swiftly as possible—and go to her aid. But if she became conscious, and he was revealed to her, she might be able to recognize and identify him later when suspects were sought after the explosion. Caught between the desire to help and the fear of danger, Hurtado wished the security guard would return and spot her and revive her. But the watchman would not be returning for another twenty minutes, and he would be passing at some distance from the grotto area, and might overlook her inert figure.

As the inner debate continued to worry Hurtado's mind, something unexpected happened below.

A second figure had appeared, on the run, a young man, going directly to the woman who had fainted before the grotto, and quickly kneeling beside her. He was making an effort to revive her, rubbing her limp wrists, patting her cheeks, pulling her up to a sitting position. At last she moved her head, shaking it, regaining consciousness. The man continued speaking to her, until she finally nodded. The man jumped to his feet, bounded to the water spigots, collected some water in a cupped hand, and hastened back to her. He dabbed the water on her face with a handkerchief, and at once she was fully conscious and speaking. The man was helping her to her feet, and on her feet she seemed completely revived, yet confused in some way. There was something odd about the way she reached out a hand, as if trying to feel her way, before the young man took a grip on her arm and led her from the grotto.

It was during this that Hurtado realized the woman who had been praying so fervently at the grotto was probably blind. Trying to recall the moment he had set eyes on her at the hotel, Hurtado remembered that he had thought then that she was blind. He had completely forgotten it.

Hurtado cursed beneath his breath. Her affliction meant that she would not have seen him if he had chosen to leave the area fifteen minutes earlier. Now he was uncomfortably stuck on the hillside near the grotto until the pair had gone, and the guard had come again and gone once more. Hurtado watched the couple leaving. He tried to understand their relationship. She had undoubtedly told her boyfriend that she was going to the grotto by herself, and had made an appointment with him to pick her up at a certain time, and he had come to get her just after she had fainted.

The pair was gone now. But the guard could be seen at a distance on his patrol. Gradually, Hurtado began to crawl down the hillside, to be ready to depart once the guard was out of the way.

Near the bottom of the hill, Hurtado waited for the guard to have his smoke, and to start patrolling again. Seven or eight minutes passed, and Hurtado knew that the man would now be on his long amble around the domain. Hurtado carefully picked his way down the remainder of the hill and was relieved to be on level terra firma once more.

Satisfied with his exploration, despite the delay, and pleased that everything was set for his final act, which would bring the Basque nationalists closer to success, he strode hurriedly past the eerie grotto and the towering Upper Basilica, and made for the street ramp and the Hôtel Gallia & Londres.

Leading the grateful girl—he had learned her name was Natale and that she was Italian (the best kind)—into the hotel lobby, ignoring the reception desk that he had left unattended, Anatole took her to the elevator that was waiting. She thanked him for the hundredth time, and insisted that she could make it up to her room by herself, but he was equally insistent that he wanted to escort her safely to her room.

Going up in the elevator with her, Anatole was pleased with this lucky break. After she had left the hotel, he had intended to go back behind the desk and resume his nap. But all interest in sleep had vanished. His mind had been filled with images of the girl, those tits, that ass, undressing her, putting it into her, and his erection had not abated. At last, he had determined to seek her out at the grotto, speak to her, try to seduce her. He had convinced himself that she might want a warm body, a French lover, and that she might be impressed by his pursuit of her in the early hours of the morning. His intention had been to encourage her to invite him to her room or to invite her to his own room several blocks away from the Gallia & Londres, for a few drinks and finally some real lovemaking. But finding her in a faint, being the big hero who had saved her, had been more than he had counted on. Now he had her gratefulness, and this would make her vulnerable. He knew that he need but ask her if he could stay the night, and he would have her immediate compliance.

His erection, briefly down, was growing once more.

The elevator had stopped and they were on the second floor. "Let me see you to your room," Anatole said. "What's the number again?"

"You needn't bother. I know my way."

"Well, I've brought you this far, so let me get you to where you're going. The number?"

"Room 205," she said.

At the door of the room, she fished inside her purse, found her key, and put it in the lock.

Aware of his continued presence, she said, "Thank you."

She unlocked the door, pushed it open, and went inside. He followed her, shutting the door behind him.

"I thought I'd see you safely inside," he said.

"You have," she said. "I appreciate it."

"Are you all right?" he asked.

"I'm fine. I'd better get to sleep. Thank you again." She put out her hand, and taking it, feeling the warm flesh of her hand, he was further aroused.

He held her hand tightly. "Any time," he said quietly. Abruptly, he pulled her to him, and pressed his rough lips against hers, kissing her hard. She struggled, tearing herself free.

She was breathing fast. "What are you doing?" she gasped.

"Natale, I just wanted to kiss you. I—I'd like to stay here tonight."

"You can't. I don't want anything like that. Now please go."

"Come on, be a sport, Natale. You owe me. Don't you want to do something for me? Sure you do."

"Not *that,*" she said, her voice rising. "I don't owe you that." She tried to contain herself. "You were nice to me, and I appreciate it, but now you're not being so nice, and I don't like it. I'd suggest you not cause any trouble. Just be a gentleman and leave right now."

"All right, you win," he said with mock contriteness. "But you are something special, so don't blame me for trying. Sorry it didn't work out. Good-night."

"Good-night," she said with finality.

Anatole walked to the door, opened it noisily, and then banged it shut firmly, but remained in the bedroom. Soundlessly, he eased himself against the wall beside the closed door.

She stood at the foot of her bed a few moments, sagging with relief. Then with a sigh, she felt her way along the bed to the closet, reached inside for her white nightgown and threw it on the bed.

Anatole held his breath, wondering whether or not she was aware that he was still in the room.

Then he was sure that she was not aware of him, was certain that he had left and that she was quite alone.

Through narrowed eyes, he watched her. She had unbuttoned her dress and was pulling it off. She was wearing only a flimsy brassiere and tight string bikini briefs now. She turned away from him to hang her dress in the closet, and then stepped back to the bed, unhooking her bra. The bra was off now and those fantastic firm breasts, with the great brown buttons of nipples, bobbed free, were facing him. She was reaching down to take off her panties. He caught his breath, his heart hammering with excitement, and the bulge at his crotch about to burst.

Her bikini panties were coming down now, she was lifting one bare leg and then the other to step out of them, and the triangle of curly pubic hair was visible, and Anatole was out of control, unable to restrain himself a second longer.

He zipped open the fly of his trousers, let his full erection burst out, and charged across the bedroom toward her.

Mikel Hurtado, having left the elevator at the second floor, proceeded down the corridor toward room 206. He had just passed the door of 205, and was nearing his own door, when he heard a muffled scream, a scream from somewhere nearby.

Startled, Hurtado halted in his tracks, listening intently.

Another muffled drawn-out scream, high-pitched, a woman's, and definitely from inside the room next door to his.

Next door. The blind girl, the blind girl at the grotto. The beginning of another scream, abruptly choked off. Something was going on in there, something terribly wrong, and Hurtado did not bother to think, did not hesitate.

Whirling around, he rushed back to the door of 205. He could clearly hear scuffling. He had grabbed at the doorknob, meaning to grip it and heave himself against the door to break it down, when the door, unlocked, flew open.

Hurtado was inside the room.

Instantly, he saw what was happening—the young girl naked on the bed, beating with her fists, as some animal, the palm of one hand clamped over her mouth, trousers half down, was trying to get on top of her and between her legs.

Rape, savage attempted rape, was what Hurtado saw. Neither of them on the bed, in their struggle, was aware that someone else was in the room.

Enraged by what he was seeing, in a mindless fury at what the monster was trying to do to this helpless girl, Hurtado hurtled himself across the room to the bed. His hands clutched at the assailant's shoulders, yanking him off the girl, and throwing him on the floor. Anatole, stunned by surprise, scrambled to his feet, hampered by the trousers around his ankles, too amazed to lift his hands. Hurtado was on Anatole in a single motion, driving his right fist to the assailant's jaw and smashing his left fist into the rapist's abdomen. As Anatole groaned, doubling up, Hurtado unleashed more punches, battering the other's head and face. Anatole began to crumple, and Hurtado kept landing his pile-driver punches.

Anatole lay sprawled on the rug, half senseless, blood trickling from his mouth.

Hurtado reached down, hooked his hands under the man's arms and dragged him across the room and through the doorway into the hall. There, he dropped the dazed rapist. Briefly, Hurtado considered whether he should summon the police, but quickly decided against it. He wanted no contact with any police while he was in Lourdes.

Instead, he kicked the rapist in the ribs, and in a low voice, so as not to awaken any guests, he warned him. "You get out of here, you fucking bastard, you get out of here and get out fast, or I'll grind you into a meatball."

With effort, fright showing in his puffed eyes, Anatole climbed to his feet clutching his trousers, dribbling blood and nodding. He turned, almost tripping, and staggered toward the staircase. Snatching at the rail, he plunged down the stairs and out of sight.

Hurtado grunted, and slowly went back into the girl's bedroom. She was standing in a bathrobe, tying the sash, and groping for her dark glasses on the bed and putting them on.

"Don't worry, señorita, he's gone," Hurtado said in Spanish. She asked him something in Italian. He said in English, "I don't understand Italian. You speak English?"

"Yes, English . . . Did you call the police?" she asked, still trembling.

"Not necessary," Hurtado said. "He won't be back. I think he's the fellow who works as a night receptionist downstairs. But I'm sure he won't be back on the job or even stay in town. Are you okay?"

"Just scared," she said.

"Don't blame you," Hurtado said. "That's an awful thing to have happen. How did it happen?"

She explained what had taken place, how she had gone down to the grotto by herself to pray, how the spiritual intensity had made her faint, how this person had come out of nowhere to revive her and bring her back to her room, how he'd tricked her into believing that he had left the room when he had actually remained inside determined to rape her.

"Thank God for you," she concluded. "How you got in here in time I don't know, but I owe you a lot."

"It was sheer luck," Hurtado said matter-of-factly. "I was out for a late night walk, was coming back to my room to go to sleep—I have the bedroom next to yours—when I heard you scream. I was going to break in to see what was happening, but the door had been left unlocked." He paused. "Are you better now?"

"Much better," she said with a wonderful smile. She came hesitantly around the bed toward him, stumbling once, righting herself, apologizing. "I—I'm blind, you know."

"I know," he said.

She put out her hand. "I'm Natale Rinaldi, from Rome."

He took her hand, shook it, released it. "I'm Mikel Hurtado," he said, "from—from Spain."

"Pleased to know you," she said, "to put it mildly. Are you here for the Virgin?"

He hesitated. "For a cure, an arthritic condition."

"Maybe both of us will be fortunate."

"I hope so," he said.

"Well, I don't know what more to say except thank you again. Thank you a million times."

"If you really want to thank me," he said sternly, "you can do so by promising never to let strangers see you to your room—and by keeping the door locked from the inside from now on."

She held up one hand. "I promise," she said.

"Now you get some sleep, Natale, and I will, too."

"Good-night, Mikel."

"Good-night," he said, and he went through the doorway, closing the door.

He listened for the lock to turn. The lock turned. He put his mouth close to the door, and said, "Good girl."

He heard her say, "I hope we run into each other again."

"We will," he assured her. "Good-night."

At his door, unlocking it, he knew that he wanted to see her again. She was a delicious girl, so lovely, so sweet. He had never met a young woman quite like her, and he did want to see her again. Maybe he would. But he reminded himself he was here for business not romance.

He must be all business from now on. No diversions. No failure.

Euskadi was his life. The freedom of Euskadi came before anything. There was work to do. Sorry, Natale, he thought. There is only one love, the homeland I've never had, and will have yet.

Behind the steering wheel of her venerable Renault, Gisele Dupree, her blond hair tied in a neat ponytail, her features scrubbed and shiny and without makeup, drove unhurriedly through Tarbes and on the highway toward Lourdes. Sergei Tikhanov sat uneasily in the passenger seat beside her. His uneasiness came from Gisele's disturbing habit of turning toward him when she spoke instead of keeping her eyes on the road.

But then he realized that the deeper uneasiness he felt came from an unnerving happening that had occurred last night. With a shudder, he relived it—

Last night, asleep in the Dupree apartment, Tikhanov had awakened from a terrible nightmare in a cold sweat at four in the morning. Once fully awake, the nightmare had swum vividly before his eyes. He was running frantically from members of the KGB, desperately trying to find a place to hide.

Sitting up in bed, turning on the lamp, he found that the horror of the nightmare had blurred slightly, and in the light he sought reason. What had brought on the scare? General Kossoff and the KGB weren't chasing him. They were, in reality, honoring him. He was their star, soon to be the most shining star in the Soviet Union. But he had tried to hide from them in the nightmare—and immediately he'd understood that aspect of the nightmare and tried to interpret it.

The hiding part had to do with the present risk he had undertaken, and his total failure to sublimate his fear of being found out.

By coming to Lourdes, he had put himself in a precarious situation, watching each step he made in his frontal move on faith and the hope for a cure. Yet, intent on this daring effort, he had neglected to protect his flank sufficiently. He had neglected to keep in touch with those in the Soviet Union who might need him most any minute and not be able to find him. What if they searched for him, and somehow managed to find him here?

A tremor went through Tikhanov.

And then he realized he could prevent any suspicions by simply being in touch with his colleagues by phone before making himself visible to them once more in person.

At the first opportunity he would contact the Soviet Embassy in Paris. He would call there, supposedly from Lisbon—no, he had called from Lisbon already—better to have returned to France to meet secretly with an arm of the Communist apparatus near Marseilles.

Having decided this, he felt a weight lifted off him. For now, he had better concentrate on what was before him, meaning his absolute anonymity in Lourdes.

Worriedly, he glanced at his talkative driver behind the wheel.

Tikhanov was in no mood to engage in conversation with anyone, let alone this country girl. He wanted only to restore his health, and get to the seat of power that awaited him in the Kremlin as soon as possible. From a corner of his eye he saw a road sign. Twenty kilometers to Lourdes. Last night, in the taxi, the journey had taken a good half hour. At the rate the Dupree girl was going, it might take almost a full hour —and give her too much time for conversation.

As if reading his mind, she turned her head and said, "No hurry. It's just after eight and I don't have my first tour until nine this morning. It is such a glorious day, not hot like yesterday." She inhaled the fresh air through the open window. "On days like this I could stay here forever." Then she added enigmatically, "But I won't." She looked at him. "Have you ever been to Lourdes before, Mr. Talley?"

At first he was unaware that he had been addressed, his mind drifting, and he did not respond. He had forgotten that he was Mr. Talley, but with a start he remembered his acquired name. Hastily he became more alert as he replied. "No," he said, "no, I have never been anywhere near here."

"When did you get here?" she inquired. "Oh, yes, it was yesterday when you were trying to find a room."

"Yes, yesterday late."

"From Paris?"

"I stopped over in Paris, yes, I have friends in Paris."

"And you came here for a cure you told me last night. Is yours a recent illness?"

He was uncertain of how to answer her. He said, "Something I've had off and on for several years."

"What made you finally decide to come here? The news about the Virgin Mary reappearing?"

"I suppose that inspired me. It made me curious. I thought I would give it a try."

"Nothing to lose," she said with a lilt. "Possibly everything to gain."

"I am hoping."

"You will remain the entire week?"

"If necessary. I hope to go back home no later than next Monday. My vacation will be nearly over."

"Home," she said, eyes now on the road. "Where do you make your home in the States, Mr. Talley?"

He thought quickly. He had not anticipated personal questions and had not thought about this before. He tried to recall some remote places he had visited in the American East, places a person like Samuel Talley might have come from. He recalled a weekend trip he had made to a small town and resort called Woodstock, Vermont. "I come from Vermont," he said. "My wife and I have a modest farm in Woodstock."

"I've heard of it," she said. "I've heard it is picturesque."

"It is, it is." Tikhanov was worrying. He wondered if she had detected an accent in his English. He had better cover the possibility. He went on casually, "Actually, my parents emigrated from Russia, separately, when my mother was fourteen and my father eighteen. They met in New York at a social event, and fell in love, and were married. My father had been a farmer, and he found this property in Vermont and bought it. I was born there." Very casually, the next. "Growing up, I learned to speak Russian. It was natural. There was always Russian, as well as English, spoken around the house."

"I love languages," Gisele said. "I speak four but Russian is not one of them."

"No loss," said Tikhanov.

"And you work the farm?" inquired Gisele.

This girl was too inquisitive and smart. It was no use lying. She might see that his soft hands were not those of a farmer. He forced a short laugh. "Me labor on the farm? No, no. The truth is I'm a professor." He was feeling his way now. "Uh, a professor of the Russian language. I went to Columbia University, in fact majored in Russian and linguistics. After I got my doctorate, I became a member of the language department at Columbia. I teach Russian there."

"How do you manage to do it? I mean, live in Woodstock and teach in New York?"

Traps, everywhere there were traps, but as a diplomat Tikhanov was used to avoiding them. "Quite simple," he said. "I keep a small apartment in Manhattan to use during the school year, but maintain our home in Woodstock, and commute there whenever I can. My wife stays mostly at the Vermont house these days. She's a Vermont native and we have a son at—at the University of Southern California. He is studying theater arts." In an effort to leave the fictitious past behind, he made a transition into the present. "My wife was a Catholic, so I became a Catholic, too. I am not too religious, as I mentioned last night. Still, enough so to come to Lourdes."

"But you work in New York City?" she said.

"Yes, of course."

"I love New York, absolutely love it. I can't wait to get back."

Tikhanov was worried again. "You've been to New York?"

"I've *lived* there," she said cheerily. "I had the best time ever. There is so much to do in New York. I lived in New York for over a year."

Tikhanov tried not to be too interested. "You did? What were you doing there?"

"I had a secretarial job at the United Nations."

"At the United Nations?"

"With the French delegation. I'd met the French ambassador to the UN in Lourdes. He hired me to be one of his secretaries, and took me along when he moved to New York. It was a memorable experience. I can't wait to go back. I made so many friends there. Some of my best friends are Americans. One of them was in the United States delegation to the UN. As a matter of fact, if I remember right, he was a graduate of Columbia University. Maybe he was a student of yours, for all I know. His name is Roy Zimborg. Does that ring a bell? Did you ever have a Roy Zimborg in any of your classes?"

A big trap and danger. "I have had so many students it is difficult to remember names. Maybe he did not study Russian?"

"Probably not," said Gisele.

Tikhanov could see that they were approaching Lourdes, and he was relieved. He could not wait to get away from this country girl who had lived in New York and worked at the United Nations where he had appeared and spoken so often. Her inquisitiveness and persistent prying made him uncomfortable. Sooner or later she might catch him out in some error or inconsistency. He must rid himself of her.

Presently, they were on the Avenue Bernadette Soubirous, and entering the parking lot of number 26, which was connected to the Hôtel Gallia & Londres.

"What's this?" Tikhanov asked.

"The hotel where Edith Moore and her husband are staying," said Gisele, getting out of the car. "I told you last night about Edith. She's our miracle woman, had a miracle cure of cancer right here in Lourdes. You'll find it encouraging to talk to her. You still want to, don't you?"

"Certainly I do."

"Let me see if she's in."

He watched the French girl go into the hotel. His resolve had hardened. He must separate himself from her and from her prying. If he continued to lodge in Tarbes with her family, he would have to commute to Lourdes with her every morning and evening, and answer a continual outpouring of questions, and inevitably be tripped up. He had to find a room of his own in town as soon as possible. That was the immediate priority.

Gisele had returned, and was slipping into the driver's seat. "Edith is at the Medical Bureau, checking in, but she'll be back at the hotel for lunch. I left her a note, and told the girl at the desk to reserve two places at Mrs. Moore's table for twelve o'clock noon. How's that, Mr. Talley?"

"Perfect."

"What are you going to do with yourself until then?"

"You are the expert on Lourdes. What do you suggest?"

"Well, you're here for your health, aren't you? You're after a cure? You're serious about that?"

"Most serious."

Gisele started the car. "Then here's what I suggest. Go through all the routine that every ailing pilgrim goes through. First, go to the grotto and pray."

"I'd like to. How long should I give it?"

She blinked at him. "Why, that's up to you—five minutes, sixty minutes, whatever you feel. After that, walk over to the second trough, the one past the grotto, turn on one of the faucets and drink some of the curative water. Finally, next door you'll find the bath houses. Go inside, shed your clothes, and take a dip. And think of the Virgin Mary when you do so. The baths have proved to be the most effective remedy yet."

"The water cures?"

"No," said Gisele, shifting gears, "the water has nothing in it to cure. But your head does. Don't forget to meet me in front of this hotel for lunch. Now I'll drop you off at the domain, Mr. Talley."

"My thanks," said Tikhanov. "I'll do everything you say, Miss Dupree."

Amanda Spenser had not been in a hurry to leave Eugénie-les-Bains and return to Lourdes. She had enjoyed a leisurely breakfast at the table on the balcony of her suite, thinking constantly of Ken, his illness, and finding it inconceivable that Ken, the fool, could have left this elegant paradise for that hovel in Lourdes. After breakfast she had dressed in pants, blouse, sandals, and taken a long stroll over the hotel's lawn.

The drive from beautiful Eugénie-les-Bains to miserable Lourdes had taken an hour and a half, but as she neared Lourdes, its monotony and accompanying depression had been alleviated by one valuable tidbit of information from her elderly balding driver. The driver had known a good deal about the Lourdes story and especially Bernadette herself. In passing, as they drove, he had mentioned Bernadette's early illness, and Amanda had been attentive. Amanda had known that Bernadette had been a frail youngster, but she had not known that the little girl had suffered so seriously from asthma.

"It is a curious thing," the driver had said, "that when Bernadette sought a cure for her severe asthma attacks, she did not go to the grotto. By the time Bernadette had seen the seventeenth apparition of the Virgin Mother, there had already been four miracles cures at the grotto. But in truth, Bernadette did not herself believe in the curative powers of the grotto. Instead, when she was so sick, she went to Cauterets."

"Cauterets?" Amanda had said. "What's that?"

"A mere village. But also a fashionable spa in those days, not far from Lourdes. There was a healing spring, a thermal bath, that was supposed to be useful for an asthma cure. So Bernadette went there, not to the grotto, for her cure. Of course, she was not cured, but she tried."

"But not at the grotto," Amanda had mused. "She really did not believe in it?"

"Not for cures, no. She went to Cauterets instead."

"What's Cauterets like today?"

"It is still there, less fashionable perhaps. It's nearby. You drive up the valley into the mountains. I believe that there is even a shrine to commemorate Bernadette's visit."

"How interesting," Amanda had said. "I'll have to remember

that." If Bernadette did not believe in a cure at the grotto, she would dare to ask Ken, why should he?

Now, in the reception lobby of the hotel, she wanted to find Ken. Perhaps he was still kneeling hypnotized before the grotto. Or perhaps he was in their awful room getting some rest. Maybe the plump receptionist at the desk, the one called Yvonne, would know.

Amanda went to the desk. "I'm Mrs. Clayton," she said. "We had to go out of town last night. My husband, Mr. Ken Clayton, came back this morning. I wonder if you've seen him around?"

"Actually, I did," said Yvonne. "He's asked me to arrange for him to have lunch downstairs at Mrs. Edith Moore's table. He should be in the dining room right now. You know where it is?"

"You said downstairs. I'll find it. You can send my bags up to our room."

Amanda made for the staircase near the elevator, and hurriedly descended to the entry to the dining area. She could see the main dining hall, plain, every table filled with nondescript pilgrims, with a second narrower dining hall beyond it, and alcoves and booths off that room for more private dining.

A maître d' materialized to inquire if she was a resident of the hotel, and Amanda gave her room number. "I'm told my husband is lunching here now, and he's expecting me."

"His name?"

"Mr. Kenneth Clayton."

"Yes, of course, he is dining at Mrs. Moore's table. Please follow me."

Amanda was brought to an oversized round table at the far side of the main dining hall. She spotted Ken immediately, and he wobbled to his feet to greet her. She went around to embrace and kiss him. "I'm back, darling," she whispered.

"I'm glad," he said. "I hope you'll join us for lunch?"

"I'm famished."

Clayton signaled the maître d' for another chair, then took Amanda by the elbow and introduced her to the others at the table. "This is my wife, Amanda," he announced. "Amanda, I want you to meet my friends. Right here we have Mrs. Edith Moore, from London. And this is Mr. Samuel Talley, from New York. And Miss Gisele Dupree, who works in Lourdes as a guide."

When her chair was in place, between Ken and Mr. Talley, Amanda tried to orient herself to the strange mixed group. Edith Moore was obviously the dominant, central personality, although everything about her from her flat, square countenance to her unadorned, inexpensive dress was commonplace. The Talley gentleman was more distinctive with his beady eyes, bulbous nose, and flowing mustache. The Gisele youngster resembled a French starlet on the make.

Ken was speaking to Amanda. "You remember, I met Mrs. Moore on the train from Paris to Lourdes. The miracle woman—"

"Oh, now," Edith protested modestly.

"I wanted to hear her whole story," Ken continued, "and I invited myself to lunch with her. She was kind enough to have me."

"I'm pleased to help anyone I can," said Edith.

"I hope I'm not interrupting anything," said Amanda, apologetically.

"We've hardly started yet," said Ken. "We just ordered our lunch. Do you want to see the menu?"

Amanda felt oppressed by the ordinary dining room and the company. "I—I'll have whatever you're having."

"We're all having the same," piped up Gisele. "For the main dish it's grilled steak and potatoes today. Is that all right?"

"Suits me perfectly," said Amanda, without enthusiasm.

Gisele gave the order to the maître d', and then directed herself to Edith Moore. "Anyway, Mrs. Moore, you were telling us that your malignant tumor of the iliac bone was discovered five years ago."

Edith gave a deprecating wave of one hand. "Well, if you're sure you want to hear all that—"

"Mrs. Moore, I am anxious to know how your cure came about." said Tikhanov.

"Yes, do tell us about it," added Ken.

Amanda kept her lips compressed. She wanted to tell them all that despite what they heard from Edith Moore about a cure at the grotto, Bernadette herself, the instigator of all this miracle nonsense, had put no faith in the powers of the grotto, had instead been taken to a spa called Cauterets. But Amanda maintained her silence. She would not diminish the glory of this ordinary Englishwoman, and certainly she did not want to upset Ken, not right here in this odd group.

"To make it brief," Edith Moore was saying, "I had been forced to quit my job with a movie talent agency, and I could get around only with the use of a crutch, when Father Woodcourt—the very one on the train yesterday—suggested I join his next pilgrimage to Lourdes. Although I was a believer, I did not have much hope, nor was I given any great hope by Father Woodcourt. But I had reached a state where I was ready to try anything, you understand."

They all, except Amanda, bobbed their heads with full understanding. Ken, Amanda observed, most vigorously of all. Edith Moore halted her recital to allow the first course of the lunch to be served. The moment the plates were on the table, the English lady resumed, and Amanda found herself irritated by Edith's monotonous voice, no inflections whatsoever, and her colorless language. Nevertheless, Amanda made a pretense of being extremely attentive.

"The first visit to Lourdes produced no change in me," Edith Moore recited. "Perhaps the visit was too brief, and I did not pray enough, even permitted doubts to enter my prayers." Her gaze went around the table. "One must believe," she said. She chewed her shrimp piously, and resumed with her mouth full. "The second visit, four years ago, I was determined to try harder. To stay longer and try harder. I prayed by the hour at the grotto. I drank water from the spring without stop. I immersed myself in the baths. On my final day, being assisted out of the bath, I found that I could stand and walk without aid. I went to the Medical Bureau and was examined. Over the next three years I returned to Lourdes, and realized I was cured."

"It was verified?" asked Tikhanov.

"By sixteen different doctors," said Edith. "Even the iliac bone, which had degenerated, began to grow back to normal. There are X rays to prove it."

"A miracle," said Ken with awe.

"It has already been declared a miracle," chirped Gisele enthusiastically.

Edith Moore retreated behind a modesty that Amanda was sure she did not possess. "The miracle is not official yet," said Edith. "I have one more examination with a famous specialist in Paris, Dr. Paul Kleinberg, who will be arriving here this week to confirm my—my full recovery."

"But that's open and shut," said Gisele, employing one of her favorite Americanisms. "Everyone in Lourdes knows you are the one, the latest, of a favored group closest to Saint Bernadette."

"Oh, I don't know," said Edith with a seraphic smile, but not actually denying it.

"So it does happen," said Ken with continued awe. "It can happen to *anyone.*"

"If they have pure faith," pronounced Edith as high priestess.

Amanda, bending over her plate, felt sick to her stomach, with no desire to eat and with the single desire to get Ken away from the banal, stupid Englishwoman.

Tikhanov, his voice serious, said, "You attribute it all to the baths?"

"To everything here, to belief in the Immaculate Conception above all else," said Edith. "But my cure happened after the bath on the last day of my second visit."

As Edith finished speaking, a rather large, florid gentleman—he reminded Amanda of pictures she had seen of Phineas T. Barnum—had appeared behind Edith, stooping to kiss her on the cheek.

"Reggie—" said Edith, pleased. "Everyone, this is Mr. Reggie Moore, my husband." She proceeded to introduce Reggie to everyone at the table, one by one.

"Edith," Reggie said, "I hate to interrupt your tête-à-tête, but I must see you alone on something that's come up."

"But Reggie," Edith complained, "I haven't had my dessert yet."

He was half lifting the miracle lady out of her chair. "I'll treat you to some ices later. Please come along." He saluted the others. "Glad to have made your acquaintance, everybody. Hope to see you again soon."

Pushing and then pulling, he was leading the reluctant Edith out of the room.

"So it is the baths," mumbled Tikhanov to no one in particular. He twisted toward Gisele. "You heard. She said it happened after the bath."

"Well, you're on your way," said Gisele. "You started your baths this morning."

"I am afraid I did not," admitted Tikhanov. "I prayed by the grotto, but I did not go in the baths."

"Then go this afternoon, Mr. Talley."

"I shall. But first I must find a room in the city." He added quickly, "It is a pleasure to room with your parents, Gisele, but it is too far from here, too removed. I want to be close to the baths. I must find a hotel room in this city. I have tried, and I will try again."

Gisele eyed him shrewdly. "Is that all that's bothering you, a hotel room in Lourdes?"

"I know it is impossible, but it is important."

"Maybe I can find you a hotel room, but it'll cost you extra. Are you willing to pay extra?"

"I will pay anything reasonable."

"Say four hundred francs, for me to give to a reservations clerk."

"I will pay it."

"Let me see what I can do," said Gisele, rising. "As a matter of fact, I'm moving into town myself tonight. One of my girl friends is going to Cannes for the week, and she's turning her apartment over to me. I have to be here for the overload of work. I'll walk you to the baths now, and you can start in. You can meet me in front of the Information Bureau at five o'clock, and we can drive to my parents, pick up our things, and both move back to Lourdes tonight. If I can get you that hotel room."

"You will?"

"I think so," said Gisele. She waved to Ken and Amanda. "Excuse us. You heard our heavy business. Pleased to have met you both. Good luck."

Amanda watched the trollop leave with the older man, and finally she turned to Ken, intent on bluntly telling him what the taxi driver had told her, that Bernadette had never believed in the grotto or that its waters could cure, and had gone to another village to seek her own cure. But facing Ken, Amanda saw his expression. Oh, Christ, she thought, he's been lofted to another plane, all spirituality and faith in his future.

"Mrs. Moore is quite a lady," he murmured. "She's done a lot for me, she's renewed me."

Je-sus, Amanda said under her breath. This was no time to shake him up with the truth.

Besides, she told herself, she had better be sure of the taxi driver's story about Cauterets. She had better go to Cauterets and find out for herself if what she had been told was actually a fact. Telling Ken about the incident could wait a day longer.

"Ken, maybe you should go up to the room and rest for a while."

"I'm going back to the grotto," he said doggedly, starting to rise.

Amanda stared at him. That her man, sharp and brilliant attorney, athlete and handball player, marvelous lover, had been reduced to this puddle of piety was almost impossible to believe. But here it was, and she would somehow have to deal with it, with him, a tougher case than any she had ever encountered as a clinical psychologist.

She sighed and stood up. "Very well."

"See you for dinner early."

She wondered what she would do in the desert of the afternoon. Maybe buy her future mother-in-law a souvenir, a plastic Virgin Mary.

Going up in the elevator to the fifth floor of the hotel, Reggie Moore had been uncharacteristically quiet, but Edith knew that he had something on his mind. She knew that he was waiting for the privacy of their room before speaking to her.

Once they were in their room, the door shut, Reggie all but pushed his wife into the straight chair at the table as he remained standing over her. Dutifully, Edith waited, letting him have the floor, prepared for him to speak what was on his mind.

He spoke. "Edith, I had to get you off alone. I felt there was something I must discuss with you."

"Couldn't it wait a few more minutes? Those lovely people at lunch, they were hoping to hear more about my cure."

"That's just it," said Reggie emphatically, "the very thing I want to talk to you about."

"I don't understand. What do you want to talk about, what very thing?"

"Your cure," said Reggie. "The minute I came on you with all those people, I knew those freeloaders had cornered you to get some advice and inspiration."

"But they weren't freeloaders. That nice Mr. Talley said he would pay for my lunch."

Reggie showed his exasperation. "Edith, I didn't mean money. I meant they were freeloading from your—your mind."

"I don't know what you mean."

She was used to Reggie speaking to her as if she were a child, and she was ready to endure it now.

"I mean everyone wants to use you," Reggie answered. "Everyone wants to draw strength from you for themselves, selfishly in a way. My point is you shouldn't be going around giving away your story for free. You shouldn't do it."

"But why not?" she asked, utterly bewildered. "What's wrong with it? If the story of my cure gives people inspiration, gives them hope, why shouldn't I tell it to them? I'm an example to them, a fortunate one who was blessed with a miracle. They want to hear that it's possible. Why shouldn't I tell them?"

Reggie was momentarily without an easy or logical answer. "Well, because—" he said hesitantly, "because—well, I'd feel better about what you're doing once the miracle is officially confirmed."

"Oh, that," she said, dismissing it, "if that's all you're worried about, you needn't bother. My cure has been confirmed, really. It'll be officially confirmed—a technicality, as we both know—the day after tomorrow. I spent the morning with Dr. Berryer at the Medical Bureau. He's obtained the services of one of the two best men in the field—one with much experience in sarcoma cases—a Dr. Paul Kleinberg in Paris, who is arriving tomorrow to review the papers on my case and have the final look at me."

"Tomorrow?"

"Absolutely. Dr. Berryer will phone me after Dr. Kleinberg arrives, and let me know when to see him on Wednesday. Dr. Kleinberg will then confirm the miracle and it will be announced."

"Well, in that case," said Reggie, displaying his relief, "that's different, and I shouldn't be worrying. Since that's happening, I guess it's all right for you to talk about your cure."

"Of course it is, Reggie. I'm glad you agree."

"Yes, I'm sure it's all right," said Reggie smoothly, "and, as you say, it does give so many suffering people the belief that they can be cured, too. Yes, I'll go along with you, Edith. You are doing wonderful missionary work, just like the first apostles, spreading the word of miracles." He paused, his face lighting up. "In fact, we should celebrate again. Jamet has finished remodeling the new restaurant—it's a grand place now—and he and I are having our reopening tonight—we're plastering the town with handbills announcing the great event—"

"How wonderful!"

"—and I want you right there beside me to greet the guests. There should be a huge turnout. We'll have a special table and we've invited eight or ten important people, not just from Lourdes, but pilgrims from everywhere, to join us. I know they'll all be thrilled to meet you. And you can answer their questions. They'll be inspired to hear every detail of your story. What do you say, old girl?"

"Of course I want to be there, and tell them whatever they want to know. I don't mind if you're sure you don't mind."

"I insist on it," said Reggie with a half smile. He bent over and kissed Edith's cheek. "You're my little lady, my miracle lady. We're going to go far together."

8

. . . August 15

It was early afternoon, and Mikel Hurtado was sound asleep in his room on the second floor of the Hôtel Gallia & Londres, and he might have slept much later into the afternoon if the insistent ringing of the telephone on his bedstand had not awakened him.

It rang and rang without stop, until Hurtado finally shook himself awake, realized it was the telephone, and reached for the receiver, almost knocking the phone over as he brought the receiver to him.

"Yeah?"

"Mikel Hurtado, please." It was a faintly familiar female voice asking for him in English. "Mikel, is that you?"

"It's Mikel. Who is this?"

The events of the early morning hours came back to him, the attempted rape next door, his own role in beating up the rapist, the gratefulness of the beautiful and helpless blind girl next door, her name was Natale, and at first he thought that it was this Natale phoning to thank him again.

But the voice on the other end of the line was deeper and now speaking to him rapidly in Basque. "I've been ringing a long time," she was saying, "and I was just about to give up, when you answered. Mikel, don't you know who this is? This is Julia. I'm calling from San Sebastián."

Julia Valdez, his colleague in the Basque underground, calling long distance.

He was immediately annoyed, becoming angry.

"We agreed you were not supposed to call me in Lourdes," he snapped out. "I want no calls here. Are you crazy?"

"I *had* to call," Julia implored. "It is important."

Resigned, he said, "What can be so important?"

"Your life," said Julia, lowering her voice.

She had always had a tendency to be melodramatic, he told himself, being so young and immature. So he remained calm.

"My life?" he said. "What are you talking about?"

"It's my fault, in a way," Julia was saying. "I'd better explain. Augustin came looking for you this morning."

Augustin Lopez, as leader of the ETA, rarely had time to meet with him unless it involved some pending action. Hurtado wondered if the assassination of Minister Bueno had been revived. He was instantly alert. "Do you know what he wanted?"

"He said that he must see you. Luis Bueno has set a conference on our autonomy to begin in Madrid right after the reappearance of the Virgin. The minister is so confident the reappearance will occur that he has set a definite date for talks. Augustin wanted to inform you, and to consult with you about a strategy and agenda for the talks."

"The talks," Hurtado said with contempt. "Augustin really thinks they will take place and amount to anything? He's becoming senile. Julia, that's what you called me about?"

"Mikel, no, I am calling about what followed. Augustin kept insisting that he must see you. I couldn't tell him where you were, of course. So I tried to stall. But he's pretty smart, the old man is, and he started becoming suspicious. He pressed me to tell where you were, when you'd be back in the apartment. I told him soon, promised him you'd be back in a few days. Mikel, he kept pushing me. 'Back from where?' he kept saying. 'Where has he gone?' He knew that I was hiding something. He pressed me and pressed me, and was beginning to lose his temper—and you know his temper, Mikel—and he started saying I was keeping something from him, and he demanded to know what, and would force an answer out of me unless I was honest with him. I had to tell him—"

"So you told him the truth," Mikel interrupted bitterly. "You told him where I was. You told him I went to Lourdes."

"Mikel, I had no choice but to be truthful," she begged. "He'd see through any lie. He always does. I was forced to say you'd gone to Lourdes to—to see what was going on. Augustin saw through that at once. He wouldn't let me get away with it. 'You mean our Mikel has suddenly got religion, hopes for a chance to see the Virgin Mary?' He was shouting at me. Then he said, 'Bullshit! He's gone there to cause some trouble, to do something, anything, to keep me from negotiating with Bueno, to force me to approve of direct action, of terrorism.' Augustin kept saying that, words like that, trying to make me confess that I knew what you were up to. When I refused to confess, he lost his temper grabbed me by the wrist, twisting it—"

"That doesn't sound like him."

"I know. But he was really out of control. He kept on shouting. He said, 'If Mikel has gone crazy, thinks he can get anywhere with an act of violence in Lourdes, he's got to know that all he'll blow up is our chance for a peaceful settlement with Spain. He is going to try something violent, isn't he?' Mikel, he was hurting me, painfully. I had to tell him the truth."

Hurtado's own anger rose. "You told him the truth?"

"I had no choice. Then Augustin said, 'Do you know where to reach him?' I said I did, but I'd never tell. I told him he could kill me first. He said, 'The minute I leave, you reach him. You find Mikel. You order him to stop whatever he is planning, to stop in my name. You order him to return to San Sebastián immediately That is a strict order. If he attempts to defy it, he will be disciplined. I expect to hear from him today.' Mikel, those were his very words. Please listen to them. Augustin knows best."

Hurtado was furious. "Fuck Augustin. Fuck you, too, for being so stupid as to tell him what you did."

"Mikel," she pleaded on the phone, "be reasonable. He's smarter than I am. He knew without my telling him. He's just too smart."

He's also your father figure, your authority figure, and you want him to love you, Mikel thought, and he gave himself seconds to simmer down and be reasonable. "All right, Julia, I shouldn't blame you. I know you were on the spot."

"I was, Mikel, I *was*. I'm glad you understand."

"But I'm not forgiving him, not forgiving his sudden softness," Hurtado went on implacably. "He wants my answer today? You can give him my answer today, in fact right now. Go and tell him I am not returning to San Sebastián, tell him I am not leaving Lourdes until I've done what I've come here to do. Got it?"

There was silence on the other end. Julia's voice finally filled the void. Her tone was a tremble. "Mikel, you—you're not actually going to—to do what—what you told me you were going to do?"

"You're damn right I'm going to do it."

"Mikel—"

"Stay out of this, Julia. I'm going ahead. No one is going to get in my way."

Julia's response was hushed. "Mikel, if you could have seen him, you'd know. He won't let you. *He* will stop you. He'll say it is for the good of the cause. But he won't let you go ahead. He will stop you."

Hurtado gave an angry laugh. "Let him try."

With that, he hung up.

He remained seated on the bed, his legs still under the blanket, trying to think. He did not like what was going on, but what the whole matter came down to, Mikel felt convinced, was that Augustin would not move to undermine a fellow fighter in the movement. In the end, Augustin would be reasonable himself and loyal. It had been an empty threat to display authority. Augustin Lopez would make no real effort to stop him.

Feeling better, Hurtado looked out the window into the sunny afternoon. The grotto would be teeming with visitors right now. He would wait a few hours, wait until the crowd in the domain thinned out before dinner. Then he would carry his goodies down to the grotto, and there, at the first opportune moment, secrete them in the small forest above. After that, he would walk back to the hotel for a hearty dinner, and after dinner bide his time until midnight, maybe an hour or so after midnight, to return to the grotto to do the job.

After the satisfactory lunch at the Gallia & Londres hotel, spurred by the incentive of a 400-franc bonus from Sergei Tikhanov if she could find him a hotel room (and certain that she could find him a room), Gisele Dupree decided to drive with her affluent client to Tarbes right away to collect and move their belongings to Lourdes. There was still time, Gisele could see, better than two hours, before she was scheduled to guide a Nantes pilgrimage group to the grotto. Tikhanov readily agreed with her new plan.

On this trip she drove the red Renault fast, at breakneck speed, and they arrived at her parents' apartment in Tarbes in almost no time at all. Inside, she was able to pack her two suitcases swiftly. Tikhanov, who had unpacked very little the night before, was in the living room and ready with his single bag when she came out with her suitcases and a note to leave for her parents.

Again, with minimal traffic on the highway to slow them, Gisele covered the distance between Tarbes and Lourdes at high speed, as Tikhanov sat stiffly and nervously beside her. Once inside Lourdes, and having swung into the Rue de la Grotte, heading for their destination near the foot of the Château Fort, she broke her concentrated silence.

"We're just about there," she said to Tikhanov. "I'm taking you to the Hôtel de la Grotte. Very elegant and merely ten minutes from the domain and the sanctuaries."

"Are you sure you can find me a room there?" Tikhanov asked worriedly.

"Do not be concerned, Mr. Talley. I have the best connections."

Indeed, she did have a good connection at the Hôtel de la Grotte. She had done favors for the main receptionist, Gaston, and, in turn, he had done favors for her. They had an understanding about a spare room that was usually available for a guest prepared to pay for it with a bonus.

The huge white stucco five-story hotel, with the lettering HÔTEL DE LA GROTTE strung across the top of its roof, loomed before them. Gisele drove her Renault through the open black wrought-iron gates, entered the blacktop forecourt that curved past the blue awning and glass doors of the front entrance, and bore right into the half-filled guest parking lot.

"You wait here," said Gisele, leaving the car. "I have to see my friend and find out about the room."

"I'll be here," said Tikhanov. "Where else would I be?"

Gisele strode rapidly back to the hotel, and once inside turned right to the reception and key desk. It was unattended, but then she saw her friend Gaston coming from the blue lounge beyond the main lobby and returning to his station.

"Gaston!" she called out, and the diminutive figure in the black suit and bow tie halted, searched off and recognized her. His face broke into a show of pleasure, as he minced toward her. They hugged, kissed each other's cheeks, and parted for business.

"Gisele, my child, it has been a while."

"But well worth waiting for. Listen, Gaston, I need a room. Do you have one?"

"It depends," Gaston said warily. "This is a very, very busy season, you know."

"I have an important American client out in the car," said Gisele, "a New York professor. He offers a four hundred–franc bonus for a spare room. Half for you, and half for me."

"I will check. I think there is a space available on the third floor."

Pleased, Gisele clapped her hands, signaled a bellboy to follow her, and dashed out to the parking lot.

A few minutes later she came back with Tikhanov in tow, grandly introduced him with a short biographical sketch to Gaston, whispered to her client that it was the moment to deliver the bonus. Waiting while

Tikhanov peeled off the 400 franc notes, she slipped 200 francs to Gaston, and held on to the rest. Once Tikhanov had been safely registered, he was off to the elevators to be shown to his room by the bellboy.

"See you around, Mr. Talley," she called after Tikhanov.

"Thank you, Mademoiselle Dupree," he answered.

Once more in her car, noting that she still had time for her next two stops before taking on her afternoon tour, Gisele drove to her first stop, parking on the Avenue du Paradis, around the corner from the Café Jeanne d'Arc. Walking to the café, she peered inside and made out her friend Dominique clearing a table near the bar.

Gisele went inside. "Dominique, is the apartment free? I'd like to move my things in."

"All free and ready for you," said Dominique, plucking a key from her pocket and handing it to Gisele. "You can give it back to me when I return late Sunday night." Dominique had been invited by a wealthy patron, a Lebanese Christian, to accompany him on a five-day vacation to Cannes.

"I'll be waiting for you," promised Gisele. "Right now, can you get me an espresso and a pastry? I see there's a table outside."

Buying a copy of *Le Figaro*, Gisele went to the outdoor table, sat down in the yellow wicker chair as Dominique came up with the coffee. Sipping her espresso, Gisele placed the Paris newspaper before her. The front page was dominated by the photographic portraits of three Russians. The heading above them posed the question: WITH THE SOVIET PREMIER SERIOUSLY ILL, WHO WILL BE HIS SUCCESSOR?

Gisele's attention went to the lead front page story. Based on a brief report from TASS, the Soviet news agency, Premier Skryabin, head of the Soviet Union, was in a Moscow hospital. His condition was regarded as serious. Although the TASS announcement made no mention of an actual successor, there was speculation that the Politburo was considering three veteran Russian politicians for the high post.

Gisele's attention shifted to the photographs of the likeliest candidates for the premiership. Two of the pictures and names meant nothing to her. But the third one gave her a flush of excitement, for she recognized his name and vaguely his face. He was identified as Sergei Tikhanov, the longtime foreign minister of the Soviet Union. Gisele remembered, during her year at the United Nations, seeing the great Tikhanov speaking to the UN members from the podium. His stolid presence and self-assurance had made a lasting impression, and briefly, afterward, she had gone with her employer and lover, Ambassador Charles Sarrat, to a cocktail reception for Tikhanov. Staying close to Sarrat, as he had gone to shake the foreign minister's hand, she had actually seen Tikhanov from three feet away, but now remembered only his stony profile, his fat nose, and beneath it on his upper lip an over-sized brown wart. And now, this man she might once have reached out and touched, could be the next ruler of the Soviet Union.

Immediately, Gisele's mind was off once more on another of its countless journeys to her stay at the United Nations, and she knew more than ever that New York was where she belonged. She vowed again to save the money for translator's school and to get another job at the UN as soon as she had her diploma. But she realized that it could not be very soon, at least not at the rate she was saving. She hoped for tips and bonuses at the end of her guided tours, but with the exception of an occasional Samuel Talley, the pilgrims and tourists who came to Lourdes were either poor or ungenerous. It was going to be difficult, finding that extra money she needed, but she was determined.

She glanced at her watch. Barely time enough for her one more stop, to unload her suitcases at Dominique's apartment and hasten to meet up with her Nantes Pilgrimage and one more deadening tour of this tiresome city. She finished her espresso, paid her bill, stuffed the newspaper into her purse, and headed for her car and Dominique's apartment.

At last alone in the privacy of his own hotel room on the third floor of the Hôtel de la Grotte, Sergei Tikhanov did not waste a moment on his surroundings, but made straight for the telephone. Taking up the white-and-red telephone book on the shelf beneath the phone, he turned to the blue pages that offered information on the PTT system. Scanning the French text, he was pleased to learn that calls inside France from Lourdes could be made *automatique,* meaning he could direct-dial Paris without worry that the origin of his call would be suspect or possible to trace.

Immediately, he dialed the Soviet Embassy in Paris, gave his code name, and was put straight through to the Soviet ambassador. After an exchange of amenities, Tikhanov said that he was phoning from Marseilles and was not on a safe phone and therefore would be brief and imprecise. He was just checking in, before returning to a vital meeting with their country's friends outside Marseilles. He was calling to make only two inquiries: Had the general at home tried to reach him? And how was the premier?

Tikhanov was relieved to hear that General Kossoff of the KGB had not tried to reach him, knowing that he was busy with party affairs.

"The premier has not called either. But I hear he is in his usual good health."

For a moment, Tikhanov was puzzled, then remembered the open phone line. "Ah yes, of course." Tikhanov thanked the ambassador, and was about to hang up, when the ambassador suddenly asked, "If the general *should* want to talk to you, can I tell him where you're staying?" Tikhanov had been ready for that. "You'll tell him I had to leave the city to meet with our friends in a place where I cannot be reached. You can tell the general I'll be done with our business by the weekend, and I'll be in touch with him directly on Monday or Tuesday."

With that, the crucial call was finished, and his disappearance protected, and Tikhanov felt better than he had at any time since his arrival in Lourdes.

Slowly unpacking, he had time now to take in the single room he had been provided with, and he pronounced it satisfactory, although he was used to luxurious hotel apartment suites. His brief confinement with the lowly Duprees in Tarbes had been depressing, and he was glad to be away. But better than that, even more of a relief than escaping them, was his freedom from the inquisitive presence of that little hustler, Gisele, who had once worked at the United Nations and who might have eventually put him in jeopardy. To be shed of her, to be on his own, was the ultimate relief.

While waiting for the order he had placed with room service—he had not eaten enough at lunch in his concentration on Mrs. Moore—he began to pile his neatly folded shirts, undershirts, socks, pajamas into the drawers of the antique fruitwood chest on the wall across from the twin beds. Despite the crucifix hung on the wall between the beds, despite the pseudo-antique white Directoire chairs with their plastic upholstery, the room was acceptable. The marigold yellow drapes, and the French doors opening on a tiny balcony with a soothing view of trees, made the atmosphere lively and refreshing.

Tikhanov finished his unpacking just as the swarthy waiter arrived with his order. After the waiter had left, Tikhanov pulled a chair up to the table on which the tray rested next to the television set, unfolded the copy of *Le Figaro* he had requested, and drank his double vodka on the rocks.

The first thing he saw on the front page was the picture of himself, as a candidate for the premiership of the Soviet Union, and he stared at it with mixed emotions. His immediate sensations were of surprise and pleasure, surprise that TASS had so quickly announced that Skryabin was ill beyond recovery and would have to be replaced, and pleasure in the official word made public from Moscow that he, Sergei Tikhanov, was one of the choices for his nation's highest post. It did not bother him that there were two other candidates mentioned. They were party hacks, and their mention was merely a subterfuge until the real announcement could be made, and when it was made—as KGB head General Kossoff had assured him—there would be but one name for premier and it would be his own.

On the other hand, and this was the mixed part of his emotions, it was not wise to have his picture on the front page of a leading French newspaper while he was still lingering in France, and of all places, in Lourdes. But automatically patting his shaggy false mustache, he felt reassured that he would not be recognized. His disguise had not been penetrated and could not be. That, as well as his unlikely presence at a Catholic shrine, gave him sufficient protection.

Draining his glass of vodka, he wolfed down his salad and *omelette au jambon* as he read every word of the story released from Moscow. When he had finished both his meal and the story, his complacency was disturbed by a reminder of one thing. He was an ailing man, and his glory would not be long-lived unless he could be cured in this spot so publicized for its inexplicable cures. Actually, he had come here with no blind faith in a possible cure. What had given him an iota of hope, a trickle of faith, had been his luncheon encounter with the plain Englishwoman, Edith Moore, who had been cured of cancer by a visit here.

Cured by a visit to the baths.

It defied Tikhanov's orderly sense of logic, such a cure, yet it had taken place and been attested to by the most respected members of the medical profession. He had personally met the recipient of such a magical cure. This was no time for questioning or demanding logic. This was a time for believing.

He rose from the table. The day was short, and so was his time on earth, unless he gave himself over to magic. So it was off to the baths.

Taking the elevator downstairs, Tikhanov headed for the reception and key desk. The Dupree girl's friend, the receptionist Gaston, was there engaged in a conversation with another gentleman. Tikhanov prepared to inquire of Gaston how one reached the bathing area from the hotel.

Before Tikhanov could speak, Gaston greeted him warmly. "Ah, Professor Talley, there is someone here you must meet . . . Professor, this is Dr. Berryer, the gentleman in charge of the renowned Lourdes Medical Bureau."

Briefly, Tikhanov considered the one whose hand he was shaking. Dr. Berryer had deep lines in his forehead, eyes like poached eggs, a faintly aloof and clinical air, and appeared solidly built in his old-fashioned suit.

"Pleased to make your acquaintance," said Tikhanov.

"The pleasure is mine," said Dr. Berryer. "Gaston had mentioned your arrival. We are always flattered to have academics here. I hope you've found Lourdes to your liking."

"I haven't had time to find out yet," said Tikhanov, "but with the town's credentials, I'm sure I'll like it very much." He turned to Gaston. "In fact, I thought I would try the baths today. I'm not sure how to get there."

"You need only follow Dr. Berryer," Gaston said.

"Yes," acknowledged the physician, "I'm going in that direction right now, to the Medical Bureau. It is not far from the bathhouses. You can come along with me, just a short walk."

"Delighted," said Tikhanov.

They emerged from the hotel, and started west on the Rue de la Grotte.

"This is kind of you, Father Berryer," said Tikhanov.

Dr. Berryer offered a glacial smile. "I am not a priest. I am a layman, a physician, and a Catholic."

"Forgive me. The Medical Bureau of course. It becomes confusing."

"There may be more doctors in Lourdes than priests," said Dr. Berryer. "You have come here for your health, Professor Talley?"

"To see what can be done for my muscular dystrophy."

"Umm. It is possible. Who knows? You will be in the hands of the Virgin. There have been miraculous cures in many similar cases, as you know."

"I met a miracle cure earlier today. Mrs. Edith Moore. I was extremely impressed."

Dr. Berryer nodded. "Mrs. Moore, our latest, an inexplicable cure certified by medical science. I had examined her myself. A remarkable recovery, instantaneous and complete."

"She informed me that it occurred after she had bathed in the spring water," said Tikhanov. "Therefore it encourages me to undertake the baths today."

"The baths," murmured Dr. Berryer. "You know about them?"

"I am ashamed to say, not a thing, except that since the time of Bernadette they have cured."

"True, they have," said Dr. Berryer. "You may be interested in the background, how the baths came about, before you undertake them."

"I am most interested."

As they continued to walk past the souvenir shops, Dr. Berryer launched into a subject that clearly fascinated him. "The baths had their beginning on February 25, 1858, when Bernadette went to the grotto and saw the Virgin Mary for the ninth time. There was a crowd of four hundred onlookers on hand to observe her. The Virgin Mary spoke to her. Bernadette recalled it after. 'The Lady said to me, "Go and drink at the spring and wash yourself in it." Not seeing any spring, I was going to drink from the Gave. She told me it was not there. She pointed with Her finger to the spring. I went there but saw merely a little dirty water. I put my hand in it but could not get hold of any. I scratched and the water came, but muddy. Three times I threw it away; the fourth time I was able to drink some.' Actually, Bernadette not only drank some of the muddy water, but washed her face with it. Then, as she later claimed she was instructed, she attempted to eat a handful of weeds. She tried to do this but was forced to spit them out and vomit. Many spectators were revolted by her behavior, and they shouted that she had lost her mind and was insane. But by the next day the trickle of muddy water had miraculously become clear water and was coming out through a hole that was enlarging. The spring grew until it was a pool, and soon many visitors were drinking from it and washing in it, and there were numerous cures that resulted. Gradually, a series of con-cealed pipes were built to bring the spring water up to spigots and faucets from which pilgrims might drink and to bathhouses where the ailing might be immersed in the water."

"But this water is known to cure?" Tikhanov inquired, wanting to be certain.

"No doubt about that," Dr. Berryer assured him. "But here we are together, a man of science and a learned scholar, so I cannot be anything but candid with you. And in candor I must tell you that chemically there is no medicinal or curative element in the spring water, none at all."

"None?"

"None. In April of 1858, Professor Filhol, a scientist at the University of Toulouse, was asked to analyze the water. He did so and reported, 'The result of this analysis is that the water from the grotto of Lourdes has a composition that may be considered as a drinking water similar to most of those found in the mountains where the soil is rich in calcium. The water contains no active substance giving it marked therapeutic properties. It can be drunk without inconvenience.' In short, the spring water was ordinary drinking water. Through the years a concern grew that the water might actually be harmful. In 1934, my predecessors sent samples of the bath water to laboratories in Anvers and Tarbes, and to a laboratory in Belgium. Each analysis report was in agreement with the other. The Lourdes bath waters were extremely polluted—yet utterly harmless, for the billions of bacilli found in the water were inert. As the aged president of the Hospitaliers, Count de Beauchamp, used to say, 'I have drunk a whole hospital full of microbes, but I have never yet been sick.' "

"What you are telling me," said Tikhanov, "is that the drinking and bath water at the grotto in itself contains no properties that are helpful."

"Exactly."

"Then what makes the waters curative?"

Dr. Berryer shrugged. "What can I say? As a physician I can say it is the psychological element that cures. As a Catholic I can say it is an inexplicable spiritual cure fostered by the blessed Virgin. I know this one fact. The waters have cured, do cure, will continue to cure."

"So you would recommend the baths."

"What do you have to lose with your illness? You did speak to Mrs. Moore. Surely that is enough."

Tikhanov smiled apologetically. "It is encouraging."

As they strode along, Tikhanov saw that after crossing the bridge they were no longer on the Rue de la Grotte but on the Avenue Bernadette Soubirous, and ahead the spire of the Upper Basilica was in view.

"Let me prepare you for the baths," Dr. Berryer was saying. "About thirty thousand gallons of the grotto spring water is piped daily to the taps from which pilgrims drink and to the men's and women's bathhouses. Water is also held and released from two storage tanks. Now, you may have heard some skepticism about the cleanliness of the bath water—"

"I have heard no such thing," said Tikhanov hastily.

"No matter. The fact is that well over a hundred pilgrims bathe in the same water before it is changed at noon. There is often worry that the residue of the ailing may infect the healthy who bathe, and that this might result in a typhoid or cholera epidemic. But have no fear. There has never been an epidemic, and, to my knowledge, no one has ever been infected from water used by previous bathers. However, there have been cures, cures that I, myself, have verified. Invalids have gone into the baths for their one-minute immersions and climbed out under their own power perfectly healthy."

"Have you ever used the baths?" wondered Tikhanov.

"Me? Not ever, not once. But thank God I've had no need for a cure. I remain healthy." As they meandered down the ramp, Dr. Berryer remembered something. "But other physicians have lotioned themselves, as some call it, in the bath water. I remember particularly a predecessor of mine in the Medical Bureau, Dr. Jean-Louis Armand-

Laroche. He used the baths whenever he was in Lourdes, although he did not find them particularly hygienic. Someone asked him why then did he use the baths. Dr. Armand-Laroche replied, 'I do it as a believer. I do it in humility, in the spirit of penance and as a spiritual exercise.' "

Dr. Berryer cast Tikhanov a sidelong glance. "But you have more in mind."

"I hope to be cured."

Dr. Berryer said, "Then try the baths."

They had crossed the Rosary Esplanade. Dr. Berryer gestured off to the left at the archway. "Past the grotto, past the second drinking fountains, you will find the baths. I must go back to the Medical Bureau, so I will leave you here. I leave you in the best of hands. Remain optimistic. Good luck."

Tikhanov watched Dr. Berryer go, at last turned in the direction of the grotto, girding himself for the strange ordeal ahead.

The baths proved easy to find. There was a low, long, austere building with a marble front, entrances on one side for males, and entrances on the other side for females. There were some portable railings about for crowd containment, and four rows of metal chairs at each of the entrances. Nearby, there was also a black-robed, bearded priest of indeterminate nationality standing in front of a group of pilgrims and saying the rosary with them.

There was a short queue at the nearest entrance to the men's bathhouse, and Tikhanov fell into line, his heartbeat quickening with the knowledge that, for his grave illness, he was at the spiritual clinic of last resort.

The line of men was shuffling forward, and Tikhanov with it. They entered the bathhouse, stood in a corridor, off which were a series of blue and white curtains. A cheerful volunteer, a brancardier, spoke to them in an Irish accent. He explained that there were 2,000 men—and 5,000 pilgrims on the women's side—who came through here every day, so no time could be lost. Behind the curtains, he said, were the dressing rooms, and these led to the baths.

Tikhanov was directed to the first dressing room. He shoved aside the damp curtain and went into the cubbyhole. Three men, in their shorts, were seated on a bench awaiting their turns.

A French brancardier, on post at the exit curtain, called over to Tikhanov, "You are American or no?"

"American," Tikhanov answered.

The brancardier switched to English. "You will disrobe, like the others. Leave on only your undershorts."

Nervously, Tikhanov began to take off his shoes and socks, shirt and trousers, until he was down to his maroon shorts. He had hung up his clothes, started for the bench, when he saw that it was empty. He was about to sit down, but the volunteer beckoned for him to come across the dressing room. There, the volunteer wrapped a soggy blue towel securely around his waist, then ordered him to remove his shorts underneath. "You will have them back with your clothes when you leave the bath. When you finish with the bath, do not wipe yourself with this towel. You do not dry yourself. You leave the water on your body, and put your clothes on again over it. You will dry soon enough in the sun. Now, the bath."

He took Tikhanov by the elbow and sent him past the curtain to the bath itself.

Tikhanov teetered on the edge of a long rectangular sunken stone tub, filled with water that he was positive was foul. Two husky brancardiers wearing rubber boots and sporting blue aprons over their shirts and trousers, took his arms from both sides and assisted him down slippery stone steps into the tepid water. One of them signaled him to wade to the far end of the tub. Tikhanov did as he was told.

Wading to the opposite end, Tikhanov found himself confronting a Madonna on the wall and a large crucifix bound in rosary beads. A robust attendant leaned over and asked him what language he spoke, then handed him an enameled metal card with lettering. "A prayer for you to say in English, and after that make your silent request to God." Tikhanov mouthed the prayer to himself, and, handing back the card, tried to think of a request to make of the Highest Power. But he could only think of the brackish water and the billions of bacilli populating the water.

The attendants' outstretched hands grasped Tikhanov's hands while he was reassuringly told to sit down in the tub. Tikhanov lowered himself into the water, which covered his white torso up to his abdomen. One attendant ordered Tikhanov to ease back in the water, to lay back, immersing himself up to his neck. Tikhanov tried to do so, sank down, the water rising to his neck, and then suddenly he slipped, and his entire head went down underwater with the rest of him. He swallowed a mouthful of the putrid water, and struggled to sit up, coming to the surface choking and sputtering and sucking for air.

The attendants solemnly reached down to help him out of the tub, and quickly he was led back to his shorts and his clothes. Tikhanov was soaking wet from the top of his head to his toes, and he wanted to dry himself, but there were no towels. With difficulty, he got into his shorts, which clamped tight to the moisture of his torso, than yanked on shirt and trousers, socks and shoes, everything immediately becoming soaked through by the water on his body.

And then, dazed, he was outdoors again, confronting two palm trees, the bank of a hill, and a statue dedicated to "St. Margaret, Queen and Patroness of Scotland." He glanced about, seeking a way of escape, wanting to put as much distance as possible between himself and the miserable bathhouse. Then he saw a way out, back to the mainstream of people leaving the baths area for the grotto. Walking uncomfortably in the sun, his clothes clinging to him, he wondered if the immersion had cured his ailment. He could not tell. He was still walking stiffly, as if on stilts, and desired only to be dry once more.

He came to a stop in an unpopulated section beside the grotto, where what was left of the sun could still be enjoyed.

He remained there a moment, absorbing the sun, still feeling sticky and constricted. He shook himself like a wet dog to loosen up the clothing plastered to his body. As he did so, something untoward and unexpected happened. Something fell against his mouth and chin and fluttered to the ground.

Puzzled, he stared down at his feet, and was instantly horrified at what he saw. Automatically, his hand went to his shaved upper lip, felt its total smoothness except for the wart. His huge shaggy mustache, loosened by his immersion in the bath water, had become unglued and fallen off. Afraid to look around, to see if he had been seen, to note if his unmasking had been witnessed, he quickly stooped, snatched up the mustache, and in a flash pasted it back on his upper lip where it belonged. When he felt it was precariously in place again, he gulped and peered around to see if anybody had witnessed his brief exposure.

He stared straight ahead, and what made his receding horror change to shock was what he saw. He saw Gisele Dupree, the bitch of a tourist guide, pointing a camera at him. His eyes widened at the sight, but then as his shock, too, receded, he realized that she might not have been focusing her camera upon him. Just before him, slightly to one side, was a grouping of pilgrims, perhaps a dozen, posing for their guide Gisele, as she shot another picture of the members of her latest tour.

Confused, Tikhanov remained rooted to where he stood across from the grotto. He couldn't decide whether Gisele had actually taken a shot of him after his mustache dropped off, or if it only seemed that she had been shooting in his direction and had actually been focused on her tour group gathered not many feet away.

He could not be certain.

He wanted only to turn and flee, but before he could do so, he saw

Gisele lower her camera with one hand as she recognized him and smiled broadly. She waved to him with her free hand.

"Mr. Talley!" she called out. "How are you?"

"Fine, fine."

"You tried the baths?"

"I did."

"You must continue to do so," she called out, "if you want to be better." She winked. "Hope to see you again soon."

She went to join her group, and Tikhanov pivoted sharply away and put her and the grotto behind him as fast as possible. Retreating, he tried to revive the words that she had spoken to him. There had not been even a hint that she had taken his picture. She had simply been surprised and pleased to see him, and that was all.

He had been reacting like the worst kind of paranoiac.

She had not seen. No one had seen.

He was safe.

And he would be cured.

Reggie Moore had attired himself in his Sunday best, the pin-striped blue suit with the vest that he had last worn on the occasion of the dinner in London celebrating his partnership with Jean-Claude Jamet. Tonight, Reggie exuberantly had reminded his wife, there was to be an even bigger celebration, the reality of the partnership that would make them rich, the official opening of their remodeled and expanded restaurant in Lourdes. Before leaving London, Edith had packed her most expensive dress, the polka-dot purple satin, which she took out of the closet and put on.

They had been walking from the hotel for two blocks up the Avenue Bernadette Soubirous. Despite the pleasant evening, the thoroughfare was less crowded at this hour. It was just seven o'clock, and most pilgrims and tourists were dining before attending the nightly procession in the domain.

At five minutes after seven, Reggie brought Edith to a halt and pointed at a corner restaurant across the street. "There it is, luv," he said, "our very own pot of gold at the end of the rainbow."

Edith stared at the restaurant, freshly painted dark blue and orange, and she showed pleasure because Reggie was so proud and pleased. "It looks so three-star," she said.

"It is, it is," Reggie promised her, pulling her arm more tightly inside his as he started her across the street. "After the partnership was final, Jean-Claude didn't have much time to renovate. But he'd always had plans ready. So, with my approval, he gave it a fresh paint job outside, a modern decor inside, and added to the cocktail lounge and second dining room. He threw it open the day we arrived in Lourdes, and business has been smashing ever since."

"I'm so glad, Reggie."

"But tonight makes it official. From tonight on there's a special cover charge and special menu."

"Will people pay?" Edith wondered.

Reggie smiled at her naïveté. "They'll be glad to pay anything for a number of reasons. One, it's not merely a routine dining room connected to a cheap hotel. Two, it is one of the few separate luxury restaurants. Three, and this is most important, we have something to offer that no one else has." He was guiding her alongside the restaurant, and pointed upward. "Look."

Edith raised her eyes, and saw a tall neon sign glittering on and off over the glass entrance. The sign read: MADAME MOORE'S MIRACLE RESTAURANT.

Reggie's eyes were on his wife, as her mouth fell open. "What—" She stood bewildered. "What does that mean?"

Reggie grinned. "There's only one Edith Moore in Lourdes and I have her."

Edith stood hypnotized by the sign. "Madame Moore's Miracle Restaurant," she read aloud with disbelief.

"Doesn't that make you happy?"

"I—I don't know, Reggie—I think I'm embarrassed. I mean, my name in lights. Maybe that shouldn't be. Maybe it's—"

"You deserve it, you've earned it," said Reggie. He tugged at the door. "But that's not all. Wait till you see what's inside."

They were inside the doorway, and Reggie watched his wife as she took in the main dining room. It was a large room, splashed in dark blue and orange, blue walls and booths, and round tables covered with orange tablecloths. Each table was adorned with a pink rose in a slender silver vase, and each table was spotlighted by a chrome bullet light overhead. The dining room was crowded, with an overflow in the cocktail lounge beyond.

"It's wonderful," said Edith.

"It's ours," said Reggie with pride. "Now let me show you the real surprise."

As they wove their way between the tables, they were intercepted by Jamet, who had come rushing forward. His Gallic countenance was wreathed in a broad smile. "Welcome, Edith," he greeted her, lifting her limp hand and kissing the back of it. "Now the evening can begin. Reggie and I will take you to your table."

It was the largest circular table in the dining room, and the only one still vacant. Propped on a holder was a white placard with gold lettering. The gold lettering read: *Reserved for Edith Moore, the Miracle Woman, and Her Guests.*

"Oh, no—" Edith blurted, covering her mouth.

"You deserve it," Reggie persisted as he and Jamet showed Edith to her chair behind the placard.

"I—I really *am* embarrassed," Edith protested, forced into the chair. She surveyed the vacant nine chairs around the table. "And guests, what guests are we eating with?"

"Why, people who want to meet you, who are excited to meet you and hear your marvelous story," exulted Reggie. "We printed handbills and passed them out all around Lourdes today. Dozens of visitors phoned in for reservations, enough to fill this table every night this week. Jean-Claude has never seen anything like this before."

"But, Reggie, what happens after next Monday?"

"What about next Monday?"

"I won't be here. We'll be going back to London."

Reggie hesitated momentarily. "I—I was rather hoping I might persuade you to stay another week."

"But I have my job. Still, even if that could be postponed—who will you have here after the second week?"

Reggie swallowed. "We are thinking of a stand-in."

"A what?"

"Someone to replace you, someone we'll say is a close friend of yours and will have rehearsed your story, the story of your cure. Maybe she'll also pass out photographs of you, photographs you've signed, and people will feel blessed."

Edith was openly distressed. "Oh, Reggie, that sounds terrible."

"They'll be getting their money's worth anyway, believe me," Reggie said urgently. He had turned and clicked his fingers, and Jamet hastened over holding a menu aloft as he would a flag.

Reggie took his partner by the sleeve. "Jean-Claude, my wife wants to know if our guests will be getting their money's worth in the meal. Tell her."

"A feast, a pasha's feast," said Jamet, opening the menu, prepared to read aloud from it. "This is a deluxe dinner for this table, for this table only." He read from the menu. *"Melon Rafraîchi et Jambon Cru de Pays.* Followed by *Aiguillettes de Canard Persillées.* Then *Fromage des Pyrénées.* For dessert, *Profiterole au Chocolat.* And finally *Corbeille des Fruits."*

Edith held out her hand. "Let me see the menu."

Jamet glanced at Reggie, then shrugged and handed it to her. Her eyes skimmed it and she looked up with disapproval. "What you're charging for that—I can't believe it. And the huge cover charge besides."

"But at this table there is a special attraction," said Jamet, "and everyone is ready to pay. Now excuse me, I must summon the guests who are waiting."

Edith was glaring at Reggie. "I won't have this, Reggie. I can't have this. Using people like this. It is outright exploitation."

Reggie showed his exasperation. "Edith, for heaven's sake, you'll be helping people who need help, who want to be inspired by your case."

"Helping people is one thing. But it should be done for free. Not by making them pay through the nose." She shook the menu. "This cheapens the wonder of what happened to me. I don't think the Lord will look kindly on this."

"He'd look kindly on a wife trying to give her husband a hand," Reggie said desperately. He glanced off. "We'll discuss it more later. Jean-Claude is coming with the guests. Edith, be nice to them. Tell your story. Answer their questions."

Jamet was already seating the guests, and introducing them to Edith and Reggie as they took their chairs. Jamet reeled off the introductions smoothly. "Mr. Samuel Talley from New York, whom I understand Mrs. Moore has already met . . . Miss Natale Rinaldi from Rome, and Mr. Mikel Hurtado from Madrid. It is Madrid, isn't it? . . . Mr. and Mrs. Pascal from Bordeaux . . . Mrs. Farrell and her son, Master Jimmy, from Toronto." Jamet moved in behind Jimmy, a nine-year-old boy in a wheelchair. "Here, Jimmy, let me pull away the regular chair and get you in to the table properly. *Voilà.* And the other guest next to Mr. Moore, with whom both Mr. and Mrs. Moore have had a five years' acquaintance, is Dr. Berryer, the distinguished head of the Lourdes Medical Bureau. Now you know one another. If you will excuse me, I must tend to the other tables."

There was an awkward void after Jamet left, but Dr. Berryer quickly filled it. "How are you, Edith? I must say you are looking more fit than ever."

"I'm fine, thank you, Dr. Berryer," Edith said, a trifle sullenly.

"She's better than fine," Reggie boomed out. "She's great."

"The red-letter day is the day after tomorrow," said Dr. Berryer. "The specialist from Paris, Dr. Kleinberg, is arriving in Lourdes late tomorrow night. You'll have an appointment to see him Wednesday morning, but I will phone you before then to confirm the hour."

"Thank you," said Edith.

Dr. Berryer took in the man next to her. "You are Mr. Talley from New York," he said. "We met in your hotel. I showed you to the baths. Did you find them?"

"I took a bath," said Tikhanov, somewhat disgruntled. "I found the process extremely uncomfortable."

Here Edith could not help but interject herself. "It is not necessary that you be comfortable, Mr. Talley. Ideally, you should come here to do penance. Back in 1858, when Bernadette had her eighth visitation from the Virgin Mary, the Virgin told her, 'Go and kiss the ground as a penance for sinners.' Mr. Talley, you must regard the discomfort of the baths as a similar penance."

Tikhanov nodded solemnly. "You were kind to me at lunch. I came to this dinner for added reinforcement from you. Now I have it. I will go to the baths again tomorrow."

At this point, Natale spoke up. "Mrs. Moore, let me tell you why I am here. You are aware, of course, of my affliction."

"I am, Miss Rinaldi."

"When I returned from the grotto late this afternoon," said Natale, "my friend and helper, Rosa Zennaro, accompanied me to my hotel room, but had to excuse herself before dinner. As she left, a neighbor in the hotel who has been nice to me—Mr. Hurtado who is sitting next to me—was entering his room and he overheard Rosa and offered to bring me dinner. Meanwhile, he was showing me into my room when he found the handbill under the door about dinner at this restaurant and the opportunity to meet you, Mrs. Moore. I was enthusiastic about the prospect, so Mr. Hurtado offered to bring me here."

Hurtado gave off a shrug. "Also, I was very hungry."

Natale laughed, and addressed herself in Edith's direction once more. "Mrs. Moore, what I wish to discuss with you is this. I have devoted all of my time here to praying at the grotto. I have not gone to the baths because I thought it would be difficult."

"There are women attendants to help you," said Edith, and added with compassion, "You must try the baths."

"I come to this question—are the baths the most important means of achieving a cure?"

"That cannot be answered exactly," said Edith. "Speaking only for myself, I was instantly cured after bathing in the water from the spring. But others have been miraculously cured after praying at the grotto, after drinking the water, after marching in the procession. Dr. Berryer is really the authority on the cures."

Dr. Berryer dipped his head toward Natale. "You can even be

cured after departing Lourdes and upon your return home. It has happened. There are no rules, no formula, for how and when the cure will happen, if it does happen."

"So it can happen after any act or profession of faith," said Natale.

"Apparently," said Dr. Berryer. "When I first came to Lourdes, I made a study of all the sixty-four cures from 1858 to 1978 recognized as miraculous by the church. It will interest you to know, Miss Rinaldi, that the very second cure authenticated as miraculous was for a fifty-four-year-old man afflicted, at least partially, as you are. Louis Bouriette of this city had suffered an eye injury twenty years earlier, and for two years had actually been blind in his right eye when his sight was restored at the grotto."

"The cure really happened?" said Natale eagerly.

"It certainly happened, defying all medical explanations," said Dr. Berryer. "All those sixty-four miraculous cures I studied defied medicine—a young woman with a leg ulcer with extensive gangrene, a nun suffering pulmonary tuberculosis, a woman with cancer of the uterine cervix, an Italian gentleman with Hodgkin's disease, an Italian youth afflicted with sarcoma of the pelvis, such as Edith Moore had—all given up by their doctors, yet cured because of the shrine and by miraculous means. To be sure, most of these miracles occurred after bathing. But authenticated miracle cure number fifty-eight, that of Alice Couteault, and cure fifty-nine, that of Marie Bigot, took place during the Processions of the Blessed Sacrament. Yet others, among the first sixty-four, occurred after prayer before the grotto. I am still studying several that have happened since, and at least one of these cures I recall took place in the midst of prayer at the grotto. You would be wise to try everything available to you, Miss Rinaldi, not only praying at the grotto, but drinking the water, visiting the baths, even walking in the processions if you can manage it."

"But certainly the baths, you must try the baths," insisted Edith.

From across the table, the doughy Canadian mother, Mrs. Farrell, spoke up. "You were saying you, yourself, were cured after bathing."

"That is correct," said Edith.

"It would be a true revelation to us, to my son and myself," said Mrs. Farrell, "if you would tell us how the miracle happened to you."

"Go on, Edith," Reggie urged his wife, "tell them how it happened. I'm sure everyone here wants to know."

Edith shot him a lethal glare, and then, tuning back to the others she affected a transformation as neatly as an actress, offered one and all an engaging smile, and ignoring the food being served, she patiently went into her practiced recital.

As the guests sat mesmerized, only Dr. Berryer constantly bobbing his head in confirmation, Edith spoke of the gradual onset of her illness, the endless tests in London, and the final verdict that she had been suffering a sarcoma. Then, when all hope seemed lost, her parish priest, Father Woodcourt, had suggested a visit to Lourdes with his pilgrimage group.

Listening intently to her familiar story Reggie tried to judge his wife's temper from her tone. So aware was he of every nuance of her speech that, even though the listeners might be deceived, he knew Edith was straining to be level and even-tempered. Beneath there boiled a lava of displeasure with him that might erupt at any moment. While pretending to be closely attentive, Reggie glanced off toward the cocktail lounge and caught Jamet's eye. Reggie nodded mysteriously. Jamet, as if understanding, nodded back, and disappeared into the lounge.

Reggie appeared to hang on every word his wife was speaking, but from the corner of his eye he was on the lookout for something else. Then Jamet reappeared leading a cleric toward the table, keeping to the rear of Edith. The clergyman, a tall, imposing figure in a Roman collar and dark suit, came quietly to a chair Jamet had placed behind Edith. The clergyman settled into it, and cocked his head the better to hear what Edith was telling the others.

The courses came and went, and Edith's story progressed to her second Lourdes visit, to the last day of the visit and the final bath, when she had emerged no longer disabled, totally cured and free of her crutch, fully ambulatory.

Reggie noted, and was pleased, at the reaction of the first-night audience to Edith's opening performance. The American Talley was grunting his pleasure, the blind Italian girl's angelic countenance reflected happy wonder, the Canadian mother and the French couple were delighted with the miracle. What followed from his wife, Reggie knew, the certification of the cure from the many doctors at the Lourdes Medical Bureau, was anticlimax but an added sweetener more delicious than the profiteroles everyone had just finished consuming.

Then it was over, the dinner and Edith's miracle, and the adults were rising, thanking her profusely, everyone inspired and grateful, and leaving now in a rush for the domain and the evening procession, everyone with reinforced optimism that they too might be saved in this momentous Reappearance Time.

When the last of the guests disappeared, Edith and Reggie were alone at the oversized table. Immediately, Edith turned on her husband. Her bland face was contorted again in anger. "Now are you satisfied?" she demanded.

Reggie did not reply directly. Instead, he touched his wife's shoulder, and said, "Edith, you have one more guest who wanted to hear you. Look behind you."

Puzzled, Edith jerked around in her chair and saw the priest rising from his seat.

"Father Ruland," Edith murmured.

Reggie beamed, observing yet another and expected transformation on his wife's face. Her entire expression had softened. Reggie was aware that Father Ruland, the most intellectual and urbane of the Catholic churchmen in Lourdes, was a particular favorite of Edith's.

"Delighted to have you back in full health, Mrs. Moore," said Father Ruland in his courtly manner, bending his head without displacing a strand of his long sandy hair in a bow of appreciation, "and do forgive me for eavesdropping. I'd never heard your story in company, and I wouldn't allow myself to miss it. You asked your husband if he was satisfied. I am sure he is, and I can tell you that I certainly am. It was inspiring, both to me and to everyone in attendance. I, for one, want to thank you for sharing it with us."

If a person could melt in a puddle, Edith had done so. All anger had evaporated. Her countenance reflected only the purest joy. "Father Ruland, you are too generous. This coming from you means so much to me."

"You have earned and deserved whatever we humble members of the church can offer you," Father Ruland went on suavely. "You were blessed by the Holy Virgin, and all of us, through you, are secondarily blessed. I want to congratulate you on the verification of your miraculous cure, which will take place this week. I pray that the Virgin Mary will consider you as the one to whom She may show herself."

"Oh, I pray that might be so," said Edith fervently.

"Also," added Father Ruland, "I want to thank you on behalf of our entire order for foregoing your privacy and cooperating with your husband and Mr. Jamet in giving of yourself to the great number of pilgrims who wish to join you nightly at your dinner table. I trust you will not find it too much of an ordeal."

"It's an honor, and a pleasure, Father Ruland," said Edith breathlessly. "If I could be sure I am worthy of all this fuss and attention—"

"You could do nothing better, I assure you, Mrs. Moore," said Father Ruland.

"Oh, thank you, thank you."

Reggie had come to his feet. "Let me see you out, Father." He looked over his shoulder. "I'll be right back, Edith."

"I'll be waiting, darling," said Edith sweetly.

Reggie walked Father Ruland across the dining room to the door. Speaking in an undertone, Reggie said, "Father, you know how much Jean-Claude and I appreciate that. You have our everlasting thanks." With a touch of levity, he added, "As I told you, from now on all your dinners are on the house." Then serious again, "Father, you saved my neck. Maybe I'll be able to do something for you one day."

"Maybe you will."

Reggie reached out to clasp the priest's hand. "Anyway, once more, thanks. You've served a good cause."

Father Ruland smiled. "It's our cause, one and the same cause."

And he went out the door.

Long after dinner, and after he had left Natale at her room, and gone to his own, Mikel Hurtado prepared to return to the grotto area.

It was before midnight when he finished packing his sticks of dynamite, wiring, detonator, and other equipment, into a shopping bag. He had selected his locations above the grotto, and all that remained was to plant and wire his explosives in the darkness and quiet of the night. It should be safe, he told himself. The shrine would be emptied of pilgrims and tourists, who would be asleep. The security setup, as he had seen, was practically nonexistent.

The act was open and shut. He would lay down the explosives. He would set the time clock for the detonation. He would bring his single suitcase to the European Ford he had rented under another name, using the doctored passport and driver's license of his French Basque colleague. He would be many kilometers out of town, and free, when the grotto blew up.

Good-bye grotto. Good-bye Virgin Mary. Sorry, good believers, but there was a cause more important for the grotto to serve—a cause that meant good-bye to Spanish enslavement of the Basques.

Once his shopping bag was filled, Hurtado stepped out into the corridor, proceeded past Natale's door, thinking briefly of her and of her warmth and ravishing beauty (what a pity he would not see her again), and went to the elevator.

He rode the elevator down to the reception lobby, holding the shopping bag tightly at his side, and left the hotel. The Avenue Bernadette Soubirous was completely empty of life. He walked down the avenue, and strode to the corner of the Boulevard de la Grotte. At the corner, about to cross over the ramp leading down to the grotto, he stopped in his tracks.

Across the way, at the head of the ramp, there was life. Gathered at the top of the ramp was a group of men in blue uniforms, members of the Lourdes police, standing near two of their white and red squad cars, two station wagons with flashing blue lights on top.

Glancing to his left, Hurtado saw that the café, Le Royale, was still open, and the tables empty, but apparently it was near closing time. Hurtado considered wandering over to the café and taking a table for a cup of coffee, but quickly vetoed the move as making him, a loner with his bag, too conspicuous.

If the police saw him watching them from this corner, they might become curious. No, this was too conspicuous, also.

Rattled, he turned around and started walking up the avenue toward the darkened stores. He felt certain that this police gathering would soon break up and it would be safe to go down to the Rosary Esplanade and the grotto and do what he had planned to do all evening.

Hurtado slouched along by himself for fifteen minutes, and finally turned back and took another fifteen minutes to retrace his steps to the corner. This half hour would be enough to rid the area of police and clear the way for him.

But once he had arrived at the corner, he was surprised again. The police had not dispersed at all. In fact, their number had increased. There were ten men in blue uniforms there now at the head of the ramp. And one of them, a beefy officer with a map in one hand, appeared to be speaking to the others.

Hurtado pulled back out of sight completely. He decided that it would be unwise to hang around, to be seen alone at this hour, possibly to be questioned.

He tried to think why the police were there, and then he remembered having overheard, in the afternoon, in some shop, that Lourdes had been invaded by pickpockets, common thieves, even prostitutes from other cities, mostly from Marseilles.

No wonder the police had gathered, while it was quiet, to plan their strategy for law enforcement.

Hurtado turned away once more, and trudged toward the Hôtel Gallia & Londres.

There was no choice but to rest one more night, and wait for tomorrow. He would do it all tomorrow. He would get lost in the mass of humanity going down to the domain during the day, and slip up into the foliage above the grotto to hide his shopping bag. Then he would return tomorrow night at this same hour and set the detonator.

What the hell, the Virgin Mary deserved a day's reprieve.

9
Tuesday, August 16

Father Ruland himself had arranged the site for the first and only press conference that the church would hold in Lourdes during The Reappearance Time, the little-used but solid-appearing building known to the townsfolk as the Palais des Congrès—Palace of the Congress. It was a rectangular red building fronted by topiary landscaping where, from time to time, meetings were conducted by a cardinal from the Vatican or the mayor of Lourdes.

The arrangement inside, Father Ruland had decided during the selection process, was perfect for convening the international press. There was a great central auditorium that held as many as 800 visitors in individual chairs. Two steps led up from the stage to the semicircle of the wooden rostrum upon which was centered a lectern and microphone.

With the bishop of Tarbes and Lourdes promised as the representative of the church and the main attraction, the press conference had been called for nine o'clock in the morning.

Now, in a private office of the Palace of the Congress, the wall clock told Father Ruland it was eleven minutes after nine.

Michelle Demalliot, head of the Sanctuaries Press Bureau, came breathlessly into the office from the auditorium, nervously running a hand through her dark-blond hair and announced, "They are all in their seats, a large turnout, and waiting. And getting restless." She cast about, looking past Father Ruland and Jean-Claude Jamet, representing the Lourdes Merchants Association, and she asked, "He's not here yet?"

"Not yet," said Father Ruland. "However, I spoke to the bishop just last night and he assured me that he would be here at nine."

"Listen," said Jamet.

They could hear someone approaching the side door. Father Ruland stepped over to the door and pulled it open, and was relieved to see Bishop Peyragne parting from his driver, a young priest, and nearing the door.

As the lanky, elderly bishop of Tarbes and Lourdes came into the office, they all welcomed him. Father Ruland was particularly pleased to see the bishop so aristocratic in appearance with his elaborate pectoral cross hanging on a gold chain against his black cassock. Ruland liked his bishops tall and gaunt or round and pudgy. They looked more like princes of the church. And especially when they were attired in their vestments. The bishop would awe and contain the journalists.

"Sorry to be a few minutes late," the bishop said, "but I was delayed by a call from Rome. Well, now, I suppose I'm ready. Do you want to bring the reporters in?"

Father Ruland swallowed. "Uh, I'm not sure that would be possible, Your Excellency. There are at least three hundred journalists in the auditorium waiting for your press conference."

The bishop's long face darkened. "Press conference? What are you saying? When you spoke to me of seeing the press, I assumed you were arranging for me to meet with a half dozen reporters at most. But a press conference—"

"I'm sorry I was misunderstood," said Father Ruland. "But we had no way of limiting it—"

"I don't like circuses," the bishop growled.

"Your Excellency," Father Ruland continued, unruffled, "the world press is here in great numbers for the same reason we are here, to await the miraculous return of the blessed Holy Mother."

"No member of the international press could be denied," added Michelle. "We could not show favoritism in the invitations."

Jamet moved closer to the bishop. "Your Excellency, not only do those newspaper and magazine reporters deserve to know what is expected at the grotto, so that they can write about it, but they will write about Lourdes as well. The eyes of the entire civilized world are on Lourdes this week. The well-being of our town, our shrine, depends very much on your cooperation. What the press reports will help sustain the town of Lourdes as well as of the domain itself."

The bishop grunted, and spoke to Michelle. "Who's out there? Where are those people from?" he demanded.

"From everywhere and the most important," said Michelle. "International television reporters, of course, but no cameras in accordance with our policy. Also newspaper and magazine reporters from the *Times* in New York and the *Times* of London. Reporters from *Der Spiegel* of Hamburg, *Aftonbladet* of Stockholm, *La Prensa* of Buenos Aires, *Asahi Shimbun* of Tokyo, *La Stampa* of Turin, *Newsweek* of New York, our own *Le Figaro* of Paris. There is even a priest-informer—as the Vatican calls its reporters—here to cover this for *L'Osservatore Romano.*"

Mention of Vatican City's own semiofficial newspaper seemed to affect the bishop favorably. "Well, now, perhaps I should start with a personal statement about the impending Reappearance."

"Not necessary, Your Excellency," said Father Ruland. "I'll lead you out onto the rostrum and introduce you. Then I will request the members of the press to raise their hands if they have questions. You will point to certain reporters at random, and each will rise and pose a question. You will answer as briefly or as fully as you desire. I warn you, some of the questions may not be worthy of reply, but—"

"Never mind," said the bishop. "How much time am I expected to give them?"

"A half hour or so will do," said Father Ruland. "Longer only if you wish. At any rate, I'll approach the lectern at the end of a half hour."

The bishop fingered the pectoral cross on his chest. "Very well," he said gruffly, "let's go in and get it over with."

Liz Finch, wearing her pale-blue linen suit, sat expectantly in the second row of the auditorium, open notebook in her lap, pencil in her hand, waiting as the good-looking priest, Father Ruland, finished his introduction of the bishop of Tarbes and Lourdes.

"Now His Excellency will reply to your questions," announced Father Ruland over the microphone. "Those of you with questions, please raise your hands to be acknowledged. When you are addressed, please rise, give your affiliation, and state your questions as clearly and briefly as possible. Ladies and gentlemen, I turn the conference over to the bishop of Tarbes and Lourdes."

Father Ruland stepped aside and gracefully retreated to the background, and Liz watched the bishop, a towering warhorse bedecked in black robe and gold cross tramp to the microphone at the lectern.

As hands began to shoot up around the crowded auditorium, Liz kept her own hands resting on her notebook. She had only one question to ask, and it would be best to save it for the end, when most of the pious nonsense was over with.

The bishop was pointing to a man in the front row. The man came to his feet. "Toronto *Star* of Canada," he said. "Your original announcement was that the Virgin Mary would reappear in Lourdes between August 14 and 22. Here we are on the morning of August 16. How would we know if she had already been seen?"

"The event would have been announced immediately after it occurred. Obviously, it has not occurred yet."

Another man, next to the Canadian, had raised his hand and was already on his feet. "But you are certain the Virgin Mary will reappear here during one of the last five days of The Reappearance Time?" He added, *"Die Welt* of Hamburg."

The bishop offered a bleak smile. "Since the Virgin confided the approximate date of Her return to Saint Bernadette, I feel certain that the Virgin will keep Her word."

"But perhaps Bernadette miscalculated?"

"No," the bishop replied, "Bernadette was exact in her journal—this year, this month, these eight days." The bishop pointed to someone in a back row. "Yes?"

A youngish woman rose. "Your Excellency, I'm with *Le Monde* of Paris. When the Virgin Mother appears, will she be seen by only one person or more than one?"

The bishop shrugged. "I cannot say. If it is the same as it was in 1858, the Virgin Mother will be seen by only one."

Liz Finch heard a movement and glanced over her shoulder. The man seated behind her had come out of his chair.

"BBC, London. Will the apparition show herself only at the grotto once more, or could she be anywhere in Lourdes?"

The bishop answered, "Her message was explicit as to place, and it is likely that She will not only appear within the domain, but at the grotto itself. After all, it is familiar to Her."

A woman at the rear had been acknowledged and was standing. *"Il Messaggero* of Rome. I wonder what she will be wearing?"

Liz Finch could see the bishop repressing a smile, as he answered. "When it comes to fashion, I am out of my depth." There was laughter in the auditorium, immediately hushed by the bishop's solemnity. "Bernadette originally saw the Virgin Mary garmented in white. As Bernadette stated, 'I saw a Lady dressed in white, wearing a white dress, a blue girdle, and a yellow rose on each foot, the same color as the chain of Her rosary: The beads of Her rosary were white.' " The bishop paused, and added dryly, "It is unlikely the passage of almost a century and a third would have much effect on the Lady's attire. Next question?"

A Japanese gentleman was waving, standing. "From Tokyo *Asahi Shimbun,*" he called out. "Have you speculated about what the Lady may have to say to the one who sees her?"

The bishop shook his head. "Only God knows—God, His Son, and the Virgin Mary. When it happens, we too shall know."

Liz Finch listened intently to the unreality of the continuing questions and answers.

"Your Excellency, I am from *O Globo* of Rio de Janeiro. Excellency, our readers wonder—when the Virgin reappears, will she cure someone who is an invalid?"

"Yes, She told Bernadette She would. On the other hand we know that long ago when Bernadette was ailing, even though she saw the Virgin Mary, she was not cured. Indeed, Bernadette sought a cure elsewhere." Liz Finch blinked, and began to scribble a note. The bishop was going on. "As the Virgin told Bernadette, 'I do not promise to make you happy in this world but in the next.' "

"Your Excellency, I represent *The New York Times.* In the event of a nonappearance . . . if the Virgin Mary does not appear—that is to say, is seen by no one—what will be the Church's position?"

"Sir, the Church will not need a position. We devoutly believe in the Holy Mother, and She has promised that She will appear in Lourdes this week. Of that, no one in the Church has a doubt. Each of us dedicated to God, from the Supreme Pontiff of the Universal Church in the Vatican to all of his servants, fervently believes that the Immaculate Conception will reappear in one of the five days ahead."

Liz Finch stirred in her seat, eyes on the dial of her wristwatch. This was the moment for her own question. She must pose it before the conference ended. There were many hands beckoning for attention, and Liz quickly lifted her own hand.

To her surprise and relief, the bishop was pointing at her.

Liz jumped to her feet. "Bishop Peyragne, I'm from Amalgamated Press International of New York, from the Paris Bureau, and I have this question. Taking into account Bernadette's age at the time of the apparitions—fourteen, I believe, an adolescent, and unlettered—could it not be possible that the secret she heard from the Virgin Mary and noted in her private journal might have been more—more wish than factual reporting?" Ignoring the brief stir in the audience, Liz reiterated her question in another form. "In short, Your Excellency, how can the

Church be positive that what Bernadette set down in her journal about the Virgin's reappearance this year, this month, these days, was actually what she thought that the Virgin had told her?"

The bishop of Tarbes and Lourdes, from his elevated place, was staring down at Liz, and there was a long pause. At last, he spoke. "Madame, if we know nothing else about Saint Bernadette, we do know one thing that is absolutely beyond question. Bernadette was honest, she was unfailingly honest. She was tested and never once found wanting. She was ever truthful. She sought neither monetary gain nor fame. She wished only to be the conduit of a voice and message brought down from heaven. She would not enter anything in her journal that the Virgin Mary had not told her. She would enter only the truth."

Writing, Liz Finch felt the bishop's eyes were still piercing her. She looked up and saw that his concentrated stare was holding on her. Momentarily, he was inattentive to the other hands in the auditorium. He seemed to have something more to say to Liz herself.

He bent closer to the microphone. "Let me add this word. I am well acquainted with Bernadette, but I would not claim to have delved as deeply into her life as others. If you have any doubts about Bernadette's integrity, I would suggest that you speak further to one who is a scholarly historian of Lourdes and a biographer of Bernadette." He gestured behind him toward Father Ruland who was seated calmly between Michelle and Jamet. "I would suggest you see Father Ruland. I am sure he can dispel any doubts you may harbor." The bishop looked off at the forest of arms. "Now let us proceed. I see there are more questions."

Father Ruland was at the lectern, thanking the journalists and adjourning the press conference.

The bishop, followed by Jamet and Michelle, was exiting from the stage. As he did so, there was an unaccountable smattering of applause from the assembly of reporters.

Liz Finch watched the bishop leaving, and in her mind she continued to feel the intensity in his burning eyes when he had stared at her. Those Holy Joes, she thought, with their fanatical fever of piety. The unbending strength of their belief made her shudder.

Then she directed her attention to Father Ruland, still at the lectern, observing the breakup of the press conference. Somehow, he seemed to be lingering, and she wondered if it could be for her.

Scrambling to her feet, tucking the notebook and pencil into her purse, Liz hastened down the aisle to the stage.

She strode up to Father Ruland, and, indeed, he appeared to be expecting her.

"Father," she said, "I'm Liz Finch. Perhaps you remember that the good bishop suggested I speak to you about Bernadette."

Father Ruland's mouth crooked slightly. "Yes, Miss Finch, I do remember."

"Perhaps you can spare me a few minutes now, or would you rather I make an appointment for later?"

"Miss Finch, crowded as my calendar is with appointments, I think I can fit you in right now for fifteen or twenty minutes, if that will do?"

"It will do fine."

"Follow me."

She trailed his imposing figure off the platform and went with him as he entered an austere office. The priest signaled Liz to the chair in front of the desk, then stood at the desk reaching into a jacket pocket. "Do you mind if I smoke?"

"Not if you don't mind if I do." She sat, digging into her purse, came up with her packet and shook free a cigarette and put her lighter to it. He'd found his box of cigarillos and busied himself putting a match to one.

She held her gaze on him, trying to assess him. If he had not become a priest, he might have been a matinee idol. He was much too male and attractive to be wasted on celibacy. His long sandy hair and eyelashes, the faintly Mongolian cast to his eyes, the sensuous lips, really too much. But there was more, she sensed. A suavity colored by a brush of cynicism. Perhaps a politician priest, as well as a historian. Surely a worldly priest. But what was he doing, then, cooped up in a provincial tank town like Lourdes? Why not in Rome and in the Holy See itself? But then she realized that Lourdes was more than a tank town, far more, a notable adjunct to the Vatican in fact. Here was also where the action was, especially in this elongated week, a municipal stage for exposure and action. The Pope would know who his most effective servants were. Presently, for certain, this Father Ruland would wind up in Rome where he belonged.

Liz came out of her reverie to realize that Father Ruland was seated across from her, puffing his cigarillo, and contemplating her with mild amusement.

She was briefly disconcerted. She sat up, taking one more pull at her cigarette, leaning forward to grind it out in a ceramic ashtray on the desk. "I—I am glad you could see me, Father. Perhaps I'd better tell you exactly who I am, what I do, and what I'm after in Lourdes."

Father Ruland's voice was lazy. "I know who you are, Miss Finch, I know what you do, and I know what you are after here. So we can bridge all that."

"What am I after?" she challenged him defiantly.

"You are after Bernadette," he said pleasantly. "You want her scalp. At least, so I heard before the press conference. Your question for the bishop confirms it. You regard Bernadette as a fake. Well, Miss Finch, it may relieve you to know you are not alone. For in her own time, Bernadette, at least at the outset of the apparitions, was very much doubted and considered a fake by many authorities."

Ah, he's one of those smooth snakes, thought Liz, one of those in the business of disarming. The tactic was not unfamiliar to a veteran interviewer. Utter frankness and candor that made you lower your guard. Then *whamo,* straight to the chin. She had dealt with the Father Rulands, those without Roman collars, before, and often. Still what made this appetizing and fun was that he did wear a Roman collar and he was ready to join an American muckraker in disparaging a saint of the church.

"No kidding?" said Liz, playing along. "Some of her contemporaries actually considered Bernadette a fake?"

"Absolutely," said Father Ruland. "After Bernadette had seen the first apparition of the lady in white, she intended to keep it to herself. She did not mean to tell anyone about the visitation. Then her younger sister, Toinette, wheedled it out of her. The sister spilled out the story to their mother Louise, 'Bernadette saw a white girl in the grotto of Massabielle.' Louise demanded to know exactly what Bernadette had seen. Bernadette told her mother about the lady. Louise, considering the troubles the family had already had—failures in business, evictions from homes, a period in prison her husband had served—angrily struck Bernadette with a stick, and cried out, 'You didn't see anything but a white rock. I forbid you to go back there.' Her father, François, also forbade Bernadette to return to the grotto. Nevertheless, three days later, after her confession to Father Pomian, who treated what she had seen more seriously, Bernadette went back to the grotto and saw the Virgin a second time. Bernadette fell into such a deep trance, that an adult, a miller, had to be summoned to lift her and bring her away."

"But her parents eventually came around?"

"Eventually, but not immediately," said Father Ruland. "In fact, the following day, after the word had spread to Bernadette's school, the Mother Superior demanded to know if she was through with her 'carnival extravaganzas,' and one of the nuns actually slapped Bernadette on the cheek. Nevertheless, Bernadette was drawn back to the grotto a third time, this time accompanied by two curious women who insisted that she have the apparition write down its name. For a third time the apparition appeared, and Bernadette reported that she asked the white lady her name and the lady replied, 'It is not necessary.' And then added, 'Would you have the graciousness to come here for fifteen days?' Bernadette agreed. By her sixth visit, as many as one hundred people came to watch her in prayer and her mother was among them."

"But there were those who doubted the girl's stories?"

"Yes, definitely," agreed Father Ruland again. "As I told you, there were important personages in Lourdes who doubted her, regarded her as a faker, a daydreamer, an ignorant youngster suffering hallucinations. One of these was the town's police commissioner, Jacomet, and he hauled little Bernadette in for an interrogation. After learning that she was no more than fourteen, unable to read or write, and had not made her First Communion, Jacomet said to her, 'So then, Bernadette, you see the Holy Virgin?' She snapped back, 'I do not say that I have seen the Holy Virgin.' Jacomet exclaimed, 'Ah, good! You haven't seen anything!' Bernadette persisted, 'Yes, I did see *something* . . . Something white . . . That thing has the form of a little young lady.' The police commissioner pushed on. 'And that thing did not say to you, "I am the Holy Virgin"?' Bernadette would not retreat. 'She did not say that to me.' Jacomet's interrogation went on and on. Finally, he lost patience and said, 'Listen, Bernadette, everyone is laughing at you. They say that you are crazy. For your own sake, you must not go back to the grotto anymore.' " Father Ruland leaned forward against his desk, and went on speaking. "Bernadette insisted that she must go back, that she had promised the white lady she would return for fifteen days. Jacomet had been writing down everything Bernadette had recounted, and now he read his notes to her. 'You stated, the Virgin smiles at me.' Bernadette objected. 'I didn't say the Virgin.' Jacomet read further. Bernadette interrupted once more. 'Sir, you have altered everything on me.' At last, the police commissioner lost his temper, shouting at Bernadette, 'Drunken sot, brazen hussy, little whore! You are getting everyone to run after you.' Bernadette replied calmly, 'I don't tell anyone to go there.' But Jacomet would continue to oppose her, and she would continue to defy him."

Liz Finch could not help but be impressed. "She was a nervy little girl."

Father Ruland nodded his agreement. "She saw what she saw, and was unshakable in describing what she had seen."

Liz wanted to know more about the opposition. "And were there others in Lourdes at the time, I mean persons whom people looked up to, who also believed that Bernadette was a fake?"

"Many, many," said Father Ruland. "The Imperial Prosecutor Dutour interrogated her. He wanted her word that she would not return to the grotto, since it was disrupting the community. Bernadette told him that she had promised the lady she would go there. Dutour said, one presumes acidly, 'A promise made to a lady that no one sees isn't worth anything. You must stay away.' Bernadette replied, 'I feel a great deal of joy when I go there.' Dutour said, 'Joy is a bad counsellor. Listen instead to the Sisters, who told you that it was an illusion.' Bernadette replied that she was drawn to the grotto by an irresistible force. Dutour threatened her with prison, but finally gave up. A number of priests cross-examined Bernadette. One, a Jesuit named Father Negré, insisted that she had seen the devil. Bernadette replied, 'The devil is not as beautiful as she.' There was even some talk in town, among the intellectual doubters, that she might be insane—"

"Insane?" said Liz with surprise.

"Oh, yes. So in due course three well-known doctors in Lourdes were asked to examine Bernadette. They did so. They found her nervous and, of course, asthmatic, but anything but insane, in fact quite normal mentally. The doctors wrote off her visions as a not-uncommon childish hallucination. Speaking of Bernadette's first vision, the doctors reported, 'A reflection of light, no doubt, caught her attention at the side of the grotto; her imagination, under the influence of a mental predisposition, gave it a form which impresses children, that of the statues of the Virgin that are seen on altars.' The three doctors concluded that once the crowds ceased giving her attention and following her, Bernadette would forget the illusion and settle down into her normal way of life and routine." Father Ruland smiled. "Which tells us something about how wrong doctors can be, or could be in those days. But the most important resistance to Bernadette's story came from the leading priest in Lourdes—"

"Father Peyramale," interjected Liz, to let Ruland know that she had done some homework and was not entirely uninformed.

"Yes, Peyramale," said Father Ruland. "From the first, he was the strongest doubter. He simply would not take Bernadette's visions seriously. He was a powerfully built man, mid-fifties, impatient, short-tempered although decent and kindly underneath. It was after the thirteenth time that Bernadette had seen the apparition that she came before Father Peyramale, accompanied by two aunts. She had a message from the lady in the grotto. The lady's message was, 'Go and tell the priests that people are to come here in procession and build a chapel here.' Father Peyramale was not charmed. He addressed Bernadette sarcastically. 'You're the one who goes to the grotto? And you say you see the Holy Virgin?' Bernadette would not buckle under. 'I did not say that it is the Holy Virgin.' Peyramale demanded, 'Then who is the lady?' Bernadette replied, 'I don't know.' Peyramale lost his temper. 'So, you don't know! Liar! Yet those you get to run after you and the newspapers say that you claim to see the Holy Virgin. Well, then, what do you see?' Bernadette answered, 'Something that resembles a lady.' Peyramale roared, 'Something! So, then! A lady! A procession!' He glared at her aunts, whom he had thrown out of a church society for becoming pregnant while unmarried, and spoke savagely to them. 'It is unfortunate to have a family like this, which creates disorder in the town. Keep her in check and don't let her budge again. Get out of here!' "

"What disorder was Bernadette responsible for?" Liz wanted to know.

"The crowds at the grotto were growing. At first a few had watched Bernadette's trances, then 150, then 400, and soon 1,500 people gathered to witness her visions, and finally as many as 10,000."

"Did she ever see Father Peyramale again?"

"Frequently," said Ruland. "In fact, the very evening after he had thrown her out, she returned to see him once more. He had calmed down somewhat, and he asked Bernadette about the lady once more. 'You still don't know what her name is?' Bernadette replied, 'No, Reverend Father.' Peyramale advised Bernadette, 'Well, then, you must ask her.' After the fourteenth apparition, Bernadette returned to the rectory and said to Peyramale, 'Reverend Father, the lady still wants the chapel.' Peyramale said, 'Did you ask her for her name?' Bernadette said, 'Yes, but she only smiled.' Probably, Peyramale smiled, too. 'She is having a lot of fun with you! . . . If she wants the chapel, let her tell you her name.' When Bernadette saw the lady for the sixteenth time, she boldly asked the lady, 'Madame, will you be so kind as to tell me who you are?' According to Bernadette, the lady bowed, smiled, clasped her hands at her breast and replied, 'I am the Immaculate Conception.' Bernadette raced to the rectory and repeated what she had heard. Peyramale was thunderstruck. 'A woman cannot have that name,' he gasped. 'You are mistaken! Do you know what that means?' Bernadette had no idea what it meant. Actually, the dogma of the Immaculate Conception of the Blessed Virgin Mary—that Christ's purity at birth extended to his mother Mary at birth—was a highly sophisticated dogma announced by the Pope only four years earlier to help create a religious revival. That anyone as unschooled and ignorant as Bernadette could know about it seemed impossible. Father Peyramale was stunned. In my opinion, from that moment on, Peyramale was no longer a doubter. He believed everything that Bernadette had reported to him and would continue to tell him. From that moment on, he was on her side, one of her main backers."

"And that's what did it," said Liz.

"Not quite, but Peyramale's conversion was indeed a turning point," said Father Ruland. "But there were other factors, too, that dissipated doubt, and weighed the scales in favor of Bernadette's honesty. There was the cynical Dr. Dozous, who went to the grotto to watch her, saw her hold a burning candle in her hands while the flame crept down to her fingers. Afterward, when the doctor examined her hands, they showed no burns. There was the highly respected tax inspector, Jean-Baptiste Estrade, who mocked Bernadette until he saw her at the grotto, and who thought her performance was greater than any by the French actress Rachel, and that convinced him she was honest. Estrade came away saying, 'That child has a supernatural being in front of her.' Then the whole succession of early miracles."

"What miracles?" Liz wondered.

"The son of a tobacco seller who had sight in only one eye. He drank some of the water from the spring Bernadette had discovered and was able to see with both eyes. There was Catherine Latapie, who had fallen from a tree and partially paralyzed her right hand. At the grotto, after she dipped the hand in the stream, her paralysis disappeared. There was Eugénie Troy, whose vision was impaired and whose eyes were bandaged. She embraced Bernadette and was cured. Perhaps the most publicized cure was that of Napoleon III's two-year-old son, heir to the French throne, who had suffered a serious sunstroke in Biarritz. There was fear that the sunstroke might lead to meningitis. His governess traveled to Lourdes, spoke to Bernadette, filled a bottle with the spring water, and sprinkled it on the suffering prince. With that, his sunstroke vanished. And with that the Emperor ordered Lourdes and the grotto opened freely to the public. From then on, it became the most attended religious shrine in the Western world."

"Sounds to me like the cures really did it," said Liz.

Father Ruland hiked his shoulders, and said casually, "Make what you want of the cures, but Bernadette herself never thought too much of them. She was a very sick little girl, as you know, suffering from severe asthma and undernourishment. When she was extremely ill, she did not go to the grotto. She had no faith in its curative powers. Instead, she traveled to the village of Cauterets, thirty kilometers from here. It was a spa and she went there for the thermal baths. But they did not cure her."

"Still, Bernadette went there."

"Because the spa was highly spoken of in her day."

"I might look in on it, if I have time."

"It's not very interesting, but if you go there have a look at the church, Notre-Dame de Cauterets, and especially the modern chapel inside the church, the Chapelle Sainte Bernadette. Request the local priest to show you around—I forget his name—Father Cayoux, I think, I'm not sure. But, I repeat, there's not much else to see." He took out his box of cigarillos, and sought a fresh one. "Anyway, there it is, the whole series of events that made Lourdes what it is, the succession of events that happened and, of course, the cures for so many except Bernadette."

Liz had been jotting something. She put her pencil and notebook away, slowly, allowing a few seconds of silence to elapse, and then she inquired innocently, "Wasn't there something more that made the grotto notable?"

"Something more?"

"I read that politics played a major role in its fame."

"Politics—" repeated Father Ruland, knitting his brow. "Ah, you mean the showdown for control between Peyramale and Father Sempé. Is that what you mean?"

"I think so. What happened?"

"Well, to put it in a nutshell, after the area's bishop, Laurence by name, had appointed a commission of inquiry, and the commission had declared that Bernadette's visions had been authentic, the bishop felt that Father Peyramale was too local and provincial to be the promoter of Lourdes. The bishop appointed four members of the nearby Garaison order, led by Father Sempé, to take over Lourdes and the shrine. Whereas Peyramale's plans were limited to building a basilica above the grotto, Father Sempé envisioned Lourdes as the world's center for pilgrimages. It was he and his order who obliterated Peyramale in their rush for bigness. They created, at the edge of Lourdes, the Domain of Our Lady. There they funded the vast esplanades, staged real processions, completed the basilicas. They fought Peyramale to the ground, eventually obliterated his reputation, and in effect made the shrine what it has become today. Is that what you mean by politics?"

Liz Finch could not fault Ruland for lack of frankness. He apparently had covered everything for her, yet had not confessed to any real chicanery and hype. A little, but not much. A bone of contention to nibble at, but nothing to take a real bite out of. Smart man, clever man.

"I suppose—yes, I suppose that is what I meant by politics."

"Well, there you have it all." Ruland pushed himself to his feet. "Now I must be on my way, but if there is ever anything else you wish to inquire about, feel free to call upon me."

Five minutes later, when Liz stood in the morning sunlight before the Palais des Congrès, she realized that she had scribbled only three useful lines in her notebook, and those at the very end of the session. She read what she had scribbled:

"Bernadette did not believe in the cures at the grotto, and for her own cure she went to the village of Cauterets. *Be sure to go to Cauterets and check that out, and ask for Father Cayoux.*"

She stuffed the notebook into her purse. You're damn right she was going to Cauterets, in fact this very afternoon.

Following the address on the slip given to her by Yvonne, the hotel receptionist, Amanda Spenser at last came upon the Marian Car Rental, a side-street front office with a small automobile lot behind it.

Going inside, Amanda found one customer ahead of her, a weird-looking woman with orangish hair, studying a map spread on the counter. The clerk, a Frenchman too young to grow a full mustache, was drawing a red line on the map to give his customer directions to somewhere.

The young clerk straightened up. "There you are, Miss Finch. Just be certain you get on highway N21 going south. After that you'll have no trouble. It is not much of a drive, merely thirty kilometers."

"Thank you," said the customer, accepting car keys from the clerk. "Let me go over the route once more. No, you needn't do it with me. You can attend to the other lady."

The clerk moved sideways, and greeted Amanda questioningly, as she stepped closer to the counter.

"Can I help you, madame?" the clerk inquired.

"Yes, you can," said Amanda, setting the slip in front of him. "The receptionist at my hotel suggested I come here. She thought you might have a car available for rental this afternoon."

The clerk took on a mournful expression. "I am sorry, madame, so sorry. Our last available vehicle was just taken minutes ago."

"Dammit," muttered Amanda.

This was frustrating. She had spent much of the morning bored to tears at the grotto, while Ken had silently given himself over to prayer before the stupid hole in the hill. After lunch she had decided she couldn't do a repeat visit, and had sent Ken off to the domain alone. She had determined to use the afternoon better by resuming her pursuit of

Bernadette. She had to prove, the sooner the better, that the peasant girl from Lourdes was more fit to be a patient of a clinical psychologist than to be a saint whose visions could save people. Then, remembering the bit of historical gossip that the taxi driver from Eugénie-les-Bains had given her, Amanda had made up her mind to spend the afternoon driving to the village where Bernadette had actually gone for her cure. And now, no car.

"Dammit," she repeated aloud, "and all I wanted to do was to go to some little town near here called Cauterets. Sure you couldn't find a car somewhere for a few hours if I gave you something extra?"

"Madame, in a week like this one, no cars no matter for how much money."

Crestfallen, about to leave, Amanda heard the rustle of another person beside her. It was Miss Orange Hair.

The other one was asking her something. "Did I hear you say you wanted to go to Cauterets?"

"That's right."

"I'm Liz Finch, the lady who hired the last car, the one you wanted. And I'm about to drive to Cauterets." She hesitated. "Are you, by any chance, a member of the press?"

Amanda dismissed the notion with a short laugh. "Press? Me? Anything but. I'm Amanda Clayton, here from Chicago. I'm visiting Lourdes with my husband, who's hoping for a cure. I wanted to do some—some sightseeing in my time off, and I heard that Cauterets is worth a short visit."

"Well, in that case," said Liz Finch, "be my guest. I've got the BMW, and we're both headed for the same spot, so come along, if you want to. I could stand some company on the road."

Amanda was delighted. "Do you mean it? That's very kind of you. I'll be glad to share your expenses."

"You heard me say be my guest. I have no expenses. I'm here on an expense account." She folded her map. "Come on, let's get the show on the road."

They settled into the slick and clean BMW sedan. The women strapped themselves into their seats, and Liz nimbly took the car through the traffic. About a half mile from the main square, they drove past the Palais des Congrès and Les Halles on the Avenue du Maréchal Foch, and then swung left and merged into the highway labeled N21 and headed south.

Liz, who had been concentrating on her directions, now relaxed. "Here we go," she said. "Thirty kilometers to Cauterets. That's eighteen miles or so. Shouldn't take long, except the clerk back there said

the last ten kilometers climbs up a canyon and might slow us down."
She glanced at Amanda. "Why'd you pick Cauterets as a place to visit?
I'm told it's not much."

"We-ll—" Amanda hesitated briefly. "If you want the truth—but
first I'd better find out something. Are you a Catholic?"

"I'm an out-and-out atheist. Why?"

Amanda was relieved. "I wanted to tell you the reason I'm going
to Cauterets, and it would have been difficult to tell a believer. I'm not a
Catholic, either, just a run-of-the-mill convert and by profession a
clinical psychologist who doesn't believe in miracles. Or in supernatural
visions."

Liz grinned. "I think we're going to have a good trip."

"But my husband, Ken Clayton—well, he's really not my husband
yet, he's my fiancé—well, he's a fallen-off Catholic who suddenly got
religion again. Not that I fully blame him for reaching for something.
You see—let me explain—we were in love, were soon to be married,
when it was discovered that Ken had a malignant tumor on the upper
thigh."

"Sorry about that," said Liz. "That's dreadful."

"He was supposed to undergo surgery. But surgery in that area is
iffy stuff. Nevertheless, it was his only hope. Then, in the Chicago papers, he read the story about Bernadette's secret—that the Virgin Mary
is returning to Lourdes this week."

"It was probably my story he read," said Liz.

Amanda was surprised. "You're a reporter?"

"With the Paris Bureau of Amalgamated Press International of
New York. I filed The Reappearance Time story that ran in most U.S.
papers. Your Ken probably read my story."

"Probably," agreed Amanda.

"Anyway, go on," urged Liz. "What happened to Ken after he
read my piece?"

"He got religion, put off the important surgery, and hightailed it
here to Lourdes to see if the Virgin Mary could cure him."

"And you came along?"

"To try to bring him to his senses. The longer he puts off surgery,
the less chance for survival he has. I'm trying to convince him he's
wasting his time here. I don't think the Virgin Mary is coming back,
because I don't think she was here in the first place."

Liz shot her companion a look of delight. "Hey, Amanda, you're a
girl after my own heart."

"That's why I wanted to go to Cauterets. I want to prove to Ken
that Bernadette herself did not believe the grotto could cure. I heard a

rumor to that effect, that when Bernadette was ill, she didn't pray at the grotto. Instead, she went to Cauterets to take thermal baths. If I can verify that's true—"

"It *is* true, I assure you," interrupted Liz.

Amanda sat up. "You know it's true? For sure?"

"I can guarantee it's a fact, as given to me by the best Bernadette authority in Lourdes. That's Father Ruland, a bigwig priest there, close to the bishop of Tarbes and Lourdes, and a sort of an expert on our grotto girl." She laughed. "Now I can tell you why *I* am going to Cauterets. You won't believe it, but it's true. I'm going for the same reason you're going. To prove Bernadette was a phony."

"Well, I don't know if she was a deliberate phony. She may have believed she saw all those apparitions. She may have been hallucinating."

"Whatever, what difference?" Liz sang out. She pointed from the open driver's window. "It's a beautiful day out there, and getting more beautiful. Look at that scenery."

They had been driving through a wide river valley, the ripe green hillsides dotted with chalets. A bit of Switzerland in France, Amanda thought, especially with those snow-capped mountain peaks, like irregular sentinels rising in the distance. She had noticed that they had passed through a village named Argelès-Gazost, and now they were entering another village called Pierrefitte-Nestalas.

Liz was speaking again, as she maneuvered the BMW through the town. "I interviewed Father Ruland in Lourdes this morning, and he's the one who told me that Bernadette did not believe her grotto could cure, or at least she had no interest in its curative powers. When she felt ill, she traveled to the spa in Cauterets to take the thermal baths and hoped to be healed. So it is probably a true story, coming as it did from Ruland. But still, when you're writing an exposé you want to be superpositive. I made a telephone call to Cauterets and arranged to interview Father Cayoux, the parish priest there." She paused. "Yes, I'm trying to do what you also want to do. Expose this Bernadette for what I suspect she was. A sicky or a liar, one or the other. People have *wanted* to believe her for so long that nobody's really looked carefully at the facts. Everybody takes her story—well, on faith. I want to do a big number out of here, a big blast, and if ever, this is the week to do it. But when you go worldwide like that, you'd better have the goods. And I hope to find it, some of it or all of it, in Cauterets." She gave Amanda another grin. "We have the same purpose. Only different motives. So it's going to be a fun day. Can't wait to get there. Oops, we must be in the home stretch, because we're climbing."

A sharp turn out of the village had brought them up a steep road, a winding mountain road, along a precipitous cliff, and past a few miniature waterfalls. Liz was driving at a slower speed. They crossed a high bridge over a gorge through which a river—the map told them it was the Gave de Cauterets—rushed. The valley before them was widening now and they could make out the village of Cauterets, resembling a French resort town, nestled beyond.

Soon they were in the town, and passing two thermal-bath buildings identified on their more detailed map as Thermes de Cèsar and Néothermes.

"There they are," said Liz, "the places Bernadette considered more useful for her health than the grotto."

Next, they found themselves in the Place Georges Clemenceau, the main square. Over the rooftops and beyond they sighted the spire of the church, Notre-Dame de Cauterets, their destination.

Liz indicated the spire. "That's where we're headed."

"In the footsteps of Bernadette," Amanda said almost gayly, filled with optimism at finding what she wanted to know.

They reached a narrow one-way street, Rue de la Raillere, that wound up to the church. At the top, they realized that the tiny square in front of the church also served as a parking lot. They emerged from either side of the BMW, both stretching as they studied the church. The church was encircled by a wrought-iron fence built into dirty-white stone blocks.

Liz was reading her watch. "On time," she said, "actually five or ten minutes early for my appointment with the parish priest. Might as well go in and find him."

They walked in step across the square, which they saw was the Place Jean Moulin, noted the statue of a French soldier and the plaque listing the names of the town's dead in World Wars I and II, and continued on up a steep flight of steps and into the church entrance.

Indoors, there was a handful of worshippers, and Mass was coming to an end. They held back, and Amanda surveyed the interior. The altar area ahead, past the pews, was surprisingly bright and modern, circular marble steps leading to a beige-carpeted platform and a cheerful blond-painted square altar.

The Mass had ended, the parishioners and tourists leaving, when Amanda saw Liz step out to intercept a downy-cheeked youngster, with the look of a choir boy, who had come up the aisle.

"We have an appointment with Father Cayoux," Liz said in French. "Is he around?"

"I believe he is in the presbytery, madame."

"Would you be kind enough to tell him that Miss Finch is here from Lourdes to see him?"

"Gladly, madame."

As the boy hurried off, Liz, followed by Amanda, began to inspect the decorations along the inner walls of the church. Beside a doorway near the altar area, Liz halted to examine a curious old Vierge—a fourteen-inch-high statue of the Virgin Mary—blue and peeling, set under a glass bell on a wooden ledge.

Amanda pointed to the plaque beneath it. "Look at that."

Bending to the plaque, Amanda translated aloud in English. "In the year of our Lord 1858, between the seventeenth and eighteenth apparition, the little Lourdaise, the humble prophet of Massabielle, Bernadette Soubirous, came to Cauterets for her health, said her rosary before the statue of this Vierge."

"Well, that confirms it all right, what Father Ruland told me," said Liz with pleasure.

The downy-cheeked boy had reappeared. "Father Cayoux is in the presbytery. He will receive you. I will show the way." But he did not move, instead pointed his finger to the statue of the Virgin Mary on the ledge. "You are interested in Saint Bernadette's visit?"

"Very much so," said Amanda.

"Here, I will let you see the room dedicated to her."

The boy hurried up some carpeted steps through a doorway, and Amanda and Liz followed him.

"Chapelle Sainte Bernadette," the boy explained.

It was a narrow, starkly modern room, with patterned carpeting, maroon-covered armless bench chairs, a few small sculptured holy figures on the plain light-brown walls.

"Very nice, but very nothing," Liz said to Amanda. She put her hand on the boy's shoulder. "Take me to your leader." When the boy looked puzzled, she added, "Let's see Father Cayoux."

A few minutes later, they entered the presbytery and found the priest on his feet, at a table that served as his desk. He was pouring hot tea into three Limoges cups.

Liz went to him, extending her hand and addressing him in French. "I'm Liz Finch from the American syndicate in Paris. And, Father Cayoux, this is my friend who has accompanied me, Amanda Clayton, also an American visiting Lourdes. Her husband is ill."

Having welcomed them both, Father Cayoux waved them to two of the three straight-backed chairs near his table. As he passed out the cups of tea, and a plate of cookies, Amanda took him in. Father Cayoux was quite fat in his black clerical robe, rotund and short. A fringe of black hair detracted from his partial baldness, and he had a carbuncle of a face dominated by protruding yellow teeth. Amanda guessed that the frown he wore was perpetual. Although friendly enough, Father Cayoux gave her the impression of someone who might be irritable and fussy. Setting the plate of cookies on the table, he selected one, and balancing his own cup of tea, he settled with an exhalation in the chair beside Amanda, with Liz next to her.

"So," he said to Amanda, now speaking in English, "you are in Lourdes to see your husband cured. How do you like Lourdes?"

Amanda was at a loss. "I—I haven't had time to find out. Well, it is rather unusual."

Father Cayoux snorted. "It is awful. I dislike it. I rarely go there."

He had an abrupt manner, and seeing Liz beaming at him, he addressed her. "On the telephone, Miss Finch, you said that Father Ruland had told you that the petite Bernadette had gone not to her grotto but came to our thermal baths hoping for her cure. You wondered if the story was true. That you could speak of this interested me, that you could wonder even for a moment whether our well-known Ruland was being truthful."

"As a newspaperwoman, I had to be—"

"No, no, I understand," said Father Cayoux. "And every abbé cannot be trusted, to be sure, and you would have a right to wonder about a salesman like Ruland. When you questioned that story of his, I decided to see you. As to Bernadette and her visit here, you will recall I said come here and see for yourself. Now you have seen?"

Liz bobbed her head. "We have seen the Vierge, Father, and the inscription below."

Father Cayoux tasted his tea, then blew on it, and spoke. "In Bernadette's time our Cauterets was a fashionable spa, with the best of healing springs. You have seen the thermal baths?"

"Yes," said Amanda.

"They are less of an attraction today, but in Bernadette's time they made our town a resort of importance. In contrast, Lourdes was a minor impoverished village. But that petite peasant girl changed it all, made the world turn upside down. She made Lourdes an international center, and reduced us to a half-forgotten way station. Actually, her own role in this was innocent, perhaps—perhaps. Her promoters saw the opportunity and took advantage." He blew on his tea once more, sipped, nibbled his cookie thoughtfully. "No, Bernadette did not believe in the curative value of her grotto. She was always ill from the start, touched by a cholera epidemic that had taken others, a pitiful child with secondhand clothes, underfed and weakened by chronic asthma. She could not imagine, I suppose, that she could be healed by her own creation, the holy grotto, so in a period between her last two visions, after suffering a serious and lingering cold, she came here to Cauterets for treatments, to bathe in the water, to pray. In fact later that year, when the apparitions had finally ended, she came here a second time still hoping to be healed." He snorted, placed his empty cup on the table. "The inventor did not believe in her invention."

"What do you mean by 'her invention'?" Amanda quickly asked. "Are you being literal, Father?"

"I'm not sure," Father Cayoux mused. "I'm not quite sure," he repeated, staring into space. "I am a devout priest, a Marianist, perhaps closer to my faith than some of those ringmasters and publicity seekers who wear the cloth in Lourdes. I believe in God, His Son, His Holy Mother, and all the rites of our church, beyond question. I am less certain about miracles. They exist, have happened, I would imagine, but I have yet to see one in my time, and I wonder if Bernadette saw one or any in her time. You see—" His voice drifted off, and he was silent, lost in thought.

Amanda was excited, and a glance told her that Liz was, also. During Father Cayoux's recital, Amanda had perceived what was responsible for his crustiness and skepticism. He resented Lourdes, the big show, the brassy big time, the success, that overshadowed his parish and caused his good works to be overlooked. He was jealous of Lourdes, and he was angry with its high-riding hierarchy. All because of a little girl's fancies. His own obscurity, the changed character of his parish, was due to a—possibly—unbelievable little scamp, and the machinations of a cabal of church promoters.

There might be much here, Amanda thought, indeed everything that she and Liz wished for, if Father Cayoux could be persuaded to continue. Perhaps, what he had been saying, had been about to say, had frightened him, made him think that he had better cease and desist. But no, Amanda told herself, this was a man who did not frighten easily.

She determined to encourage him to go on. She broke the silence. "You were saying, Father? This is all so fascinating. You were wondering about Bernadette and her visions."

Father Cayoux's head bobbed up and down. "I was thinking about it, the miracles," he said. His eyes focused on his visitors, and he addressed them directly. "You see, visions and miracles come cheaply to the villages of these Pyrenees valleys, as they do to so many young visionaries in Portugal and in remote parts of Italy."

"Do you mean that others like Bernadette had entertained similar visions?" asked Amanda.

Since Father Cayoux was apparently incapable of laughing, he met the question with a familiar snort. "Others like Bernadette? Countless others like Bernadette before she came along and in the years since. I have heard that between the years 1928 and 1975 there were at least eighty-three persons, in Italy alone, who claimed to have seen the Virgin Mary. You have heard about the incident at La Salette near Grenoble?"

"I think I read about it in passing," said Liz.

"I haven't," Amanda told the priest.

"La Salette was one of your typical rustic villages," began Father Cayoux with relish. "On September 19, 1846, two children of the village, shepherd children, Mélanie Calvet, fifteen, and a boy of eleven, Maximin Girand, saw the Virgin Mary and heard prophetic secrets from Her. The boy was manhandled by the police, but refused to reveal the secrets. Both of the youngsters were interrogated for fifteen consecutive hours, but would not reveal the secrets. Instead, four years later, they sent the secrets that the Blessed Virgin had given them to Pope Pius IX, who did not reveal them. The authenticity of the vision seen by the pair was hotly debated. Mélanie was abnormal in some ways, ignorant, and even Catholic apologists admitted that she was lazy and careless. Maximin was worse, a known liar, but clever and vulgar. Both were characterized as repulsive young people. Nevertheless, the Ultramontanes, the conservative church-over-state Catholics, bought their stories completely. After forcing the children out of sight—the girl was placed in a convent in England, the boy with the Jesuits—the good Fathers promoted the La Salette miracle, put it over, and the pilgrimages began and the community prospered. Sound familiar?"

"Incredible," said Amanda.

"La Salette was before Lourdes. The miracle at Fátima in Portugal came after. Three shepherd children, Lucia dos Santos, ten, Francisco, nine, and his sister, Jacinta Marto, seven, on May 13, 1917, saw the Virgin Mary in a bush and once a month for six months thereafter. As usual, they heard secrets, and there was skepticism among the clergy and the children were even put on trial. But the children and their visions prevailed and Fátima became a miracle shrine second only to Lourdes."

"The Fátima youngsters must have known about Bernadette," said Liz, "as Bernadette probably knew about La Salette."

"Very likely," agreed Father Cayoux. "In Bernadette's case, however, she must have drawn her scenario, if such it was, from Bétharram."

"Bétharram?" said Amanda blankly.

"It is a town on the Gave de Pau, not far from Lourdes. It is a place where miracles supposedly occurred for many centuries. The Virgin Mary in white materialized there a number of times. The most dramatic apparition took place when a little girl fell into the river, and was certain to drown. The Virgin Mary appeared on the bank, held out a sturdy branch for the sinking girl to grasp, and she was pulled ashore and saved. Bétharram had its own wonder worker in Michael Garacoïts, who became Father Superior at the local seminary and was a splendid teacher. He also had the ability to levitate. He died in 1863, and was canonized as a saint in 1947. Anyway, it was from Bétharram that Bernadette may have fashioned her own Lourdes scenario."

Amanda was intrigued. "How?" she wanted to know.

"Bernadette was attracted by Bétharram and used to visit the church there often. The Bétharram church acknowledged that Bernadette was there praying for a number of days, four or five, before she had seen her first apparition. The very rosary Bernadette used at the grotto was the one she had purchased in Bétharram. Michael Garacoïts was still alive during and after Bernadette's apparitions. She was sent to see him and he believed her story from the start. When someone told him, 'This Lourdes may overshadow your Bétharram,' Garacoïts was alleged to have replied, 'What does it matter, if Our Lady is honored?' He visited the grotto many times before his death." Father Cayoux paused. "Well, the obvious point is that Bernadette could easily have picked up the Virgin Mary apparition idea at Bétharram and imported it to Lourdes."

Liz leaned forward. "We appreciate your forthrightness, Father. Many priests might not be as realistic and candid. Clearly, you are a man of faith yet one who holds the Bernadette story suspect."

"I'm afraid that is my feeling," said Father Cayoux.

"Bernadette's frequent visits to Bétharram certainly give reason for holding Bernadette suspect," said Liz. "I wonder if you have any other evidence that might indict Bernadette?"

Father Cayoux backed off slightly. "That might indict her? No, I have no proven evidence against her or her honesty. Just suspicions, just circumstantial evidence that makes her story questionable."

"Any of this you wish to speak about?" pressed Liz.

"There is too much, far too much," said Father Cayoux. "For one thing, Bernadette's parents. François and Louise Soubirous are portrayed, in those pretty color booklets they sell you in Lourdes, as impoverished, struggling, but industrious parents, perhaps too generous and charitable. Nonsense. They were both terrible drunks. I do not mean to visit the sins of the parents on the children, but just to show you what an unstable background Bernadette had. Nor did she have a decent home or a decent meal in all the years before she saw the apparitions. Her father was not fit to make a living. Bernadette was famished most of the time. The food she ate was mostly cornmeal porridge, watered-down vegetable soup, cornmeal and wheat bread sometimes mixed with rye. She often threw up her food. She might have suffered from ergotic poisoning as well."

"Which can make people hallucinate," interjected Amanda.

"It can," said Father Cayoux. "But even without such poisoning, her stomach was empty and her head was light. All the family starved. Bernadette's brother was seen scraping candle wax from the church floor for food. Bernadette, unlearned, constantly hungry, constantly ill with asthma, and without dependable love was certainly a candidate for —as you suggested, Mrs. Clayton—hallucinations."

"Yet," said Liz, "Bernadette was so exact in what she saw and what she heard. And this made a favorable impression on most believers."

Father Cayoux nodded. "Well, let's examine how our heroine might have come to what she saw and heard. The Virgin Mary that Bernadette saw was very young, too young, skeptics thought, for a Mother of Christ. As one English skeptic, Edith Saunders, explained—" Father Cayoux reached for a folder on his desk, and located a sheet of paper inside. He began to read from it. " 'Bernadette looked into the grotto and saw hard reality. She was despised and rejected and had no way of making herself admirable. Life had cast her disarmed into its competitive arena. She was fourteen years old, but so small and young-looking that she appeared to be only eleven. . . . The ideal of a little girl is naturally a little girl, and the apparition had the form of a girl of dazzling charm and beauty. She appeared to be about ten years old, and in being even smaller than Bernadette she consolingly proved that one could be very small and yet be perfection itself.' "

To Amanda's analytical mind, this was all insightful. Bernadette had been suffering from reactive psychosis, the obvious result of real environmental pressure. Bernadette had undergone a total flight from reality. In order to escape the problems of living, she had lost herself in imaginary satisfactions that made her existence more endurable.

Father Cayoux deserved praise. "That information, that's very good," Amanda told him.

"There is more, much more," Father Cayoux promised. "The Virgin that Bernadette saw was wearing a pure white dress. Well, that's more or less traditional. And Bernadette herself admitted that the Virgin was dressed much like the Children of Mary, a group of young

Catholic women volunteers in the village who were very beloved and were often attired in pure white dresses."

"What about the Immaculate Conception bit?" Liz interrupted. "The Virgin informing Bernadette that she was the Immaculate Conception, a concept that Bernadette could not have known about."

Father Cayoux uttered one of his characteristic snorts. "Bernadette knew about the Immaculate Conception, that I guarantee you. She may not have understood the concept, but she knew about it. After all, when Bernadette was staying in the town of Bartrès a few months before her visions, she attended or saw the Feast of the Immaculate Conception celebrated there as a holy day. The Feast of the Immaculate Conception was also a holy day in Lourdes itself. Bernadette certainly absorbed this."

"Yet, Bernadette carried it off, presented it all as something new to her," Liz said.

"Possibly with some help," Father Cayoux added mysteriously. He proceeded to clarify and expand on his remark. "There may have been a degree of stage management."

"Meaning?" Liz prodded.

"While Father Peyramale would not allow his fellow priests to attend Bernadette's exercises at the grotto," said Father Cayoux, "he did permit Bernadette to have constant contact with these clergymen in the confessional. These clergymen, in Lourdes and Bartrès, were Marians, strongly pro Mary and in favor of the Immaculate Conception dogma, and one of them once pointed to Bernadette, saying, 'If the Blessed Virgin were to appear to anyone, that's the sort of a child She would choose.' Furthermore, her Lourdes confessor constantly advised Bernadette, despite all restrictions, to continue to go to the grotto. In short, there were members of the church pushing for the acceptance of the visions. Nor were Bernadette's parents as far removed and as innocent of the happenings as has been made out. Once, when Bernadette came down to the grotto, with a great crowd on hand, perhaps four thousand people, Madame Jacomet overheard François, Bernadette's father, whisper to her, 'Don't make any mistake today. Do it well.' "

"Wow," said Liz. "Is that really true?"

"It was noted firsthand," Father Cayoux assured her.

Amanda, whose mind was on her Ken, went to something else. "But the original cures, like the Troy girl," she said to the priest, "what about them?"

"Many of the cures were not ascertained," said Father Cayoux. "You've cited a perfect example. Eugénie Troy. Twelve years old. She had been blind for nine years. She went to Lourdes, to the grotto, from

Luz, and was embraced by Bernadette, and came away with her sight fully restored. Shortly after, her priest in Luz revealed that Eugénie had never been totally blind, had always been able to see and to work at her job. There had been no cure at all, and besides, the doctors in 1858 were very limited in their knowledge, and unscientific."

"But they are scientific today," Liz challenged him, "and cures supposedly occur."

Amanda turned to Liz. "There is wish fulfillment, self-hypnosis, and there are so many diseases that physicians still don't know enough about, and many are eventually—especially under certain stimuli—self-curing."

"Precisely," agreed Father Cayoux. "There can be cures, but they need not be regarded as miraculous." With a grunt, he lifted his bulk out of the chair and stood over the two women. "After the cures began, and Lourdes had its foothold in fame, there was a problem. The problem was the young Bernadette, who was growing up as a legend. What to do with her? Continual exposure to the public, long after the visions had ceased, might lead her to contradictions, unvisionary behavior, might erode her legend. The masters of Lourdes encouraged her to remove herself from the public eye, become a relatively faceless nun. To this end, her masters encouraged her to leave Lourdes forever. She decided to go to Nevers, enter the convent of Saint-Gildard, become a cloistered nun. Before Bernadette was removed to Nevers, an eligible young man, an aristocrat and medical student, who had fallen in love with her, came to Lourdes to propose marriage. Bernadette was never told about that. The young man was rejected by her guardians, and she was spirited out of sight to the convent."

The women had come to their feet. "Might there be anything of interest for us in Nevers?" Liz wondered.

"I don't know," said Father Cayoux. "It is true that Bernadette's novice mistress in Nevers, Mother Vauzou, did not believe in Bernadette's visions. Mother Vauzou also treated her little nun harshly, almost sadistically, because she considered Bernadette too self-important and vain. However, this may have been Mother Vauzou's problem and not Bernadette's. At any rate, that was in the old days. I have no idea how the sisters up there regard Bernadette today, probably highly since she was elevated to sainthood after her death in 1879." He was fussing about his tabletop now, obviously eager to return to his duties. "You might go up there and see for yourself."

"We just might," said Liz. "Father, I don't know how I can thank you enough, for Mrs. Clayton and myself, for the time you've given us and for the balanced picture you've given us of Bernadette."

"My pleasure, I've tried my best to help," said Father Cayoux grumpily. "Good luck to you both."

After they had left the presbytery, exiting from the front entrance into the waning afternoon, they paused to light cigarettes and then looked at each other.

"Well, what do you think?" Amanda wanted to know.

"What do *you* think?" countered Liz.

"For me, fascinating stuff, a healthier view of the Lourdes matter," said Amanda. "Maybe I'll try to repeat some of it to Ken. Only—"

"Only what?"

"Only I'm not perfectly sure about our fat priest friend," said Amanda. "It crossed my mind that much of his cynicism, backbiting, might have been caused by pique and jealousy of Lourdes, and the way it has outstripped Cauterets as an attraction."

"No doubt about that," agreed Liz. "Still, it doesn't make what he gave us any less true."

"But you haven't told me what you really think," said Amanda.

"True or not—and I'd guess most of what Cayoux told us has some basis in fact—it's mainly a conversation piece, peripheral material," said Liz. "None of it adds up to an API exposé story. I still need some piece of hard central evidence that shows Bernadette up as a charlatan or an adolescent nut. Unless I have that piece of provable evidence, I can't file a story."

"Maybe you're right," said Amanda.

Liz started down the steps to the Place Jean Moulin and its parked cars, with Amanda falling in beside her. "Let's head back to Lourdes before it gets dark," Liz said. "Once we're there, I'll find out how to get to Nevers. I believe it is nearer to Paris than Lourdes. If we want to spend tomorrow there, we may have to leave tonight. You game?"

"Why not?"

"We can't miss a bet," said Liz. "Nevers may give us the key—the key that'll open up the grotto and show us Bernadette's big secret."

"If there is a secret," said Amanda.

"Are you kidding?" said Liz.

Rarely in his life had Mikel Hurtado felt more frustrated and puzzled than he felt this evening as he once more trudged back to the Hôtel Gallia & Londres.

For the third time this day, he had been blocked in his efforts to plant the dynamite and detonator beside the grotto.

Retreating slowly to the hotel, Hurtado reviewed his forays and failures and tried to make sense out of them. Early in the afternoon,

armed with his shopping bag of explosives, he had confidently undertaken his first effort of the day. He had wended his way down the
crowded Avenue Bernadette Soubirous to the corner, intent on following the stream of pilgrims crossing the street to the head of the ramp,
and going down the ramp into the domain.

Stepping off the curb, he had stopped dead in his tracks. Past the
pedestrian traffic, across the way, at the top of the ramp, were the police
and one of the white-and-red squad cars with a blue light on its roof.
The police were strung out, barring access to the ramp and the domain,
observing visitors, apparently halting and questioning some. Hurtado
could not make out clearly what the police were up to, but they were
there all right, exactly where he had seen them gathered last night.
Realizing that he did not dare go closer, considering the contents of his
shopping bag, he had backed off yet again and returned to the hotel.

In his hotel room, he had taken a deck of cards from his suitcase
and devoted himself to endless games of solitaire. Tiring of this paste-
board masturbation, he had picked up a paperback novel by Kafka,
flung himself on the bed, and read until he had dozed off. Awakened by
the sound of singing outside the window, the late afternoon procession,
he had squinted at his bedside clock. Five-thirty. By now, he had hoped,
the police would be done with whatever they were doing. He had
washed his face and hands, retrieved the shopping bag, and for the
second time this day had strolled over to the Boulevard de la Grotte.
Across the thoroughfare, the hub of the scene had been a replica of
what he had witnessed four hours or so before. There was the milling
crowd, vocally annoyed by the slowdown while going into the domain,
and the uniformed police apparently examining each worshipper and
tourist passing through a temporary barrier at the ramp entrance. Once
more, Hurtado knew that he dared not risk it, until he was certain that
the police had left.

Returning to his hotel room, he had disposed of the shopping bag
and, feeling a pang of hunger, he had taken the elevator down to the
dining room for dinner. At the table for eight where a place was reserved for him, he had seen that his neighbor and new friend, Natale
Rinaldi, was already there, eating, and that the chair next to her was
unoccupied. He had taken his place, greeting Natale and the other
guests, all French, apologized for being late and ordered his dinner. The
guests, along with Natale, had been deeply engaged in discussing some
of the more dramatic cures that had occurred in the last ten years at the
grotto and baths. Disinterested, Hurtado had not deigned to be drawn
into the conversation, but consumed his meal moodily, his mind constantly intent on getting into the domain.

Not until the dinner was over, and the others were rising to leave and go to the nightly procession, had Hurtado attempted to speak to Natale. He had offered to escort her to her room, and she had thanked him and accepted. In the elevator, going to the second floor, Natale had asked him what he had done with himself this day. He had invented a lie about hours of shopping to find a suitable gift for his mother in San Sebastián. Leaving the elevator, he had inquired politely how she had spent her day. At the grotto, of course, she had told him, at the grotto, praying. He had seen an opportunity of finding out about the swarm of police there and inquired if she had run into any trouble getting to the grotto. She had told him she'd had no trouble and wondered why he had asked. He had told her about the police at the ramp, and the long delay in reaching the domain, and was curious about the sudden gathering of gendarmes. At the door to her room, Natale had remembered that this had been briefly discussed at the beginning of dinner by several of their dinner partners. Yes, there had been some police, and those who had discussed it assumed that the police had been trying to spot veteran pickpockets and prostitutes. While the table speculation had proved nothing, still Hurtado felt it was something, and after seeing Natale into her room, bidding her good-night, and going back to his own quarters next door, he had felt encouraged.

Once in his room, he had decided to try again, and felt that he would make it. Certainly by now, by nightfall, the police would have found their petty criminals and dispersed so that the pilgrim traffic could resume at a normal pace. Preparing for a third advance on the domain, meaning to take the shopping bag with him, Hurtado had hesitated about carrying it, had felt unaccountably cautious. He had decided that he would examine the terrain, just to be sure that the path was clear, and once assured that it was clear, he would hasten back for his shopping bag and once more go to the domain and the grotto, and lose himself there, and do his preparatory job.

For the third time he had walked to the corner, and for the third time the scene had not changed. He could see the delayed lines of visitors pushing toward the ramp, and the bulwark of uniformed Lourdes policemen at the head of the ramp. Dismayed, but unencumbered by his explosives and feeling safer, Hurtado had determined that this time he would have a closer look and see what this was all about. He had strolled into the street to the café Le Royale, found a seat and table near the curb, ordered a Cacolac, and fixed his sight on the activity directly across the street. Pulling at the straw in his drink, he had finally been able to make out something of what was going on. The police, he could observe, were stopping only those pilgrims and tourists with packages and shopping bags, unwrapping the packages and searching the bags, then passing the people through to the ramp. Odd, Hurtado had told himself. What in the devil were they looking for? One thing for certain, he had been glad he had not attempted to enter the domain with his own shopping bag.

Now, still puzzled, he was returning to the hotel.

Inside the entrance, calling for the key to 206 from the special key desk, taking it, going into the reception lobby, he became aware of the lone receptionist, the plump French lady known as Yvonne, behind the desk busy as ever with some kind of ledger. The moment he saw her, he knew what to do. She would know what was going on—most hotel personnel like this one knew everything, all the town news and gossip—and she would tell him.

Hurtado detoured from the elevator and strode to the reception desk with a cheerful smile.

"Hello, Yvonne," he said to her.

She raised her head from the ledger and smiled back. "Good evening, Mr. Hurtado. Why aren't you down at the procession?"

It was a perfect opening, and he took it. "Too hard to get down there. Police at every entrance. What's going on?"

"Well . . ." But she was reluctant to answer.

He summoned up his most flirtatious smile. "Aw, come on, Yvonne, you know everything."

"Not quite everything—but some things."

"So you're not going to give a poor pilgrim a break?"

"Well, it's confidential—if it could be strictly between us—"

"You have my promise on the head of the Virgin."

"Really, Mr. Hurtado—"

"In fact, in return for enlightenment, I promise to treat you to a drink this week. If I don't keep my word, I'll owe you two drinks, even three."

She rose and leaned across the counter conspiratorially, and he cooperated by putting his head closer to hers. Dropping her voice, she said, "You won't break your word, now? This is absolutely confidential. I have it from my closest girl friend, Madeleine—she, uh, has a special relationship with Inspector Fontaine, who is the head of the Lourdes *gendarmerie*—"

"Yes?"

Yvonne whispered, "The police have had a tip that a terrorist may attempt to blow up the grotto, of all things, this week."

Hurtado felt the clutch at his heart. He tried to keep his voice even.

"I don't believe it," he said. "Nobody would do that, certainly not this week. A tip, you say?"

"It was an anonymous call. The inspector did not tell Madeleine more. But he has stationed gendarmes at every entrance to the grotto, and they search everyone going into the domain for explosives. They are taking it seriously all right. In fact—" She lowered her voice even more. "They are now checking the foreigners in every hotel. I—I'm not supposed to tell, but they are right here in the Gallia & Londres this very minute. The inspector himself and a large contingent of police. They have keys to all rooms, to open the rooms right now unoccupied and inspect what is in them and to examine the possessions of guests who are in their rooms."

Hurtado's throat was dry. "They're here, now, the police?"

"They started on the first floor about fifteen minutes ago, and they are working their way up."

Hurtado shook his head. "I can't believe it, a police search in Lourdes in a week like this."

Yvonne shrugged. "There always could be some crazy one loose."

"Thanks for the gossip, Yvonne. I owe you one drink." About to turn away, something occurred to him. He addressed Yvonne once more. Casually. "By the way, almost forgot to tell you. I have to be out of town for a day or two. A friend's birthday. But hold my room. I'll be back to use it. And—oh, yes, if the police want to know why 206 is unoccupied—you can assure them it's still occupied. Okay?"

"No problem."

He pivoted toward the elevator, and tried to appear unhurried, but in fact his legs were leaden. The realization of what had probably happened struck him all at once. He had half forgotten Julia's telephone call from San Sebastián yesterday morning, her call confessing that she'd told their leader, Augustin Lopez, what he was up to. He remembered defying Augustin on the phone with Julia, and he remembered her warning him that if he insisted on going ahead Augustin would try to stop him. He *had* insisted on going ahead, and that sonofabitch Augustin Lopez had anonymously phoned the Lourdes police and warned them of a possible terrorist act.

Hurtado knew that he must reach his room on the second floor before the police did. He must get rid of the explosives.

Real danger.

He felt the warm moisture of perspiration on his brow.

He waited for the elevator.

Hurtado was inside his room, the door shut behind him, falling against it to control his breath.

He had poked his head out of the elevator cautiously, praying that the police were not already there. If the police were there, he had made up his mind to get downstairs, get his car, and make a run for it. He might have a head start before they found the dynamite and detonator in his room, and before they issued an all-points bulletin for his arrest. But when he had come out of the elevator, and quickly scanned the second floor corridor, he realized that it was empty and he was momentarily safe. Immediately, he had made a dash for his room, unlocked the door, and thrown himself inside.

Now, breathing hard, exhaling in gasps, he waited for his body to settle into some degree of normalcy. In these fleeting seconds, he tried to figure out his next move. The first thing to do was to get the explosives and his person out of the room, out of the hotel. But then what? Another hotel? A boarding house? Neither promised any more refuge. He would go for his rented car, drive out of Lourdes to some neighboring town, Pau maybe, and hole up there. He could safely commute to Lourdes, scout the domain, and soon enough the police, empty-handed, would give up their vigil, determining that the anonymous call had been a crank call. The moment the lawmen let down their guard, he would slip in with his explosives and do the job.

Fuck you, Augustin Lopez, he shouted in his head to his betrayer. I said you couldn't stop me and you won't.

But ahead of anything else, he had to put distance between himself and the hotel. Flinging himself away from the door, he lifted his suitcase, put it on the bed, and opened it. Then he went for the shopping bag of dynamite, and by maneuvering his sparse effects around, was able to make room to fit in the explosives. He looked around the room to see if he had missed anything, and then remembered his toothbrush, toothpaste, and shaving kit in the bathroom. He scooped them up, stuffed them into the suitcase, and shut it tight.

Not another second to lose.

Lifting the suitcase off the bed, gripping it, he opened the door and glanced up and down the corridor. Empty. Time was still on his side. Relieved, he went out into the corridor, closed the door, and started swiftly toward the elevator. Reaching the gate, hoping that the elevator would be there, he saw that it was not there but in use by somebody else. No choice then but to take the staircase next to it down the two floors to the lobby. As he moved to the head of the stairs, he heard sounds, the tramping of footsteps ascending from below and a voice addressing someone else. The voice spoke in French. He eased himself to the side of the staircase, and peered down into the stairwell. He had the briefest glimpse of blue uniforms one flight below.

Trapped though he was, Hurtado did not panic. He had escaped at least a half-dozen similar close calls in Spain during his underground years. There was no time to think. There was only his survival instinct. If there was no exit, and no place to hide his suitcase, there might still be one uncertain refuge.

Hastily, he strode back toward his room, but stopped at the door just before his room, the door numbered 205. He could only hope that she was still inside where he had deposited her after dinner. He could only hope that she had not left to grope her way to the grotto alone once more.

His knuckles rapped the wood door panel. No reply. About to try again, he thought that he heard some kind of movement behind the door.

More certainly, he could hear the heavy footsteps off to his left tramping up the steps to the second floor corridor.

And then he heard Natale's voice on the other side. "Who is it?"

He tried to keep his voice down, yet above a whisper. Pressing against the door he said urgently, "Natale, it's Mikel—Mikel Hurtado. I—I need your help. Open the door."

Almost instantly, as the French voices to his left filled the corridor, her door came away. Without another word, he slipped into her bedroom and shut the door, locking it from the inside. He wheeled around and saw her standing a few feet from him, wearing no more than a diaphanous low-cut, sleeveless white nightgown. No dark glasses this time. Just her blank, unseeing eyes fixed in his direction.

"Mikel," she said, "it is you?"

"It's me—" He set his suitcase against the wall.

"You sounded so—you sounded like you were in trouble. Are you all right?"

He stepped close to her, gripping her bare arm. "I am in trouble, Natale. The local police have been alerted that there's a terrorist loose. They're making a room-by-room search of the hotels. They're in this one now. They've just come to this floor. If they find me, a Basque— they might take me for a suspect. Wrongly. But I could be in trouble. I had to find someplace to hide. Is there anyplace in this room I can hide?"

"Mikel," she said helplessly, "I don't know what's really in this room. What do you see?"

He'd forgotten her blindness, and now he used his eyes. The room was four ungiving walls. A closet, like the one he'd had, too shallow.

"Maybe the bathroom," he said, "the shower."

She was shaking her head. "No. When they come, it's the first place they'll look." Her face came alive. "I know how you can hide. Do as I say, quickly. Take off all your clothes—"

"What?"

"Mikel, no matter, I can't see you. Undress, fast. I've undone the bed. Crawl into it. Get beneath the covers and pretend you're asleep. Put your clothes on a chair—"

"I brought my suitcase."

"Under the bed."

He grabbed the suitcase and shoved it out of sight.

"Are the lights on?" she asked.

"Yes. The chandelier."

"Turn it off."

He turned off the overhead lights. "There's still a dim lamp the other side of the bed."

"Leave it on. Are you undressing?"

"I will." He yanked off his corduroy sport jacket. He unbuttoned his shirt and hung it on the nearest chair. Kicking off his shoes, he unbuckled his belt. Awkwardly, he stepped out of his trousers and dropped them on the chair. He stood naked except for his jock shorts and socks.

"All right," he said, "I'm undressed."

"Now get into bed. Cover yourself. Close your eyes. Be asleep." He stepped to the bed, had begun to get into it, when he saw her feeling her way along the foot of the bed and around it to the other side.

She sat down on the side of the bed. "I'm getting into bed with you. We're married. When the police knock, I'll get up and answer. You'll be asleep. Leave the rest to me." She was under the covers beside him, and he could sense her nearness and imagine her body. It would have been erotic, exciting, but he was too tense and worried to allow his mind to be stimulated by it.

"I have an acute sense of hearing," she whispered, "and I'm sure they're very near. So pretend sleep, and be very still, and don't stir when they knock. Leave everything to Natale. I used to be an actress, you know."

The suspense was full in his throat, almost gagging him, but he lay there unmoving, playing slumber, and waiting for the knock on the door.

Perhaps a minute or two had passed in silence.

And then it came. Three sharp knocks on the door. Three more knocks. A male voice speaking French. "Anyone in the room? If so, open the door. It's the police."

Natale sat up in the bed. "Yes, I'm here," she called out. "I was asleep—"

"Come, open the door. It is the gendarmes. We just want a few words with each of the guests. Nothing to worry about."

"I'm coming," called out Natale, leaving the bed. "One second."

Hurtado kept his eyes shut, drawing the blanket up to his chin. He could hear Natale padding around the bed to the door. He could hear the lock turning. He could hear the bedroom door creaking slowly, until a thin shaft of light from the corridor fell across the bottom of the bed.

Through the slit of one eye, Hurtado had a glimpse of the confrontation. He could see Natale, in her transparent nightgown, in the partially open doorway, and facing her, towering over her in the corridor two police officers.

The foremost of the officers, the older one, was speaking to Natale apologetically. "I'm Inspector Fontaine of the Lourdes Commissariat de police, and I'm sorry to disturb you like this, madame. But it is a necessity. We have received a warning that there is a terrorist loose in the city, probably armed, and we must treat it seriously. Now, with the assistance of our police colleagues from Pau and Tarbes, we are making an overnight sweep of Lourdes, searching every hotel."

Natale had reacted with fright. "A terrorist, you say?"

"Don't worry, madame, we have many on the search. There is nothing to fear. You are alone here? Or are there others in the room?"

"Only my poor husband, so exhausted from a long plane trip to join me in Lourdes that he's already fallen asleep. But of course, if you must, you can come in and wake him. Are there many of you to search my room? I can't tell. I can't—I'm unable to—to—" She had let her helpless voice drift off.

In the bed, under the blanket, feigning sleep, Hurtado steeled himself for what might happen next. But he guessed, without being able to look, that Natale had somehow indicated her condition.

He listened. Apparently she had, for he heard a second and different male voice, higher pitched, probably the first policeman. "Inspector, I believe the young woman is blind."

Natale was confirming this sadly. "Yes, I'm afraid I am. I've come to Lourdes to seek help from the Virgin. Nevertheless, you can—"

The inspector's voice broke in. "Never mind, madame. Forgive us." He tried to be jocular. "I'm sure you're not our terrorist person."

"Nor is my husband," Natale said coolly.

"Neither of you, I'm certain," said the inspector. "Sorry to have awakened you. Just doing our duty. You can go back to sleep now. Sorry to have disturbed you. We'll be moving on to finish the rest of the floor. Good-night, madame."

Hurtado heard them march off, opened his eyes as Natale shut and locked the door. In the semidarkness he watched her navigate around the bed once more and waited as she crawled under the blanket.

"How was that?" she asked proudly.

He rolled onto his back, pushing the blanket off his chin. "Bravo, you were wonderful, Natale." He added, "I never attended a better performance."

From her pillow, she was smiling. "It was easy. It didn't need much acting. Others are always embarrassed and uneasy when they confront someone who is blind." She paused. "Are you?"

"Embarrassed and uneasy? Of course not."

"No, not that—I meant, are you the one they are after, Mikel? Are you some sort of terrorist?"

"I'm not quite what the word implies. But the police might think so. What I am really—"

"You needn't tell me."

"—is a fighter for the freedom of my homeland, the Basque homeland presently in Spain." His eyes held on her delicate pale face framed by the spread of her shiny raven hair on the pillow. "Are you afraid of me?" he asked.

"How can I be afraid of someone who saved me from a rapist?"

"It was natural to want to protect you. I'd never let anyone hurt you."

"In the same way, I'd never let anyone hurt you."

"You're marvelous, Natale." He lifted himself on an elbow. "I want to thank you once more." He leaned toward her, to peck a kiss on her cheek, but at that moment her head moved and the kiss found her full soft lips.

Quickly, he pulled away. Throwing his part of the blanket aside, he abruptly sat up.

"What are you doing, Mikel?"

"I'd better get dressed and leave you alone. I'll be on my way."

"Mikel—" She had reached out, fumbling for his bare arm, holding it. "You can't. It's still too dangerous. Where would you go?"

"I'm not sure yet, but I'd better leave you."

"No," she said, gripping his arm more firmly, "you needn't. You might be stopped in the corridor, in the lobby, in the town. I won't have you risk it. You can stay here until morning, and then see if it is safe. If it isn't yet, you can stay with me until it is safe."

Hurtado hesitated. "Well . . ."

"Please."

His hand covered hers. "Well, maybe—maybe I could just sleep on the floor."

"Don't be foolish. You can stay right here in bed with me."

Briefly, Hurtado was bewildered by her invitation and her frankness. It was not the way with women he had known in his country. He said quietly, "Are you sure you can trust me?"

She said simply, "Are you sure I want to trust you?" She removed her hand from his arm, took the fringe of the blanket and threw it off her. She sat up and then in what seemed a single gesture, lifted her nightgown, drew it over her head and luxurious hair, and flung the nightgown aside. She faced in his direction, utterly naked, her small but full nippled breasts exposed to him, the fold in her soft stomach, the generous thighs, with only the upper portion of her pubic hair visible.

He sat speechless, unable to move.

"Mikel, what is it? Does my blindness inhibit you?"

"God, no—"

"Because it need not. In love, I don't have to see. Feeling is enough."

Her arms were outstretched, and he tore off his shorts, came to his knees, and fell into her arms, embracing her.

His entire body was shaking as he pressed to her, and she felt it. "You are shivering, Mikel," she said. "Why? Because of the police?"

"Because of you, it's you," he gasped, holding her tightly, feeling the hardness of her nipples, conscious of his own growing hardness.

Her mouth was at his ear. "Don't worry about virginity," she whispered. "I—I'm not exactly one—there were youthful episodes, but child's play. I've never made love with a man, a beautiful man."

"I—I'm not anything," he tried to tell her in a strangled voice.

Her fingertips were passing over his face. "For me you are beautiful, what I want." His hand guided her hand over his features, continued to guide her hand as her fingers touched his neck and the soft hairs of his chest. When his hand released her fingers, her hand continued downward on its own. "You are young and strong and wonderful," she whispered, her breath catching.

Her warm fingers had found his hard erection, and her warm fingers curled around his penis.

"You want me," she whispered breathlessly.

"I want you, darling—more than anything in the world—I want you . . ."

"Love me," she whispered, sinking back on the bed and into the pillow, and drawing him down with her, atop her. "Love me, darling Mikel."

Her knees had come up, and her legs had spread, and he reached to touch the long stretch of sweet pubic hair, to caress the distended clitoris, to find the wetness between her legs.

His penis was swollen larger and stiffer than he had ever known it, and he guided it to the moist vulva, and easily slid into it deeply, groaning as he did so, and hearing her short cries and gasps as his hardness rose and sank within her.

Her hands had been clutching his shoulders, but now her arms clamped around his back, and she was squeezing her fleshy thighs against the friction of the perpetual motion of his body, until she lifted her legs higher and entwined them around his back.

They were together now, as one, in perfect unison, rising and falling, she all liquidity below, he perspiring and panting.

He had known many women intimately, enjoyed the couplings, the physical stimulation and excitement and release, but he sensed the difference now. The others had been only one half of lovemaking, physical, nothing more, but what he was experiencing with this young woman was total lovemaking.

There had been no easing in their coupling, only a rising crescendo, she heaving her hips uncontrollably, rolling her buttocks, pushing and pulling him, and he in and out, almost peaking, both peaking, near bursting.

Then bursting.

With outcries and sighs and utter relief. Holding and kissing and loving, each closer than they had ever been to another opposite human being.

Long minutes after, drained, lying on the bed separately but together, hands touching, exchanging endearments, Mikel realized that his Natale was silent. He looked closely, and saw that she had fallen deeply asleep in her own special darkness, asleep with a smile on her lips. Smiling down at her, tenderly, he drew the blanket up over her shoulder.

At last, he lay back to be with himself. He had not known such a period of peace in years. He marveled at the absence of his anger. There was left in him, pervading his entire being, merely the residue of love he had felt for this young woman.

Gradually, in his drowsiness, he sought the purpose of being in this bed in this town of Lourdes. Reality, the larger reality, slowly surfaced.

It was not easy to superimpose reality on, even obliterate briefly, the love that he felt. It was difficult to bring harsh hatred and his reason for being here back to his consciousness. But images of his Basque childhood and adolescence, his father's murder, the masters of his slavery, evoked anger and hatred once more.

With regret, he considered the child woman he adored in slumber beside him. What he was feeling contradicted all that he felt for her. She, this dear one, was a person of unblemished faith in a fairy story that she fervently believed could restore her to normality and living. He, by necessity, remained an enemy of that faith that was now misleading his people into compliance with inevitable treachery and certain continuous enslavement. To free his people, he must destroy the symbol of faith that might lead to their deception and endless thralldom. By his act of destruction, he would also destroy forever Natale's foolish hope and her love.

But, he saw, it must be done. He owed himself—and the loss he must endure—to an even greater love.

Oh, Natale, Natale, when it is over and I have succeeded, try to understand.

But, he knew, she would never understand.

At the same time, it suddenly occurred to him, considering that he had been forced into hiding, that he might never succeed. The police were everywhere, and might continue to be everywhere until the eight days had ended.

How could he blow up the grotto if he did not have the means of bringing the explosives into the domain?

Then, an idea, an inspiration came, a means, something he could do tomorrow. If it worked, he might succeed, and turn away the Virgin Mary forever.

10

Wednesday, August 17

At ten minutes to nine in the morning, Michelle Demaillot, of the Sanctuaries Press Bureau, was briskly leading the way across the Rosary Esplanade of the domain to the Medical Bureau. Following her were the town's latest arrivals, Dr. Paul Kleinberg, and his dependable nurse, Esther Levinson.

It was Kleinberg's first real view of any portion of Lourdes in the daylight. Despite the sight of so much religious statuary, the number of invalids in wheelchairs and stretchers, and his misgivings about the shrine, he had to admit that the parade ground, or whatever it was supposed to be, offered up an aura of pastoral peace and serenity on this sunny summer's day.

Dr. Kleinberg and his nurse had caught the last Air Inter flight from Paris late yesterday, and when they had left the plane at the Lourdes airport it had already been nightfall. The press lady, with her car, had been waiting. During the short drive to their accommodations, Kleinberg, who had come straight from his Paris office to Orly Airport to this Pyrenees village, had been too exhausted to bother to glance out the car window as they had passed through Lourdes. At the Hôtel Astoria, in the Rue de la Grotte, ordinary single rooms had been reserved for them. After telephoning his wife, Alice, in Neuilly, to tell her and the boys that he had arrived safely and to let her have the number where he might be reached, he had gone straight to bed and slept without a break for nine hours.

Now, as they walked, Kleinberg noticed how rigid and aloof his nurse was. Knowing her, the orphaned daughter of German parents gassed and cremated in the Nazi holocaust, he knew how uncomfortable she was when confronted by any sort of fanaticism, political or religious. Kleinberg felt no similar discomfort in these surroundings. His parents had moved from Vienna to Paris long before the rise of Hitler, and had become naturalized French citizens. He himself had been born a Frenchman, and despite a persistent degree of muted anti-Semitism among a minority in France, Kleinberg felt that he belonged and was a part of this land. His knowledge of French culture was broad, although his acquaintance with the Catholic shrine at Lourdes was limited. He had read about Bernadette and the apparitions and the grotto from time to time in newspapers and magazines, and also had read with mild interest about the occasional cures attributed to Lourdes.

Besides such casual reading, Kleinberg's only knowledge of the holy town had come from his careful perusal of three books involving Dr. Alexis Carrel—one of the books was about Carrel, two written by him—each going into the great physician's one visit to Lourdes in 1903. Kleinberg had acquired and read the Carrel books after he had been invited to join the International Medical Committee of Lourdes, which was assembling in Paris to review and ascertain the so-called miraculous cure of an Englishwoman, Mrs. Edith Moore, suffering from a sarcoma.

Kleinberg had been unable to assist the committee because of a previously scheduled medical meeting in London, but upon his return to Paris the Lourdes people had contacted him again. The members of the International Medical Committee had been favorably disposed toward granting Mrs. Moore's case miraculous status, but had withheld their final approval until they could have the vote of a specialist in sarcoma. Kleinberg was one of the two foremost specialists in France treating malignant growths. The other, Dr. Maurice Duval, whom Kleinberg knew and respected, had been too involved in experimental researches to cooperate. So there was only Kleinberg to bring in as a final consultant, and he had been reluctant to become involved in anything of a religious nature. Yet, learning that Dr. Alexis Carrel had once visited and investigated Lourdes, Kleinberg had given the matter some second thoughts. As a student at the Cochin School of Medicine, attached to the University of Paris, Kleinberg had admired the writings and career of Dr. Carrel. Kleinberg recalled that the scientist had kept an open mind about Lourdes and spent some time there. Kleinberg reread Dr. Carrel, and verified his student recollections. The great Carrel had, indeed, treated Lourdes seriously.

So Paul Kleinberg had agreed to accept the invitation of the International Committee, and go to Lourdes to review the incredible cure of the woman named Edith Moore.

"Here we are," he heard Mademoiselle Demaillot announce.

Where were they? Kleinberg stopped, and looked about to orient himself. They were on a sidewalk on the opposite side of the Rosary Esplanade. They were at the double doors of the entrance to a building made up of rugged large stone blocks. Above the entry, white lettering on a blue sign, were the words: MEDICAL BUREAU/SECRETARIAT.

"Let me take you inside," the press lady was saying. "I'll introduce you to the bureau head, Dr. Berryer, then leave you with him."

Kleinberg and Esther followed Mademoiselle Demaillot inside and found themselves in a spacious anteroom, with two office doors on the right. The press lady gestured off to the second door. "Let me tell Dr. Berryer's secretary you've arrived."

After the press lady had disappeared into the office, Kleinberg and Esther took their bearings. The walls of the anteroom were decorated with what resembled the artifacts of a medical museum. After a quick glance, Esther avoided a closer look at the artifacts, and immediately occupied the corner of a sofa, sitting tight-lipped, eyes on the floor. But Kleinberg was more interested. He began to go around the anteroom, studying the displays.

The large display on the nearest wall was a framed, glass case and bore the name DE RUDDER at the top. Closer inspection of the glass case revealed two copper casts of a man's leg bones, one showing the tibia seriously broken, the other showing it fully healed. Kleinberg read the explanatory legend. Pierre de Rudder, of Jabbeke, Belgium, had fallen from a tree in 1867, and in the fall had broken the tibia in his lower left leg. The bone had a three-centimeter separation or gap at the fracture point, and would not heal. For eight years, de Rudder had been a cripple. Then, after a visit to a replica of the Lourdes grotto in Belgium, de Rudder had been instantly and miraculously cured, his sundered bone totally put together again. After his death, twenty-three years later, three doctors had performed an autopsy on de Rudder. They had found that the three-centimeter gap had, indeed, closed. "The broken bone edges fitted closely. The bone preserves a very obvious mark of the fracture, but without any foreshortening." De Rudder had been declared Lourdes' eighth official miracle cure in 1908.

Kleinberg wrinkled his nose, and saw his unconscious reaction reflected in the glass of the case, and assessed that his reaction was more of surprise than of doubt.

Since their escort had not yet reappeared, Kleinberg continued to wander around the anteroom, studying the framed photographs on the three walls, and the printed histories of most of the officially recognized miraculous cures of invalids who had sought help from the Lourdes shrine. The earliest was dated 1858. The last one framed and hung was a picture of Serge Perrin, who had suffered "recurring organic hemiphlegia, with ocular lesions, due to cerebral circulatory defects." He had been miraculously and fully cured at the age of forty-one in 1970, and his miracle cure officially recognized in 1978. Kleinberg knew there had been more cures since then, but perhaps the Medical Bureau had not yet had time to mount them.

Kleinberg heard his name called, and wheeled around.

The press lady was advancing toward him. "Dr. Kleinberg, it appears that Dr. Berryer will be a little late for your appointment. There is a message, and I contacted him by phone at his meeting, and he promises he will be here in ten or fifteen minutes, and offers his apologies."

"No matter," said Kleinberg.

"Maybe you'd prefer to wait in his private office? I'll show Madame Levinson to the examination and X-ray rooms, where you'll find her after your interview. Then I must leave you both."

"Thank you, Mademoiselle Demaillot."

He allowed her to show him into Dr. Berryer's office, and watched her leave. Once he was alone, he set down his medical bag, and again tried to get his bearings. It surprised him to see how small and Spartan was Dr. Berryer's office. No more than eight feet by eight feet, with a desk and chair in the middle, two chairs for visitors, a crammed bookcase. All neat, no disarray. Kleinberg noticed a mirror, and planted himself before it to see if he was presentable. He frowned at the brown receding hairline, at the smallish hooked nose made more prominent by the sunken cheeks. The bags under his eyes had been earned, and were all right, and his sharp chin was still one chin at forty-one. He straightened his knit tie, squared his narrow shoulders, and decided that he was as presentable as he would ever be.

He took a chair to await his tardy host, and realized a feeling of unease, which he had not felt outdoors. It was the displays in the anteroom that had thrown him off a trifle, all those miracles, all so unscientific and alien to his nature. He wondered how one like Dr. Alexis Carrel had coped with it.

Dr. Carrel had been severely criticized by fellow scientists for deigning to pay attention to a religious center that claimed miracles and for having confessed that he might have actually witnessed a miracle himself. Carrel's colleagues in science—persons who had once respected him as a member of the faculty of medicine at Lyons University— turned against him for having given credence to Lourdes by visiting it and by having given serious consideration to the inexplicable cures that were going on there. Carrel's colleagues condemned him as "a credulous pietist."

Dr. Carrel had defended his interest in the so-called miracles in the press: "These extraordinary phenomena are of great biological, as well as religious, interest. I consider, therefore, that any campaign against the miracles of Lourdes is unjustified and opposed to the progress of medical science in one of its most important aspects."

Actually, rereading the controversy so many years later, Kleinberg could see that Carrel had been uncertain about the cures at Lourdes and had incurred the anger of the clerical community just as he had provoked the scientific community. For one thing, Carrel had been unhappy about the Medical Bureau. "There is a rosary on the examining table, but no medical tools." Carrel had been equally unhappy about one of Dr. Berryer's predecessors, Dr. Boissarie, who had published best sellers about his medical study of the cures. "He has written these works as if he were a priest rather than a physician," Carrel had complained. "He has indulged in pious consideration rather than scientific observations. He has shunned rigorous analyses and precise deductions."

But the sudden—miraculous?—cure of a French girl, Marie Bailly, swept most of his reservations aside. He had tried to defend what he had witnessed before the scientific community: "At the risk of shocking both believers and non-believers, we shall not discuss the question of belief. Rather, we shall say that it makes little difference whether Bernadette was a case of hysteria, a myth, or a madwoman. . . . The only thing that matters is to look at the facts; they can be investigated scientifically; they exist in a realm quite outside of metaphysical interpretation. . . . Science, of course, must be continually on guard against charlatanism and credulousness. But it is also the duty of science not to reject things simply because they appear extraordinary or because science is powerless to explain them."

This from the man who had become a giant at the Rockefeller Institute for Medical Research, who had won the Nobel Prize in 1912 for suturing blood vessels, who had experimented in 1935 with an artificial heart designed by Charles Lindbergh.

Sitting there in the stillness of Dr. Berryer's office in the Medical Bureau, Kleinberg closed his eyes. *Do not reject things simply because they appear extraordinary.* Dr. Carrel's own words. At once, Kleinberg felt more relaxed, less disturbed about the miracles heralded in the anteroom and by his very presence in the playground of the Virgin Mary and the site where he was to reaffirm the miraculous cure of a woman named Edith Moore.

Kleinberg heard the office doorknob turn, and came to his feet as a preoccupied, squarish older man barged into the room.

"Dr. Kleinberg?" the man said, offering a handclasp. "I'm Dr. Berryer, and pleased to meet you. Forgive the delay, but bureaucratic matters can often take more of one's time than medicine."

"No need to apologize," said Dr. Kleinberg affably. "I'm delighted to be here."

"Do sit down," said Dr. Berryer, going around his desk and standing over it to review the various messages waiting for him.

Kleinberg sat down again, and waited as the head of the Medical Bureau swept his messages into a corner, and settled into his swivel chair.

"So glad you could make it," said Dr. Berryer, "knowing how busy you must be."

"I repeat, I'm delighted."

"Is this your first visit to Lourdes?"

"I'm afraid so."

"Well, the Moore examination today shouldn't take up much of your time. You'll be able to have a look around. Do you know anything about Lourdes?"

"Very little, a layman's knowledge," said Kleinberg. "I've seen a few articles on it. Of course, I read the International Committee's summary report on Mrs. Moore. And I've read Dr. Alexis Carrel's memoir on his visit here."

"Ah, poor Carrel," said Dr. Berryer with a forced smile. "For the rest of his life, after leaving here, he waffled between belief and disbelief at what he had seen."

"Understandable, for a man of science."

"I, for one, have never had trouble reconciling religion and science," said Dr. Berryer. "Pasteur had no problem about that. Neither did Einstein. At any rate—" He had folded one hand across the other on top of his desk. "—since there is a little time before Mrs. Moore arrives and you are occupied with her, perhaps I can bore you with a brief fill-in on how we work here—medically . . . that is, scientifically —so that you will feel more at home."

"I'd be pleased to learn what I can."

"Let me give you a bit of background on the process you are

specifically involved in, the process ascertaining cures," said Dr. Berryer. "You are acquainted with this process?"

"Only vaguely," said Kleinberg. "It would be interesting to know more."

"Very well. Briefly then. To give you a better understanding of why we summoned you in the case of Edith Moore and her sudden cure."

"Her miracle cure," said Kleinberg, with a friendly curl of his lips.

Dr. Berryer's eyes, almost sunk behind the puffy cheeks, fixed on his visitor. His tone became less conversational, more pedagogical. "I am not here to define a cure in Lourdes as miraculous. As a doctor, I can merely define such a cure as unusual. It is for the Church to decide if any cure is related to a divine intervention, one that can be recognized as a sign of God. Our doctors affirm that a healing is inexplicable in the realm of science. Our clergymen confirm it can be explained as the work of God. In the Medical Bureau, those are the ground rules."

"I understand."

"The Church has always been less generous than our doctors in its claims. From the time of Bernadette to this day, the Church has claimed less than seventy cures to have been genuinely miraculous. But our doctors, even after rigorous examinations, have been more generous in announcing unusual cures. There have been about five thousand confirmed cures to date. About sixty times more cures than miracles. Why all have not qualified as miracles I cannot say. The clergy has its own standards. While millions and millions of visitors have come to Lourdes since 1858, most have been pilgrims seeking spiritual comfort or tourists wishing to satisfy their curiosity. The number of actual invalids who arrive each year represents a small minority. The statistics break down as follows—about one medical cure for every five hundred patients who arrive here, and about one miracle for every thirty thousand patients who show themselves."

Listening, Kleinberg realized that Dr. Berryer's voice had flattened out, lost its inflections, settled into a lecture given many times over.

"Now as to the criteria governing a cure," Dr. Berryer went on. "The illness must be serious, inevitable, incurable. The illness must also be organic, not functional. An organic illness involves a lesion at the organic level, whereas a functional illness—"

Mildly annoyed, Dr. Kleinberg interrupted. He was being treated to a layman's lecture, and not as a medical colleague. "I am acquainted with your criteria, doctor," he broke in.

Momentarily thrown off his verbal rut, Dr. Berryer stammered slightly. "A, yes—yes, of course—well, now—Mrs. Moore's hip sarcoma—an organic illness, certainly, and a permanent cure. The last hip sarcoma cure we had, before Mrs. Moore's, dates back to 1963. I have no doubt—and certainly as a specialist in this area, you will agree—that the cure of such sarcoma will be less unusual in the future, as medicine progresses."

Kleinberg nodded. "Great advances are being made already. Dr. Duval in Paris has conducted successful experiments on animals to arrest and cure sarcoma medically."

"Exactly, Dr. Kleinberg. At one time, medicine could not deal with tuberculosis. But today, there are medical means to treat tuberculosis, and so that is one serious illness which depends less on the grotto. But in the present state of science, many sufferers continue to look to the grotto, to prayers, the water, as a means of recovery. Edith Moore, afflicted by hip sarcoma, was such a one." He paused. "You know how she was cured by a visit to the baths during her second visit here? You know her instantaneous cure was confirmed by sixteen physicians, both in London and in Lourdes."

"I do."

"Now as to the process that followed. First, the Medical Bureau here. In the beginning there was no Medical Bureau. There was Dr. Dozous, assisted by Professor Vergez of Montpellier, to sift all claims of cures. There were twelve cases considered, and seven of these were determined by Bishop Laurence's canonical commission in 1862 to be cures that could be attributed to the work of God. The word miracle was not then in use for such cases. After that, as visitors to Lourdes increased, as more patients claimed cures, something had to be done. Dr. Saint-Maclou, who had settled here, established a reception center for visiting doctors to inspect evidence of cures. That was in 1874 and the center was called the Office of Medical Verifications. Gradually, the Verifications Office was enlarged to the present-day Medical Bureau. Shortly after 1947, the National Medical Committee was established and in 1954 this became the International Medical Committee, the one you were invited to sit in on earlier this year."

"And the International Medical Committee has the last word?"

"Medically speaking, yes. The process goes as follows—our Medical Bureau in Lourdes confirms a cure, and then passes the dossier on to the International Committee. There are about thirty members on the committee, physicians from ten different countries, all appointed by the bishop of Tarbes and Lourdes, and they meet for one day a year, as they recently did. During the most recent meeting, the dossier of Edith Moore was presented. The member doctors discussed it at length. A vote was taken, with a two-thirds vote usually enough for approval. After that, the dossier was returned to the bishop of Tarbes and

Lourdes. Since Mrs. Moore's diocese was in London, the approved dossier was sent to the bishop of London. He, in turn, appointed a canonical commission to judge if Mrs. Moore's cure was miraculous. As you know, Mrs. Moore's cure was approved by all hands—"

"Yes."

"—but it was not officially announced because the International Committee did not have a sarcoma specialist at their meeting. You were invited, but you were away. Dr. Duval was invited, but he was occupied with his experiments. The International Committee then cast its favorable vote subject to your confirming its judgment. Rather than convene the committee again, it was agreed that if you came to Lourdes and saw Mrs. Moore in person, then the official announcement could be made."

"Well, here I am, ready, willing, and able," said Kleinberg.

Dr. Berryer considered the white digital clock on his desk. "I made an appointment for Edith Moore to meet with you. She should be in the examining room in about a half hour." He stood up. "I know you've studied the report on the case, but that was a summary, and you may prefer to see the diagnosis of each doctor involved."

"That would be useful," said Kleinberg, rising while Dr. Berryer went to the bookcase and removed a handful of manila file folders.

"I'll take you to the examining room, and leave these with you. You'll have time enough to browse through them before your patient arrives."

Kleinberg followed Dr. Berryer out of the office to the examining room. In the undecorated room, between the leather examining table and a wooden cabinet against the wall containing medical instruments, Esther Levinson sat in a chair, leafing through a French magazine. As they entered, she came to her feet, and Kleinberg introduced his nurse to the head of the Medical Bureau.

Inside the door, Dr. Berryer handed the layer of folders over to Kleinberg.

"For your reading pleasure," he said. "When you've confirmed the reports, please let me know."

"I certainly will."

Dr. Berryer had his hand on the knob of the open door, about to leave, when he hesitated and turned back.

He stared at the folders in Kleinberg's hand and then fixed his gaze on Kleinberg himself. Dr. Berryer gave a short cough. "You understand the importance of this case, doctor. Father Ruland, who represents the bishop and the Vatican itself here in Lourdes, thinks it would be of great value to be able to make the announcement of Mrs. Moore's miraculous cure during this exciting Reappearance Time—a confirmed miracle—a lovely present to welcome the return of the Blessed Virgin. So—" He hesitated once more. "Uh, I trust you will judge the reports in your hand—rather open and shut, I would say—entirely on their scientific merit."

Kleinberg's eyebrows went up. "But how else would I possibly judge them?"

Without blinking, Dr. Berryer said, "Well, whatever we say, we are dealing with what my church agrees is a miracle cure. And—I do know that people of your persuasion don't have much belief in miracles. Anyway, I am sure you will adhere to the facts."

With that, he left the room, closing the door between them.

Dr. Kleinberg's face had darkened as he glowered at the door. "People of your persuasion," he mimicked. "Did you hear that, Esther?"

He turned around to see Esther's features flushed. "I heard," she said. "Maybe you should have told him that someone else of your persuasion, a man named Moses, was involved in a few miracles."

"Never mind. Who gives a damn about a narrow-minded country lout like Berryer? Let's look over these reports, see our Mrs. Moore, and get out of here as soon as we can."

Then, minutes later, as an afterthought, Kleinberg tried to forgive Berryer slightly, remembering that Dr. Alexis Carrel, while not a bigot, had been an Aryan-lover and a race supremacist as well.

An hour and a half had passed, and Dr. Paul Kleinberg was still seated in the examining room alone, once more studying the before-and-after medical reports on Edith Moore's malignant tumor while she was finishing her new work-up and X rays next door.

Fascinated, Kleinberg studied the diagnostic reports on Mrs. Moore's osteosarcoma of the left ilium. It was all there in the seemingly countless microphotographs, the blood tests, the biopsies, the X rays. There was the destructive sarcoma—and then it wasn't there, a total disappearance of the infiltration of the marrow, and reconstruction of the bone elements.

Definitely amazing. In his years of practice, Kleinberg had never seen a self-cure such as this one.

Absolutely miraculous—even to a person of his persuasion.

He laid aside the evidence, pleased for the nice, dull English lady. Well, there was nothing left, except for the latest examination and a final new set of X rays and then he would be done. He would be able to confirm to Dr. Berryer and the clergyman called Father Ruland that

God was on their side, after all, and that they could announce their miracle with fanfare to the entire world. With that publicity, and the presumed return of the Virgin Mary to Lourdes, they would have not five million faithful pouring into Lourdes next year, but six or seven million, at least.

The door opened, and Kleinberg came to his feet as Mrs. Moore entered, pushing her belt through a last loop on the waistband of her skirt and fastening the buckle.

"All done, and I'll bet you're glad," said Kleinberg, not knowing what else to say to a miracle recipient.

"I'm pleased it's over with," she said with a happy heave and a sigh. Her bland countenance had color in it and she was definitely repressing considerable inner emotion. "Miss Levinson told me to tell you she'll have all the X rays for you in five or ten minutes."

"Good. I'll just have a look, and then I'll inform Dr. Berryer and prepare my final report. You needn't wait around any longer. I'm sure the Medical Bureau will be in immediate touch with you. Thank you, Mrs. Moore, for enduring all this discomfort one last time."

She took her summer jacket off a wall hanger. "My pleasure, believe me. I appreciate everything. Good-bye, Dr. Kleinberg."

Esther Levinson arrived with the fresh X rays, turned on the lights in the view box on the wall and pinned up the four X rays for his scrutiny. Kleinberg rose, and with a practiced eye he studied the negatives, while Esther hovered nearby awaiting his approval.

"Umm, this one," Kleinberg said pointing to the third negative, "it's a bad shot, unclear, somewhat blurred. She must have moved."

"She did not move at all," Esther countered. "She's very professional. She's been through a million X rays. Mrs. Moore was in position, perfectly rigid."

"Well, I don't know—" Kleinberg murmured. "Tell you what. Remove all of the negatives except this poor one. Pin up two of the other X rays, the previous ones, taken of this area of the iliac bone after her cure. You'll find them in the dated folders."

As his nurse went to rummage through the folders, Kleinberg continued to inspect the new X rays. Presently, Esther was beside him, taking down three of the negatives and replacing them with previous shots for comparative purposes.

When she had finished, and stepped aside, Kleinberg bent closer to the illuminated X rays. He studied them in silence, clucking his tongue several times.

Straightening his back at last, he said, "I'm sure it's all right, but I'd still like to get a better picture from this particular angle. Maybe I'm being too much of a perfectionist, but when you're dealing with a so-called miracle, you want to see the results of the miracle one final time."

"We can shoot her again, if that's what you wish."

Kleinberg nodded. "That's what I wish, Esther. Just to do it right. We'll get a better picture, and then we can honestly crown our patient as a miracle woman. Tell you what. Go and see Berryer's secretary. She'll know where to locate our patient. Have her call Mrs. Moore and bring her back for another X ray at two o'clock. Will you do that?"

"On my way," said Esther.

"I'll meet you in the anteroom in a few minutes. Let's take a look at the town, and I'll treat you to lunch. Then we'll come back and finish with Mrs. Moore and head for Paris. How's that?"

"That's great," said Esther with a rare smile.

Mikel Hurtado awakened with a start. Something had brushed his cheek, touched his lips, and startled him out of a deep sleep. When he opened his eyes, he saw that it was Natale kneeling over him, kissing him a third time.

Reaching for her, to bring her closer, he saw that she instinctively knew that he would do so, and had pulled away. She retreated to her side of the bed, feeling her way to the far edge, groping for her dark glasses on the bedside table. When she found the glasses, and had slipped them on, she swung off the bed and stood up.

"Are you up, Mikel?" she called.

"You bet I'm up."

"I just wanted to be sure, because I wanted to tell you—I love you."

He was sitting now, staring at her. She presented an incongruous sight. She was totally nude from her head to her knees—the rest hidden by the bed—her firm, unblemished being seemed to glow. And she was wearing sun-glasses.

"I love you, too," he said softly.

She was groping and finding a fresh brassiere and panty briefs on the chair. "You are the most marvelous lover on earth," she said.

"How would you know?" he asked chidingly.

"I just know," she replied. "I know how I enjoyed you. I know when I'm happy."

The sight of her jiggling breasts and brown nipples, the navel in her flat belly, the triangle of pubic hair between the generous thighs, was beginning to arouse him. "Natale, come back to bed."

"Oh, I want to darling, but I can't, not yet. Later, but not now. First things first—"

"What comes before us?"

"Mikel, I've got to bathe and dress and go to the grotto to pray. What time is it?"

He picked up his watch. "Just past ten-thirty, morning."

"I'll have to hurry. Rosa takes me to the grotto at eleven-fifteen every day."

"Rosa?"

"She's that friend of my family in Rome who comes to Lourdes every summer as a handmaid. She's been taking care of me."

That instant, Hurtado remembered what had last been on his mind before falling asleep.

First things first. He, too, had a priority and an idea of how to pull it off.

"I'll take you to the grotto," he said. "Let's go together."

"I'd like to but—Mikel, what about the police? Maybe you should stay away from them or go out of town."

"The police," he said. "They're mistaken. I should tell you what's going on." He couldn't tell her the truth, that he was here to destroy what meant so much to her. Yet, he rationalized, she didn't need the grotto to achieve her hopes. She had faith. That was enough. Nor need she ever know his role in what was soon to happen. He was prepared to make up some fanciful story for her, a mistake in identity, a false lead from an enemy, something. "Let me explain—"

"You don't have to explain anything to me," she said firmly. "I told you that before. I don't need it. I trust you. You still want to take me to the grotto? You think it's safe?"

"Of course it is. Yesterday I didn't want to be questioned in my room. But it's safe now." And he believed it was. He was positive that whatever Lopez had done, he had not given the Lourdes police a description of the terrorist. Obviously, Lopez wanted to frighten him off, not get him caught.

"Then we'll go. We can leave Rosa a note on the door—"

"I can write it for you."

"Yes. Write, 'Dear Rosa, a friend has taken me to the grotto. You can find me there. Natale.' Now I'd better have my bath and dress."

He watched her making her way to the bathroom.

First things first, he reminded himself.

"Natale, is there anything else I can do for you? I see your flight bag, your carry-on, sitting on the table. There are some plastic bottles and a candle in front of it. Are they going to the grotto?"

She was at the bathroom door. "Yes, I meant to pack them in the flight bag. I want to light my candle. And fill the bottles with water to take back to my relatives."

His heart skipped. "I'd be glad to pack them."

"Would you?"

"Right away. Write a note to Rosa, and pack your flight bag. Have I got it all?"

"And love me," she said lightly, and she closed herself in the bathroom.

Tempted as he was to go after her, carry her back to the bed, love her as he had never loved anyone before, he restrained himself.

After he heard the tub water running, he crawled out of bed. He scribbled the note to leave behind for the woman named Rosa. He knelt, pulled his suitcase out from under the bed, and unlocked it. Tenderly, he lifted the packages containing the sticks of dynamite, detonator, timepiece, wiring and carried them to the table. As he had planned—rather hoped was possible—he laid his wrapped explosives inside Natale's flight bag. Then, he stuffed in a folded shopping bag, and he covered his packages with her large candle and plastic bottles. He drew the zipper on the flight bag.

He was waiting, smoking, when she emerged, clad in her brassiere and panties. He intercepted her on the way to the closet, to embrace and kiss her fervently.

"Oh, Mikel, I want you so," she breathed, but drew away. "Later. After. I'd better get dressed."

"Later," he agreed. "I'd better get ready, too."

He sought his travel kit in the suitcase and brought it into the bathroom. After brushing his teeth, he shaved, then quickly bathed, dried himself, combed his hair, and dressed.

"Ready, Mikel?" he heard her call.

"Be right with you."

In seconds he emerged, and saw her fumbling at the table.

He snatched up the packed bag before she reached it. "I have your bag," he said. "And I have the note for Rosa."

With his free hand, he took her arm. "Now, to the grotto," he said.

Ten minutes later, as they neared the ramp leading to the domain, Hurtado had his plan formulated.

The police had their cordon across the top of the ramp, again, and they were stopping only the pilgrims and tourists carrying anything, and were searching through each package or bag before passing the visitors through.

Crossing the street, Hurtado said to Natale, "We'll have to get in line here and go through a police inspection."

"Will it be all right?" Natale whispered.

"No problem," he said.

He hoped.

They were inching ahead, and getting close to two of the police-men. This was the moment to make his move as he had planned it.

He took Natale's arm once more. "*Querida,* do you mind if I leave you for a few seconds? I forgot my cigarettes—and even if they don't like smoking down there—I'd feel better to have a pack handy. Here, you take your bag for the moment. I'll run across the street to the café. Catch up with you along the ramp." He handed her the bag. "You've got just ten steps to take before you reach the police."

"All right, Mikel," she said, grasping the handle of the flight bag.

Quickly, he stepped away from her, and retreated to the back of the line of visitors, making sure to fall in where he had a full view of the police inspection. If something went wrong, he wasn't certain what he'd be able to do for her. But he felt nothing would go wrong. Police, like most authorities, had a weakness for a number of human afflictions.

He craned his neck to keep Natale in view, and then he saw her standing with the bag before two uniformed policemen. He saw her hand groping in front of her, trying to find out if she had arrived at the police guards. He saw the two policemen observing her, looking down at her bag, then up at her face. He saw one policeman make a gesture toward his eyes, plainly indicating that she was blind. He saw the other policeman nod understandingly, and put his hand on Natale's shoulder, sending her on her way down the ramp uninspected.

Hurtado exhaled, and breathed easily once more.

In a few minutes, he was before the officers, empty-handed. They glanced at him, and one waved him through. Despite the pebble in his shoe, and the limp that resulted, Hurtado went swiftly down the ramp, and near the bottom he caught up with Natale.

"Here I am," he said. He took the flight bag from her. "Everything all right?"

"Thanks for taking the bag," she said. "I didn't know it would be so heavy."

"My fault," he said cheerfully. "I stuffed a camera and a pair of large binoculars under your things. Wanted to get a picture and closeup view of the domain area from a distance. Natale, one day you'll be able to look through both of them yourself."

"If the Blessed Virgin takes notice of my prayer," she said uncer-tainly. "Anyway, you must tell me what you see."

"I will," he promised.

Now that they had managed to get his explosives through, he felt elated. He was closer to his goal and success. Guiding Natale toward the grotto, he saw that it was swarming with worshippers. There were even police spotted about. He would be able to ascend the hill next to the grotto and secrete the explosives, of that he was sure, but setting the explosives in place behind the statue of the Virgin Mary, and wiring it to the detonator, would be impossible in the daylight. He would have to return when it was dark, around midnight, and the worshippers were asleep and the police guards had gone off duty.

Ahead, at the rear of the many benches facing the grotto, he saw an elderly woman rise from her seat and move away. Hurriedly, he led Natale to the bench and settled her into the empty place.

He told Natale exactly where he had seated her, and her position in relation to the grotto. "You just sit here and pray," he said. "I'll take the bag with me, and see that your candle is lighted. And I'll fill the bottles with water."

"You're so sweet, Mikel."

"I do this for all my loves," he said lightly, and bent down and kissed the smile off her lips. "Be back soon."

Slowly, easily, he picked his way through the crowd on the far side of the grotto. No one was paying any attention to anything except the cave in the hillside. It was almost too easy to drift away, and be interested in the foliage of the hillside, and move up it unhurriedly inspecting the plants and gradually disappear behind a group of trees.

He continued climbing a short distance, until the grotto itself was hidden from view. He sought the depression behind the large oak tree he had spotted earlier, and he found it filled with fallen leaves, broken branches, bits of other vegetation. Setting down Natale's flight bag, he knelt and began using both hands to scoop the debris out of the hole. When he had finished his excavation, he was pleased. The depression would be deep enough to hold and hide his equipment.

Emptying Natale's bag of the bottles and candle, he gingerly took out his own packages containing the sticks of dynamite, the detonator, the clock, the wiring, the tape, and the shopping bag. Casting about to see if he had by chance been followed, or, indeed, if there were any other climbers in the vicinity, he was satisfied that he was quite alone. He resumed work, lowering his packages into the hole, covering them with the folded shopping bag. Quickly, he scooped up the debris beside the hole, the dead leaves, branches, brush, and covered the shopping bag with them until the explosives and other materials were completely buried out of sight.

Rising, he examined his handiwork. The leafy surface of the ground looked untouched, as if it had been arranged by nature. Carefully, he restored Natale's bottles and candle to her flight bag. Then, with one hand, he dusted all signs of the foliage from his jacket and trousers. Taking up the bag, careful of his footing, he began his descent, noting every obvious landmark that would guide him on his return late that night.

When he came off the hill, he was sure that almost no one had seen him, or if they had, they would have small curiosity about this nature lover and exercise freak. Ready to melt into the crowd surrounding the grotto, he became aware of the flight bag in his hand. He had told Natale that he would take care of her candle and her plastic bottles. He searched off toward the baths, saw the rows of flickering candles nearby, and went to them and piously lighted Natale's candle and placed it alongside the others. Next, dutifully, he approached a water gutter with a spigot at either end where pilgrims were lined up taking their turns filling a variety of containers. Finally, his turn came. He uncapped each of Natale's empty plastic bottles, several shaped like the Virgin Mary, and filled all of them, one by one, with the supposedly curative water, and then capped each bottle and set it in the flight bag.

All there was left to do was to return to Natale, and guide her back to the hotel for lunch.

Weaving through the people milling about the grotto, he thought of Natale, of how attracted he was to her. He thought of her vivacity and her magnificent body and her passion, and suddenly he was impatient to take her to the hotel, get lunch over with if she was hungry, and return to her room for another memorable coupling. Anticipating this, he wondered about something else. He wondered how serious he was about her, and how much he wanted to deal with her in the future. Was she the woman he had always fantasied about and hoped to live with for the rest of his life? Was it possible to devote one's years to an afflicted person, one who would forever be afflicted? He did not know, or even know if she was interested in giving her own life over to an unseen Basque revolutionary—and a struggling author. Well, he told himself, it would all work itself out some way.

He had expected to find her on the bench as he had left her, occupied with silent prayer or meditating behind those dark glasses. Instead, when she came into sight, he saw that she was engaged in an animated conversation with a vaguely familiar older woman, a rather tall woman with black hair drawn back severely into a bun, who was seated beside her.

Puzzled, he advanced upon the pair. The older woman was speaking now, and Natale listening, as Hurtado came upon them. He waited for the other woman to finish, and then he stepped closer, and touched Natale on the shoulder.

"Natale," he said, "It's Mikel. I have all your bottles—"

Natale twisted toward him, a smile on her upturned face, as she reached for his hand. "Mikel, you must meet someone dear to me. The lady I'm talking to is Rosa Zennaro, our family friend from Rome and my helper here in Lourdes."

"Yes, of course," said Hurtado, offering her a bow and a smile, "the one for whom we left the note. Pleased to meet you, Signora Zennaro."

"The pleasure is mine," said Rosa. "Natale has been telling me all about you—"

"Not quite all," said Natale to Hurtado, blushing.

"—and that you are competing to replace me by becoming her brancardier," Rosa finished.

"I'm sure that would be impossible," said Hurtado. "I saw you two deep in conversation, and I really didn't mean to interrupt."

"Nothing important," said Rosa. "I was merely telling Natale about the statue of the Virgin Mary in the niche beside the grotto." She pointed off. "There it is. You can't miss it."

Hurtado peered off guiltily, unable to admit that he knew it well, had been closer to it than either of them, and the plans he had for its demise. "Yes," he said. "Quite attractive."

"But Bernadette didn't think so, Mikel." Natale turned, fumbling for Rosa's arm and tugging it. "Rosa, tell Mikel about the statue—he'll be so interested."

Without protest, Rosa launched into telling the story a second time. "There had been a plaster statuette of the Virgin in the niche next to the grotto, placed there by the townsfolk. Two sisters in Lyons, much devoted to the grotto, wanted to replace it with a larger and more accurate statue of the apparition that Bernadette had seen. They commissioned a well-known sculptor, Joseph Fabisch, of the Lyons Academy of Arts, to prepare it. Fabisch traveled down to Lourdes to interview Bernadette and get a description from her of what the Virgin had looked like when She had announced that She was the Immaculate Conception. To describe what Bernadette had seen, Fabisch later recorded, 'Bernadette got up with the greatest simplicity. She joined her hands and raised her eyes to heaven. I have never seen anything more beautiful. . . . Neither Mino da Fiesole, nor Perugino, nor Raphael have ever done anything so sweet and yet so profound as was the look of that young girl, consumptive to her fingertips.' Somewhat according to Bernadette's specifications, but allowing himself a degree of artist's license, Fabisch carved his large statue out of Carrara marble. When Father Peyramale received the statue in Lourdes, and showed it to Bernadette, she exclaimed, 'No, that's not it!' "

Natale was delighted. "Bernadette couldn't pretend about anything."

"Bernadette did not withhold her criticism," Rosa went on. "She considered the statue too tall, too mature, too fancy, and she insisted that by making the Virgin raise her eyes but not her head to heaven, the sculptor had given her a goiter. Nevertheless, the statue was placed in the niche with great ceremony on April 4, 1863. Bernadette was not allowed to attend, presumably because curiosity-seekers might bother her. But I suspect that she was kept away because she might be too frank and make a negative remark about the statue."

"Very amusing," said Hurtado, feeling guiltier than ever. "Well, shall we all have lunch? You'll join us, won't you, Mrs. Zennaro?"

"Thank you," said Rosa. "I'd enjoy that."

"Mikel, you go ahead of us, please. I want a few moments alone with Rosa, to discuss something personal. We'll be right behind you."

"Okay," said Hurtado, starting away.

But before he was out of earshot, he could overhear Natale and Rosa conversing in stage whispers. They were still speaking in English.

Natale was saying, "Rosa, isn't he wonderful? I'd give anything to see him. Do you mind—would you give me some idea what he looks like?"

Rosa was answering, "He's ugly as sin, like something monstrous out of Goya. Pop eyes, squashed nose, crooked teeth, and as big as a gorilla."

"Now I know that's untrue," said Natale laughing. "You're joking, aren't you?"

"Joking completely, dear one. He's as handsome as you could have wished for. He looks like an artist—"

"He's a writer," said Natale.

"I can believe that. He is perhaps five foot ten, slight but sinewy, strong face with dark soulful eyes, straight longish nose, full lips, determined jaw, and close-cropped dark auburn hair. Very intense all around, like one who knows what he is after and is going to get it."

Listening, Hurtado mouthed a soft amen, and trudged on up the ramp.

For Gisele Dupree, it had been a leisurely morning. She had had no tour group to guide until early afternoon, so after lying abed late, she had decided to dress and go out and take care of a few odds and ends.

On the Avenue Bernadette Soubirous, she had stopped to purchase some cosmetics—eye-liner, lipstick, moisturizer—to bolster her new resolve to begin wearing make-up again. Then she had gone along the Rue de la Grotte until she reached a leather store that had a red wallet she liked, and she had decided to buy it. At the last moment, about to stock up on food, she had remembered the roll of film that she had taken of her Nantes pilgrim group at the grotto the day before yesterday. For a gratuity, she had been guaranteed a forty-eight-hour delivery. She had detoured to the camera shop, picked up the color prints, and promised herself to drop them at the tour group's hotel after lunch. Tucking the packet of prints in her purse, she had set off for the food shops, determined to cut her lunch and dinner bills by eating at Dominique's apartment for the remainder of the week.

In the tiny dining room of the cool apartment, after heating some tomato soup, preparing a chopped egg salad, and putting jelly on a croissant, she sat down with a few days of accumulated copies of *Le Figaro* to catch up on the news that was already old. She had started to read when she recalled the packet of photographs and decided to see if they had all come out well, since she had never been one of the world's best photographers. Finding the packet in her purse, she took it back to the table, pulled out the prints and resumed digging into her salad.

The prints of the group, mostly posed and static, had come out fairly well, at least each one was in focus. As she turned them over, one by one, she counted nine of them. Then, to her surprise, there were three more photographs of a complete stranger, some lone older man standing in the sun near the grotto. The pictures had been shot in rapid succession, the first of the older man just standing in the sun, his suit clinging to him, obviously because he'd been in the baths, with a slight blur resembling the feathers of a small bird fluttering in front of his shirt. The second picture showed him bending down, picking up what might have been the bird with outspread wings. And finally the third picture showed the man fastening the bird—no, not a bird, but a mustache—to his upper lip, and with that photograph he was no longer a stranger. She recognized him.

He was Samuel Talley, her former client, the professor from New York.

Instantly, recollection came. As she had been photographing the tour group, she had seen Talley standing alone near them. As a lark, she had diverted the lens of her camera to focus on him and had taken three automatic fast snapshots of him. Perhaps she had done it for fun, to please him with a record of his visit to the grotto, which could be plainly seen in the distance behind him, or perhaps there had been an ulterior motive, to please him in order to wheedle another tip from him. She had a long way to go to reach that translator's school in Paris, but still those tips added up, each one counted.

Anyway, the pictures of Talley were crazy.

She had ceased eating to consider each picture again. At first the sequence made no sense, and then she realized that it did. The crazy thing was the mustache, the flowing Talley mustache. It was false, a false mustache. She recreated the scene. He had come out of the baths, and his mustache had fallen off, because he had been immersed in the water. He had stooped to retrieve it. He had pasted it back on his upper lip.

Funny.

But odd, also. She had thought his shaggy mustache real. But here she could see it was false, a disguise.

Why on earth would a nobody professor from far away want to wear a disguise in a place where he was a foreigner and unknown?

Unless, of course, he didn't want to be recognized, and was therefore not unknown, and therefore a visitor who might be known but preferred to be in Lourdes unknown.

The intrigue side of her mind was going a mile a minute now—a favorite expression from America—and her curiosity was thoroughly aroused.

Why the devil would a nonentity of a professor worry about being seen in Lourdes? Maybe he was trying to avoid a onetime French girl friend who might be here? Maybe he was trying to avoid a local creditor in Lourdes whom he owed for a previous extravagance beyond his means? Or—

Maybe he wasn't Samuel Talley at all. Maybe his name was false just like his mustache. Maybe he was someone else, someone more important, someone who for some reason did not want to be identified with Lourdes.

Someone important?

Gisele threw aside the second and third photographs, and concentrated on the first one, the one of Talley sans mustache, the older man with his face exposed, looking as he really looked. Gisele brought the photograph up closer, narrowing her eyes, staring at the Slavic countenance in the picture. There were thousands and thousands of important faces in the world, and she knew only a few of them, mainly those that belonged to entertainers or politicians she had seen featured in the daily newspapers. Yet this particular photograph of the man who called himself Talley, the man who had lost his false mustache, had a look of familiarity about him.

It was as if she had seen him somewhere before.

The obviously Slavic features, now with the upper lip growth out of the way. An upper lip with a wart. Slavic features on a man who had told her he was an American of Russian parentage and taught Russian at Columbia University, and yet might be somebody else. But—

Gisele blinked. Why not Russian, really Russian?

Then like a bolt it struck her, recognition struck her.

She had seen this man before, or his double, in person, in the newspapers. She ransacked through recent memory, the UN months. Yes, that's where she had seen the face with the wart. Her lover, Charles Sarrat, had taken her to a UN reception, and she had seen the great man, had been awed to see him up close. And again, just the day before yesterday, on the front page of *Le Figaro*.

Her hand streaked to the backlog of unread copies of the newspapers. The day-before-yesterday's edition, the front page, and there it was, and there *he* was on the front page before her. One of the three candidates being speculated upon as the possible successor to the ailing premier of the Soviet Union. There he was in the paper, the very face in the color photograph she had taken at the grotto.

Sergei Tikhanov, foreign minister of the Union of Soviet Socialist Republics.

It couldn't be, it just couldn't be. But it might be, almost certainly it might be.

Quickly, she had the faces side by side, the one in the Paris newspaper, the one in the photograph she had taken playfully yesterday at the grotto, and she was comparing them.

Absolutely, they were one and the same. Samuel Talley, of the false mustache, was actually the renowned and mighty Sergei Tikhanov.

My God, Holy Jesus, if this were true.

The clever and deductive side of her mind was racing now, outlining possibilities, one logical possibility.

The successor to the leadership of the Union of Soviet Socialist Republics was ill. As Talley, he had admitted that he was ill. He was in line for the top job in Russia. But he was ill, and maybe doctors didn't give him much hope. So he was trying for any cure, and Lourdes had been in the headlines these past weeks. In desperation, he had made the decision to visit Lourdes. But as a leader of the biggest atheistic state in the world, he dared not let it be known that he was indulging in a romantic and wild enterprise like seeking succor from the Virgin Mary at the foremost Catholic shrine. Therefore, he had come here under a pseudonym, and wearing a disguise.

Gisele sat back, shaken by the enormity of her discovery.

If true.

The discovery was a prize, but it had to be true, verified, proved. There could be no mistake. Her only evidence was the very clear snapshot of Talley-Tikhanov taken near the grotto, and the one in the photograph resembled the image in her memory of the Soviet foreign minister she had seen up close briefly at the United Nations reception. But memory could be faulty, inexact. Then there was the photograph in the newspaper, clear yet not totally clear because it was reproduced on cheap newsprint.

What additional evidence did she need?

For one thing, a better photograph of Tikhanov that would be clearer than the one in the newspaper, a real print that she could hold beside her own clear snapshot taken at the grotto.

And one more thing. Absolute evidence that Talley, the name, was fake, that it was not his own name but as much a disguise as his mustache. It that could be proved, that Talley wasn't Talley, and a truer picture of Tikhanov showed him to be the one at the grotto, then there would be no more doubt. She would be able to expose someone who, at any cost, did not want to be exposed. She would be on to a big one, the biggest break in her young life.

But first the evidence.

Gisele considered the next step, actually two steps, and in moments she knew exactly what to do.

First, the truer photograph of the actual Foreign Minister Tikhanov. Once she had that evidence, she could take her second step. The first step, the better photograph, had to come from somewhere, obviously a photo agency or a newspaper photo file. That was a problem. Lourdes had no photo agency and its newspaper would be too small and too limited to have a folder of portraits of a Soviet foreign minister in its files. Only the big city papers would have such files. Like Marseilles, Lyons, Paris. If she could contact one of those newspapers—and then she had an idea how to do so.

Her good friend, Michelle Demalliot, head of the Sanctuaries Press Bureau, might be the one person to help her.

Gisele had an eye on the clock. There wasn't time enough to go down to the press center and talk to Michelle, and get back into town in time for her tour. Well, she needn't do it in person. The telephone would be enough. Pushing aside her half-finished salad, she went into the living room, found the white and red telephone book titled *Hautes-Pyrénées* which listed telephone numbers in Lourdes and Tarbes. Finding the listing for the Sanctuaries Press Bureau, she sat next to the phone and dialed the number.

An unfamiliar female voice answered.

"Is Michelle Demalliot there?" Gisele asked.

"She's just going out the door to lunch. I'll try to catch her."

"Please! Tell her Gisele Dupree is calling."

Gisele held on, and then was relieved to hear Michelle's voice on the phone.

"Hello, Michelle, it's Gisele. I don't want to make you late for lunch, but I need a favor."

"Of course. What?"

"I need some still photographs of the Soviet Union's foreign minister, you know, Sergei Tikhanov. I need them as soon as possible."

"Whatever for?"

"Because—because when I was at the United Nations—remember? —I saw him and met him, and some small magazine has asked me to write a short piece on him, but they won't buy it without a picture. So I wondered if you had any press people still coming to Lourdes, today, tomorrow, whom you might talk into bringing a few pictures of Tikhanov along? Can you think of anyone?"

"Well, everyone is mostly here waiting for the Reappearance, but there may be a few more—wait, let me see."

Michelle left the phone for thirty seconds and then she was back on the line.

"I just checked. You may be in luck. I have someone coming in this evening from Paris, a photographer from *Paris-Match,* to do a layout of the activity here and hang around to photograph the person who sees the Virgin Mary, if someone does. I could call him at *Paris-Match,* probably catch him. If I do, you want a photograph of Sergei Tikhanov?"

"A good clear glossy portrait of his face from their file. I'll pay for it. If I can see a couple of shots all the better. Can you call me back? Here's the number I'm at." She read off Dominique's phone number.

"All right, Gisele, let me call Paris right this second. If I can't pull it off in five minutes, I'll let you know. If he can bring your pictures, I won't bother to call back. You'll know they'll be here tonight. You can pick them up at the Press Bureau around eight tonight. How's that?"

"Super. You're a doll, Michelle. Thanks a million!"

She hung up thinking, A million, a million, God knows what it might be worth if it was true.

She sat there beside the phone, hoping it would not ring. She sat waiting for five minutes, six, seven, ten. No ring.

That meant her friend had reached *Paris-Match.* That meant the photographs of Tikhanov would be in her hands tonight.

Step one on its way.

Next, step two. To find out if Talley really was Samuel Talley, a professor in the language department at Columbia University. Gisele knew exactly how to find out. Her old American friend Roy Zimborg had graduated from Columbia University. She glanced at the mantel clock. She had no time for the call to New York now. She'd better be off to her job. Besides, it would be terrible to wake Zimborg at this early hour in New York. It would be better late tonight, maybe midnight, when it would be six in the evening in New York and when she had already seen the *Paris-Match* photograph and had ascertained that it was the same person she had caught in her own amateur's snapshot at the grotto.

She sat very still, a smile wreathing her face.

A miracle was happening in Lourdes, after all, a personal miracle all her own.

By tonight she might have her ticket and her passport to the United Nations. She could not think of it as blackmail. Only as good fortune to one who was so deserving.

11

. . . August 17

They were coming out of the parking lot on the Rue de Lourdes in Nevers, where they had left their rented Peugeot and were starting uphill toward the Saint-Gildard Convent, Bernadette's last resting place and their destination.

Early this morning Liz Finch and Amanda Spenser had taken an Air Inter flight from Lourdes to Paris, rented the car, and driven down to Nevers in three hours.

Walking now in the midday heat, Amanda spoke. "Do you think anything will come of this?" she wondered. "Maybe it's a wild goose chase."

Liz shrugged. "Never can tell. In my profession, you don't miss a bet. You just keep burrowing and burrowing, and hope for a gleam of gold. I don't expect we'll find anyone here as bitchy as Father Cayoux. Yet, we might find something—we just might."

They had reached the eight-foot-high convent wall that led to the open gates at the entrance. A diminutive middle-aged nun, in gray habit, short skirt, standing inside the gates, was waiting for them. She had a broad smooth brow, unlined peach complexion, bright intelligent dark eyes, and a gentle smile.

"Miss Liz Finch? Miss Amanda Spenser? You are the Americans we are expecting?"

"None other," said Liz.

"I'm Sister Francesca—"

"Who speaks perfect English," said Liz.

"I hope so," said the nun, "coming, as I do, from an American father and a French mother. Well, welcome to Saint-Gildard Convent." She paused. "I understand you are writing a story on Saint Bernadette, Miss Finch, and that Miss Spenser is your assistant. We are glad to cooperate. You'll have to give me an idea what you want to know. Saint-Gildard Convent was, of course, Saint Bernadette's last station on earth. Do you want me to show you around first?"

"Definitely," said Liz. "Miss Spenser and I want to see everything related to Bernadette. After that, we'd like to spend a little while with you asking some questions."

"I hope that I have the answers," said Sister Francesca. "But let's begin with a brief guided tour."

The nun was leading them past a long bank of lavender-colored flowers, and they followed her until she slowed down.

"*La Grotte de Lourdes,*" Sister Francesca announced.

To Amanda's surprise, they were standing in front of a replica of the original grotto at Lourdes, smaller than the real one, but hardly miniature, either, a replica of the real grotto created on a slope that ran uphill to street level.

"For outdoor Masses," the nun said.

Then Amanda realized that, behind them, but facing the duplicate grotto, were rows of benches for pilgrims, and that a horde of pilgrims was this moment leaving the benches and filing out toward another exit on the side.

"Those are the members of a German pilgrimage from Cologne and Dortmund, about four hundred of them," the nun explained. "They have finished their religious services now and are going across the Boulevard Victor Hugo to our Abri du Pèlerin—our pilgrim shelter or dormitory for visitors. This group will remain for tonight and then go on to Lourdes itself."

Amanda was examining the replica grotto once more. There, at the upper right, inside the niche, was a blue and white statue of the Virgin Mary.

"The plaque beneath the statue," said Sister Francesca, "tells us that the little piece of rock mounted on it is an actual rock fragment from the real grotto of Massabielle in Lourdes. Now, let me show you our convent church and Saint Bernadette herself." She had started away from the replica grotto toward a courtyard, and was beckoning

Liz and Amanda past a tall, white marble statue of the Virgin Mary to a side door of the church.

Once inside the convent church, and proceeding down the center aisle between pews, Sister Francesca resumed speaking in a hushed tone. "This church was constructed in 1855. It was modernized twice, the last time in 1972. The white altar ahead is concrete."

Except for the modernity of the church's interior decoration, Amanda felt that she had been inside this church before. She had visited at least a hundred churches in Europe, and they were always the same. High above the altar the arched ceiling and the multicolored windows. Behind the altar a crucifix, a bronze Jesus on a pale wooden cross. Immediately on either side of her, the rows of oak and walnut pews and a scattering of worshippers in silent prayer or meditation.

Liz and Amanda had arrived at the two steps leading up to the altar, and halted with their nun guide. Sister Francesca's voice dropped lower. "After the apparitions, Bernadette was at a loss as to what to do with herself. True, she was going to school at last, and sometimes acting as a baby-sitter to earn money for her parents, but she was constantly the object of attention from both neighbors and the endless stream of visitors coming to Lourdes. She could not be alone. She was daily exposed to intruders with their questions. By 1863, her mentors had decided that she needed a vocation, and suggested she enter some holy order as a nun."

"Maybe the church people just wanted her out of sight," said Liz provocatively. "By then, she was a growing legend, yet she sometimes did not behave like one. She had a streak of stubbornness, I've heard, and she disliked discipline, enjoyed playing pranks, had too lively an interest in fancy clothes. Maybe the churchmen wanted to get her off the streets and out of the way. To them, probably a convent seemed a convenient place to put her."

In this setting, Liz's assessment seemed harsh, and Amanda wondered how their nun guide would react. But Sister Francesca reacted nicely. "Some of that may have been true," she agreed, "but actually many convents considered her a prize and were after her, although with reservations because her health was so poor and her fame might disrupt their routines. The Carmelites and the Bernardines were both after her. She rejected the latter because she did not like their ungainly headdress. When she settled on the order in Nevers, she remarked, 'I am going to Nevers because they did not lure me.' The mayor of Lourdes wanted her to become a dressmaker, but she told him she preferred to be a nun. On July 4, 1866, at the age of twenty-two, she left Lourdes forever, and took a train, her first and last train ride, to Nevers and entered our order. She remained here until her death on April 16, 1879, at the age of thirty-five. She was elevated to sainthood in 1933." The nun paused, smiled, and said, "Now we can have a look at Saint Bernadette herself. She rests in the chapel near the altar."

Trailing after the other two, Amanda could not imagine what to expect.

They were facing the chapel, a restricted alcove, a narrow room almost sterile in its simplicity. The ceiling was a Gothic arch, the high windows dark blue, the three walls gray stone, and the centerpiece of the chapel was a large glass-and-gold casket, and inside it lay the body of a young woman, the object of their quest.

"Bernadette," the nun whispered.

Unaccountably, Amanda found herself drawn closer to the casket. When she had approached the low railing that protected the chapel, her emotion had been combative, as if she were about to come face to face with the other woman, this woman who stood between Ken and herself and their planned life together. But now, preceding Liz and Sister Francesca to look closely at the casket, Amanda found that her anger had dissipated. She was enveloped by a sense of awe at what this young woman, little more than her own age, an unlettered peasant girl, had achieved, the unswerving beliefs she'd held, the indomitable strength of her belief.

The casket itself was trimmed in gold, with glass sides, quite ornate, and rested on a carved solid-oak stand. Inside the reliquary, attired in the black and white habit of her order, eyes eternally shut, hands crossed on her breast as if in prayer, lay Bernadette. She seemed like one asleep, and at peace, after a long wearying day.

"It's really Bernadette?" asked Amanda softly, as Liz and Sister Francesca joined her.

"Yes, the blessed Saint Bernadette," said the nun, "all but the face and hands, that is."

"All but the face and hands?" Amanda said, surprised.

"In truth those are wax impressions of her face and hands that were fitted after her third and final exhumation."

"No wonder she looks so smooth and unblemished," said Liz.

"I'd better explain," said Sister Francesca. "Bernadette's physical condition was poor at the time of her death—bed sores on her back, a knee swollen from tuberculosis, lungs collapsed—therefore what followed is all the more remarkable. Her corpse was displayed for three days after her death. Then she was placed in a lead coffin, which was set in an oak coffin, and this was buried in a vault beneath a garden chapel. Thirty years after her burial, when efforts were first being undertaken by an episcopal commission to start Bernadette on the road to saint-hood, her coffin was opened. That was in 1909."

"Why?" Liz wanted to know.

"To observe her condition," said the nun. "Most bodies of ordinary corpses suffer putrefaction. But a church tradition has always held that the body of a candidate for canonization would escape decay, be found in good condition. Well, when the coffin was opened, Bernadette's remains were found to be in an excellent state. The report by the examining doctor read: 'The head was tilted to the left. The face was matte white. The skin clung to the muscles and the muscles adhered to the bones. The sockets of the eyes were covered by the eyelids. The brows were flat on the skin and stuck to the arches above the eyes. The lashes of the right eyelid were stuck to the skin. The nose was dilated and shrunken. The mouth was open slightly, and it could be seen that the teeth were still in place. The hands, which were crossed on her breast, were perfectly preserved, as were the nails. The hands still held a rusting rosary.' "

"What happened next?" asked Liz.

"Bernadette's body was washed, dressed, reburied. There were two more exhumations as sainthood came closer, one more in 1919, and the last one in 1925. Each time the body was found well preserved, a good sign of sanctity. But after all those exposures to air and light, the body began to be affected and blacken. So impressions were made of Bernadette's face and hands, and in Paris a mask of wax was made for the face and wax covers for the hands. I will admit the artist took a few minor liberties—in the face mask he straightened Bernadette's nose a wee bit, plucked her eyebrows a little, and he added polish to her fingernails on the hand covers. Finally, the mask was fitted, Bernadette's body was wrapped in bandages and dressed in a fresh habit, and she was ready to be shown to the world. Here she has rested ever since. If there is anything else you would like to know—"

"I have a few questions," said Liz firmly.

A man with an armband had come into the chapel from the altar area and held some kind of photograph over the casket. In a few seconds he left.

"What was that?" Amanda wanted to know.

"Probably a supplication," said Sister Francesca. "Some pilgrim sending in the picture of a loved one who is ill, and by this, hopes for a healing, and a guide agreed to take it right to the casket to have it blessed, in a sense, by proximity to Bernadette." She glanced at Liz. "You have some questions?"

"Yes," said Liz.

"Very well. I think it best if I try to answer them outside the church. Less disruptive. Let's go back to the courtyard."

The moment that they left the church and emerged into the sunlight, and gathered together at the foot of the statue of the Virgin Mary, Amanda had a question of her own to ask, before allowing Liz to begin her promised interrogation.

"I was wondering," said Amanda, "what Bernadette did with herself in her thirteen years here at Saint-Gildard. Was it all prayer?"

"Not quite," said Sister Francesca. "True, the nuns here today—they live in the upper floors of the convent and keep to themselves—devote their time largely to prayer and various household tasks. Some few of us, of course, work with the tourists. But in Bernadette's time she had many things to do. Her main job was in the infirmary, serving as assistant infirmarian. She loved to nurse ailing patients. She never fully escaped public exposure, of course. Her fame grew steadily during her lifetime, and notable visitors came and went. Sometimes biographers sought to see her, speak with her. And don't forget, she was frequently ill and bedridden, several times on the verge of death."

Impatient to try out her own questions, Liz aggressively stepped nearer to the nun. "I've also heard that Bernadette was pretty busy in the convent fighting with her superior, the Novice Mistress Mother Marie-Thérèse Vauzou. Is that true?"

"Not exactly fighting," said the unruffled Sister Francesca. "After all, Mother Vauzou was Bernadette's superior. Bernadette would not have dared to fight with her."

"Let's not quibble," said Liz. "I've heard from good authority that the two of them were on the outs from day one."

"I would put it another way," said Sister Francesca, still not flinching. "Allow me to be strictly factual based on what we know. At first Mother Vauzou welcomed Bernadette as 'the privileged child of the Virgin Mary.' But then she had certain reservations about her new novice. For one thing, she never quite believed that Bernadette had actually seen the apparitions of the Virgin. Moreover, she did not like the whole Virgin Mary cult that was growing, since her own devotions were based on the all-importance of Jesus Christ. As to the talk that the mistress of novices treated Bernadette severely, even making her kiss the ground, that was common in those days. The task of the superior was to teach all novices humility and make them do penance."

Liz persisted. "I heard that Bernadette was afraid of Mother Vauzou."

"Some witnesses say that is true. But Mother Vauzou had her reasons to treat Bernadette a trifle harshly. She worried about what some call the Bernadette legend, that the keen interest in Bernadette may have gone to her head, that she had become too vain and prideful to become a proper nun. Also, Mother Vauzou believed that Bernadette lacked frankness, once describing her novice as 'a stiff, very touchy character.' Above all, I repeat, Mother Vauzou may have had lingering doubts that Bernadette had ever seen the Virgin Mary. She could not imagine the Virgin coming before such a simple girl with so lowly a background. Mother Vauzou remarked of Bernadette, 'Oh, she was a little peasant girl. If the Holy Virgin wanted to appear somewhere on earth, why should She choose a common, illiterate peasant instead of some virtuous and well-instructed nun?' On another occasion, Mother Vauzou said, 'I do not understand why the Holy Virgin should reveal Herself to Bernadette. There are so many other souls more lofty and delicate! Really!' When there was talk of introducing Bernadette's cause, it was set aside in the period when Mother Vauzou was promoted to superior general of our convent. When her successor came along and mentioned the possibility of sainthood, Mother Vauzou begged her, 'Wait until after I am dead.' "

"Wasn't that enough to put down the Bernadette legend?" asked Liz.

"Not really," said the nun. "Because on her death bed Mother Vauzou confessed that her doubts were created by her own weakness and not Bernadette's. Mother Vauzou's last words indicated that she had capitulated to Bernadette and to the reality of Lourdes. Her last words were, 'Our Lady of Lourdes, protect my death-agony.' "

Liz herself seemed to capitulate at this point. "All right," she said, "enough of that. But there's one more thing I must ask you. It touches on church politics, the desire by some to get Bernadette out of Lourdes and tucked into relative anonymity in Nevers. You know, of course, that someone of high social standing wanted to marry Bernadette before she became a nun?"

"I do," said Sister Francesca.

"Well, I for one would like to know why the church did not permit the suitor to propose to Bernadette, or even tell her that someone had asked for her hand? Wasn't that because the church didn't want her to remain in the open, become as normal as any other young woman, but preferred to keep her from view in order to maintain her legend and to build the fame of the shrine at Lourdes?"

"No, that wasn't so," said the nun. "I'm afraid you have it quite wrong."

"Then tell me what's right," said Liz testily.

"What's correct is this: A young nobleman and medical student in

Nantes, Raoul de Tricqueville, wrote Monsignor Laurence, the bishop of Tarbes and Lourdes, in March, 1866, and stated that the only thing he wanted in this world was to marry Bernadette, and would the bishop intercede for him. The bishop replied somewhat tartly that any marriage for Bernadette was opposed 'to what the Holy Virgin wanted.' Shortly after Bernadette came to Nevers, the young man pressed his suit again. This time he wrote to Bishop Forcade, and asked if he could visit Bernadette and propose marriage to her in person. 'Let me at least ask her myself to marry me. If she is as you say, she will refuse me; if she accepts, you will know she is not truly suited for the vocation she has chosen.' The bishop replied that Bernadette was, indeed, perfectly suited for her vocation, and he did not intend to disturb her peace of mind. He did not bother to tell Bernadette about the young man or the proposal. There is not one shred of evidence that either of these refusals was engendered by a church plot or politics. Bernadette's superiors were merely looking after her best interests."

"If you say so," said Liz grimly.

"The facts say so," said Sister Francesca with equanimity. "Now I had better get back to my duties. You'll be driving to Lourdes?"

"To Paris to catch the last flight to Lourdes tonight," said Liz.

"Let me see you to the front gate," said the nun.

They strolled in silence to the gate, and were about to part company, when Amanda held back.

"Sister, just one last thing, if you don't mind," said Amanda.

"Please, go ahead."

"About Bernadette's private journal," said Amanda. "I've heard everyone refer to Bernadette as illiterate, unable to write. So how could she keep a journal?"

Sister Francesca nodded. "She was illiterate and unable to write at the time of the apparitions. After that, preparing for her First Communion, Bernadette went to school, studied at the Hospice in Lourdes, and learned to write very well. She then wrote a number of accounts about the apparitions. She wrote numerous letters, including one to the Pope in Rome. She wrote quite easily, not in French at first but in her regional language. Eventually, she did learn French."

"But this journal, the one that was recently found," said Amanda, "I read that it was written by her right here in Nevers, in this convent."

"So I am told," agreed Sister Francesca. "She kept this journal toward the end, setting down all she could remember of her young life before the apparitions and more detail of what she could recall of her visions at the grotto. Before her death, she sent the journal to a relative or friend as a memento."

"How was it discovered after so many years? And where?"

"I know only that it was located in Bartrès, and that someone from Lourdes acquired it—or at least the latter part of it—for the church."

"Acquired it from whom in Bartrès?" Amanda wondered.

"I don't know." For the first time, the nun appeared evasive. "You might ask Father Ruland when you return to Lourdes."

"I may do that," said Amanda. "Anyway, thank you for everything."

"God go with you," said Sister Francesca, and left them.

Liz glared after the nun. "Thanks for nothing, Sister," she muttered. "What a bust. The straight party line."

They started away.

"I don't know," mused Amanda. "There may have been something. I keep thinking of that journal."

"You can be sure it's authentic," Liz said grouchily. "The Pope would never have announced its contents unless he was positive it was genuine."

"Not that, that's not what I'm thinking. I'm thinking about the rest of the contents. The church announced only the part about the apparitions, especially the one apparition where the Virgin passed on her secret to Bernadette. But you heard Sister Francesca. There was more to the journal than that. There was all kinds of material Bernadette set down about her early life."

"So what? Where will that get you? Forget it. We've reached a dead end. Admit it. We've lost. I've lost with my boss, Trask. And you've lost with your boyfriend, Ken. We're through."

Amanda shook her head slowly. "I don't know. I'm still not quitting. I'm going to follow up."

"On what?"

"On that journal. I want to know more about the journal that brought us all to Lourdes."

"Oh, that," said Liz. "Believe me, you're not going to get anywhere."

"We'll see," said Amanda.

Edith Moore had kept her second appointment of the day at the Medical Bureau in Lourdes exactly on time. She had come, and in less than a half hour she had gone, and Dr. Paul Kleinberg had barely seen her. He had thanked her for coming in again, apologized for the X-ray botch, and turned her over to Esther Levinson for another set of X rays.

Now Kleinberg paced restlessly in the examination room of the Medical Bureau waiting for Esther to hang the X-ray negatives and turn on the view box. It was all mechanics now, routine, and he would be through with the case and in Paris again by evening.

"Ready for you," Esther said, turning on the view box.

She stepped aside as Dr. Kleinberg moved toward the X rays. "This won't take more than a minute," he said absently.

But it took more than a minute.

It was ten minutes before Kleinberg came away from the X rays and wandered over to the chair and sat down heavily. Briefly, he was lost in thought. When he looked up, he saw his nurse's worried expression.

"Didn't they come out again?" Esther wondered.

"They came out very well," Kleinberg said.

"Then you can confirm our miracle woman?"

"No, I can't," said Kleinberg flatly.

"What?" Esther came forward with surprise. "What are you saying?"

Kleinberg met his nurse's stare, and shook his head. "She's not a miracle woman. Probably never was. The sarcoma is plainly there. Either the tumor has come back—something I've never seen happen before—or it has never gone away. Whatever took place, Mrs. Moore is not cured."

The nurse's poise had evaporated entirely. "But, doctor—that—that can't be."

"It's a fact, Esther."

"Those other X rays." She was almost pleading for Mrs. Moore. "The previous pictures, the recent ones, they don't show the sarcoma. And the negative biopsies—what about them? She must have been cured."

Kleinberg was shaking his head again. "I can't explain this. It makes no sense."

"Unless the other doctors—in their zeal, or whatever—maybe they tampered with the previous X rays? But no," she corrected herself instantly, "that wouldn't explain it either, because Mrs. Moore became well, from an invalid she became a healthy person again."

"I can't dispute that," Kleinberg agreed, "but Esther, pictures don't lie. She's suffering the cancer once more—or still. Soon she won't be functioning. The condition is sure to worsen, to deteriorate. There was no miraculous cure. Our miracle woman simply isn't."

"That's terrible, doctor. You—you'll have to tell Dr. Berryer."

"I can't." Kleinberg amended his response. "Not yet." He added, "This diagnosis might not be acceptable—from a person of my persuasion. They'd all think a nonbeliever is trying to obstruct them."

Esther's fingers touched the nearest X ray. "This picture is also a nonbeliever. It doesn't obstruct. It's ruthless. It tells the truth."

"Not to everyone, and not that easily," said Kleinberg. "A general physician might overlook what a specialist in sarcoma can see."

"There can be no mistake about what you see?"

"None whatsoever, Esther. Our miracle woman is in trouble."

"You just can't leave it at that."

"I won't. But I haven't the heart to break this to Edith Moore. I think her husband should do that, and then I'll follow up. If you can get Berryer's secretary to locate Mr. Moore—Reggie Moore—tell him I'd like to see him as soon as possible."

In the ten-minute period in which Esther was gone, Kleinberg stood up and studied the X rays once more. When he was through, his diagnosis had not altered. The British lady was, indeed, in trouble. He tried to think what could be done. She was doomed unless some effort was made to deal with the sarcoma. Of course, only one possibility existed. Surgery. Normal surgery would not promise much hope in this case. But what came to mind was his colleague, Dr. Maurice Duval, the other major specialist in this field who had been experimenting with a new kind of surgery involving genetic engineering. Judging from the recent scientific papers on the subject that Kleinberg had studied, Dr. Duval seemed on the verge of stepping out of experimentation on animals and moving closer to surgery on human beings.

Kleinberg's thoughts were interrupted by the return of his nurse.

"I'm sorry, doctor," Esther was saying, "but we can't locate Mr. Moore anywhere. We only know that he and possibly his wife will be at a restaurant they own in Lourdes around eight this evening for dinner."

"Then we'll have dinner there, too."

"What if Mr. Moore is with his wife. What will you tell her?"

"I'll have to stall her until I've been able to inform her husband about what's happened. Make the reservation for the two of us, Esther. It won't be a digestible dinner, but make the reservation for eight-fifteen."

It was a warm evening in Lourdes, and many pilgrims were on their way to dinner, some hastily in order to eat quickly and catch the nightly procession in the domain. Among those going more leisurely, perhaps hesitantly, along the Avenue Bernadette Soubirous were Dr. Kleinberg, in a freshly pressed lightweight tan summer suit, and his nurse, Esther Levinson, wearing a striped cotton dress.

Kleinberg was noting the street numbers they passed. "We must almost be there," he said. "Probably across the intersection, on the corner."

They crossed over to the corner. Kleinberg sought the address, and checked his watch. "Here it is," he said, "and we're just on time."

Going to the entrance, he abruptly stopped, his eyes on the sign above. He read it aloud. "Madame Moore's Miracle Restaurant." Kleinberg sighed. "Well, they'll have to change only the name—not the cuisine."

The dining room was spacious, expensive, and filled with chattering customers. The maître d', formally attired, took Kleinberg's name, consulted the reservation list on a stand, and immediately led his guests through the room to a vacant table along the far wall.

After ordering their drinks, Kleinberg settled back and tried to size up the room's occupants. He made out the main table, and Edith Moore commanding it, at once. She was holding sway, the dominant figure, speaking animatedly to the others and full of obvious good cheer. Except for two empty chairs, the table was occupied by guests who were listening to her intently.

Someone, a woman, had suddenly appeared from the adjacent bar and was blocking his view. Kleinberg looked up. After an instant's blankness he recognized her, just as she identified herself. "Michelle Demaillot, your friendly press officer," she said gaily. "How are you, Dr. Kleinberg? And you, Miss Levinson?"

"Very well, and you, Miss Demaillot?" replied Kleinberg, half rising, then lowering himself to his seat again.

"I'm glad you could find time for our favorite restaurant," said Michelle.

"Yes, very nice," said Kleinberg.

"I'm sure you've been busy at the Medical Bureau," Michelle went on. "I presume you'll have some news for us any minute?"

"Any minute," said Kleinberg uncomfortably.

"You know, of course, your patient Edith Moore is here. Her husband is one of the owners."

"I've seen her," said Kleinberg. "By the way, is Mr. Moore at the table with her?"

Michelle stepped back, half turning to take in the table. "He's there, all right. The one to her left."

Kleinberg narrowed his eyes and found the beefy, ruddy-faced Englishman in the plaid sports jacket next to Mrs. Moore. To Kleinberg, Reggie Moore appeared an amiable sort, and perhaps one who would not be too difficult to deal with after dinner.

"I see him," Kleinberg said. "Do you know any of the others at the table?"

"Sooner or later I get to know everyone," said Michelle. "The others, counterclockwise are Ken Clayton, an American lawyer, the empty seat is probably for his wife, Amanda. Next there is Mr. Talley, an American professor. He's been here every night. The French couple beside him are the Marceaus, in the wine business, they own a vineyard. Then the lovely girl is Natale Rinaldi, Italian. Poor thing, she's blind. With her is a friend—I don't know his name—but obviously he's Spanish or Latin American." Michelle was momentarily distracted by two tardy arrivals coming through the front door. "Ah, the two others for the table. Amanda Clayton, whom I mentioned. And her companion is one I've talked to every day. Liz Finch, an American correspondent in Paris. I know she went to Nevers early this morning."

"Why Nevers?" Kleinberg wondered. "It's a bit of a distance from here."

"Miss Finch is doing some stories about the events of the week. She most likely wanted a look at Bernadette. Our saint lies in state, visible to all, in a Nevers chapel."

"Who would want to go that far to see a corpse?" Kleinberg said.

Michelle raised her shoulders. "Americans. They must visit everything. Well, I see you have your drinks and menus. I won't hold you up. *Bon appétit.* And, Dr. Kleinberg, we await your confirmation with, as they say in the novels, bated breath."

Dr. Kleinberg watched Michelle return to the bar, and once more gave his attention to the Moore table. The travelers back from Nevers were being greeted. The attractive one, Amanda, was kissing her lawyer husband, Mr. Clayton, and quickly introducing her companion, the rather unattractive woman correspondent, Liz Finch, to the others around the table.

That instant, Kleinberg realized that Edith Moore, in a moment's respite, inspecting the room, had noticed him and was waving for his attention.

Kleinberg forced a weak smile of greeting.

In a silent body gesture, Edith Moore was transmitting a question. The gesture was clear: Any news yet?

Kleinberg tried to respond. With exaggeration, he mouthed one word: Soon.

He looked away, pretending to join Esther in consulting the menu she had opened.

He grunted. "Suddenly, it's a bit close in here." He indicated the menu. "Let's order. I want to meet Reggie Moore and have it over with."

"All right," said Esther, "but this is a crazy menu, doctor. There are two set meals at fixed prices. The cheaper one is unreasonable enough. But the other one, supposedly deluxe, is really expensive—because, for its dessert, so to speak, you are guaranteed an opportunity to be personally introduced to the latest miracle woman of Lourdes, namely Edith Moore." Esther wrinkled her nose. "Such blatant exploitation. By her husband, I'd guess." She met Kleinberg's eyes sympathetically. "I'm afraid that's not going to make things easier for you."

"I knew this would be an indigestible dinner," muttered Kleinberg. "But who says I have to eat? All right, pick out the meal we're to have and let's be done with it."

An hour later, Kleinberg and Esther were almost done with it, in the middle of their coffee, when Kleinberg became aware that someone was rising at Edith Moore's table. It was, he saw, Reggie Moore apparently setting out to make the rounds of some of the other tables and exchange a few words with customers of his acquaintance.

Kleinberg set down his cup. "I'm going to speak to Mr. Moore at once, while she's not in the way. Esther, you pay up. I'll reimburse you later. Don't wait for me. See you in the hotel lobby for a nightcap."

Kleinberg was on his feet, throwing down his napkin, and heading in the direction of the affable Reggie Moore. Kleinberg slowed, waiting until Moore had left one table and was starting for another, and then he intercepted the Englishman.

"Mr. Moore?" Kleinberg said. "I'm Paul Kleinberg, your wife's consulting physician—"

"I know. She pointed you out. Pleased to meet you. Would you like to come over to our table, say hello?"

"No, not right now."

"I know Edith's eager to hear the good news from you."

"I'll be speaking to her," said Kleinberg. "You're the one I want to speak to now."

"Oh, sure, whatever you—"

"Not here," said Kleinberg. "I'd prefer privacy. Do you mind if we take a little stroll outside?"

For the first time, Reggie's features showed puzzlement. "I can't imagine what we need to discuss in private, but—"

Kleinberg already had Reggie by the arm, and was propelling him to the door. "I'll explain," Kleinberg said, and he followed the Englishman out to the sidewalk.

They started walking. "I hope this is about Edith," Moore said.

"It is." Kleinberg saw a sidewalk café directly ahead. The Café Jeanne d'Arc. Most of the yellow wicker chairs at the curb were empty. "Do you mind sitting down for a few minutes?"

"Whatever," said Moore.

They were no sooner seated, than a waiter was upon them. Kleinberg ordered a pot of tea, which he didn't want, and Reggie Moore ordered a Perrier.

Reggie continued to wear a perplexed expression. "If it's about Edith, I hope it's the news we've all been waiting for."

Kleinberg girded himself. How many times, in his particular specialty, he had been the bearer of bad tidings, not exactly like this one but with the same miserable results to be announced. "Mr. Moore, I'm afraid it is not good news I have to report."

Reggie's expression of puzzlement was immediately replaced by an expression of fear. His watery eyes seemed to have frozen. "Not good news. What does that mean?"

"She has the sarcoma again. Either it's come back—or it never completely went away."

"That's insane." Reggie's cheeks began to quiver. "I don't believe it. How can you be sure?"

"Mr. Moore, my practice deals with sarcoma. It's my specialty. Her tumor is evident, at an early state, in the X rays."

Reggie had become aggressive, defensive. "She was cured, and you know it. The cure was a miraculous one. It has been attested to by sixteen doctors, leading doctors from everywhere on earth."

For Kleinberg, this was painful. He didn't want to argue with the poor bastard. But he had no choice. "Mr. Moore, they could have been wrong, overlooked something."

"You're a doctor, and you can be as wrong as you say they are."

Kleinberg tried to ignore the attack. "Or it could have been something else. Assuming she was cured, and her case history seems to support that, still each diagnosis was made previously, at another time. My diagnosis has been made today. I saw her. I saw sarcoma once more. She's ill and—"

"She's perfectly well, totally cured," Reggie interrupted, raising his voice. "You can see, she gets around perfectly. No more pain, no more trouble. She's one hundred percent okay."

"I'm sorry, but she won't be. Her condition will deteriorate. I have no choice but to tell you it will happen. I thought it would be easier all around, if I told you and you found a means of telling her, to soften the blow. As her husband you would know how to handle her."

Reggie glared at Kleinberg several seconds. "Doctor, I don't intend to tell her and upset her, especially since I don't believe you. I refuse to believe you know better than the best in the medical profession."

Kleinberg held his temper in check, tried to remain low-key. "I'm not here to debate my diagnosis. I'm here to inform you that your wife is going to be very ill—and to add that there is something you can do about it. What you can do is take your wife straight to Paris—or London, if you prefer—and avail yourself of the latest surgical advances. There is a colleague of mine in Paris, Dr. Maurice Duval, also a specialist in this field, who has had some remarkable success with an entirely new kind of surgery encompassing genetic engineering. I don't know if he's prepared to use the technique on human beings, but if he is, Mrs. Moore would be in the best of hands and have a real chance to survive. I even put in a call to Dr. Duval before dinner to learn if he was able to get involved. But I was told that he was out of Paris, and that he'd return tomorrow early and call me back. With surgery, Mrs. Moore could have a chance."

"Have a chance?" Reggie was outraged. With effort he tried to control the pitch of his voice. "A chance for what? Don't you know my wife was totally cured here in Lourdes by a miracle and she's remained cured? She is applauded everywhere as the new miracle woman. Give her surgery, and she's like everyone else, she's nobody. Repudiate the miracle and she's ruined, I'm ruined, we'll lose everything, lose our business, every pence we have!"

Kleinberg eyed the Englishman coldly. "Mr. Moore," he said measuring his words, "the subject at issue here is not your having a nonmiracle wife—but your having any wife at all."

Reggie leaped to his feet, furious. "Never mind that! I have a wife. I'll keep on having one. Because every expert knows she's cured. Everyone except you. The high-ups will get someone to replace you and certify Edith. They won't trust you anyway—they can't—they know of your—your background—"

"My religious persuasion," Kleinberg helped him.

"They won't trust you because you're a nonbeliever."

"Mr. Moore, apparently I have failed to penetrate your thick skull. If I had, you would understand that this is not a matter of religion. It is a matter of science."

"It *is* a matter of religion," Reggie snapped. "My wife was saved by an absolute miracle, and one incompetent doctor isn't going to make things different. Good-night to you, Dr. Kleinberg, and thanks for nothing."

He swung his barrel of a body around, stepped down into the street, and stormed off.

Kleinberg sat very still, thinking. He was sorry for the poor lady from London. If her husband didn't give a damn about her welfare, then it was his own duty, as a doctor, as her doctor, to do something about her fatal illness. He would do something tomorrow, take the whole affair into his own hands.

He reached for the lukewarm cup of tea. He needed a drink very much. But this wasn't it. He needed something much stronger. He picked up the check, put it down with some francs atop it, rose to his feet and started for the hotel and the hotel bar.

It had been an unexpectedly long evening for Gisele Dupree, yet despite the agonizing suspense, she had not minded the drawn-out prelude to what could be a high point of her life. She had likened the delay to one of those evenings in New York when she had gone to bed with Charles Sarrat and they had made love. She had wanted the pleasure of release immediately, yet had savored the extended buildup knowing that the climax would come and it would be all the more welcome and pleasurable for the waiting.

It was this kind of buildup that she had enjoyed through the long evening. Only she had not been positive that it would end in the desired climax.

Leaving the taxi and entering her borrowed apartment near the domain, she had relived the buildup.

Having finished guiding her Irish pilgrims around Lourdes, Gisele had routinely checked into the travel bureau office to turn in the money received and to learn if she was on call for a nighttime tour, which was rarely the case. But this time there was a nighttime tour on tap, a pilgrimage of two dozen Japanese Catholics, and the group was assigned to Gisele. This tour was to begin sharply at eight o'clock and finish at ten.

At first, Gisele had tried to talk her way out of the assignment, since it got in the way of her own plans. But her talking got her nowhere. Not another guide was available for those hours, and the Japanese pilgrims could not be disappointed. Moreover, they were paying the agency at the special evening rate, a sum too profitable for Gisele's employer to consider rejecting.

The one important thing for Gisele to know before she collected her Japanese tour, was how late the press office would be open after eight o'clock. She had been promised the fateful pictures from *Paris-Match* at eight o'clock, and she would be unable to pick them up until after ten. She had telephoned Michelle Demaillot at the press office, and prayed it would be open late. Michelle herself had answered, and told her not to worry, the press office was staying open until eleven throughout this busy week. And yes, Michelle added, she had spoken to her friend at *Paris-Match* and he had promised to bring some Tikhanov pictures to Lourdes. He would drop them off at the press office when he came in from the airport. "So they should be here, Gisele, don't worry. I won't be here—I'm going to Madame Moore's Miracle Restaurant for drinks and a bite—but my assistant will have the pictures for you."

Relieved, less resentful of her overtime assignment, Gisele had rushed out to get something into her stomach before going to work. It was too late for a real dinner, but there was time for a heated brioche and coffee in a café to carry her over until she could cook something for herself at Dominique's apartment after her job was done.

Now, at nearly ten-thirty in the evening, the climactic moment was nearing. She set down the precious manila envelope that she had picked up at the press office—she had not examined its contents until she could be in the privacy of Dominique's dining room—and sought the key to the apartment in the navy leather purse dangling from her shoulder.

She found the key, and retrieving the manila envelope, she let herself into the seclusion of the apartment.

Hungry as she was, Gisele put off any thought of food until she could satisfy a more urgent craving. To know if Samuel Talley and Sergei Tikhanov were one and the same.

Dropping the manila envelope and her purse on the dining room table, Gisele hastened into the bedroom where she kept the packet of pictures she had taken at the grotto. She had carefully placed them in her friend Dominique's drawerful of lingerie. Emptying the packet, Gisele found the snapshot of Talley without his fake mustache, and she brought it back to the dining room.

She settled into a chair and, with a clutch in her stomach, she unfastened the large manila envelope from *Paris-Match*. She pulled out the two pictures inside. They were enlarged black-and-white glossies, both head close-ups of the world renowned Soviet foreign minister. They were extremely sharp, and almost the same. But Sergei Tikhanov almost always looked the same in all photographs. The look could best be described as stony. Here he was in each—stony, etched from granite —the lined low brow, piercing eyes, bulbous nose, thin lips, upper lip with its brown wart, clean square jaw. The only difference between the photographs was that they had been taken a year apart, one last year outside the Élysées Palace in Paris, the other the year before inside a hall of the Albertina in Brussels. Since Tikhanov's face filled each photograph, the backgrounds were actually unidentifiable, except for the typed captions that explained the settings on the rear of each shot.

Gisele felt sure, but she had to *make* sure.

Lovingly, she laid the two enlarged photographs of Tikhanov a few inches apart on the table top, and then she reached for her snapshot of Talley near the grotto and carefully set it down between the two larger ones. She inspected the Paris photograph of Tikhanov and her own Lourdes snapshot of Talley. She examined the Brussels portrait of Tikhanov and her own Lourdes snapshot of Talley.

Her pulse raced.

All three, one and the same. Hair, forehead, eyes, nose, lip and wart, mouth, chin, all features alike and the same.

Professor Samuel Talley of New York and Minister Sergei Tikhanov of Moscow were one man.

If so, Gisele told herself once more, the snapshot of the Soviet foreign minister near the Lourdes grotto could be a scandal of such proportions in his homeland, that Tikhanov would pay anything to erase the evidence.

But being sure was not enough, Gisele knew. When you dealt in a possibility as sensational as this, you had to be positive.

After all, Gisele reminded herself, the world was populated by a fair number of look alikes. Two men, separated by a geographical distance, could appear to be the same man but might very well be two utterly different men. Occasionally, nature made its Xerox copies. Talley and Tikhanov could be to the eye as one, as if identical twins, yet be in fact two different individual human beings. Two different men who looked exactly the same? Or one man, the same man, playing a second role?

There was only one way to be positive: Find out if Professor Samuel Talley, instructor in Russian in the language department of Columbia University in New York City, really existed. Gisele knew beyond doubt that Sergei Tikhanov existed and was the foreign minister of the Soviet Union and a candidate for the premiership. But his look alike, Samuel Talley, an actual professor at Columbia University in New York, a professor and separate entity from the Soviet foreign minister?

If there was a Talley at Columbia, a real Talley who looked like this, then Gisele knew that it had all been an incredible coincidence, and that she had lost. The gate to freedom for her would remain closed.

On the other hand, if . . . she did not want to speculate further. She wanted the truth and she would find it soon enough.

She peered at the electric clock that rested on the polished bureau holding the table linens.

The hour was ten forty-six in the evening in Lourdes.

This translated to four forty-six in the afternoon in New York.

Too early. Her old United Nations friend, Roy Zimborg, would still be hard at work. He would not be back in his apartment until six. Tempted as she was to phone him at the UN, she repressed her desire. You don't take a person away from an important job to ask a favor. You would want them in a relaxed mood. Nice as Roy Zimborg was, she still had to be considerate.

Gisele decided to restrain herself, wait until it was midnight here and six in the evening in New York. That would be a sensible hour to ring Roy long-distance at home.

To hurry the time between now and midnight, she had to occupy herself, do something, distract herself. She did not want to dwell any further on the future. She would contain herself until the future became a reality. Dinner, that was something to do. She would busy herself with dinner although she was no longer hungry.

For an hour Gisele puttered about the kitchen, cooking, preparing dinner, carrying it into the dining room, trying to eat slowly, her attention always given to the three photographs spread on the table.

When she had finished eating, had washed the dishes and put them away, it was still fifteen minutes before midnight and she could not contain herself any longer. She would call Roy Zimborg in New York, and pray that he was already home from work.

Five minutes later, when she had his breathless voice on the line, she knew that he had arrived just as the phone began ringing.

"Roy," she repeated, "it's Gisele—Gisele Dupree—calling from France. Roy, I'm so glad I caught you in."

"Gisele, by God, no kidding? What time is it? Lemme see. Yeah, ten to six. Well, just walked through the door and heard the phone. I had to run for it." He exhaled. "Hey, Gisele, it's really you? That's great. Where are you?"

"Still in Lourdes, still the girl guide. What about you?"

Distantly, Zimborg exhaled noisily again, as if to regularize his breathing. "Me? At the UN, still with the U.S. delegation. No change. Who else would want a French into English translator?"

"I may be joining you one day soon at the UN, like old times."

"That would be great!"

"Well, it's not certain yet, Roy, but there's a good possibility of getting out of here. First, I'd have to go to the translator's school in Paris. Then I'll probably be able to get a job with the French delegation to the UN. But before that I've got to have enough money to go to the translator's school. There's a chance I can get it all at once, without waiting forever. There might be an angel who'll sponsor me."

"Oh, yeah?"

"An American academic, seems prosperous, who is here in Lourdes right now. He's taken a special interest in me. I want to ask you a favor, Roy. It's about this man."

"Anything I can do, just name it," said Zimborg.

"It has to do with Columbia University. If I remember correctly, you graduated from Columbia, didn't you?"

"With honors, sweetie."

"While you were there, did you ever have or know or hear about a member of the faculty named Professor Samuel Talley?"

"Spell it, the last name."

Gisele spelled it out.

"That's Talley, Samuel Talley," said Zimborg. "No, it doesn't ring a bell. Why do you want to know?"

"This man I met, Professor Samuel Talley, claims to be in the language department of Columbia University."

"Could be," said Zimborg. "There are a million professors and associates at Columbia. I just may not have heard of this particular one. Or he may have come on since my time. After all, I haven't been at Columbia for some years."

"Do you still have any connections at the school, Roy?"

"You mean contacts? Someone I know? I know a number of faculty members quite well, now that I'm a bigshot at the UN. I see them for lunch, dinner, well, at least a couple of times a year."

"Would it be imposing on you, Roy, to ask if you could get in touch with one of your contacts at Columbia tomorrow? It would be sort of complicated for me to call Columbia directly. But if you could—"

"No problem whatsoever. What do you want to know? You want to know about this Professor Talley?"

"Exactly. I want to know if Talley's there, as he says he is."

"Hold on a sec, Gisele. Lemme get a piece of paper and a pencil, so's to be sure I've got it right. Just hold on." She held on briefly, and then heard his voice again. "Hi, Gisele. Okay, give it to me slowly once more."

"I want to know if currently, or recently, there is or was a Professor Samuel Talley in the language department at Columbia University. He has an apartment in Manhattan, and a permanent residence in Vermont. I just want to verify that he is who he says he is, and is on the faculty at Columbia. Can you do that?"

"No sweat, honey. I can find out at lunchtime. I'll call you with the info. When should I call you?"

"Let's see, the time difference is six hours. When it is one in the afternoon in New York, it is—what?—it is seven in the evening in Lourdes tomorrow. Can you call me at one tomorrow your time? I'm at someone's apartment. I'll give you the number. It is right in Lourdes. The phone number is 62-34.53.53. Do you have it?"

"Got it," chirped Zimborg. "I'll be back to you with all the dope during my lunch break."

"That's a real favor, Roy. Now I owe you one. Anything I can do for you, Roy, let me know. Whatever you want."

"Do you still look like you used to look, sweetie?"

"Of course, the same. Maybe better."

"Then you know what I want."

She grinned at the mouthpiece of the phone. "Just help me get there," she said, "and you've got it."

Mikel Hurtado had patiently waited until it was nearly midnight before leaving the hotel to visit the grotto one last time. Hopefully, at this late hour, the last of the pilgrims would be gone and asleep, and the police would have lifted their intensive security and abandoned the area. He would have plenty of time in which to climb the hillside beside the grotto, assemble his equipment, wire it to the dynamite, plant the dynamite behind the statue of the Virgin Mary in the niche—and then set the timer for the explosion and be off and far away before it blasted sky-high.

During his short walk to the ramp, his purpose was undimmed, tinged only with one regret.

Less than an hour ago he had finished sleeping with Natale, making passionate love to her, for the second time this day. The last coupling had been incredible, perfect, and when he left her sound asleep in bed, it pained him to see her there, in innocent repose, so giving and trusting—it pained him not only because he was going off to destroy an object of veneration that she held so holy, but because in departing the town in the night he might never see her again. It was a terrible thing to do to her, and to himself as well, but all the way to the ramp he did not falter. It had to be done.

At the top of the ramp to the domain, there was no one in sight except the goddam police. They were there again this night, not as many as before, but still there, three of them standing around talking and smoking.

But this time he was not daunted. He had nothing to hide or to be afraid of. Just one more pilgrim, one with insomnia, who wanted to go below and offer up more fervent prayers.

Hurtado limped along, traversing the street, and nonchalantly approaching the lawmen. When he was almost abreast of the police, the tallest of them stepped to one side to size him up. Hurtado gave a quick smile and short wave, and continued down the ramp. The policeman neither bothered to stop him nor call out to him. Good sign.

Hurtado went on down the ramp to the Rosary Esplanade, then veered around the church toward the grotto.

He strode hastily, and suddenly the grotto was in view and so were the benches in rows before it. On one of the rear benches sat two uniformed and armed policemen, chatting away.

They did not see him, but he could see them, and they looked like they would be there until dawn.

Hurtado cursed under his breath.

Impossible. When would those goddam bloodhounds be tired of their unremitting surveillance and be through with it? When would they give up and go back to their normal duties and leave him alone? Again, he cursed them—and Augustin Lopez.

Turning away, he hiked wearily back up the ramp to the street and the hotel.

Entering the reception lobby, wondering how he could find out when the domain would be free of security and he would have an all-clear, he saw Yvonne seated behind the reception counter. She wasn't dozing. She was reading a book. He reminded himself that it had been Yvonne who had unwittingly and originally alerted him to the police search for a terrorist. She'd had the tip from a girl friend who was bedding down with Fontaine, the superintendent of the Lourdes police. Possibly, now, she would know more and not mind repeating it.

Hurtado wandered over to the reception desk.

"Hi, Yvonne," he said. He took out his cigarette package and shook one free. "Want to have one?"

"No, thanks, but I appreciate your thoughtfulness." She put a marker in her book. "When do you ever get sleep?"

"I felt like going to the grotto tonight and praying by myself. But no use. Police all over the place. I don't like company when I'm praying. So I just gave up. It's just no use. They're there every night. When are they going to give up this security crap?"

Yvonne put down her book, and came to him. She leaned over, whispering. "They're giving it up."

"They are?"

"You'll soon have the whole grotto to yourself to pray as long as you want to."

"When's that happening?"

"The police are giving it two more days and nights. Then they're calling it quits. They're lifting super security and going back to normal on Saturday. Inspector Fontaine told my friend that the phone tip was probably from some crackpot anyway. And he's tired of keeping his force on overtime, and overworked. You know, we're not supposed to say, but the police really have their hands full at those campsites out of town—you know, where all the people who couldn't get rooms in Lourdes are staying. You'd think people coming to see the Blessed Mother would behave better, wouldn't you? Anyway, my friend said Inspector Fontaine threatened to call in the soldiers if he couldn't pull his men off crackpot duty. If nothing happens tomorrow or the day after, he's pulling everyone off the special shift the day after that. So that's my word for you."

Hurtado bent over the counter and kissed Yvonne on the cheek. "Thanks for good tidings," he said "When I get down there again, I promise to say an extra prayer for you. Good-night."

He limped to the elevator, disgruntled that he would have to wait for two more days, but happy that the deed could finally be done. There was one benefit in the delay. He could be with Natale that much longer.

12

Thursday, August 18

Throughout the day Gisele Dupree had led her two tours about Lourdes like a somnambulist. Her mind was in faraway New York trying to imagine the progress or lack of progress that her faithful friend Roy Zimborg was making. Sometimes her mind floated back to Lourdes, to some fringe of the town where her prey, her Dr. Jekyll and Mr. Hyde, her Dr. Talley and Mr. Tikhanov, was innocently (but secretly) going about his rites for self-rejuvenation.

When the second tour had ended, and as she rested in the agency for the third tour to begin, Gisele had begun to display signs of a migraine headache. No Rachel or Bernhardt could have matched her subdued histrionics. At last, knowing that a replacement tour guide was available, she had begged off further work, insisting that the pain behind her forehead was excruciating and that she must take medication and go to bed.

Once released, she had staggered out to the first available taxi, and had directed it to Dominique's apartment beyond the domain.

Safe in the living room of the apartment at last, with plenty of time before the crucial long-distance call was to come, her simulated migraine had happily disappeared. She had sat next to the telephone, and willed it to ring.

The appointed time had come with no ring. The appointed time had gone. Still no ring.

And now, almost a half hour later, she was beginning to suffer a real headache, one formed of tension and fading hopes.

Then, like a clarion call, the phone rang out.

Automatically, Gisele stumbled to her feet to take it, realized the telephone was beside her, and sat down hard, snatching the receiver from the cradle.

As if through a wind tunnel, she heard dear Roy Zimborg speaking, distinctly enough, from the far-off land of spacious skies and amber fields of gold. "Gisele? This is Roy. Can you hear me?"

"Loud and clear," Gisele half shouted from outer space.

"Sorry to be late, but—"

"Never mind, Roy. Just tell me if you found out anything."

"I really tried my best, Gisele, but I'm afraid you're going to be disappointed."

Gisele's heart sank to her stomach.

She did not want to hear, but said, "Tell me."

"I made calls to my faculty friends at Columbia. I had them call me back. I even used an early lunch break to trek out to the school to do some research digging myself. As I said, I'm sorry to disappoint you. That fellow in Lourdes who told you he's Professor Samuel Talley in the language department at Columbia University—he's lying. He's just trying to put the make on you. I hate to give you bad news—"

Gisele regarded the telephone as if it were the Kohinoor, just handed her on Christmas morning. For the moment she was unable to handle such riches. She wanted to kiss Roy for the Kohinoor, but it would be too long and too difficult to explain the truth. So she kept controlled, her voice feigning disappointment as she hid her wild elation.

She interrupted his consolations. "You mean there is no Professor Talley at Columbia University."

"Nobody on the faculty by that name. There is no Talley on the staff of Columbia. There is no such person teaching there, and there never has been. The person you met, the man you're involved with, he's either pretending or simply pulling your leg."

"The bastard," blurted Gisele, which was realistic and ambiguous enough.

"I'm sorry—" Zimborg's far-off voice tried to soothe her again.

"Never mind, Roy," she said, recovering. "I'll live. I'll live to see you and thank you properly in person."

"I wish it had worked out."

"You've done your part, and I appreciate it. You're a love, and I can't wait to see you. I'll write you when I'm coming to New York."

"I hope it's soon, Gisele."

"Somehow, real soon, I promise you, Roy."

After she'd hung up on him, she realized that she was smiling like an idiot and that her heart had risen from her stomach to its familiar and happier cage.

God, this was wonderful.

No more uncertainty. There was no Talley. There was only Tikhanov. There was Tikhanov here and in Lourdes and at her mercy.

Now to nail him.

Relishing what came next, she brought the Lourdes telephone book to her lap, thumbed through it until she found the telephone number for the Hôtel de la Grotte. Dialing, she wondered if she should ask to be connected to Samuel Talley's room, but decided against that. She wanted no confrontation on the telephone. She preferred to present her terms to Talley in person. It would be more threatening, more effective. She would meet with him in his room, if he was in. She would find out if he was in.

When the switchboard operator answered, Gisele asked to speak to her friend, Gaston, at the receptionist's desk.

"Reception desk," she heard Gaston say.

"Gaston, this is Gisele Dupree. How are you?"

"Gisele, dear. Never better. And you?"

"Fine. I'd like to know if one of your guests is in, the one we found the room for. You know. Mr. Samuel Talley, of New York. Is he in?"

"One moment, I can tell you." A pause. "Yes, Gisele, his key is not here. He must have it and be in his room. You want me to put you through?"

"No. I prefer to see him. I'll drop by."

Hanging up, she came to her feet, grabbed her purse, and was out the door in less than a minute.

Emerging from the apartment building, she sought a taxi. Not one was in sight. She knew that there was a taxi stand two blocks away. She made for it in quick strides. There were three taxies lined up at the curb. The familiar driver in the first one hailed her with a greeting, and started the motor as Gisele opened the rear door and climbed in.

"Hôtel de la Grotte," she ordered him breathlessly. "Make it fast, Henri."

"At your service, Gisele."

Ten minutes later they swung into the blacktop driveway and pulled up before the blue and orange awning of the white stucco hotel.

Unlatching the rear door, Gisele said, "Keep your meter going, Henri. I'll need you to go back. I won't be long."

The driver pointed off to the parking lot below and alongside the hotel. "I'll park down there."

"Be right back," she called, and hurried under the awning to the glass entrance door and pushed it open. With growing confidence, she went down the hall past the lobby and started for the elevators, which were beyond the reception desk. At the desk Gaston was taking a room key from a male guest and speaking to him.

Gisele was going past the two men when she caught a glimpse of the guest turning away to go to the hotel entrance. She recognized him immediately. The Slavic face and flowing fake mustache belonged to the estimable Samuel Talley, the professor who never was.

She skidded to a halt, put a finger to her lips so that Gaston would not address her, and pivoted to sneak up on her quarry. She fell in behind her ambulatory gold mine, matching him step for step as he moved to the door.

Suddenly, she spoke. "Mr. Tikhanov," she called out.

He stopped so abruptly that she almost collided with his back. She retreated a step and waited. He had not moved an inch. He stood very still.

She wondered if he was shocked to the roots and trying to recover his composure.

"Mr. Tikhanov," she repeated mercilessly.

Because there was no denying that he was the one being addressed, he slowly wheeled around, feigning surprise. "Oh, it's you, Miss Dupree? Were you calling me by some other name? You must have thought I was someone else."

Wearing her most innocent expression, Gisele shook her head and her blond ponytail gently. "No, I was not mistaken. It was you I wanted. Perhaps I should have addressed you more correctly as Foreign Minister Sergei Tikhanov. Now do I have it right?"

He made an effort at exasperation. "Miss Dupree, you know my name very well. We've spent enough time together. What kind of nonsense game is this?"

"I think in most countries, even yours, it is called the truth game. I suggest you play it with me. I'd like a word with you, Mr. Tikhanov."

He was beginning to show irritation. "Unless you stop calling me by that ridiculous name—I won't speak to you any further."

"I think you'd better, for your own sake," said Gisele. "I think we should sit down for a minute and talk. Please follow me."

"Really, Miss Dupree—" he protested. "I must get to dinner."

But she went back down the hall, and she knew that he was following her. She continued, without slowing, past the reception desk, and then said over her shoulder, "There's a nice little lounge here. We can have a lovely tête-à-tête in privacy."

She entered the small blue lounge as he caught up with her. He was protesting again. "Miss Dupree, I have no time to humor your foolishness. I—"

Ignoring him, she went directly to an armchair, and plumped herself down into it, reaching to draw a second armchair closer to her own. Imperiously, she gestured toward the seat beside her, and reluctantly he took it.

"You want to know what this is all about," she said in a low voice. "Now I will tell you with no embellishments. Please listen and don't interrupt. I told you once that I had worked at the United Nations. There I saw you up close briefly. I was with the French ambassador, Charles Sarrat. When you came to Lourdes at the beginning of the week, I did not recognize you. But when I was taking some photographs at the grotto last Monday, I saw you and happened to take some pictures of you just as your mustache fell off, after the baths. When I compared this snapshot of you with the photograph of you in the newspaper, and some I have seen from a magazine file, I could see that the picture of Samuel Talley near the grotto and the pictures of Sergei Tikhanov were one and the same. Now you know I know—"

"A mere happenstance," he broke in, with a short laugh. "My resemblance to Tikhanov has been remarked upon before. Every one of us has a Doppelgänger, a look alike, somewhere in the world."

"I wanted to be sure I'd made no mistake," resumed Gisele, relentlessly, "so I decided to check on the person you claim to be. I telephoned New York to inquire about the status of Professor Samuel Talley, a faculty member of Columbia University." She barely paused. "I had my reply from New York not an hour ago. There is no Professor Talley at Columbia, and there never has been. But assuredly, most assuredly, there is a Minister Sergei Tikhanov in Lourdes, France—the foreign minister, and soon to be premier, of the leading atheistic nation on earth, now begging for health at the shrine of the most Holy Blessed Virgin. I tell myself—that is incredible. I also tell myself—it need be only between us, the two of us, if you wish it so, if you are ready to be reasonable."

Gathering up her purse, she studied his drained face, and she rose to her feet with cool poise.

Never taking her eyes off him, she said, "If you want my print of the photograph of you, and the negative, and my silence, you must pay the fair market price for my initiative and cleverness. After all, as you know, I am only a poor working girl who wants to live—and let live. If you will bring yourself and $15,000 to my apartment—an apartment I'm temporarily using—at eleven o'clock tomorrow morning, you will find me there waiting to conclude our exchange. Here, I will leave you the address and apartment number." She took a slip of paper from her purse and offered it to him. He ignored it. She placed the slip on the table behind her.

"If you have the money in cash," she resumed, "it must be in francs, dollars, or pounds. If it is too much to expect you to carry around such a sum in cash, you may pay by a cashier's check on a Paris, New York, or London bank. If that can't be done, then mail me the sum in cash next week, and give me a place where I can send you the pictures and negatives. What do you say to that, Mr. Tikhanov?"

He sat Sphinx-like, both of his hands spread flat on the arms of his chair. His flinty face was raised toward hers. "What do I say, Miss Dupree? I say you are quite insane. I am not coming to your apartment at eleven tomorrow morning or at any other time. I will not allow myself to be frightened by your fiction—not frightened or blackmailed. If you expect me to submit to this madness of yours, you can wait till hell freezes over."

A tough bastard, the foreign minister, she thought, as hard as a rock. But she was certain that there was a fissure in that seeming solidity.

"Up to you," she said cheerfully. "It's your grave—to avoid or to dig. Be my guest."

Feeling good, feeling victorious, after the encounter with Tikhanov, and free of an engagement to lead another tour, Gisele had requested that her taxi driver make a detour to the photo shop. There she had picked up another package of prints of her tourists, then hopped back into the taxi and told Henri he could now take her to Dominique's apartment.

As they drove toward the domain, slowed by the evening traffic, Gisele spotted someone familiar eating in one of the outdoor cafés. Squinting through the rear window, she made out the mop of orange hair that could only belong to Liz Finch.

As Liz slid from view, and the taxi proceeded on its course, Gisele had a sudden thought.

The probability that she had been victorious in her meeting with Tikhanov was still likely, but yet not entirely certain. One shadow of a doubt had cast itself over her encounter. While she did not wish especially to expose the Russian leader—her only interest was obtaining money from him—there was always the faint possibility that Tikhanov might stand firm. He was a man of peculiar character, on the surface inflexible, and he might decide not to give in to her demand for money but instead risk having his abberation of behavior publicized, feeling that he was powerful enough to ride out any storm. Gisele believed that he would not hazard exposure, yet his stubbornness might induce him to stonewall it, another one of her favorite American expressions.

If, by chance, her prospects of getting money from Tikhanov fell through, she would be left with an empty victory, with merely the knowledge that she had destroyed a Soviet leader. In that case, she would want the money from another source, and having just fleetingly seen Liz Finch, she realized that there remained a second source.

Conjuring up her first meeting with Liz Finch last Saturday, Gisele remembered that Liz had spoken of a big story, possibly an exposé of Bernadette's veracity. When Gisele, knowing the impossibility of undermining the honesty of Bernadette, the very foundation of Lourdes, had inquired if anything else might qualify as a big story, she recalled Liz Finch's reply: *Thousands of people from all over the world have been pouring into Lourdes, and more will come tomorrow for the Virgin's encore. Maybe some of them will be newsworthy, and crazy things will happen to them. There could be a story there, too, that would be worth considerable money. Mind you, it would have to be a big story.*

It struck Gisele at once that she had what Liz Finch wanted.

The foreign minister of the Soviet Union in Lourdes for a cure by the Virgin Mary.

Certainly there couldn't be many bigger stories.

Liz Finch, Gisele realized, could be her life insurance. If Tikhanov, himself, failed to come through, there would be Liz to come up with the money.

Her mind made up, Gisele determined not to pass over this opportunity. Leaning forward, she tapped her taxi driver on the shoulder.

"Henri, I think I saw someone a few blocks back that I'd like to speak to for a minute or two. You can find a place to turn around, can't you?"

Nodding, the driver swung his car into the first side street, made a short U-turn, and drove down into the main thoroughfare and began to cover the distance they had already traveled. "Where to?" he wanted to know.

"I think it was the Café au Roi Albert," said Gisele, peering out the window and hoping that Liz Finch had not already left.

Then she saw the mop of orange hair once more, and felt relieved.

"You can let me off here, Henri," said Gisele. "Find a place to park somewhere. I'll just be a little while."

Negotiating the foot traffic in the street, Gisele could see that Liz Finch was quite alone, relaxed in a red wicker chair, munching away at a plate of *pommes frites* and sipping an iced Coca-Cola. What ghastly eating habits Americans had, Gisele thought, but she knew that she loved them nevertheless.

"Hi, Miss Finch," Gisele greeted her.

Liz looked up. "It's you. How've you been?"

"Busy as usual." Gisele pulled back a chair. "Mind if I join you for a minute?"

"Please do," said Liz. "Just having an hors d'oeuvre before dinner. Want some?"

"No, thanks," said Gisele. "How's it been going for you? Found any big stories yet?"

Liz shook her head dolefully. "Not a damn thing, nothing but pious hymn singers in this goddam dull village. I'm just hanging around the whole eight days until someone shouts hallelujah, I've seen the Virgin Mary, which seems to me most unlikely at this point. I can't wait to get back to Paris empty-handed and be fired."

"Be fired?"

"That's something else. Forget it." She held a French fry high and dropped it into her mouth. "How about you? Got any hot scoops for little Liz?"

"As a matter of fact, I may have. I thought I should have a word with you, Miss Finch."

"Oh, yeah?" Liz stopped eating and sat up. "You've come across something?"

"I think I have, maybe," Gisele said with great earnestness. "I was remembering, when we first met, you advised me to keep my eyes open for a big story. You told me if I found one, well, it might be worth a lot of money, and your syndicate would willingly pay. Is that correct?"

"It's true." Liz was alert now. "What have you got?"

"Well, Miss Finch, I may be on the verge of obtaining such a story—"

"And you're sure this is a big one? No diddling smalltown crap?"

"Miss Finch, I promise you, this is not merely a big one. It is a big, big one. The biggest, and with international overtones." She paused. "Are you interested?"

"You know I'm interested in any real news, anything super big that you can authenticate. It's not about Bernadette, is it?"

"No. More timely."

Liz pressed forward. "Okay, go on."

"It'll have to wait overnight. I'll know tomorrow if you can have it."

Liz sat back. "If it works out, if I decide it is that important, if you can prove it—all right, how much?"

"In your money, $15,000."

Liz emitted a low whistle. "You're not kidding around, I can see. You're sure this one is worth that much?"

"Maybe it is worth more, but $15,000 would satisfy me."

"I won't deny that's a lot of money, Gisele, but if the story is really a blockbuster, and you have the goods to support it, I could certainly get API to pay for it. You said you'd know tomorrow. How will I know when you have it available?"

Gisele took an agency card from her purse and wrote on it. She handed the card to Liz and stood up. "That's my phone number and address. It's a girl friend's apartment I'm staying at. Call me at noon tomorrow. I'll tell you if you have it."

"I'll be calling. Fingers crossed, for both of us."

Another Americanism Gisele adored. She smiled. "Yes, fingers crossed—until then."

Striding away, toward her driver on the corner, she felt giddy about her prospects. Now not one buyer, but two.

It was in the bag, as Roy Zimborg used to say.

Having heard in the press tent that Liz Finch had gone off to a café, Amanda Spenser was proceeding up the street, searching in every café for her. Then, at last, she saw Liz up ahead sitting at a sidewalk table with some young woman. The young woman was rising, leaving, and Amanda quickened her pace to catch Liz before she left, too.

Amanda reached the table just as Liz was cleaning up the last of her French fries.

"I'm glad I found you, Liz. I was looking everywhere for you."

"Well, this must be old home week," said Liz. "Sit down, sit down. What's on your mind?"

Amanda tentatively took a chair. "I have an appointment with Father Ruland in half an hour. I thought maybe you'd like to come along."

"I've been keeping Ruland busy myself. But anyway, what are you seeing him about?"

"Bernadette's journal. What we heard about it from Sister Francesca in Nevers yesterday. I'd like to delve into the matter of the journal a little deeper, find out more about how the church acquired it—how the church was able to be sure of its absolute authenticity—"

"Forget it," said Liz. "It's authentic all right. Like I told you before. You can be sure the church wouldn't lead with its chin unless it knew it had the goods."

"How can you be so certain?"

"Because," said Liz, "I don't let any grass grow under my feet. I met with Father Ruland on that very point early this morning. He dragged out the actual journal Bernadette had kept, the one in which she had confided the Virgin Mary's secrets. Then he displayed the various certifications of authenticity."

"Like putting it through the carbon-14 dating process?"

"No, not that—that's for ancient papers, parchment, papyrus— Bernadette's journal wasn't old enough to require that kind of test. It was much simpler, really. There were many specimens of Bernadette's handwriting around. The journal script has been compared to those by any number of prominent handwriting experts. There were also numerous other tests made—overkill really—the use of ultra-violet lamp, chemical analysis of the pigments in the ink, close studies by scholars of the style or language usage in the journal, to be positive it jibed with the style and language usage in Bernadette's previous writings, for example, her letters. No, you're wasting your time, Amanda. On authenticity, the church has an airtight case. I think we'd both better drop our researches on Bernadette."

Amanda stiffened. "You can, but I'm not ready to, not yet. Even if it is authentic, I want to know more about the journal, how the church acquired it, and from whom, and whatever else I can find out. Maybe I'll stumble on something, some lead, that'll bring Ken to his senses."

"I can only wish you good luck. For my part, I'm finished with that journal. I'm just going to sit here and wait for the apparition."

"Very well," said Amanda, annoyed. "From here on in, I'll go it alone."

They were in a quiet, plain room of the Rosary Basilica, in a sparsely furnished room that Father Ruland had identified as his office. Because Ruland was so open, so generous and cooperative, Amanda made every effort not to let him know that she was a doubter. But she perceived that he was an insightful and sophisticated man, well-versed in the understanding of human nature, and she guessed that he was aware of her doubts from the outset of their meeting.

She sat at an antique wooden table in the middle of the office, and he brought exhibits of Bernadette memorabilia from a fireproof wall

safe to impress her. And to cooperate with her on the article about
Bernadette that she had told him she was writing for a psychology
journal. Ruland's exhibits were mostly paper objects, scraps of paper,
letters, documents with writings in Bernadette's hand, as well as records
of the events at the grotto and of talks between Bernadette and various
neighbors and officials of Lourdes who had been witnesses in the year of
the apparitions and the years that followed.

"But foremost of all, you are interested in Bernadette's last journal,
the one that revealed the most dramatic and exciting of the Virgin
Mary's three secrets, and the one that brought about this Reappearance
Time," Father Ruland had said, carrying the journal from the safe and
laying it down before Amanda. "There it is, our treasure. You may have
a look inside for yourself. With care, of course, great care."

"I'm afraid to touch it," said Amanda. "Do you mind opening it,
Father?"

"A pleasure, believe me, Mrs. Clayton," said Father Ruland coming around the table. When he had bent down beside her, his handsome
and imposing presence and his worldly assurance had briefly dwarfed
Amanda's doubts, had made them seem niggling and foolish. Nevertheless, she had remained attentive.

He had pulled the leather-bound folio from its slipcase, and opened
it, spreading the pages before Amanda.

Now she was examining two of the pages, and the old-fashioned
and slanted script gave Bernadette a reality that she had not possessed
for Amanda earlier, not even at Nevers.

"Why, I can read this," Amanda said. "It's in French."

"What did you expect?" inquired Ruland.

"I'd been told she usually wrote in some native *patois* or village
dialect that no one—"

"Ah, yes, Mrs. Clayton, that much is true. She was brought up
speaking not a dialect but a special language of the Pyrenees. But by the
time she wrote this version of the events as a nun in Nevers, she had
learned the fundamentals of the French language. You know, to satisfy
many people after 1858, Bernadette made a number of accounts in
writing of her experience at the grotto, some for clergymen, others for
journalists and historians. This account was the last one she set down
on paper, to make a chronology of what happened to her one final time
before memory of the apparitions escaped her and before her serious
illness would make writing impossible."

"I'd like to know more about the journal, Father Ruland."

"I'm delighted with your interest," the priest said, closing the
bound journal, and pressing it back into its slipcase. He went to the wall

safe, deposited the precious journal and the other memorabilia inside it, shut the door, twirled the knob to lock it, and returned to the table, sitting down across from Amanda. "I'll tell you whatever you want to know."

"I've been wondering how you found the journal."

"By chance. Well, not exactly. I've been fascinated by Bernadette all my life, ever since my seminary days. There was little I did not know about her. Along the way, I began to suspect that Bernadette had completed a chronological journal of the high points in her life. There was evidence that she had undertaken such a journal, between bouts of illness, at the Convent of Saint-Gildard. But I had not been able to prove that such a journal had ever been completed or, indeed, if it had, to learn what had happened to it. The superior general at Saint-Gildard knew, of course, of my interest. Then, about two years ago, a bit more, I heard from her. In preparing for a public exhibit of Bernadette's written corpus, in gathering artifacts related to her life, the copy of a letter was found addressed to Basile Laguës, a farmer in the village of Bartrès near here."

"I've heard about Bartrès," said Amanda.

"Bernadette had written Laguës in French, then realized he might not be able to read it and she had rewritten the letter in the patois of Bigorre, the local language we spoke about. The original version of the letter, the French one, was found among Bernadette's papers. She'd written the letter in 1878, the year before her death, to tell the Laguës family, principally the elder Laguës, who was Basile, that she had finished a journal and was sending it to them as a memento and appreciation of their life together."

Amanda's brow had furrowed. "The Laguës family?"

"The relationship between Bernadette and the Laguës family played an important role in Bernadette's life," said Father Ruland. "Marie and Basile Laguës were a young couple, industrious farmers in Bartrès, to the north of Lourdes. Bernadette's father owned a mill at the time, and the Laguës were among his customers. Shortly after Bernadette was born in 1844, her mother, Louise, had an accident. A burning candle fell from the fireplace mantel and set fire to the bodice of her dress. She suffered superficial burns on her breasts, but these were sufficient to make it impossible to breastfeed Bernadette. So she scouted about for an available wet-nurse. Just about that time, Marie Laguës in Bartrès lost her firstborn son, Jean, and she wanted another baby to suckle. She agreed to take in the infant Bernadette as a temporary foster child and breastfeed her for five francs a month. After Bernadette had been weaned, Marie Laguës did not want to give her up, but at last did so after nearly a year and a half. That was the beginning of the relationship between Bernadette and the Laguës family."

"When did she see them again?" asked Amanda.

"For one more period in 1857 and 1858 when Bernadette was thirteen," said Father Ruland. "By then things had worsened for the Soubirous family in Lourdes. Bernadette's father was doing poorly, unable to earn money. There were siblings, more mouths to feed. A cholera epidemic had almost taken Bernadette's life. There was a famine on the land. Meanwhile, the nearby Laguës family had survived and fared well. They owned a large property, many cows and sheep, and having a number of children by now, they were prepared to take on an additional servant. They agreed to accept Bernadette a second time. She would work as a mother's helper and shepherdess, and in return receive shelter, food, and an education. So Bernadette moved in with the Laguës family in Bartrès. It wasn't exactly an idyllic life. There wasn't much food on the table, although more than there had been in Lourdes. And Marie Laguës had developed a kind of love-hate relationship with Bernadette. She wanted her about, but was severe, difficult, sometimes mean. Also, she often treated Bernadette as a slave. Yet, there were compensations. The altitude and air in Bartrès were good for Bernadette's health. The girl enjoyed relaxing on the hillsides with the sheep, daydreaming and building toy altars and praying. Although her foster mother did little to educate her, Bernadette gained the affection of the local parish priest, a kindly man named Abbé Ader, who tried to help her."

"I heard that he tried to influence her interest in the Virgin Mary," Amanda dared to say.

"Ah, you heard that from Father Cayoux over in Cauterets, I imagine."

"I don't remember," Amanda lied.

"No matter." Father Ruland remained unconcerned. "We don't know how much influence Abbé Ader had on Bernadette. It is true that one day, watching Bernadette, he said aloud that if the Virgin Mary ever returned to earth again, the Blessed Lady would most likely appear before just such a simple peasant girl. But actual influence on her? We don't have any real evidence of that. Ader gave her catechism lessons, but soon that came to an end. He left Bartrès to take up a career in the Benedictine order, and not long afterward Bernadette told her parents that she was tired of Bartrès and wanted to come home to Lourdes, and she did, in January of 1858, after a stay of eight months in Bartrès."

"And just a month later in Lourdes," said Amanda, "Bernadette saw her first apparition of the Virgin Mary in the grotto at Massabielle."

"Yes," Father Ruland conceded. "Anyway, after she had gone off to be a nun at Nevers, Bernadette seemed to hold some kind of residue of affection for the Laguës and the interlude in Bartrès. Especially for Papa Laguës and his three surviving children. So one last time she set down on paper her recollections of the stirring and mystical events of her short life in a journal. Once the journal was completed, Bernadette, aware of her special standing in the eyes of the Church, decided to send it to the Laguës family as a keepsake and remembrance of her. Well, when I had this clue, I went to Bartrès in search of that journal, which I'm sure the Laguës had never read, since it was in French. Marie and Basile, the original possessors of it, had long been dead. But, after a persistent hunt, I was able to trace the odyssey of this journal. It had come down from relative to relative and finally fallen into the hands of a distant Laguës cousin."

"Who was the cousin?"

"A middle-aged widow in Bartrès named Eugénie Gautier, who lived with an adolescent nephew named Jean and who was his guardian. Yes, Madame Gautier had the musty old journal somewhere around. I doubt if she had ever read it. She had no interest in the long-gone Bernadette. Her entire devotion was to her growing nephew and his support. When I approached her and asked to see the journal, and suggested that I might want to purchase it as a relic for the Church, Madame Gautier put me off briefly until she could hastily read it. Then, for the first time coming across Bernadette's revelations of the secrets that she had heard from the Blessed Virgin, especially that in the near future the Virgin would be returning to Lourdes, Madame Gautier knew what a treasure she possessed, and I soon knew about it as well. The bargaining with her was difficult and took a considerable time. Her original demands were outrageous. But at last we effected a compromise and the church purchased the journal for a considerable sum of money. Madame Gautier was left well-to-do. In fact, she bought a new house, where she lives comfortably today."

Amanda's curiosity had heightened. "This journal, did you buy all of it? I understand there was an earlier section in which Bernadette recounted some of her earlier years?"

"We had wanted to purchase it all, of course. But our primary interest was in Bernadette's final recounting of the events at the grotto. So I studied that earlier section, and it did not offer much, merely the hardships of her growing up in Lourdes, something about her daily work as a shepherdess in Bartrès, but I would have acquired it just to keep our oeuvre complete. That proved impossible. Madame Gautier was reluctant to sell it. I think she wanted to keep that section of the journal as a memento for her nephew, because it recorded what life was like in the old days in Bartrès. It was unimportant. I had what I wanted —the electrifying knowledge that the Virgin Mary would return to Lourdes this year. Now I think you know everything I can tell you about our acquisition. I hope it will satisfy you for the psychology paper you plan to write."

"It is all wonderful," said Amanda. "You've given me everything I wanted." She prepared to leave. "I was just thinking. It might be fun to drive over to Bartrès and have a look around."

"There's not too much to see, but the town hasn't changed a great deal in a century and you might get a picture of the way of life in Bernadette's time."

"Yes, I'll drive there. Did you say—does Madame Gautier still live there?"

"She's there all right. I'm told she purchased a house not far from the Laguës' Maison Burg, which is now a museum in Bartrès."

"Do you think I could meet Madame Gautier?"

"I don't know," said Father Ruland, seeing Amanda to the door. "I found her a crusty and tart lady, and not exactly hospitable. I can't imagine she's changed much. But see what you can do with her. Good luck."

There was a call Dr. Paul Kleinberg was expecting from Paris before he could proceed further in the case of Edith Moore. The call he was waiting for would be from Dr. Maurice Duval, whose secretary had notified Kleinberg early this morning that Duval would be phoning him at eight-thirty in the evening.

Ignoring his restlessness, Kleinberg slouched in the armchair of his claustrophobic room in the Hôtel Astoria, trying to catch up on his reading of recently published medical papers (two by Duval himself), while keeping an eye on the clock. When the hands of the clock told him it was eight-thirty, he shifted his attention to the telephone on the table beside him, and was grateful when it rang immediately.

He took up the receiver, hoping it was his colleague and was pleased when he heard Duval's hurried, ebullient voice.

"That you, Paul?" Duval called out.

"It's I."

"Long time, too long," said Duval. "Last place I expected to hear from you was Lourdes. What on earth are you doing there?"

"Delving into a holy miracle," said Kleinberg.

Duval gave a barking laugh. "All miracles these days take place in geneticists' laboratories."

"Not too loud. Wouldn't want them to hear you in Lourdes. But as a matter of fact, that's why I wanted to speak to you, about the scientific miracles you've been performing."

"My favorite subject, Paul," said Duval. "What's on your mind?"

"I know you abandoned routine sarcoma surgery to concentrate on experiments in genetic replacement and engineering—"

"Let me revise that slightly," Duval interrupted. "I abandoned standard sarcoma surgery, yes—as being ineffective, or at least not effective enough—but I did not abandon my primary interest in sarcoma. I have been largely devoting myself to genetic experiments, but mainly in the area of sarcoma."

So far, so good, thought Kleinberg. "I'm acquainted with the reports, the papers you've published on your experiments on monkeys, rabbits, mice. They indicate great progress."

"Enormous progress," Duval corrected him, "enormous advances in the ability to replace diseased genes with healthy ones. In two papers this year—"

"I've just caught up on your most recent published work, Maurice, and I take your word for it that there have been incredible strides in gene-replacement techniques."

"You have my word," said Duval with total assurance.

"Very well. Let me go to the purpose of my call. I have three questions for you. If your answers are what I want, I'll have a fourth question. Are you ready?"

"Go ahead."

The first question was the feeler. He posed it. "Have you ever, at this stage in your progress, performed genetic modification and replacement for sarcoma in a human being?"

"No, not yet. But I have done other gene transplants successfully. Working in the area that Dr. Martin Cline pioneered in 1980 in California, I've treated persons afflicted with beta thalassemia—the blood disorder that is potentially fatal. I've conducted genetic-replacement experiments on these cases, introduced healthy genes into the defective cells, and I've had an extremely high rate of success."

"All right, my second question," said Kleinberg. "Could you undertake the same type of surgery in a sarcoma case?"

"Certainly. For some time I've been hoping to do so. It is the exact area I've been experimenting in. That is the final step I've been preparing for. I could do it."

"Third question. What would you predict would be your chances of success—a full recovery for the patient?"

"Presuming the patient is in an otherwise stable condition, why, I'd say chances for an effective surgery, a full recovery, would be seventy percent."

"That high?" with wonder.

"I'm conservative, Paul. Yes, at least that high."

"My last question was not my last question. It was merely a comment of surprise and, indeed, pleasure. Here is my fourth question. I guess the all-important one. Would you be willing to perform such an operation on a patient I have in my charge as soon as possible?"

"Why, you need only say when and I'd arrange my schedule somehow. Assuming I have the patient's unequivocal consent."

"I don't have that consent yet," Kleinberg admitted. "I wanted to speak to you first before speaking to the patient. Assuming I obtain consent, when would be the earliest you could proceed?"

"Where are we—what day is this?"

"Thursday," said Kleinberg.

"I'm busy, you know, but I'm always busy. Perhaps the weekend would be best. Perhaps even Sunday. Yes, that might be possible."

"Would it be an imposition to ask if you could come down to Lourdes for the surgery? It would be more convenient at this end."

"Lourdes? Why not? I've wanted to visit the place ever since I read Carrel."

"It's as unusual, perhaps as remarkable, as Carrel reported."

"I'd look forward."

"Now I've got to get the patient's consent. To be honest with you, Maurice, I'm not sure I can do that. But I'm going to try very hard. She's a seriously ailing woman, but for personal reasons there may be formidable resistance. However, let me see. Meanwhile, in the event I can persuade her, you'll want to know her case history in advance."

"Certainly."

"There's an extensive file on her covering five years, right up to my own tests and X rays yesterday. It is really a unique case. Of course, I hate to bother you with all this if we can't go ahead."

"No bother, no bother. I'm eager to review the history."

"Thank you. I think what I'll do is fly my nurse, Esther Levinson, back to Paris with the file. She can deliver it to your office in the morning."

"Excellent."

One thing continued to bother Kleinberg, and he toyed with bringing it up frankly or keeping it to himself. He decided to get it off his chest. "Just one thing—"

"Yes, Paul?"

"I wonder how you can be so confident about using gene replacement on a human being when you've never attempted it on a human before?"

There was a long pause on the other end. Dr. Duval, usually so quick and direct on all questions, did not seem ready to answer this one. The silence stretched, and Kleinberg waited.

"Well," said Dr. Duval at last, "I—I can answer your question to your satisfaction, but what I will say to you must be strictly between us. This is a serious secret I am about to tell you."

"I promise you, it is between us. You have my pledge."

"Good enough," said Dr. Duval. "Why am I so confident my gene replacement can work on a human being? I will tell you. Because it *has* worked on a human being—on three, to be exact. I lied to you earlier, saying I've experimented only on animals, never on a human. I did employ the procedure, gene replacement, on three terminally ill patients outside Paris eighteen months ago. Two were sarcoma cases. All of them not only survived, but today all of them are well and active."

Kleinberg was astounded. "My God, Maurice, I never dreamed—why, I congratulate you. Once this is known, you will be nominated for the Nobel Prize. What a giant breakthrough."

"Thank you, thank you, but it will never be known. If it becomes known that I acted without permission of the medical committees, the ethical committees, I will be severely punished. No, this procedure is not supposed to be ready for ten more years, maybe longer, while those committees weigh the propriety of using it on humans. When they give permission, then it can be done publicly. Meanwhile, a lot of good people, who could have been saved, are going to die. You understand, Paul, it's medical politics in the name of judicious caution."

"I understand."

"Initiative of the kind I have undertaken is not always appreciated. To mention our Dr. Cline in California once more. He used a recombinant molecule on one case in Naples and another in Jerusalem, and when it was found out, the U.S. National Institute cancelled all of his research grants. I think he lost $250,000 in support. I couldn't afford that."

"You needn't worry, Maurice. Our medical colleagues will never know why you went to Lourdes. I've gotten a great lift out of everything you've just told me. And I really appreciate your getting involved with this case on such short notice."

"Paul, believe me, this is another opportunity and a challenge. Mind you, and at the risk of repeating myself, it must all be done on the quiet. I don't even want to chance using any Lourdes hospital personnel. I prefer to get my assistants from among formers students I have in Lyons. So you see how cautious I have to be. Once again I say, I would find personal publicity disastrous. Since, for the fourth time, I'd be ignoring going through proper channels, there certainly would be a lot of noses out of joint, and it could cause me immeasurable harm and certainly the loss of most grants. Premature, the committees would insist. But you and I know that everything is premature until it is done."

"Your name will not be made public, Maurice."

"Let's hope it works out then."

"Let's hope. I'll be phoning you again with the final word."

Finishing his call, satisfied by it, his satisfaction was clouded by what must follow. Kleinberg picked up the phone and summoned Esther from next door.

When she came in, searching his face, he replied to her unspoken inquiry. "Duval will do it. But will Edith Moore? I'm surprised I haven't heard from her all day."

"Maybe husband Reggie never told her."

"I can't believe it. But maybe. Do you mind finding Mrs. Moore for me? If she's out to dinner, call her at the restaurant. Tell her I'd like to see her at the Medical Bureau soon as she's through with dinner."

"I'll get her number. It's in my room. If I remember, she's at the Hôtel Gallia & Londres. Let me see if I can get hold of her."

Kleinberg sat speculating about Mrs. Moore's case until he heard Esther's rap. He opened the door.

"I have her on the phone," Esther said. "She was in her room. She's not up to coming to the Medical Bureau tonight. She wonders if you'd mind seeing her at the hotel. She's not feeling well. She's lying down."

"Tell her I'll be right over."

Putting on his jacket, checking the contents of his medical bag, Kleinberg wondered if Edith Moore was not well because she'd heard the truth from her husband or because she was suffering a recurrence of her tumor.

In minutes he would know what had brought her down. But whichever it proved to be, the prospect of seeing her was not one of the medical duties to which he looked forward.

With an unhappy sigh, he left the room for his confrontation.

Edith Moore, fully dressed in her white blouse and navy blue skirt but in stockinged feet, lay atop the green bedspread of the double bed watching Dr. Kleinberg. Having examined her, he was standing at the table writing a prescription.

"Get this prescription filled," he said. "It'll give you some relief."

He brought a chair up beside the bed, handed her the prescription, and then loosened his jacket.

"What's wrong with me, doctor?" she wanted to know. "I haven't felt this weak in years."

"I'll get to that," said Kleinberg. He met her eyes. "You know, I had a talk with your husband about you."

"I knew you had a talk with him. I mean, I saw you leave the restaurant last night. But I thought it was social." She blinked. "About me? Why?"

"Then Mr. Moore hasn't told you about our conversation?"

The answer came slowly. "No, he hasn't."

"I thought it would be easier if he spoke to you first on my behalf. Now I see I'll have to do it directly."

"Do what? Is this the word on my cure?"

"It is." Kleinberg steeled himself for the moment of truth, and then he uttered it. "Bad news, I'm afraid. The sarcoma has returned. The tumor is visible. The X rays show a malignancy once more. It is real, and it has to be dealt with."

He'd been through this so many times, in similar cases, and it was the part of his profession he hated the most. To examine, to test, to diagnose, those were the things he could handle best. But to face the patient with bad news, the human level, the emotional aspect, that was the worst of being a doctor.

He had told her, and next would come her reaction. The usual reaction was one of stunned silence, and inevitably there followed tears. Sometimes doubts, protests, angry protests at the unfairness, but always a breakdown of some sort and always highly charged.

Kleinberg waited for the outburst, but it did not come. Not a feature of Edith Moore's bland countenance moved or twitched. Her eyes left him to fix on the ceiling. She made no effort to speak, but simply stared up at the ceiling.

Perhaps a minute had passed as she lived through this in her mind. At last, her eyes found his.

Her voice was hardly audible. "You're sure?"

"I'm sure, Edith." Inadvertently, he had used her given name for the first time. "There's no mistake."

She licked her dry lips, silent once more. When she spoke, it was more to herself than to him. "Miracle woman," she said with a trace of bitterness. "So it's back," she said. "No miraculous cure."

"I'm afraid not."

"You can't certify me as cured because—I'm not cured. You've told Dr. Berryer?"

"Not yet."

"Or Father Ruland?"

"No."

"They kept telling me your examination was routine. Every doctor, for three years, was positive I was miraculously cured. How can you explain that?"

"I can't, Edith. I've never known a case where the sarcoma was so evident, then disappeared for so long a period—and then suddenly returned. Ordinary remission cases are not like this. The disappearance and ultimate return of the disease are inexplicable in my experience."

"You know," she said thoughtfully, "I suspected something might be wrong. Mainly because I hadn't heard from you immediately. And—well, because I began to feel sick last night—the same old weaknesses and pains, not really bad, but like it was when it all began five years ago. I started to worry about what was going on."

"You were right. I tried to tell you, as soon as I was certain, through your husband."

"Reggie," she murmured. She looked at Kleinberg frankly. "That's the worst part of it. I've been through the illness before, and for so long, I learned to live with it somehow. I lived with death so long—well, I can again, and I know I'll find a way to meet it. But Reggie's my real concern. For all his bluster and aggressive ways, he's weak underneath. He constantly escapes into a world of unreality. I suppose that is what sustains him. I've never said this to a soul before. But I know him. My God, how shocked he must have been when you told him the truth."

"He wouldn't believe me," said Kleinberg.

"Yes, that's Reggie. Poor soul. He's my only concern. For all his faults, I love him so. There's much good in him. He's a great big child, a grown child, and I love him. He's what I have on earth, to take care of and cling to at the same time. You understand, doctor?"

Kleinberg understood, and was strangely moved. There was a heart and sensitivity to this good lady that he had not perceived earlier. "Yes, I understand, Edith."

"He needs me," she went on. "Without me, he'll be a vagrant, lost, ridiculed and lost. He's failed at everything, failed and failed. His last gamble—all our money, everything—the last shred of his esteem—was invested in the restaurant. And it had begun to work." She hesitated.

"But only because I was the miracle woman. Now that I'm just a sick middle-aged woman with a terminal illness, he'll lose the restaurant. It can't support two partners without me to showcase. He'll be broke. He'll be destroyed. And soon I won't be able to work. Because I'll be gone."

"Wait a minute, Edith. There's more and it *is* important. Maybe I should have told you immediately—but I had to state your condition first. That was the bad news. But there is some extremely favorable news. You are not incurable. You need not die. Since your initial episode five years ago, a new form of surgery, a new genetic-replacement technique, has come along and can be a means of saving you. I think I'd better tell you about it."

Oddly, for Kleinberg, she offered no visible response, no expected clutch at a sudden lifeline. She just lay there, staring at him, prepared to endure listening. Under the circumstances, she seemed to have lost her will to live.

Nevertheless, he repeated the essence of his conversation with Dr. Maurice Duval, omitting any mention of Duval's secret surgeries.

He concluded, "There it is, Edith. A real chance. Seventy percent in your favor. If it works, as he promises it will, you'll be totally restored."

"But not a miracle woman."

"Unless you consider this new genetic replacement treatment a miracle, as I do."

"If I survived, I'd be there. But that wouldn't help Reggie much."

"If he loves you, he'd have you. And you'd be able to return to work."

"True, doctor. Maybe I'd live. But for all intents and purposes, Reggie would be dead."

"I think there might be more in the future for both of you. Anyway, I must have your decision on the surgery as soon as possible. Dr. Duval can undertake the operation as early as Sunday. But he must have your consent."

She shook her head slowly. "I can't give it alone. I must talk it over with Reggie."

She had still not come to grips with her unmiracle, Kleinberg saw. "I don't see the point in delaying," he said. "Unless you act, the outcome is inevitable."

"I'm still a miracle woman in everyone's eyes. It can protract Reggie's success a little longer—and maybe he'll find someone with another opinion who'll tell the church I am a miracle woman, after all."

Kleinberg could not argue this further. "It is entirely up to you," he said, rising. "But I must have your absolute decision tomorrow, certainly no later than Saturday."

"I'll speak to Reggie," she said.

13

Friday, August 19

Hypnotized by the clock on the mantel, Gisele Dupree watched as the hour hand and minute hand stood at eleven-thirty in the morning.

Her attention shifted to the apartment door, awaiting the knock that she expected would come any second.

She had returned to the apartment more than a half hour ago, standing by for the anticipated arrival of Sergei Tikhanov. She had been up and out on the town early, leading a scheduled Italian pilgrimage on the usual Lourdes tour. Finishing at ten-forty, she had been given twenty minutes to rest before taking out her next tour. Instead, she had complained once more of a migraine headache, and told the Agence Pyrénées director that she must go to her apartment to lie down. Her departure had not been taken lightly.

There had been risk in walking out on her job a second time, real risk that she might be fired upon her return. But, she had told herself, she would not have to return. She was taking a gamble, and if it worked, the risk did not matter.

She had believed, since yesterday, that her gamble was a sure thing. Mainly because her bet on her future was hedged. If Tikhanov really meant to defy her, there would be Liz Finch as an alternative source of money to buy the exposé.

If not one, then the other, she had assured herself at eleven-thirty, and she had still been certain it would be Tikhanov.

At eleven thirty-seven, she was less certain.

It was unimaginable that a diplomat of Tikhanov's stature, a candidate for the premiership of the Soviet Union, one with so much at stake, would permit an exposé to blow it all away. She was surprised that he had not shown up on time, and now wondered if he was stubborn and suicidal enough not to show up at all. Or maybe he was having trouble getting the money, which might account for the delay. Yet, she had given him an alternative.

She was beginning to worry.

She did not like her chances being reduced to one source, to Liz Finch, who might have trouble worming the necessary sum out of her American syndicate.

Gradually, the sunny prospects Gisele had envisioned, even like the sunny day outside, were darkening.

And then she whirled around. Had there been a rapping at the door? She thought so.

She called out, "Who is it?"

There was no reply. But then came three more sharp, distinct knocks on the door.

Instantly, she was revived. Casting aside any pretense of coolness and calm, Gisele ran to the door. She yanked it open. And there he was, the unsmiling granite visage, the flowing mustache, all dulled down in a heavy dark-gray suit and somber black tie.

Sergei Tikhanov.

Out of some innate kindness, and with victory in reach, Gisele greeted him warmly, "Mr. Samuel Talley, how good to see you."

"Yes, hello," he said, with a curt nod, and stepped past her into the living room of the apartment.

Shutting the door, she turned to face him. "Well?" she said.

"You win," he said simply. "I am Sergei Tikhanov."

"I was sure," she said, "from the moment I saw your picture without the mustache."

"Very shrewd of you, Miss Dupree. You are more clever than I guessed. You are to be commended. Of course, I had no choice but to see you this morning. It was foolhardy of me to come to Lourdes in the first place. But understandable. An act of desperation by a dying man. Yet, it was a mistake, and once made, I could not let word of it get out. I knew I must prevent your making my identity public."

She stared at him. "So you are here to prevent exposure. I hope not by attempting anything violent. I must warn you, I've armed myself with a gun."

Tikhanov appeared offended. "Miss Dupree, as my record makes clear, I am anything but a violent man. You have suggested a deal, and I am prepared to accept it. I am here to meet your terms. You suggested it would cost me $15,000."

Gisele felt heady, filled with a rush of greed. She had him at her mercy, and this was a once in a lifetime opportunity. "That was yesterday," she blurted. "This is today, and the terms have changed."

"Changed?"

"I now have another buyer," she said brazenly. "The other buyer might be prepared to bid higher."

For the first time Tikhanov showed anxiety. "You haven't told the other buyer what you are offering, have you?"

"Of course not. I haven't given anything away. But you'll now have to pay me $20,000. Of course, as I suggested, you could send the money next week—"

Tikhanov offered a lopsided smile. "No, I want to conclude the matter right now. Fortunately, I always travel with considerable sums in three currencies. For—for little emergencies—and payoffs." He smiled another mirthless smile. "I expected you to raise your price. Negotiating and bargaining have been my life. Adversaries with all the cards always raise the price. I have brought $20,000—actually a bit more—in American dollars."

"$20,000 will be enough," said Gisele, trying to contain the tremor in her voice.

"Here it is," he said, digging into his right-hand jacket pocket and extracting a thick wad of green bills held together by a rubber band. "All yours," he said, placing the wad of bills on the coffee table.

Gisele's eyes widened at the denominations. "You know, I never wanted to do you any harm," she said. "I have nothing against you. I just needed the money." As she started to bend over to take the money, his right arm darted out, barring her from the bills.

"Not so fast," he said. "My payment is here for you. Where is your payment for me?"

"Of course," she said breathlessly. "I'll get you the evidence, the picture—all the pictures—"

"And the negatives," he added softly.

"Yes, the negatives, too. Just wait." She spun around and hurried into the next room. "I'll get them for you."

Tikhanov watched the open door to the next room for a few seconds, and then he began to move, actually glide across the carpeted floor, moving lightly, noiselessly, with practiced quietness to the door-way.

It was a bedroom, he saw, and she was at a chest of drawers, pulling open the top drawer, concentrating on its contents, her back to him. He lifted himself to his tiptoes, poised, as a rattlesnake arches its head high before striking. His Slavic eyes were slits now, fixed on her. She was busy removing a snapshot and negative from the upper drawer.

The instant she had it out, his hand slipped into his left jacket pocket and drew out a thin hard strand of rope.

He moved quickly, so quickly, crossing the room in several long strides, uncaring about the noise he made. She had heard him, and started to turn, when he was full upon her.

The last she clearly saw of Sergei Tikhanov was the wild eyes gleaming out of the murderous face. With the rapid skill of a Red Army commando, he had the rope around her neck and was twisting it. She emitted a hoarse outcry that became a moan, and her fists beat at him to free herself and get air. Her strength surprised him, and as the nails of one hand clawed at his cheek, he weakened his grip to protect himself. In that moment, she tore away from him, and with the rope still dan-gling from her neck she stumbled out of the bedroom into the living room, fumbling for something in the pocket of her skirt. But he bounded savagely after her, as she backed into a table, knocking the telephone and a vase of flowers to the carpet.

He had the rope in his big hands again, and was twisting it tighter and tighter around her throat, steadily garroting her. Her hand stopped fumbling in her pocket, the other hand dropped limply to her side. Her eyes had bulged almost out of their sockets, her mouth had fallen open, dribbling spittle. Brutally, he continued to strangle her harder and harder.

Suddenly, her eyes closed, her head fell to one side, and her body was that of a rag doll. She began to collapse, then folded silently and slumped to the carpet. He followed her down, hands still vises on the knotted hang rope, going down with her and holding the rope taut until she was still.

At last, he released the rope ends. Kneeling, he stared down at her. He reached for one wrist to check her pulse. There was no pulse.

Satisfied, he slowly unwound the rope, lifting her loose, lifeless head off the floor and unwinding his rope. When he had all of the rope, he unceremoniously let her head fall back on the carpet. Stuffing the coil of rope into his left pocket, he took the wad of American dollars off the coffee table and slipped it into his right pocket. He saw that a small pistol—she'd actually had a pistol—had half fallen from her skirt pocket. He let it remain untouched.

Rising to his feet, Tikhanov swiftly returned to the bedroom. On the floor, at the foot of the bureau, he found the snapshot of himself without his mustache taken near the grotto, and the negative. He pocketed both. Yanking a pair of gloves out of his trouser pocket, he searched the open drawer above, confiscating the entire packet of snapshots and negatives, two large Tikhanov portrait photographs, and a newspaper clipping of himself. These he tore and tore again, jamming the scraps into a jacket pocket. Now, wiping all surfaces he might have contacted, he searched for any notepad or slip of paper that might give evidence of Talley or Tikhanov. There was nothing in the bedroom, nor in the kitchen, nor in the dining room, and finally he was in the living room once more.

He saw the telephone on the floor, and for the first time, beside it, a small red address book. Inside, under T, he saw noted in her hand the name, "Talley, Samuel," and the name and address of his hotel. He confiscated the address book also.

A farewell glance at the corpse.

The deadest corpse he had ever seen.

He was without remorse. No matter how pretty, how young, she had been no more than a dirty little blackmailer. She had tried to murder him. He had liquidated her in self-defense.

He strode to the entrance door, opened it. The corridor, back and front was clear. He was alone, unseen. He stepped into the corridor, shut the door quietly behind him, and left the building.

At exactly the noon hour, as she had been instructed yesterday, Liz Finch dialed the telephone number that Gisele had given her. The phone on the other end was busy.

Mildly disconcerted, Liz dialed Gisele's number a minute later, and when she still got a busy signal, she dialed again and again at intervals of two minutes, and each time the line she was trying to reach was busy. Waiting for the line to clear, Liz kept wondering if she was going to get the big story from Gisele, wondering what it was about and if Gisele really knew what constituted a big story.

Liz's marathon phone calls continued for over twenty minutes. At last, concluding that something was wrong with Gisele's phone, Liz dialed the operator. After an interminable exchange in French, and cooling her heels in the hotel room while the operator investigated, Liz was able to learn only that either Gisele's phone was disconnected or out of order and that the problem would be attended to as soon as possible.

Realizing that a solution to the problem might take forever, and that Gisele, unaware of what was wrong, might still be awaiting her call, Liz decided to circumvent this modern system of communication by seeing Gisele in person.

Studying her map of Lourdes as she descended to the hotel lobby, Liz realized that Gisele was located on the other side of the domain and that it would take too long to cover the distance on foot.

In the street, she hailed a taxi and gave Gisele's address. Sitting on the edge of the back seat of the cab, Liz again speculated about what kind of story Gisele might be holding for her and was prepared to sell to her. It must be something special, Liz finally decided. After all, as these local youngsters went, Gisele was surprisingly worldly and sophisticated and she obviously read the Paris newspapers. She would know what was worthy of front page coverage. She would know a real news story, and she had been definite yesterday about having got her hands on a big one. True, the story probably had a high price on it, and Bill Trask would have to buy it for API, but Liz knew that frequently the syndicate laid out sizable sums for exclusive news beats.

The possibility of obtaining a sensational story was growing in importance in Liz's mind, because she needed a story so badly. The only feature story she had in the works was one on Bernadette's weaknesses. In it, she implied that the entire validity of Lourdes was built on a shaky foundation, but there was something flaky about this feature because it lacked hard evidence. Liz planned to phone the story in tomorrow, but she had the sinking feeling that it would not impress API sufficiently to keep her at the Paris bureau instead of the luckier Marguerite Lamarche with her potentially explosive Viron scandal.

Liz needed a smasher from Gisele.

Arriving at Gisele's address, Liz paid off the taxi driver and hurried into the building. Gisele's apartment number proved to be on the ground floor, midway up the corridor. Liz hastened toward the apartment, found it, could not locate a doorbell, and so she rapped on the door.

No answer.

Perhaps Gisele was in the bathroom. Liz knocked harder, persistently, until her knuckles hurt.

She expected Gisele's response, but there was none.

From long conditioning as a reporter, Liz automatically tried the doorknob to see if the door was locked. The door eased open. It had not been locked. How thoughtless of Gisele.

Liz decided that she had the right, under the circumstances, to enter the apartment. She pushed the door aside and stepped into the living room. The room was empty.

"Gisele!" Liz shouted. "I'm here! It's Liz Finch!"

In response, there was no voice. There was silence.

At the moment, the apartment appeared to be unoccupied. Obviously, when Liz's phone call had not come through, Gisele had left either for work or to seek Liz out.

The damn phone was out of order, that's what had caused the mix-up, thought Liz. She sought the phone on some surface, and her roving eye suddenly came upon it on the floor, almost at her feet, the receiver separated from the cradle, which explained the busy signal.

Kneeling to pick up the phone, Liz's eye lighted on something so unexpected that she gasped.

There was an outstretched hand and an arm visible at the edge of a bookcase divider that hid the sofa. Gaping, Liz came unsteadily to her feet and took another step inside the room for a fuller view.

Then she saw the supine body on the floor next to the coffee table and sofa.

It was Gisele, all right, and Liz approached her and kneeled to see if she had fainted and was merely unconscious. But even as she brought up Gisele's wrist, felt for the throb of her pulse, she could see that something more drastic had happened. Gisele's congested face had a puffy unnatural awful look.

Not unconscious, Liz realized, letting go of her wrist. Dead, plain dead. The red marks were evident on the neck. She'd been strangled, murdered.

Experienced as she was at all sorts of mayhem, Liz instinctively recoiled at the sight. She came weakly to her feet, trying to understand. At first thought, the mundane passed through Liz's mind. An intruder, a robbery, and Gisele had tried to prevent it and failed. But then another thought surfaced. Yesterday Gisele had made it clear that she was onto a story . . . a big, big one . . . the biggest . . . with international overtones . . . *"It'll have to wait overnight. I'll know tomorrow if you can have it."*

Gisele had been "on the verge" of getting her story, just waiting for verification today.

Verification had to come from *someone*. Yes, someone had been here in this apartment. Yes, Gisele probably had come upon a tremendous story. But someone had learned of it and someone wouldn't let Gisele have it. Someone had done her in, viciously, monstrously.

Poor kid.

Good-bye Gisele. Good-bye big story. And, selfish realization, good-bye Liz Finch and her chance to retain her job.

Liz's immediate intent had been to flee from the corpse and the scene, but her squeamishness was subsiding and her reporter's curiosity was taking grip. If someone had been here, then someone might have left a clue. Probably not. But maybe. Nevertheless, worth a brief try. Liz felt inside her purse for her handkerchief, withdrew it and unfolded it. She wrapped it around her right hand. If she was going to make a search, she'd better not leave her own fingerprints and be implicated in the murder.

Liz started her fast but thorough search, going from room to room. But everywhere she drew blanks. Not a hint of another human presence. Not a clue. Not a scrap of writing. The apartment was eerily anonymous.

After fifteen minutes, Liz knew that she had been preceded by someone even more clever and professional than she.

Nervous that a visitor might come calling, and find her here and compromise her, Liz tarried no longer. She walked out of the apartment into the street, and found a taxi to take her to her hotel near the domain.

Arriving before the hotel, Liz decided on her next move. She felt that she owed Gisele Dupree a favor for having tried to help her. Liz owed the little guide girl one phone call. Liz meant to make it from her room, but concluded that it might easily be traced and unsafe. She asked the taxi driver where she might find a public telephone booth. He directed her to a location a half block away.

While walking to the public phone, Liz ransacked her purse for a *jeton,* found a token, closed herself into the booth. She dropped the *jeton* into the slot, and dialed the operator.

"Operator," she said in French into the mouthpiece, "connect me with the Commissariat de police. This is an emergency."

"Police secours? Appelez-vous dix-sept."

Liz hung up, then dialed 17.

Seconds later, a young man's voice answered the phone, giving his rank and name and stating that this was the police emergency desk.

Liz said, "Can you hear me, officer?"

"Yes."

"I must tell you something important, so please do not interrupt me." Liz continued rapidly and distinctly. "I went to a woman friend's apartment to meet with her. We were to go shopping together. Her door was open, and I went inside. I found her on the floor, dead, strangled to death. Let me repeat. I found her murdered. There is no question that she is dead. Take a pencil now and I will give you her name and address—"

"Madame, if you will let me interrupt—"

"I will not speak to you beyond what I am reporting. The victim's name is Gisele Dupree, a single woman in her twenties. Her address is —" Liz searched for the card on which Gisele had jotted her address, and she read it out more slowly. "You will find her body there," she added. "You have it all."

"Yes, I do. But listen, madame—"

Liz hung up the receiver, and left the public phone for some fresh air.

Liz wandered aimlessly for half an hour, until her nerves had settled down, and then she began to think about her future. She had held off the feature piece on Bernadette, hoping that she would come up with something more spectacular, something sure-fire, from Gisele. But now that this hope was ashes, there was no choice but to give Bill Trask in Paris something, whatever she had ready.

She changed her direction, and started toward the press tent. Ten minutes later, she reached it and went inside the temporary canvas cavern. There were at least a hundred desks in the tent, and unhappily she made her way to the used oak desk she shared with two other correspondents. The chair was unoccupied, and Liz hoped the others who shared the facility with her were having as poor a time of it as she was in finding something to write about.

When she brought the telephone to her, and asked the switchboard to get her API in Paris, it occurred to her that she had not one story but two that might interest her boss. In moments, she had API, and asked to be connected with Bill Trask.

Trask's gruff voice challenged her. "Yeah, who is it?"

"Come off it, Bill, who'd be calling you from Lourdes? It's Liz here, no other."

"I was wondering when you'd check in."

"Bill, it's been absolutely dullsville for six days. I've been running my ass off, doing what I can, you can be sure."

"Well, anyone seen the Virgin yet?"

"Bill, cut it out."

"I mean it."

"You know the answer is a great fat No—N-O. But, well, I have dredged up two stories for you. Won't shake the world, but they are stories."

"Okay, let me turn the machine on. I'll be listening, but meanwhile we're recording. Go ahead, Liz."

"First story, right?"

"Go on."

Liz plunged. "Murder in Lourdes this morning. Brutal murder among the holies. Everyone here to get cured, and instead a local gets herself killed. Victim's name is Gisele Dupree, single, maybe twenty-six, found strangled in her apartment near the grotto at—well, at noon. She'd once worked as a secretary for the French ambassador to the United Nations Charles Sarrat. She was in New York with him, with the delegation."

"When?"

"Two years ago."

"But now, what was she doing in Lourdes right now?"

Liz swallowed. The Trask test. "Uh, she was working here as a tourist guide."

"A what?"

"She led guided tours around Lourdes, to all the historic sites."

"All right, let's try another tack. Who murdered her?"

Feeling helpless, Liz improvised. "I contacted the Lourdes police. Murderer still unknown. They say they're running down several clues, but no suspect has been announced. I'll stay on them, if you like."

"Anything else about the killing?"

"Well, I can tell you this about the victim. She was pretty, actually beautiful, very sexy. Also—"

Trask stamped on her abruptly. "Don't bother," he said.

"What?"

"Don't bother to follow up. Come on, Liz, you know better. You know that's not a wire story for us. There are how many murders in France every goddam day? This is just another run-of-the-mill murder. What have you got there? A girl guide. A nobody killed by no one we know. That's for the French press. It wouldn't get us an inch in New York or Chicago or L.A., let alone Dubuque or Topeka. Of course, if the killer turned out to be somebody, or if somehow you dug up an international angle, we might make it work."

"I can keep trying, and see if something more breaks."

"Don't give it too much energy. I don't think this one is going anywhere. Okay, you mentioned another story. Shoot with it."

"Well, since there's been no hard news in Lourdes on the Virgin or anything, I've been poking into a little exposé on Bernadette, and what was really going on with her in 1858 and right after. Thought it might make a Sunday feature. Cause a little stir. I've banged it out."

"You can dictate. All ears on this end."

Liz exhaled. "Here goes."

She began to read her feature story into the phone.

The lead dealt with the fact that Lourdes, which normally enjoyed five million visitors a year, was in these eight days hosting the greatest number of persons ever to converge upon the holy site—and all because of the visions of a fourteen-year-old peasant girl named Bernadette, and a secret she had revealed.

While the Catholic Church had elevated Bernadette to sainthood after her death, Liz went on, a minority of the clergy as well as many scholars had questioned the veracity of Bernadette's visions. Trying to build her case against Bernadette like a prosecutor, Liz rattled off all the suspicions that existed about the peasant girl's honesty.

"Backers of Bernadette always insisted that she was not self-serving in reporting the apparitions," Liz read into the phone, "yet scholars have pointed out that as the crowds of spectators grew larger, Bernadette became an exhibitionist, playing to the crowds. On one occasion her father, François, noting the large gathering in attendance, was overheard whispering to Bernadette as she kneeled before the grotto, 'Don't make any mistake today. Do it well.' "

Pleased with that touch, Liz went on to report how Bernadette did not believe the grotto could cure her own ailments. Then Liz began to cover Bernadette's time in Nevers, where her superior, the mistress of the novices, doubted that Bernadette had seen the Virgin at all.

As Liz continued dictating the story into the telephone, she began to feel increasingly uneasy. To her own ear it sounded terribly gossipy, almost scurrilous. She wondered how Bill Trask was reacting.

She paused. "What do you think, Bill?"

"It's interesting, of course. A bit surprising. Where'd you pick up that material?"

"Well, much of it from defenders of the church—from Father Ruland here, Father Cayoux and Sister Francesca in other towns, some of the lesser clergymen in various places."

"They told you all that? They were anti-Bernadette?"

"No, mostly they were pro-Bernadette. I've been selective in what I've culled from the interviews in order to—well—to build the angle of my story. I still have another page to go. Want me to finish it?"

"Don't bother," said Trask bluntly. "Good try, Liz, but we can't possibly use it. Those so-called facts you've been reading may be valid, but somehow they add up to very little. Far too iffy and speculative, and too insubstantial to stand up against the storm of controversy they're sure to generate worldwide. Dammit, Liz, if you're exposing a saint, especially a red-hot and current saint, you'd better have the goods on her. You'd better have at least one piece of hard news with an unimpeachable source. I know you've done your best, but your story is built on sand and we need a more solid foundation. Do you understand?"

"I guess so," said Liz weakly. She had no heart to oppose her boss because she had known all along that her story was a flimsy one based on a contrived angle intended to shock.

"So let's forget it, and keep your eyes open," Trask said.

"For what?"

"For the really big story—the Virgin Mary does or does not reappear in Lourdes by Sunday. If you get that story, it won't be exclusive but I'll be satisfied."

"I'll just have to wait and see."

"You wait and see."

Knowing he was about to hang up, Liz had to get in one more question, and hated herself for having to ask it. "Oh, Bill, one other thing—just curious—but how's Marguerite progressing on the Viron story?"

"Just fine, I guess. She seems to have got very close to him. She's handing in the story tomorrow."

"Well, good luck," said Liz.

After hanging up, she wanted to kill herself. Good-bye job, good-bye career, good-bye Paris, and hello to a lifetime sentence of servitude in some small town in America's Midwest.

Surely, this was the bleakest moment of her adult life.

She heard the telephone ringing, and prayed for a reprieve.

The voice was that of Amanda Spenser.

"I'm so glad I caught you in, Liz," Amanda was saying. "I talked to Father Ruland, as I told you I would. Remember? He was most cooperative."

"About what?"

"Giving me the name of the person in Bartrès from whom he bought Bernadette's journal. I've got an appointment to see her, this Madame Eugénie Gautier. I'm just about to leave for Bartrès. I thought you might want to come along."

"Thanks, but no thanks," said Liz. "I'm afraid I've heard all I'll ever want to hear about Bernadette. The home office just isn't interested. I've had enough."

"Well, you never can tell," said Amanda.

"I can tell," said Liz. "Good luck. You'll need it."

Dr. Paul Kleinberg had propped himself up on his bed in the Hôtel Astoria, resting and reading, and expecting the phone call from Edith Moore with her decision. It exasperated him that there was a decision to make, since the poor woman really had no choice. His prognosis had been definite and unequivocal. Her illness was terminal. Unless she submitted to Dr. Duval's scalpel and genetic implant, she was as good as dead. It seemed impossible that she would risk her life depending on a second miracle, when the first had finally failed her. Yet, she was leaving her future to her husband, Reggie, who was selfish, unrealistic, and apparently insensible to his wife's fate.

Utter madness, this delay, and Kleinberg wished he was out of the whole thing and back in his comfortable apartment in Paris.

And then the telephone at his elbow, amplified by his introspection, rang out like a trumpet.

He caught up the receiver, ready to hear Edith Moore, and was surprised that the speaker was male.

"Dr. Kleinberg? This is Reggie Moore."

Considering their last meeting and parting, Kleinberg was even more surprised at the friendliness of Reggie's tone.

"Yes, Mr. Moore, I was rather expecting your wife to call."

"Well, she delegated the call to me. So I'm calling. Edith told me about your visit to her at the hotel. She wasn't well, so I appreciate that."

"You know then about Dr. Duval?"

"I do. She told me all about his new surgery."

"She couldn't make up her mind," said Kleinberg. "She wanted to talk it over with you first."

"We talked it over at length," said Reggie enigmatically.

"Have you arrived at a decision?"

"I'd like to see you first. I'd like to discuss it with you. Are you free?"

"Totally available. Your wife is why I'm here."

"When can I see you?"

"Now," said Kleinberg.

"You're at the Astoria," said Reggie. "I know the hotel. They have a nice garden courtyard downstairs where they serve coffee. Why don't I meet you there in—say—let's make it fifteen minutes. How's that?"

"That's fine. In fifteen minutes."

Kleinberg threw down his book and got off the bed. He was as exasperated as ever, and mystified as well. Why in the hell did Reggie Moore have to see him? What was there to discuss? Why couldn't Reggie have given him the decision on the phone? Then he would have been able to reserve some time in a surgical room in a Lourdes hospital or otherwise be able to pack up and go home. Nevertheless, he went to wash up, comb his hair, put on his necktie and jacket. Once refreshed, Dr. Kleinberg went downstairs.

He found the Hôtel Astoria courtyard not unpleasant, the usual splashing fountain and the area enlivened by yellow shutters on the hotel windows above the green shrubbery. There were six circular plastic tables with white slat chairs distributed around the courtyard. All of them, save one, were empty. That table was occupied by one large man lighting a cigar. Puffing the cigar was Reggie Moore.

Kleinberg hurried down the outside steps and crossed to the table. Moore shook hands without rising. Kleinberg sat down opposite him.

Reggie said, "I ordered coffee for both of us. That all right?"

"Just what the doctor would have ordered," said Kleinberg.

Reggie guffawed and sucked at his cigar. Gradually, his face transformed into something serious. When he spoke, he was almost abject, and sounded chastened. "Sorry about that little set-to we had in town. Not like me to go around shouting at anyone."

"You had reason to be upset," said Kleinberg, who did not trust small victories like this. "You seem considerably calmer now."

"I am, I am," said Reggie.

Reggie watched while the waiter set down the coffee, cream, sugar, bill, but he did not seem interested. Kleinberg discerned that Reggie had something else on his mind. And was being unhurried about speaking his mind.

Reggie lifted the cup to his lips, pinkie finger incongruously extended, and sampled the coffee. He made a face, putting the cup down. "Hate French coffee, if you'll forgive me," he apologized.

Amused, Kleinberg said, "I don't make it."

Reggie took another puff of his cigar, and propped it neatly on the ashtray, obviously getting ready for business. "Yes," he said, "me and the Missus, we had a long talk. No second thoughts about your diagnosis?"

"None. She's in trouble unless you act."

"Doctor, what is this new surgery? Is it like any surgery?"

"Yes and no," Kleinberg answered. He tried to think of how to frame it simply. "To make it more understandable, we could call the overall process surgery, because eventually there is surgery in the way probably familiar to you—cleaning away the diseased bone, implanting new bone tissue or a ball-and-socket ceramic prosthesis, or artificial hip joint, but the genetic engineering aspect is another matter. I don't know Dr. Duval's exact procedure, but I do know this crucial part would not require a surgical-style operation but actually would consist of transplanting healthy genes more in the manner of—let's say of a blood transfusion. Really, this part would consist of an injection or series of injections. Would you like me to explain a little about genetic engineering?"

"Well, would I—would I understand it?"

"You've heard about DNA, haven't you?"

"I—I've probably read about it," Reggie said tentatively.

From his tone, Kleinberg judged that he had not read about it and did not know if DNA was the name of a new government agency or a race horse. Kleinberg wondered how far he could go. "The human body consists of cells, and each cell contains 100,000 genes spread along some six feet of DNA, which is tightly coiled. When one cell goes bad, becomes an aberrant cell that triggers a cancer and starts multiplying, the body is in serious danger. Well, the findings in gene-splicing research now enable specialists to use enzymes to slice DNA strands, and replace a defective gene with a healthy one. I'm oversimplifying, but you get the idea, don't you?"

"I think I get the idea," said Reggie, who plainly didn't. "Look, doctor, it's not necessary that I know all about it, just like I don't know how a computer or a television set works, yet I accept them and use them. Okay, genetic replacement or whatever. Fine. I take your word it's the coming thing, that it has been proved to work and cure, that it can save my Edith's life."

"Seventy percent in her favor."

"Fair enough odds for a betting man," said Reggie, taking up his cigar again, knocking off the ash, lighting a match and putting it to the cigar. "And then she'd be well?"

"Like new."

"Like new," mused Reggie, "but no longer a miracle woman, meaning a woman no longer miraculously cured."

"No, she would not be miraculously cured. She would be cured by medicine—by science."

"That gives me a problem," said Reggie casually.

"A problem?"

"Like she told you, if I don't have a miracle wife, I'm bankrupt, we're both busted and flat on our backs."

"I'm sorry," said Kleinberg, "but of course that is out of my realm of specialization. That is something I can do nothing about."

Reggie was eyeing him shrewdly. "Are you sure, doctor? Are you sure you can do nothing about it?"

Momentarily, Kleinberg was lost. "Do nothing about what?"

"About helping us, letting us have our cake and eat it, too, as the saying goes," said Reggie. "Meaning saving Edith's life through surgery but still letting her be declared a miracle cure."

Kleinberg was beginning to see the light. The British promoter was propositioning, bargaining. "Are you saying that after the surgery you don't want me to mention it but just certify her as having been miraculously cured? Is that what you're asking?"

"Something like that."

"Lie to them, to Dr. Berryer and the rest, not tell them the sarcoma came back, not tell them of the surgery, just validate Edith as having been cured at the grotto and baths? I'm not fanatically bound to my Hippocratic oath, but still—"

Reggie sat erect. "Doctors do things like that all the time."

Dr. Kleinberg shook his head. "I'm one doctor who can't do that. I doubt that even the staunchest Catholic doctor would consider doing it. Anyway, I certainly cannot lie. I'm afraid that's impossible." Looking up, Kleinberg was startled to see Reggie's face. It was sunken with defeat and grief, and terrible aging had set in like a latter-day Dorian Gray. For the first time, Kleinberg's heart felt for the man, the human being across the table, and he tried to think of something softening to say. "Of course, I'm confined to the medical aspects of the case," Kleinberg said, stumbling along, "and I really have no stake in the religious part, the miracle part. I'm only interested in saving Edith medically, but if others are kept uninformed and someone else wants to overlook that aspect and declare her miraculously cured, I see no reason to stand in the way. I mean," Kleinberg found himself adding, "if someone in power wants to say that she's been miraculously cured, well, Dr. Duval and I won't interfere. We won't mention the operation. That's up to you and any clergyman you confide in. For my part, I'll simply fade away, get back to Paris and my work."

It was straw-grasping time, and Reggie had stirred himself alive. "Who—who would be able to give the word without your certificate? Who might consider Edith as miraculously cured?"

"Why, as I've suggested, someone in the church, of course, someone high up. Surely you know someone in the hierarchy?"

Reggie nodded vigorously. "One or two. One, especially. Father Ruland, the most important priest in Lourdes. He's the one who felt from the start that Lourdes needed Edith's miracle cure. He's been on her side right down the line."

"Very well, then see how much he's on her side now," said Kleinberg. "Have Edith speak to him. Take your gamble. If Edith will go to Father Ruland and tell him the truth, and Ruland doesn't object and is ready to announce her as miraculously cured, I won't block it or contradict his announcement by announcing she was saved by surgery. I'll just keep quiet."

Reggie's watery eyes began to shine. "You would, you really would?"

"Why not? I repeat, the religious end doesn't concern me. If Father Ruland hears what you are up to, then shuts one eye and makes believe it never happened, and is prepared to declare Edith's cure a miracle cure, then I'll shut one eye, too—meaning I'll shut my mouth. There you have it."

Reggie had lumbered to his feet and was pumping Kleinberg's hand. "You're a good person, a good, good person for a doctor. I'll have Edith speak to Father Ruland right away, maybe go to confession, yes, that's the best way, in confession. Tell a priest all and try to get him to speak to Ruland—get Ruland's backing, his support—an announcement."

"What if you fail to get his support?"

"Let's turn that corner when we get to it," said Reggie, and he rushed out of the courtyard.

The fifteen-minute drive to Bartrès, in her rented Renault, went smoothly for Amanda.

The only rough part of the trip was in Amanda's head.

Liz Finch's defection from their hunt for an exposé of the Bernadette legend had troubled Amanda throughout the drive. When someone as savvy and experienced in research as Liz finally called it quits, it was unlikely that anyone else—certainly not an amateur like Amanda—would ever find out anything useful. What nagged Amanda, also, was that her quest for truth was taking too long and soon would be pointless. When she went to bed with Ken every night, and held and cradled him, it was obvious to her that he was on a steady decline, becoming weaker and weaker. He was even finding it difficult to drag himself outside and down to the grotto for prayer. Only a fanatical belief in the curative powers of the Virgin Mary kept him going. No logic, no pleading from Amanda, could dissuade him from his dependence on religious faith.

And here she was speeding to a village named Bartrès, to see the custodian of Bernadette's sensational journal. This last-ditch effort in an attempt to learn one fact that would burst the Bernadette bubble and enable Amanda to take her beloved back to Chicago for a longshot surgery.

It was all depressing, and Amanda suspected that she was once more on the wildest of wild goose chases. Also, it made her feel guilty wasting her time trying to undermine Ken's faith when she should be spending the same time close to him, giving him comfort in what might be his last days.

She was on a narrow road now, passing two modern houses, then a roadside shrine—a large plaster Jesus with a bouquet of purple flowers at his feet—and next she was spinning across a valley, climbing uphill once more, and from the rise, the typical French rooftops of the small village of Bartrès lay spread below her.

Driving slowly on the descending road, with the steeple of a church in view, Amanda thought of what was waiting for her, and it did not seem too promising. She had telephoned Madame Eugénie Gautier from Lourdes and received a chilly reception. After ascertaining that Madame Gautier was, indeed, the woman from whom Father Ruland had acquired Bernadette's final journal, Amanda had requested a brief meeting with her. "For what?" Madame Gautier, sharp-tongued and a miser with words, wanted to know. Amanda said that she had come here from Chicago, Illinois, in America, and was researching a paper that she was going to write on Bernadette. Madame Gautier had snapped, "I don't want any journalists." Amanda had patiently explained that she was not a journalist. "I'm a clinical psychologist and an associate professor at the University of Chicago." Madame Gautier had said, "You are a professor? A real college professor?" Amanda had said, "Yes, Madame Gautier, I teach at the University of Chicago." There had been a prolonged pause. "What's Chicago University?" Madame Gautier had demanded to know. "I never heard of it." Amanda had assured her that it was a large and prestigious school, well-known in academic circles in America, and Amanda had quoted some statistics on the size of the faculty and the enrollment. Madame Gautier had interrupted. "When do you want to come here?" The turnabout had made Amanda stammer. "I—I—I'd like to see you as soon as possible. This afternoon, if I may." Madame Gautier had said, "I will be out until five. Come at five." Amanda had requested the address, and been given it. "Everyone knows where I live," Madame Gautier had said. "Just past Maison Burg." She had hung up on Amanda's thank you.

Entering Bartrès, Amanda could see that it was hardly even a village. Some old houses, in disrepair, on either side of the road, no main street with shops or businesses anywhere in evidence. Keeping an eye out for someone to direct her, Amanda's eye caught the dashboard clock. The time was four thirty-two, and Madame Gautier would not be home for her until five.

Wondering how to spend the extra time, Amanda saw that she was approaching the old church, and that directly across from it was a café with a sign identifying it as À LA PETITE BERGÈRE, which Amanda translated as "At the Little Shepherdess"—still and most assuredly Bernadette country. The café offered a respite and an opportunity to find out how to reach Madame Gautier's residence.

Amanda parked alongside a fence that protected a schoolyard, and took an outdoor table in the shade at the café. A young waitress materialized, and Amanda ordered an espresso and toasted white bread with butter. She sat waiting, then sipped her espresso and munched her toast, as she tried to map her strategy for dealing with Madame Gautier, actually trying to define what she was after.

Finished, she located her check, summoned the waitress, paid up, and inquired if the young woman could direct her to Madame Gautier. The waitress pointed in the direction that Amanda had already traveled. "Around the curve of the road, not far past the Maison Burg, the farmhouse where Bernadette lived. There is a museum there now. Just beyond is Madame Gautier's place, the newest residence off the road, two stories high. The rich one is seeing you?" Amanda nodded. "I have an appointment." The waitress smirked. "You must be someone special. Otherwise she would not see you. Have an enjoyable stay."

Purse clasped under her arm, somewhat refreshed but still apprehensive of the woman she was about to meet, Amanda tucked herself into the Renault, made a U-turn, and headed in the direction that the waitress had pointed out.

Presently, driving past a cluster of buildings she identified as the Maison Burg, Amanda realized that this had been the old Laguës farmhouse. Here, once long ago, the thirteen-year-old Bernadette had sat and daydreamed of a better life—a month before returning to Lourdes and to eternal glory. Strange, strange story, Amanda reflected. Maybe she would learn more of it very soon. Slowly, Amanda kept driving.

Even without the address, Amanda would have found Madame Gautier's abode with little difficulty. It was the newest and most splendid residence in the area. The gray stucco two-story house with freshly painted green shutters was perched near the top of a small rise, and a paved driveway circled up the rise to the front entrance. Amanda ascended the driveway and left her car at the door.

The woman who answered the bell was no more than five feet tall, and she had just come from the hairdresser's. A mound of purple-white hair sat on her head like an iron wig. The thick lenses of her spectacles magnified the pupils of her eyes. Her nose was as sharp as a hawk's beak and her mouth was pinched. She was a bony Gorgon of a woman.

She opened the door only partway, sizing up her visitor. "You are Madame Clayton from Lourdes?"

"And from the United States," Amanda added. "Madame Gautier?"

"Come in."

Amanda had to ease herself past the reluctantly opened door, then waited as Madame Gautier shut it, turned the deadbolt, and led her through the dark entry into an underfurnished living room bearing several imitation Louis XIV pieces. There was a stiff divan, and Madame Gautier directed Amanda to it. Then she brought a low straight-backed pull-up chair in front of Amanda, and sat down in it like an inquisitor. Briefly, she scrutinized her visitor.

"Who gave you my name?" Madame Gautier wanted to know.

"Father Ruland in Lourdes."

Madame Gautier sniffed. "That one," she said without further elaboration.

"Actually, I asked for the name of the person who sold him Bernadette's journal."

"Why?"

"I—I'd visited Bernadette's old convent in Nevers. I heard from a nun there that the church had acquired only the main part of Bernadette's last journal, the part in which Bernadette had set down her account of the eighteen apparitions. I was told that the church had not bothered to acquire the earlier part of the journal, the part in which Bernadette wrote about her upbringing in Lourdes and her stay here in Bartrès with your ancestor. When I mentioned that to Father Ruland, he confirmed it. I wondered if I might see the seller, and he gave me your name."

The slits behind the thick lenses were appraising Amanda. After brief consideration, the French woman spoke. "You mentioned on the telephone that you were doing a paper about Bernadette. This is a doctoral thesis?"

"No, indeed. I already have my doctorate. This is a professional paper on the psychological state of Bernadette at the time she began seeing the apparitions. I hope to have it published soon."

"You are a Catholic?"

Amanda was uncertain if she should tell the truth or lie. She could not guess what was expected. She decided that the truth was safer. "No, I am not exactly. Although—"

"You are a nonbeliever." This was said flatly, without accusation.

"Well, I am a recent convert. Sort of—"

Madame Gautier's head wagged impatiently. "No, I mean in Bernadette's visions."

Trapped once more, Amanda voted for truth. "Like any rationalist, I am uncertain about visions and miracles. But I'm interested in how some people get them, particularly how Bernadette had them. I want to know what—what her frame of mind was at the time she first went to the grotto."

Madame Gautier's countenance appeared to relax ever so slightly. The slits had become eyes, and the mouth unpinched. "You are a nonbeliever," repeated Madame Gautier.

Amanda was still uncertain. "I am a scholar."

"Who wants to know about Bernadette's earliest years?"

"That would be vital to my investigation. After all, what Bernadette was thinking or doing before she had her visions would be of paramount importance. Obviously, it was not of importance to Father Ruland or he would have gone to greater lengths to purchase that part of the journal from you."

"He could not purchase it because I would not sell it."

Amanda frowned. "Perhaps I misunderstood him, but I had the impression you had shown him those early pages of the journal and he had read them and considered them of little interest, except as a museum piece, and felt they were not worth pursuing further."

"He lied to you," said Madame Gautier. "I don't know why. Maybe as a historian, to prove he saw and read everything. But you have my word—he saw not a single page in which Bernadette wrote about her life in the Gaol at Lourdes and her life with the Laguës in Bartrès."

"How curious," said Amanda. "Didn't he want to buy the first part along with the second?"

"Of course, he did. But I knew that if he saw the first part, he would not buy the second. I wanted to sell the second because I needed the money for myself and for Jean." She paused. "Jean is my sixteen-year-old nephew. I consider him my son, my only child. I want the best for him."

Amanda had felt a thrill of excitement as Madame Gautier spoke. Amanda had caught something. She uncrossed her legs and came forward on the divan. "Madame, did I hear you say you wouldn't sell or even show Father Ruland the first part of Bernadette's journal because if he saw it he would not buy the second part?"

"Correct."

"But what is there in that first part, the part with Bernadette's stay in Bartrès, that might have made Father Ruland not want to buy the second part about the visions? Can you tell me?"

"You must tell me something first. You are a professor in an American university, this university in Chicago, you said on the phone. Is that right?"

"You asked if I was a real professor, and I said I was, indeed. I am a professor."

"This Chicago University, it has students who study science?"

The digression made no sense to Amanda, but she humored Madame Gautier. "We have a real strong department of biology, and—"

"Biochemistry?"

"Absolutely. The department of biochemistry is widely known. There are undergraduate courses in everything from nucleic acids to protein synthesis to bacterial viruses to genetics. A graduate student can also gain a Master of Science degree or work for a Ph.D."

"This is so?"

"I'm not sure what your interest is, but I can have the latest school catalogue sent to you."

"Never mind." Madame Gautier studied her guest. "For now, I must know something else. You are influential?"

"I'm not sure what you mean. Am I influential at the school?"

"At this Chicago University."

Puzzled, Amanda said, "I am on the faculty. I know everyone in the administration. I'm on good terms with all of them. Why do you want to know?"

"You will see," said Madame Gautier enigmatically. "Now we return to your question. Why I would not show Father Ruland the first part of Bernadette's journal."

"Why wouldn't you?" asked Amanda eagerly.

"I told Father Ruland that the first part was not for sale, so there was no point in showing it. I told him it was not for sale because it dealt with Bernadette's stay with my family ancestors in Bartrès, and I wanted to retain it for sentimental reasons, to preserve it and allow Jean —the last of our line—to inherit it. Father Ruland accepted that reason. But the reason I gave for holding back the first part of the journal was not the real reason I did so, not the truth."

"You said if he saw the first part, he might not have bought the second part."

"That is the truth."

"Madame Gautier, I must know, it is imperative that I know, what there is in the first part of the journal that would have made the second part unsaleable."

"I will tell you."

Amanda waited.

Madame Gautier adjusted her glasses, and focused squarely on Amanda's inquiring face. "Because in the first part, what Bernadette wrote makes it clear—if she knew it or not—that she was a little faker."

"A what?"

"What would you call someone who sees things that do not exist—sees them all the time?"

"A hysteric," said Amanda quickly. "A person who has hallucinations—in psychology we sometimes relate it to eidetic imagery—a vivid perception of something as though it were really there."

"Bernadette," said Madame Gautier.

"My God, what are you saying?"

"In writing in her journal of her experiences in Bartrès, Bernadette claims that in her seven months here while tending the sheep she saw Jesus three times and the Virgin Mary *six times*—saw the Virgin six times before she saw her eighteen times a month later in Lourdes. Bernadette was afraid to tell anyone in Bartrès. The Laguës were not people who would stand for such nonsense. They would have thrown her out. But luckily Bernadette soon found the people of Lourdes more gullible."

"She was seeing the Virgin over and over again—before going to the grotto? And seeing Jesus as well? Unbelievable!"

"You can believe she said that—in her own words. I will show you."

Madame Gautier almost bolted from the chair, went to the wall behind Amanda, and removed the framed color print of Versailles from the wall. In the wall, there was a metal safe, similar to the one Ruland had used. Madame Gautier quickly spun the dial, and the door sprang open. She reached inside and pulled out a cheap blue-covered school-type notebook. She began turning the pages as she came back to the divan. "The journal was two notebooks. This one about her early years. The other notebook about what happened at the grotto. Here, see for yourself. Can you read French?"

"Yes."

"Read pages twelve and thirteen, where I have it open." She handed the notebook to Amanda. "Read it."

The slanted handwriting of Bernadette covered the two pages of lined paper. Amanda found it difficult holding the notebook still as her eyes traveled across the pages.

It was there, all there, Jesus seen three times and the Virgin Mary seen six times among the sheep by a lonely rejected little girl, evidence of an absolutely unstable emotional neurotic.

"I must have it," said Amanda, looking up as Madame Gautier took the journal from her. "I want to buy it. I'll pay you any reasonable sum I can afford."

"No," said Madame Gautier.

"Are you afraid of Father Ruland and the Church, what they would say?"

"They can say nothing. Certainly not have their money back. They paid for an authentic part of Bernadette's journal and they got it. If Bernadette made a fool of them earlier, it is not my concern."

"Then what is it? Why do you refuse to sell?"

"I don't say I refuse to sell. I say I refuse to sell merely for a sum of money. While I am not as rich as they say, I don't need more money for myself. What I want is to secure my nephew's future. For that, I need an adequate sum for Jean's tuition at a good school. But it is more than that. Jean wants to study biochemistry in a modern American university. It is his dream. Perhaps he could apply and get in by normal means, but I am told it is sometimes difficult. I want to ensure his future. I want to know that he can go to an American university, like your Chicago University. If you can—"

"Of course, I can," said Amanda. "If Jean's grades are acceptable—"

"The best," Madame Gautier interrupted. "He is brilliant. I will show you."

She darted out of the room, and returned moments later with a folder, which she opened on Amanda's lap.

"You can see for yourself," Madame Gautier said proudly.

Amanda quickly scanned the reports containing Jean's school grades, and the glowing comments by his various instructors. It was obvious that the young man *was* brilliant.

Smiling, Amanda handed the folder back to Madame Gautier. "I can see he is special," agreed Amanda. "No problem. I do have the contacts to get him into the University of Chicago. I can promise—"

"You must guarantee," said Madame Gautier. "For that I will sell you this journal."

"Guarantee what? My guarantee that he gains entrance to the University or another of equal standing and—what?—I pay his tuition? What else?"

"That, no more. I want him there. I want him to have the opportunity."

Amanda was brimming with excitement. "Your nephew shall have his opportunity. I promise you. Give me the journal and I promise—"

Madame Gautier shoved the notebook into the safe and locked it. "A promise is not enough. This is business. I want a guarantee on paper, a signed contract between me, the seller, and you, the buyer."

"Anything!" exclaimed Amanda.

"Let me call Monsieur Abbadie—"

"Who?"

"An old friend and a retired *avocat*—attorney. It must be legal. He will prepare the contract." She headed for another room. "You wait."

Amanda could not sit still any longer. She was on her feet, pacing about the living room, projecting what this tremendous find meant. At first, it meant only the breakthrough with Ken. She would show him the journal. He would read it, see for himself, and see that he had duped himself into worshipping a hallucinating child. Ken would leave and return with her for his operation immediately. If there was a chance for him to be saved, he would be saved.

As Amanda paced, the find acquired a second value. With this exposé, there was another who could be saved, her new friend Liz Finch, who would have one of the stories of the decade and hold onto her job in Paris. Amanda could see the headlines around the world—and then she could see something else, and she halted in her pacing. She could see the end of Lourdes. She could see Lourdes a ghost town, a shunned hamlet. She felt a pang of sorrow and guilt for being the Attila who destroyed it, but—what the hell, she told herself. In her world of reality, there should not be any sick and false faiths that corrupted and, in their own way, misled and destroyed people. Most likely, she told herself, if there were no Lourdes, people would invent one, another one. None of that was her affair. Her concern must be only for her loved one, Ken, and incidentally her friend, Liz Finch.

She realized that Madame Gautier had returned to the living room. "My neighbor, Monsieur Abbadie, was not at his home. He has gone to visit his grandchildren for the day. But I chased after him by phone, spoke to him in Pau. I told him what this was about. He said to me that the contract will be simple to make. He will be back in Bartrès in the early morning. He will draw up the contract and come here with it and you can look it over at lunch."

"Tomorrow?" said Amanda.

"You can go back to Lourdes and return in the morning. It is not far. Or you can stay and have dinner with Jean and myself, and sleep overnight at a British children's hostel we have nearby, Hosanna

House. It is not normally done, but I can make an arrangement for you."

"I'm sorry, I can't. I have to go back to Lourdes. It's my husband, you see. He's—"

"Praying for a miracle?"

For the first time, Madame Gautier's features softened. "Go to him. You will have the journal in your hands tomorrow. That I promise."

In the early evening, Edith Moore stood at the base of the statue of Father Peyramale, curé of Lourdes in Bernadette's time and the first important clergyman to accept the peasant girl's vision, and tilted her head back for a view of the belltower in the illuminated steeple of the Church of the Sacred Heart. It was comforting for Edith to remember that this church, in 1903, had finally replaced Father Peyramale's original parish church. His remains had been interred in a crypt in the basement and his original wooden confessional box had been moved there, too.

It was also comforting to Edith to know that Father Ruland himself had scheduled her confession. Father Ruland had taken an interest in Edith's case three years ago, and he had befriended both Edith and Reggie throughout that time. Reggie, after learning of his wife's meeting with Dr. Kleinberg and after seeing Kleinberg himself, had telephoned Father Ruland to be absolutely certain that a priest would be on hand to hear her confession. Reggie had hinted that the confession was an important one for his wife. He had told Ruland, Edith's wish was to undertake the confession not in a chapel in the domain but at the Church of the Sacred Heart in the Old Town. This, for sentimental reasons. Because it had been in the Church of the Sacred Heart that Edith had gone to confession three years ago, hours before her cure. If all this prearrangement had been a bit unorthodox, it apparently had not bothered Father Ruland in the least. He had been cooperative about both of Reggie's requests. The place and time had been set, and the time was now.

Limping noticeably, Edith crossed the Rue St.-Pierre, went down the Rue de l'Église, climbed the steps to the church entrance, and went inside. There was a handful of worshippers in the pews, and Edith slid into an isolated pew, knelt, and offered up a prayer of contrition.

"Oh my God, I am heartily sorry for having offended you," she whispered, "and I detest all my sins, because of your punishments, but most of all because they offend you, my God, who are all good and deserving of all my love. I firmly resolve, with the help of your grace, to confess my sins, to do penance, and to amend my life. Amen."

Rising, limping down the aisle, Edith made her way to the confessional box where Father Ruland had said a priest would be waiting. Advancing toward it, Edith tried to speculate on the priest's reaction to her confession. Since Father Ruland knew a clergyman would be there to hear her, there was some hope that the priest might be as broadminded as Ruland himself. Reggie had always said that of all the priests in Lourdes, Father Ruland was the most practical, and reasonable, the priest most aware of the difficult ways of the world. Perhaps his appointee would be equally reasonable and flexible tonight or perhaps he would be offended. She could not guess which.

Inside the confessional booth, Edith knelt once more and addressed the openwork lattice set in the wall.

"Father, I need help."

An avuncular voice, slightly muffled, came through the lattice. "You may proceed."

From frequent practice in recent years, Edith went directly into the confessional procedure. "Bless me, Father," she began. "I confess to Almighty God and to you, Father, that I have sinned. It is almost a week since my last confession. I accuse myself of a single sin that occurred earlier today."

There was no response from the other side of the lattice, but Edith knew that the priest who was there was attentive. Edith resumed, feeling confident that what she was about to say was protected by the seal of the confessional. "Father, my recovery, which the Medical Bureau accepted as a miracle cure, and which my archbishop in London told me would be announced as such, is a failure. The last physician brought here to give final validation has found that the cure was temporary. The tumor is growing once more."

There was a brief silence. Then the priest spoke in an undertone. "You are sure of this? Your doctor is certain?"

"Yes, he is certain."

"Has he reported this to Dr. Berryer?"

"To no one but me, just Reggie and me."

"And your sin? You are ready to confess it?"

"I am, Father. Dr. Kleinberg informed me that my condition would worsen, would prove fatal, unless I submitted to a new kind of treatment that a certain doctor has been experimenting with secretly. This doctor is prepared to come to Lourdes tomorrow to try it on me Sunday. I am told I would have a seventy percent chance of recovery. If

I am healed by surgery, I can no longer be called miraculously cured, can I?"

The priest evaded the question. "Your sin?"

"I am fighting temptation, Father. As long as I am regarded as a miracle woman, I can help my husband. Right now he is doing wonderfully with our restaurant. But all of my inheritance is invested in this business. The minute that I am not a miracle woman any more, the business will deteriorate and eventually we will lose everything. Reggie and I put our heads together and we came up with a plan. This is my real sin, Father. I sent Reggie to Dr. Kleinberg to ask whether, if I submitted to this medical treatment and it was successful, he could shut his eyes to it and tell the Medical Bureau that I had been miraculously cured. We asked him to lie on my behalf."

"And Dr. Kleinberg, what did he say to this request?"

"He said that he could not validate me as miraculously cured. Only the church could do that. He said that if I found someone in the church who was willing to overlook the treatment—assuming I had it—and state that my cure had been miraculous, he would not interfere or mention the operation. He suggested I ask someone in the church to consider announcing that my cure was a miracle." Her voice was hesitant. "Is that possible, Father?"

There was a short silence. At last the priest's reply came through the lattice. "No, it is not possible. To know that you have been cured by medical means but pretend you have been cured by miraculous means would be a deceit the church could not condone. I am sorry."

Shaken, and ashamed, Edith pleaded plaintively through the lattice. "Father, I am lost. What should I do?"

"To save yourself? As your priest, I can only suggest that you offer yourself once more to the mercies of the Blessed Virgin. But I do understand the hesitation you might have about doing that, since you have believed that you were cured by Her, and for some reason unknown to us, you were not. On the other hand, your physician suggests that if you submit to medical science and surgery, you have a greater certainty of survival. You must make the choice."

"Then, Father, I should submit to surgery?"

"Why not? You may very well be healed in order to be useful on earth, but you cannot call your healing miraculous."

"Well, I guess whatever I do, I am choosing between two kinds of death. Because, even if I live, I can never be a miracle woman again."

There was a lengthier silence, and finally the priest spoke. "We do not believe that miracles are enjoyed only by ailing persons miraculously cured at the grotto. There are, in God's infinite wisdom, numerous other miracles that occur. There will be a different kind of miracle in Lourdes this week. The person to whom the Blessed Virgin appears, on Her reappearance, the person who sees the Virgin, will be a miracle person—a miracle man or a miracle woman."

"Really?"

"Certainly. That person, like Bernadette earlier, would for all eternity be known as a miracle person."

With that, Edith nodded and finished her confession. "I am sorry for my sin—my sins—asking my doctor what I did . . . and asking you. I am sorry for those sins and all the sins of my whole life, in particular my sins of selfishness and greed."

The priest responded automatically. As a penance for her sins, he assigned her to a dozen Hail Marys. Then he gave her absolution.

When it was over, Edith rose to her feet, left the booth, walked unevenly up the aisle and out of the Church of the Sacred Heart. Her course was clear.

She would phone Reggie at the restaurant where she had urged him to remain and tell him to inform Dr. Kleinberg that she was ready for Dr. Duval's new surgery—surgery and inevitable destitution—as soon as possible.

After that, she would go to the grotto and pray beneath the niche, pray fervently once more and hope that the Virgin Mary would appear to her and save her before the scalpel could touch her flesh.

Profoundly miserable, she started limping away. As she left, only one strange thing niggled at her—the voice of the priest in the confessional—it had seemed faintly familiar . . . if it had been more distinct she would have sworn that it had been none other than the voice of Father Ruland.

14

Saturday, August 20

The sun was rising this early morning in Lourdes when Father Ruland, having finished his breakfast, left the large Chaplains' Residence behind the Upper Basilica and strolled toward the ramp which would take him to his office in the Rosary Basilica.

Normally, during this walk, he was accustomed to inhaling God's good air deeply for his health, to compensate for his sedentary way of life. However, this crisp morning, he was too bemused to breathe deeply.

Strolling along, Father Ruland was lost in thought, and what occupied his mind was Edith Moore's confession last night. At almost the final moment, he had decided to sit behind the lattice in the Church of the Sacred Heart and listen to Edith's confession himself. Ruland did not know if Edith had recognized his voice, even though he had partially covered his mouth when he had spoken to her. If she had suspected or guessed at his presence, it really did not matter. What mattered had been her confession itself, which some instinct had driven him to hear.

The miraculous cure that Ruland had looked forward to announcing, a marvelous declaration for The Reappearance Time, was no more. The news had been unexpected, but there could be no doubting it. Dr. Kleinberg had been summoned here because he was among the best in his specialty, and his tests and X rays—which led to his diagnosis—could not lie. Edith Moore had been cured (probably a spontaneous remission), and now she was no longer cured.

Father Ruland turned the matter over in his mind. From a selfish point of view, it was a sad outcome. The Church could have used her miraculous cure to great advantage, heralded it far and wide, and profited from the publicity. Nor was he unmindful of the loss this was to the Moores. They had invested everything in commercializing the cure, and they would be bankrupted in many other ways as well.

He wished that he could condone the deceit that Edith Moore had begged for. He had, in his weaknesses, committed many small sins, but he had never committed a large one. In fact, it surprised him that Dr. Paul Kleinberg, a physician of impeccable reputation, had lent himself to collaborating in a deceit—but then, he really hadn't. He had really left the final decision and actual deceit to a clergyman, to Ruland himself. Ruland wondered if Dr. Kleinberg, learning of Edith's rejection by the clergy, might dare reconsider and certify her on his own, but instantly he knew that Kleinberg would not. He knew that Kleinberg was a Jew, and would have no wish to become a medical Dreyfus. Well, that was that. Poor, unhappy Edith.

Still, Father Ruland reminded himself, he had tried to help Edith Moore in his fashion. He had tried to tell her something. It had been oblique, subtle, and in no way could God truly fault him for his humanity, but Ruland was afraid that Edith Moore was too dim-witted to grasp what he had tried to tell her.

He sighed. He had done as much as an honest servant of God could do. He, too, could be absolved for having no further involvement in the unfortunate woman's case.

Aware that he had arrived at the Rosary Esplanade, he went to his office, where he planned to settle down for a long and strenuous day at his desk.

Entering his office, Father Ruland was surprised at the visitor who had preceded him, although not surprised that his visitor had located the key to the only cabinet in the office, unlocked it, found the fifth of J & B scotch, and was pouring himself a whisky straight.

The lanky bishop of Tarbes and Lourdes, Monseigneur Peyragne, came away from the cabinet with the shot of whisky in hand, acknowledged Ruland with a short dip of his head, and folded himself into the chair across from Ruland's desk. "I'm impressed by the early hours you keep," said the bishop.

"I am even more impressed by your being here earlier," said Father Ruland, occupying his chair behind the desk. "These are busy days." He studied the bishop's creased face. "Anything wrong, Your Excellency?"

"Yes, busy days," Bishop Peyragne agreed. He sipped his whisky, then lay his head back and threw down the rest of the drink. "But unproductive days. That is what troubles me."

"Unproductive in what sense?"

"You know what I mean, Ruland. This is a special week. We're here in Lourdes—at least I am—for a special reason."

"Of course, the reappearance of the Blessed Virgin."

"I know that you are the repository of all information on everything that is happening in Lourdes," said the bishop. "Is there anything happening? Has there even been a hint of the Virgin's reappearance?"

"The usual number of sightings by a few who are unstable or emotionally disturbed. Brief questioning brings an end to their fancies. It is not difficult to ferret out the truth."

"Yes, I imagine you're good at that."

"Merely experienced," said Father Ruland modestly.

"I don't mind telling you I'm troubled," said the bishop. "I was worried about this event from the moment that His Holiness ordered us to make the announcement. After all, in my lifetime, in fact since Bernadette's time, the Blessed Virgin has never appeared in this area. It gives one cause for concern. Too much pressure has built up. I don't like the atmosphere of Great Expectations."

"Still, Your Excellency, this is all the result of the Virgin's word to us."

"Through Bernadette, only through Bernadette," said the bishop unhappily. "Perhaps her writings in the journal were misread or misinterpreted."

"I have no sense of error," said Father Ruland. "I have studied the journal many times myself. Bernadette was precise in her report of the secret that the Virgin Mary had confided to her—exact as to the year, the month, the days of the Virgin's coming. This is the year, the very month, the days promised."

"Within eight days, She would reappear, the Virgin promised. This is the seventh day. That leaves but one more day," said the bishop.

"True."

"I think that gives reason for concern. What if Bernadette herself made a mistake? What if she did not hear the Virgin correctly, or in setting down what she had heard in 1858, after many years had passed, what if her memory had distorted her recollection? If some human error like that could be learned before time runs out, it could be announced and would be understood and the Church would escape censure. Yes, what if Bernadette made a mistake?"

Father Ruland would not be swayed. "I don't think she made a mistake, Your Excellency."

The bishop sat up. "Well, it's in your hands." He put his empty shot glass on the edge of the desk and rose to his feet. "I must be off. Only today and tomorrow left. I trust you will stay closely in touch." He started for the door. "I wish I were as sure as you."

Father Ruland stood up with a small bow. "Have faith," he said with a smile.

The bishop of Tarbes and Lourdes paused, responded with an angry glare, and left the office in the Rosary Basilica.

In the pleasantly decorated office of Inspector Fontaine, in the Commissariat de police de Lourdes at 7, Rue du Baron-Duprat, Liz Finch had just about finished her interview, and the page of the spiral notepad resting on her crossed knees was still blank.

It was a fruitless exercise, this interview, Liz knew, and besides, Bill Trask had already told her that he and API had no interest in the murder of a nonentity. Still, hoping for some break in the story, but mainly because she had little else to do or report and because she was becoming desperate, Liz had arranged the interview and had gone through with it.

To make matters worse, Inspector Fontaine was a typical civil servant drone. Born with a solid appearance of authority, graying now but of athletic build (she'd heard he was still captain of a local soccer team), he was an unimaginative man. She was sure that he woke early every day, shuffled papers, filled the march of hours, and enjoyed sound sleep. On the wall behind him, Inspector Fontaine had two framed photographs, one of Alphonse Bertillion of Paris, the other of Professor Edmund Locard of Lyons. They represented all the detective brain power in the room. Inspector Fontaine could not be expected to see that the brutal slaying of a gorgeous young French girl in this haven of healing might offer some possibilities for a story.

"So," said Liz, tired of the inspector's non sequiturs and digressions, "that's the latest word—no suspects."

"Because there are no clues," Inspector Fontaine repeated. "I lean to the belief that someone, some stranger, came in off the street to rob Miss Dupree, and she walked in on him, perhaps tried to stop him, and he killed her and fled."

"But if there was a robbery, something would have been stolen. The apartment belonged to Dominique, Gisele's waitress friend. Gisele had next to no possessions there. And Dominique did an inventory and told you that not a single item had been removed."

"Probably the burglar was interrupted and fled before he could take anything."

"Possibly," said Liz, but "impossibly" was the word for the Inspector, impossibly thick-headed and dull.

"What makes our work more difficult," Inspector Fontaine went on, "is that Miss Dupree knew everyone, and everyone loved her. Not one local would have had a motive to hurt her."

About to close her notepad, Liz suddenly said, "What about someone not local, maybe a foreigner, a foreign pilgrim or visitor?"

"But you can see how difficult that is," said Inspector Fontaine, "because of Miss Dupree's profession. She was a tour guide, and so many of her tour groups consisted of foreigners. They came and went, they come and go."

"Did she ever become friendly with any of these foreign tourists?"

"No, except—" Inspector Fontaine was thoughtful a moment, but Liz continued to doubt that he could think. "Now that you speak of it, there was one foreigner she knew a bit better than most. When I was forced to go to Tarbes to notify the victim's parents—terrible duty, but it had to be done—I stayed on to discuss with the Duprees any persons that their daughter might have met recently. They knew not a thing about the tourists in her groups, but I do recall that her father mentioned one pilgrim, a foreigner, an American, who had come to room with them, and their daughter had helped the American commute to Lourdes. His name . . ." Fontaine pulled a manila folder in front of him, opened it, and turned over some papers. "Samuel Talley, a professor from a university in New York, who came to Lourdes hoping for a cure. Dupree did not believe his daughter knew the American very well. Besides, Dupree said, the American was of spotless reputation. Nevertheless, we tried to find Talley and interrogate him, but by the time we located his hotel, he had checked out and taken a flight to Paris late yesterday. Routinely, we had the Paris Sûreté follow up, but Mr. Talley could not be located and it was presumed that he had returned to New York, although his name was not on any flight manifest. Of course, this could have been an airlines oversight."

"But you have no reason to suspect this Talley?"

"Not Talley, not anyone. We have not a single suspect at this stage of the investigation."

Liz snapped her notepad shut with finality, tucked it in her purse, and rose. "Thank you for your time, Inspector. If you come up with anything, I'd appreciate it if you'd call me."

He was on his feet, probably hoping that she would spell his name right, and he was seeing her to the door.

Leaving the Commissariat building, reaching the sidewalk of the Rue du Baron-Duprat and the relatively more stimulating world of the town, Liz barely avoided colliding with a pair who had turned off the sidewalk to go inside.

One of the pair, a youngish French blonde, took Liz by the arm. "Miss Finch, how are you? Michelle Demaillot—"

"Yes, the Press Bureau. Hello."

Michelle introduced a runty young man who was carrying a load of camera equipment slung over one shoulder. "This is a colleague of yours from Paris. Monsieur Pascal of *Paris-Match*. Perhaps you know each other?"

"I'm afraid not," said Liz, shaking the photographer's hand.

Continuing in her usual Chamber of Commerce manner, Michelle said, "You are finding some good stories, I presume?"

"Not much to date," said Liz. "Not much seems to be happening."

"Except one dreadful thing. Did you hear what happened to Gisele Dupree? You remember her, don't you? I saw you dining together in the Miracle Restaurant. You have heard?"

Liz nodded wearily. "Yes, I heard. I was quite shocked."

"Unbelievable," said Michelle, showing honest grief. "So terrible, especially when things were going well for her. Gisele had called me just the day before, told me she'd turned to writing in her spare time. Actually got a magazine assignment to do a piece on the famous Russian foreign minister—you know, Tikhanov—whom she'd met at the United Nations. Gisele needed a picture of Tikhanov, and I remembered Pascal here was flying in to do a layout. So I phoned him in Paris and asked him to bring along some art on Tikhanov, and he did, and Gisele picked up the photos the night before last."

Something tinkled in Liz's head. "She picked up the pictures of Minister Tikhanov?"

"Yes, I left the package for her and she picked it up."

"The article on him she was writing, had she finished it already and prepared it for mailing? Or was she still writing it?"

"Still in the process of writing it, I think."

Odd, Liz thought. After finding Gisele's body, she had gone through Gisele's apartment, hastily but thoroughly, yet had come across no notes or manuscript about Tikhanov, nor the *Paris-Match* photographs, either. If Gisele really had them, they would have been somewhere in the apartment. Gisele had no office of her own at the tourist agency or anywhere else. The Tikhanov material must have been in her borrowed apartment. But Liz had discovered Gisele's body, searched the apartment, and there was nothing. It was as if someone had been there before Liz to remove the photos—to kill Gisele and remove them.

Parting from Michelle and the photographer, Liz started back to the hotel, turning the oddity over in her mind, and gradually accelerating her pace.

The minute that she was alone in her room, she picked up the phone and put through a call to Bill Trask in Paris. She did so without hesitation, because as a loser already, she had nothing more to lose.

When she reached Trask, she said, "Bill, there's something I'd like you to have someone in the office look into for me."

"Okay."

"It is about Soviet Foreign Minister Sergei Tikhanov. I'd like to know if he's in Paris."

"You're covering Lourdes right now. What in the hell has Lourdes got to do with Tikhanov?"

"Just what I want to find out. I have a hunch that Tikhanov may have been in Lourdes recently."

"Looking for the Virgin Mary?" Trask burst out laughing. "What is this, the silly season or what? Tikhanov in Lourdes? That's plain funny."

"I think so, too. That's why I'm calling you. Because it *is* funny, the idea of it. But I have a reason for asking you to check on him."

"Well, if you have a reason—" said Trask doubtfully.

"Bill, please have someone ring the Soviet Embassy and find out if Tikhanov is there. Then buzz me right back. I'll be in my room waiting for your call."

"Okay, let me see. Stand by."

Liz hung up and literally did stand by. She was too restless to sit, so she stood up, and wondered if her wild hunch, based on an oddity, could be converted into a last-hour newsbeat that would save her job and save Paris for her.

She had just noted that six minutes had passed, when the telephone rang.

Trask wasted no time. "Liz, we called the Soviet Embassy, as you requested. Yes, Foreign Minister Tikhanov is here, which is hardly unusual, since he's always bouncing back and forth. Tomorrow he will be in Moscow again."

"No." Liz had to restrain herself from crying out. She said excitedly, "Bill, don't let him get away. He's got to be detained for questioning—"

"Questioning about what?"

"The murder of that French kid in Lourdes yesterday, the girl I told you about."

"Oh, that. How am I supposed to detain the foreign minister of the Soviet Union?"

"By getting the Sûreté to put a hold on him until he can be questioned."

"If the Sûreté were to hold him, they'd have to charge him with the crime. What evidence do you have—"

"He may have killed the girl to get back some damaging information she had on him."

"Liz, *hard* evidence, *real* evidence."

"I don't have any yet, but given half a chance—"

"Liz, I haven't quite finished what I was saying. Even if the Sûreté had such real evidence, they couldn't do a damn thing about it. Young lady, haven't you heard? Sergei Tikhanov is the foreign minister of the Soviet Union. He's a top-notch diplomat visiting France. Have you ever heard of diplomatic immunity?"

"Oh, shit, they wouldn't invoke that."

"You bet the Soviets would invoke that. Besides, what difference, you don't have the goods in hand. Listen, stop spinning wheels. You forget Tikhanov. You keep your eyes open for the Virgin Mary. You hear me? That's an order."

"All right, boss," she said in a small voice.

"An order and don't forget it," repeated Trask. "And get back to work. Get us something from Lourdes."

She heard the loud click on the other end, and hung up, also.

She lowered herself into a chair, bereft. Another hope for survival had been snuffed out. She was trying too hard, snatching at anything, becoming too desperate. Shaking out a cigarette, lighting it, smoking, she tried to calm herself. There had to be something she could file from this damn place. Her thinking cap had become a helmeted Iron Maiden. There was no reach in her head, only a buzzing pain. Well, since there was no story here, what *would* be a story, even a lousy one, but an acceptable one? Her mind clanked slowly toward the only person she knew who might be a story. Edith Moore.

Reluctantly, Liz requested the information operator to give her the phone number of that new restaurant, or renovated one, the one now named Madame Moore's Miracle Restaurant. Once she'd obtained the phone number, Liz called it. She told the woman who answered the phone that she wanted to speak to Mr. Reggie Moore. "Tell him Liz Finch of API, the American syndicate, wants to speak to him."

There was hardly any wait at all, and Reggie was on the phone, sweet as molasses in his wrong-side-of-the-town London accent.

Liz had no taste for molasses this moment. "Mr. Moore, I want to do a story about your wife, an interview with her concerning her cure and her feelings about her imminent crowning as the new miracle woman of Lourdes. This will be a top feature for our international wire. Think she'll cooperate?"

"I—I'm absolutely positive she'll be delighted."

"All right, let's make it your restaurant at two o'clock tomorrow afternoon. We'll have tea and talk healing. You produce the body and I'll produce the story."

"Happy to do so," chirped Reggie. "Tomorrow, I agree. Looking forward."

As she hung up once more, not looking forward, Liz's mind flashed to her glamorous rival, Marguerite, and her glamorous scandal story on the glamorous Andrew Viron.

And she was left with the crumbs, the dowdy Edith Moore.

For the hundredth time Liz wanted to kill herself, but then philosophically decided that a girl's gotta live, gotta earn her keep, and make the best of it. In the interim she would go out and buy a bagful of éclairs to keep her busy.

Amanda made it back to Lourdes from Bartrès in no time flat.

She had the Renault's radio on all the way, and hummed gaily to the tunes of a French medley. On the passenger seat beside her were the original and three photocopies of Bernadette's last journal, and with the journal she knew that she had everything that she needed.

Entering Lourdes she was more aware than ever of the shops in the town, the hotels and cafés, the pious pilgrims on the sidewalks, and she realized again that on the seat beside her lay the material that would devastate the community, level it for all time. In a way she was sorry it had to be done to this French Pompeii. Even if Lourdes was a fake it had made millions of gullible people throughout the world feel better about their lot and it had given most of them hope. Nevertheless, Amanda assured herself, what she was about to do to the town would be appreciated by all the rational, civilized people on earth who wanted honesty and truth.

Nearing the Hôtel Gallia & Londres, Amanda looked about for a parking place, luckily found one immediately. Grabbing the journal and the three photocopies she'd had made, she dashed into the hotel, eager to see Ken and have him read the journal for himself. She expected to find Ken on the bed, resting after another prolonged visit to the grotto.

But he was neither on the bed nor in the room. What was on the bed, instead, was a note, a sheet of stationery folded over and bearing her own name on it.

Unfolding the note, she found the handwriting barely recognizable, but realized it was from Ken. Deciphering the words, she read:

> *Amanda, became more ill this morn. The hotel arranged for me to be taken to Centre Hôpitalier General de Lourdes, 2, Avenue Alexandre-Marque, for examination and treatment. Don't worry. God will look after me.*
>
> *Love,*
> *Ken*

Amanda felt herself sag. Maybe it was too late. Maybe all her efforts, and her great find, had been for nought. Ken's potentially fatal disease was overcoming him, and now probably the hasty return to Chicago would do no good.

Amanda pulled herself together. Snatching up one of the envelopes that contained a copy of Bernadette's journal, she was immediately on the run.

Twenty minutes later, following the hotel receptionist's directions, Amanda was inside the Centre Hôpitalier General de Lourdes, hurrying along the second-floor hallway until she found the number of Ken's room. There was a sign posted on the door stating "No Visitors." Ignoring it, Amanda nervously knocked. After a brief wait, the door partially opened. A woman poked her head out and gazed at Amanda inquiringly.

Amanda said, "I'm told Mr. Kenneth Clayton is here. I must see him."

The woman bobbed her head. "You are Mrs. Amanda Clayton?"

"Yes, his wife."

"One moment, please."

The door closed once more, and Amanda waited impatiently until the door opened again.

The woman, who was in street dress, not uniform, took Amanda lightly by the arm and turned her away, moving her down the hall.

"But I want to see him," Amanda protested.

"Not yet," said the woman. "I am Dr. Kleinberg's nurse, Esther Levinson, and I will explain. We will go to the visitors' room where we can talk."

"How is he?" Amanda demanded to know.

"Better, better."

Inside the shaded waiting room, Esther pushed Amanda toward the sofa, and sat down beside her.

"Why can't I see him?" Amanda insisted.

"Because the doctor is with him," said Esther. "You have apparently been outside the city—"

"Yes, but if I'd known—"

"Never mind. Allow me to give you the sequence. When Mr. Clayton felt so ill before noon, he summoned the hotel reception to get him help. The reception telephoned Dr. Berryer at the Medical Bureau, and he said that there was a sarcoma specialist in Lourdes from Paris, my employer, Dr. Paul Kleinberg. Since Dr. Kleinberg had gone to the airport to pick up a colleague, and to pick me up as well, he could not be reached. So Dr. Berryer located a resident physician in Lourdes, Dr. Escaloma, who is with Mr. Clayton right now. As for Dr. Kleinberg, after he picked us up at the airport, he dropped me at our hotel, and went off—I do not know where—to sit and confer with his colleague. In the meantime, in our hotel, I found the message for Dr. Kleinberg from Dr. Berryer. Since I had no idea where Dr. Kleinberg was, I decided to come straight to the hospital to see what was going on and to wait for Dr. Kleinberg."

"I'm so grateful," said Amanda. "But what *is* going on with Ken now?"

"He is being examined, and being made comfortable until Dr. Kleinberg gets the message and comes here." Esther cocked her head, studying Amanda, and said, "I can be frank with you, can I not?"

"Please tell me what you can."

"There is only one thing to tell you, but you must already know it. I have seen so many of these cases, and I know Mr. Clayton's one hope is to have surgery. I am sure Dr. Kleinberg will confirm the necessity. But I am afraid Dr. Kleinberg will get no further than I did when I discussed the matter with your husband. He refused."

"He still won't consider surgery?"

"Unfortunately, he will not consider it. He is putting his life entirely in the hands of the Virgin Mary and her curative powers. But— forgive me if you are a believer—"

"Just the opposite."

"—but the Virgin Mary is not the specialist I would depend upon in a case as—as grave as this one."

"I agree," said Amanda. "I've been working every day to get Ken back to Chicago and on the operating table. I haven't been able to convince him." She touched the manila envelope on her lap, about to speak of it but decided against it. "Now I think I have the means of convincing him to submit to surgery immediately. That's why I want to see him this minute."

"Mrs. Clayton, you cannot see him this minute nor for a while. When I stepped out, Mr. Clayton was being sedated. By now he'll be fast asleep."

"When will he wake up so I can speak to him?"

"Not for a couple of hours, at least, that is my guess."

"Then I'll stay right here and wait. I want to be here when he awakens."

Esther came to her feet. "Stay if you wish. I'll let you know when Mr. Clayton is awake."

Once alone, Amanda settled back on the sofa and lightly tapped the copy of Bernadette's journal on her lap. It made her feel safer. In her mind's eye she saw Ken post-surgery, restored to health and vigor, she saw the two of them at their wedding, she saw them on their honeymoon in Papeete, and she saw them a few years later with their first child, their son.

Amanda closed her eyes to shut out all else except the sweetness of what her mind's eye sought. She tried to open her eyes, but the lids were heavy, and drooped, and she closed them again. Her body, enveloped by fatigue, gradually relaxed and soon she dozed off.

How long she slept on the waiting room sofa, she did not know, but a gentle hand on her shoulder finally wakened her.

She squinted up at the nurse, the one named Esther, who was standing over her with a smile. Amanda looked around. The lamps in the room were on, and through the shutters she could see that it was night outside.

A sudden awareness of what had happened and where she was roused Amanda to full wakefulness. She sat erect.

"What time is it?"

"After eleven, going on midnight."

"Can I see Ken now?"

"No, not tonight. He will sleep through the night. Dr. Kleinberg was here after dinner and looked in on him. Dr. Kleinberg says Mr. Clayton must rest—the best thing for him—and must not be disturbed tonight. Dr. Kleinberg will return in the morning. Then Mr. Clayton will be awake, and you will be permitted to see him. Right now I thought you should be notified and you should return to your hotel and get a good night's rest yourself."

"Yes, I guess there's no choice." Amanda struggled to her feet. "How early can I see Ken?"

"I'm sure nine-thirty in the morning will be fine. By then Dr. Kleinberg will have examined him."

"I'll be here before then. Thanks for everything."

After departing the hospital, and once inside her rented car again, Amanda realized that she still had the manila envelope containing the photocopy of Bernadette's journal in hand. But since Ken would not be able to read it until morning, she decided to bring Ken one of the other copies in their hotel room and turn this one over to Liz Finch as soon as possible. It would give Liz the story of her lifetime, and Liz deserved the break.

Instead of going directly to the hotel, Amanda detoured toward the press tent and parked her car close to the domain. The streets of Lourdes were virtually abandoned at this hour. Amanda walked toward the press tent, carrying her manila envelope, reached the entrance of the tent, and went inside.

The interior was brightly illuminated, and only three correspondents could be seen at work. Liz Finch's desk was unoccupied. By this time, Liz was certainly asleep, so Amanda decided to leave her gift on Liz's desk top with a brief note to her.

Going to the desk, Amanda sat in the swivel chair, found a red pencil and printed boldly on the manila envelope:

FOR LIZ FINCH, API.
PERSONAL AND VERY IMPORTANT

Then Amanda took up a piece of scratch paper and scribbled out a hasty note:

Liz dear,
I hit pay dirt in Bartrès. Here is a copy of Bernadette's journal I acquired—the part the church didn't see. Read it. This should give you the scoop of the year. But don't do anything about it until we talk. I'll let you know all the details. Ken's in the hospital. I'm seeing him at nine-thirty. Should be able to meet you at the hotel around eleven.

Ever,
Amanda.

Rereading her note, Amanda had second thoughts about leaving it open on Liz's desk. Other reporters who shared or passed Liz's desk might be tempted to read—and possibly confiscate—the journal. Wondering where Liz received her private mail, Amanda gave the interior of the press tent more careful scrutiny. Then she saw against a side wall

what she had overlooked upon entering. There were rows of what resembled tiers of safe deposit boxes—several hundred of them—and, at
one end, in front of them, a plump middle-aged female in the garb of a
security guard, sitting at a sturdy table, reading a book.

Hastily folding the note that she had written, Amanda placed it
inside the manila envelope. Then staggering to her feet, she approached
the security guard.

"Pardon me, madame," said Amanda, "but where does one leave
private mail for the reporters? In those deposit boxes?"

"Yes, every accredited reporter has a locked box with his own
key."

"Good. Well, I'd like to leave something personal for the American
reporter Liz Finch."

"If you give it to me, I can take care of it."

The security woman appeared bland and trustworthy, but having
come this far with her precious find, Amanda was taking no chances.
"If you don't mind, I'd prefer to leave it in her box myself."

"As you wish." The woman had pulled out a middle drawer beneath the table and was consulting some kind of cardboard directory.
"Liz Finch. Box 126." Taking out a ring of keys, the woman got up and
led Amanda past the rows of safe deposit boxes. The woman halted
before a stack of tiers, inserted her key in a metal box at shoulder
height, and opened it. "You can put your envelope in here. It will be
absolutely private."

Inside the deposit box Amanda could see some other envelopes,
Dentyne gum, several packs of cigarettes, and a tin of Altoid mints.
Smiling to herself, Amanda pushed her valuable manila envelope into
the box.

The woman closed the box and made a show of carefully locking it.
"There you are. Now you can be sure Miss Finch alone will have it."

"I thank you very, very much," said Amanda.

Relieved, Amanda watched the woman return to her table. Pleased
at having given her friend a scoop, she stretched her aching muscles,
became aware once more of her exhaustion, and then slowly she headed
for her car and the hotel, and a night of sound sleep which would
reinforce her for what the morning would bring.

At eleven thirty-two that night, having quietly left the bed, feeling
reassured that Natale would not awaken but sleep the night through,
Mikel Hurtado slowly dressed and then searched for the keys to the
European Ford he had rented. With a last backward glance at Natale's
reposeful body, and a stab of regret at their enforced parting, he slipped

out of the room, locked the door, and started for the elevator and his rendezvous with Basque destiny.

Outside the Hôtel Gallia & Londres, Hurtado turned right on the Avenue Bernadette Soubirous. Tension within him mounted as he approached the corner. He had gone to the corner twice in the past three days, and the Lourdes police had maintained their patrol of the ramp entrance to the domain below. This had not disconcerted Hurtado, because he had been alerted to expect them by Yvonne, the receptionist. Her girl friend, who slept with Police Inspector Fontaine, had told Yvonne that the police would be continuing their watch through Friday, but would end the surveillance no later than tonight.

For the past three days, Hurtado realized, he might have been out of his skull with worry and restlessness had it not been for Natale. Her very presence morning, afternoon, and night for seventy-two hours had distracted and soothed him. He had never met a young woman like her. Despite her handicap, she had been unfailingly cheerful and fun. Witty and teasing as they woke each morning and began to make love. Passionate and intense in her coupling. Serious and devout at the grotto every late morning and mid-afternoon. Fascinating and philosophical in her conversations at lunch and dinner. A totally sensual female in their evening lovemaking. Hurtado had never experienced such an ability to give wholly of the flesh from a member of the opposite sex. Natale was a wonder, a unique being, and the perfection of her beauty from forehead to toes was breathtaking. And after they had soared to a climax together just two hours ago, and after she had fallen asleep, he was hesitant for the first time about completing his mission.

In bed beside her, he had reflected on what lay ahead. To begin with, the guilt he would experience for obliterating the grotto before the last day of the Virgin Mary's reappearance, a day, he knew, during which Natale planned a marathon session to reach the only one she believed might possibly take pity on her. Natale would leave without the mystical final day in which to offer up prayer, without the grotto to kneel before, and without the young man with whom she'd fallen in love. She would return to Rome, crushed and alone.

For himself, he would be many kilometers away, hiding with fellow Basques in a village in France, awaiting the day when the French police would cease their hunt for the most blasphemous terrorist of all time, and for the inspections at the frontier to Spain, in Hendaye, to be eased. Then he would creep back into Spain, and build force and pressure against Minister Bueno and the Spanish government, and he would be able to join the jubilant crowds in the streets of San Sebastián when Basque Spain became the independent nation of Euskadi. Only then—

how long? how many years?—might he be able to set out on a lone pilgrimage to Rome, to seek and hopefully to find an older Natale. Perhaps in her disillusionment and anger she would reject him.

Lying there in bed with those thoughts, he'd had his second thoughts, considered abandoning this violent mission and praying with Natale and for her on the last day, and if nothing changed for her (and he knew that it wouldn't), accompanying her back to Rome. There he could resume his career as a writer—an author could write anywhere—and he could be with her and care for her through the rest of their lives. Let others, someday, try to free Euskadi.

But then these second thoughts seemed like real heresy, a mockery of his faith in the cause. Others were not as capable as he in the underground fight. Not even Lopez, the onetime master organizer and planner, showed persistent strength. Growing old, Lopez had been weakening, ready to compromise with that monster in Madrid. No, it was Hurtado himself who was the most qualified and needed. He could not be a traitor to the thousands of oppressed and to the memory of his dearly beloved father.

The second thoughts prevailed over selfish sentiment. He was here to bring down the obstruction to Basque freedom. Tonight was the night he would blow it to smithereens.

He hoped.

Almost at the corner, his heart and stride quickened, and although no praying man himself, he now offered a prayer to a God Unknown that Yvonne's gossip had been accurate and that the French police guards had been removed.

He was at the corner, teetering on the curb, and what he saw made him want to jump with joy. The avenue was devoid of life, no police in view anywhere, and the ramp leading down to the domain wide open.

Half-running, he was across the avenue to the top of the ramp. He peered down the paving to the bottom and the heart of the domain area. He descended fast, his confidence growing. At the foot of the ramp, on level ground, he peered out across the Rosary Esplanade to the other side, carefully searching as far as he could see for a sign of the lone security guard whom he'd observed on patrol in the late hours of the night. But even this one guard was nowhere in sight.

Trying to contain his jubilation, Hurtado swung off to his left, passing the Rosary Basilica, and circled the towering Upper Basilica which looked down on it, striding rapidly toward the grotto.

It was there, that holy hole in the mountain, seeming eerie in the light of flickering candles which also caught the image of the Virgin

Mary, the long-worshipped statue of the white-clad Virgin in the niche high above.

The niche was his target. When it was blown to smithereens, a large portion of the mountainside would come down, joining the rubble of the grotto itself.

One last time Hurtado pivoted, cautiously looking around, looking for any obstacle or potential threat. The interior of the grotto was empty. The chairs and benches empty. The area where spigots provided water from the spring and the bathhouses beyond were empty.

The long wait was over. The high moment had come.

Without another instant's hesitation, Hurtado started toward the steep rise, covered with grass, bushes, yellow buddleia shrubs, small magnolia trees, and tall oak trees, that rose sharply next to the narrow barren rock that was the grotto's surround. Hurtado was off the ground, and onto the rise, firmly planting each foot into the grassy turf as he climbed.

Going higher and higher, he was soon able to support himself by grabbing evergreen branches and the trunks of trees in the thickening forest. His breath was short now, but not from lack of stamina. He had the conditioning of an athlete. What affected his breathing was his anticipation and mounting excitement mingled with a hunter's tension.

He was at the large trees and counting off to locate the right one, and at one of the largest, he was sure he would find his treasure. He scrambled up and around the tree, tugging the pocket flashlight from his jacket, and pointing the circle of yellow light at the entwining foliage at his feet.

Then he spotted it, the depression, with the leafy camouflage he had prepared three days ago to cover and hide it. He dropped to his knees, placing the flashlight at the edge of the depression so its beam could guide him, and with bare hands he began to gather up the leaves and branches and cast them aside. The debris was moist from the night air, but this made it easier to scoop up and cast away.

The large flat folded shopping bag that he had brought here to cover the smaller packages was now before him. He lifted it off the cache, dropped it behind him, and concentrated on bringing the packages of explosive and equipment out of the hiding place.

As if he were handling precious porcelain, Hurtado laid out each piece of explosive equipment with care. From the start he had chosen an electrical timing device as the safest, the most certain, and the one that could help put the greatest distance between him and the dynamite when the explosion took place. The idea was to wire the explosive with a delayed-action fuse and attach the fuse to a clock or timer. This involved the use of a battery and terminals, as well. The clock was set as an alarm was set. The clock ticked away, and when the clock hands touched the designated position, this closed the terminals and the circuit sent an electrical charge through the detonator and the fuse connected to the dynamite. For a while, at the outset, he had considered using the plastic C-4—what the French called *plastique*—as the explosive instead of old-fashioned dynamite, but then had decided that dynamite—nitroglycerine in a sawdust mix—was simpler, as long as the dynamite sticks were fresh.

This dynamite, the sticks already neatly bound together, was new and fresh. With practiced hands—he had prepared at least a dozen of these devices to destroy sites in recent years—Hurtado unwound the coil of green wire and placed one end near the detonator and battery which were fixed to the baseboard. This done, Hurtado began to creep down the slope, running the wiring out as he descended surefooted toward the grotto. Now he shut off the flashlight as the illumination from the wax candles below flickered streaks of light across the foliage and dimly outlined in dark yellow the niche above the grotto and the marble statue of the Virgin Mary.

Briefly, between prickly bushes, he had a glimpse of the grotto area far below. His entire concentration was upon the niche as he crawled closer to it, running out his green fuse. When the niche was at arm's length, he edged even closer, bringing the package of dynamite sticks around in front of him with both hands and placing the explosive inside the niche. He prodded it gently so that it was settled perfectly behind the marble statue and out of sight.

Satisfied, he turned away on his knees, then began to retrace his path, fingering the long stretch of thin fuse as he crawled upward. In a few minutes he was back behind the large tree where the detonator and battery and clock rested. Speedily, he connected the wire to the terminal, taking care to prevent the terminals from making contact. Then he set the electrical timer. He had gauged the actual time for automatic contact in advance. He required enough time to get safely away, yet not too much time to permit the device to be exposed to someone who might accidentally notice it. Fifteen minutes seemed exactly right. Five minutes to get down from the mountainside, four minutes to hasten from the grotto to the ramp, one minute to reach his Ford (his suitcase had been packed in the trunk earlier), and five minutes to spin through the empty town and reach the back road to Pau.

By then, the grotto would be obliterated, and Euskadi would rise from the ashes. And he would have vanished from Lourdes, be in hiding far away, and protected by his French compatriots.

Fifteen minutes, starting this split second. He had finished the connection. No need to bury or camouflage the device. It, with everything else, would be blown into countless pieces.

He came to his feet, and immediately began his precarious descent downhill. Aiming his flashlight on the ground before him, gripping tree trunks and sturdy branches, he maintained his balance, slipping only once, remaining upright and steady all the way down. When he could see the bottom of the slope below, the flat ground of the area that led to and around the grotto, he doused his flashlight. He was able to move faster now, as the flat earth came closer. At the rim of the last protective foliage, he halted, and surveyed what he could of the area. No guard in sight yet, no one, and he was safe.

He stepped down to the ground, and quickly brought up his left arm to consult his wristwatch. The descent had taken him five minutes and ten seconds.

Ten seconds lost, but still he was fairly close to schedule.

Not another second to waste.

Hurrying, he swung off, starting past the grotto in the direction of the ramp.

Striding between the benches and chairs that faced the altar inside the grotto, Hurtado cast one final look upward at the statue and the niche to see if the bundle of explosives could be seen. Nothing was visible except the dumb statue.

Nothing. Perfect.

But then as his gaze dropped—something.

With a gulp, he halted in midstride, halted and stood transfixed. With disbelief he stared at the entrance to the grotto beneath the niche and could see that something was there, someone, a human being, a small human being, head covered by a shawl, kneeling, its back to him, praying. He had seen this very figure before in this headdress and posture, and it came to him, the resemblance. He had seen a photograph of Bernadette herself in this garb and this posture praying before the grotto.

In the first rush of disbelief, Hurtado was concerned with self-survival, self-preservation, keeping going, getting away as fast as he could, and to hell with this fool in prayer.

But up there on the mountain a clock was ticking, and in nine minutes the mammoth explosion would occur, and a poor human being would be blasted to shreds. At once, a stronger instinct prevailed. Hurtado wanted to kill no one here, certainly not an innocent believer. In a matter of seconds, he could save her—and still save himself. He need only warn her that she was in danger, warn her to retreat, to flee, get out of here, and then himself continue on his way.

He turned toward the grotto, racing between the chairs, and as he closed in on the kneeling woman, he threw caution to the winds and shouted, "Hey, you! Get away from there! It's going to blow up!"

He expected the kneeling woman to turn around, frightened, react to his warning, and retreat on the run from the endangered area.

But she did not stir, made no motion, remained on her knees in silent supplication, as unmoving as the marble statue high above her.

The lack of response was incredible to Hurtado, beyond all understanding, and he ran faster toward the woman, and when he was nearly upon her, ready to shout once more, he suddenly came to a jarring stop.

He had the young woman in profile and he could make her out. Natale. Natale Rinaldi. His own Natale.

He had left her asleep, but she had not slept. She had dressed in darkness, and found her way counting her steps in darkness, and sightless as ever, she had come here to undertake her last vigil.

"Oh, Je-sus," he cried out. "Natale!" he roared.

No reaction, no response, not a movement. It was as if she could not hear him.

He could see her plain now, the dark glasses, the pale waxen face, merely the slightest movement of the lips.

She was in a trance, out of this world.

He was upon her, snatching at her shoulders, grabbing wildly for a grip, trying to lift her to her feet and tear her away from here.

But she did not budge. She was deadweight, anchored to the ground, immovable.

He tugged and tore at her, trying to make her rise, attempting to lift her, but it was impossible to move her an inch.

Breathing heavily, he stopped trying. This was a phenomenon beyond his understanding. He stood over her, staring down at her, not knowing how to make contact, by what means to remove her, to propel her to safety.

And then, to his utter astonishment, he watched her shake herself and slowly rise to her feet.

"Natale!" he cried out, grabbing for her arms.

But she was smiling at him, raising one hand, removing her dark glasses. For the first time her eyes were wide and clear and luminous, and they held on him. "Mikel—you are Mikel—you must be," she said softly. "Mikel, I saw the Virgin Mary, I *saw* Her. She came to me, and spoke to me, and allowed me to see Her. I could see Her, as I can see you." She turned her head. "And the grotto, for the first time I can see it and see all the world again. The Blessed Virgin, She gave me the gift of sight again. Mikel, I can *see.*"

He stood frozen, awestricken, hardly able to comprehend the miracle and the wonder of it.

He found his voice. "You—you can see me?"

"Yes, you, everything around. It's glorious."

"You—you saw the Virgin?"

"When I knelt to pray, I was in darkness as always. And as I prayed, I could make out a cone of brightness, a light, and then I could see the opening, the grotto itself, and I saw Her, this woman in white, no bigger than I am, bowing Her head, arms extended, one hand holding a long-stemmed rose. I reached for my rosary, and the Virgin stood there, smiling graciously at me. She was as Bernadette had seen Her, except for the rose in her hand. A white veil covered Her head, and Her long dress was of the purist white, with a sash of blue, and a yellow rose was on each foot. And She said sweetly, 'You shall see again, for the length of your earthly stay, every wonder of God.' There was more but —Mikel, Mikel, it was wonderful! I love you, the entire world, life, and I love our precious Massabielle—"

She'd gone into his open arms, embracing him, but the mention of Massabielle triggered remembrance.

"Oh, my God!" he exclaimed, releasing Natale and looking at his watch.

Less than six minutes left.

He gripped the arm of the bewildered Natale tightly, and began pulling her away from the grotto, going fast, pulling and dragging her along.

"Run," he urged her, running with her along the foot of the hill and dragging her beside him, forcing her to keep up with him.

Suddenly, he halted, pushing her away.

"What is it, Mikel?" she wanted to know.

"Never mind. I'll explain later. Just do as I tell you, exactly as I tell you." He pointed off toward the bathhouses. "Go there, past the baths, as far as you can. Just go, stay away from the grotto, far away as possible. I'll catch up with you in five or ten minutes. Now, go!"

Without waiting to see her go, he leaped onto the slope and scrambled upward among the foliage as fast as the slippery footing would allow him. He kept climbing on the double, stumbling and falling, rising and falling again, but moving upward without pause. He was grasping sturdy branches, holding on to the trunks of trees, ascending steadily. Once more sprawling forward, pushing himself upright, he saw the timepiece on his wrist. Four and a half minutes had passed, and he still wasn't there.

In a frenzy, he resumed climbing, and time was ticking away, and still he wasn't there. For moments he was lost, couldn't find it, his landmark, the giant oak, and then he saw it, staggering and going down to his knees before it.

One more glimpse at his watch.

Less than a minute left. Less than a half minute.

Seconds remained, twenty-four, twenty-three, twenty-two seconds.

And on his knees, he was crawling desperately around the tree to the depression and the detonator and battery and wired clock on its baseboard.

He flung himself headlong at the device, clawing for the wiring, and tearing at it with all his strength. It would not loosen. He was a madman, yanking away until his forearm and bicep twinged with pain, certain that he had lost, awaiting the catastrophic explosion, the eruption that would bring death to Massabielle and to himself.

And suddenly the wiring ripped free, and the device was disconnected, and there was no thunder in his ears.

In the darkness he tried to make out the time on his wristwatch. Two seconds left.

The hand moved one second, two seconds, and then one second beyond what would have been the moment of hell.

He sat with the loose wiring in his dirty hands, and listened to the beautiful silence.

After a while, when breath returned, he struggled to his feet. There was work to do and it must be done. He made his way recklessly, falling again and again, not caring, and finally crawling until he could see the marble statue set in the niche above the grotto. When it was within reach, he put a hand inside, and behind the statue's base he felt the bulky packet of dynamite. With patience and caution, he withdrew the explosive from the niche. When he had the dynamite in hand, he started back to his cache, treading more carefully this time.

At the oak tree once more, he opened the heavy brown shopping bag and laid the dynamite packet inside it, and then one by one he picked up his pieces of equipment and piled them inside the bag, also.

He had stuffed the last of the loose wiring into the bag, when he was startled to hear his name.

"Mikel." He heard it again, and there was Natale standing over him.

"Natale, what are you doing here? I told you—you might have— never mind."

"I wanted to see where you were. I followed. I had to crawl most of the way. I thought I was lost, but—here we are."

He was on his feet, taking her in his arms, kissing her. "I love you," he said, "forever."

"I love you forever and more."

Releasing her, he placed one arm around her waist, the hand holding her side, and with the other hand he had the bag.

As they started down the slope, he grinned at her. "So now you can see me. How do I look to you?"

"Sinfully ugly," she laughed, "but I adore sinful and ugly men." Her expression sobered. "Mikel, you're lovely, not as lovely as the Virgin Mary, but for a mere mortal you're lovely enough."

When they had reached the bottom, he did not turn toward the grotto and the domain, but continued straight ahead toward the bridge that crossed the Gave de Pau to the meadow that spread out before them in the moonlight.

Stumbling along beside him, Natale wondered, "Mikel, where are we going?"

"To the river up ahead," he said. He lifted the loaded shopping bag. "To get rid of this, some part of my past." He smiled down at her as they went on. "For the first time, darling," he said, "I can see, too."

15

Sunday, August 21

Liz Finch was walking on air.

Actually, she was walking firmly on the carpeting of the fifth-floor corridor of the Hôtel Gallia & Londres, but for the first time since her arrival and stay in Lourdes she felt that she was walking on air.

With Amanda's manila envelope, and its contents, held fast in her hand, she was high and had never been higher. She had at her side the exposé of the decade, and certainly the most tremendous and sensational story of her career, thanks to that incredible young lady, Amanda Spenser; and she had it for her very own for the millions and millions of readers on earth who would see it and go over it absorbing every word in stunned amazement. Liz would give anything to see Bill Trask's face as she dictated it to him. Better yet, she would give more to see the face of that bitch Marguerite when she heard about it and realized that her Viron disclosures were common dross compared to this.

Amanda's room was 503, and Liz had arrived before it. Amanda's note had promised that she would be back from the hospital and waiting in her room, ready to give a full explanation of the fantastic Bernadette journal before Liz wrote and phoned in the headline story.

After that, this dreary town would be blown away, blown off the face of the map forever and all time, as it deserved to be.

There was almost a lilt in the rhythm of Liz's knocking on the door. She waited for the door to open, and when it didn't, she rapped harder, hoping that Amanda was in and had not been delayed at the hospital with Ken, whatever had happened to him.

Abruptly, the doorknob rattled, and the door swung wide, and there was Amanda in her silk nightgown, sleepy-eyed, her hair a mess, her expression confused.

"Liz, it's you?"

"Who else? Did you forget?" She held up the manila envelope. "You left this super dynamite, and made a date for me to meet you here."

"God, what time is it?"

"Eleven-thirty on the nose, as agreed."

"Dammit, I overslept. Yesterday exhausted me. I must have slept straight through when my alarm went off. I was supposed to be up at eight, and at the hospital to see Ken's doctor at nine-thirty. But mainly to see Ken and get him back to Chicago. Come in, Liz, come in while I get dressed in a hurry."

Liz went gaily inside, shutting the door as Amanda padded across the room to the bureau to pull out the drawers in search of clean pantyhose and a fresh brassiere.

Liz plopped into a chair, hoisting the manila envelope. "You ain't going to have no trouble with dear Ken, once he sees this. Say, what's he doing in the hospital anyway?"

Amanda was tearing off her nightgown. "He left me a message that he'd become worse and was carted off to the main Lourdes hospital in the Avenue Alexandre-Marqui. I went to see him right away, when I came in from Bartrès, but he was sedated and out of it."

"How is he?"

"That's what I was supposed to find out at nine-thirty." She slipped her milky-white breasts into the brassiere cups and was fastening the bra in back. "Hell, I wish I hadn't overslept. I don't even have time for a bath."

But Liz Finch was again devoted to the copy of Bernadette's last journal that she had removed from the envelope. "Amanda, you're going to have no more problem with Ken once he sets eyes on this. He'll never be a believer in any of that Lourdes nonsense any more. He'll see how soundly, or unsoundly—unwittingly—Bernadette branded herself a fake. Imagine that little peasant hysteric seeing the Virgin Mary *and* Jesus all over the place—time and again among the sheep in Bartrès— and then, after that dress rehearsal, doing her act all over again a month later in Lourdes. Wow, Amanda, the story of our time. But you didn't want me to phone it in until I talked to you, and I wanted every backup detail of how you laid your hands on it, anyway. How did you, Wonder Girl, how in the devil did you ever do it?"

"Got to go to the bathroom," Amanda said, fluttering the pantyhose she had in her hand. "Got to hurry."

"Amanda, please," Liz implored as Amanda disappeared into the bathroom, "you asked me not to file my story till I heard how you pulled it off. Will you tell me?"

"Not this second, Liz," Amanda called out. "Soon as I finish dressing, I'll tell you what I know on the way downstairs. If that's not enough time, you can drive with me to the hospital. Then I'll tell you the rest."

In a minute, Amanda darted from the bathroom, yanked on her blouse, stepped into her skirt, fastened it, was into her low-heeled shoes, snatching up a second copy of the journal in its manila envelope on her way through the door. Liz was right behind her, skipping to keep up as they went to the elevator.

Waiting for the elevator, Liz pleaded, "Father Ruland gave you Eugénie Gautier's name in Bartrès, right?"

"Right."

"How'd you know there was an earlier part of the journal?"

"Sister Francesca mentioned it in passing at Nevers. Father Ruland admitted that it existed but insisted that he wasn't interested in it. Actually, he'd never seen it. Madame Gautier confirmed its existence and showed it to me. She didn't want money, she simply wanted me to arrange to put her nephew through an American college. When I read the pages Bernadette wrote about her stay in Bartrès, how she was sheep-tending and seeing Jesus and then the Virgin Mary monthly among the woolies—how many times?—"

"Jesus three times. The Virgin six times among the sheep in Bartrès, and starting a month later, eighteen more times in Lourdes, only in Lourdes she had witnesses and her playlet went public. What a seductive nut."

"We get them often enough in clinical psychology. The flight from reality syndrome. We treat older children who've experienced hallucinatory eidetic imagery—colorful, vivid, but unreal imagery that the subject has come to believe in."

The elevator had arrived.

"Can I quote you, Amanda?" Liz wanted to know. "The eminent psychology professor from Chicago, Dr. Spenser says."

They were inside the elevator and riding down to the lobby.

"The Church'll have me burned at the stake," said Amanda, "but no matter, the truth will out. Go ahead."

Liz was jotting notes furiously. Finishing, she stepped into the lobby at Amanda's heels. "Wowie, you've made my day, my week, my life. Good-bye to miracles. This is an absolute international headliner."

As both spun away from the elevator, preparing to rush out of the hotel, they found themselves face to face with Natale and Hurtado, who had just come into the hotel and were about to get into the elevator.

Amanda looked blank for a moment, but Liz recognized the couple at once. "Mr. Mikel Hurtado," she said. "And Miss Natale Rinaldi. Aren't you lovey-dovey, though." They were close to one another, holding hands, beaming happily.

Natale said to Liz, "This is the first time I've seen you, but I recognize your voice. You're Liz Finch, the press correspondent."

"Hey, now—" Liz started to say, but her voice trailed off as she stared hard at Natale. At the same moment, Amanda had become aware of what Liz was aware of. The pretty Italian girl was no longer wearing sunglasses, no longer hiding her blindness. Her large dark eyes were shining, taking in Liz and then Amanda.

Amanda spoke first, quickly. "Did I hear you say to Liz, 'This is the first time I've seen you'? Are you telling us you can *see?*"

Natale nodded with intense pleasure. "Yes, I can see perfectly now."

Liz was puzzled. "But I'm sure you told us, when we dined together, that you were totally blind, and the ophthalmologists in Rome gave you no hope of having your sight restored."

Natale agreed. "I did tell you that. It's true. Medical science had given me up as a lost cause. So I had to pray and hope for something more than science, something supernatural, and I told you that's why I came to Lourdes."

Liz was blinking unceasingly now. "When did it happen, your regaining your sight?"

"Late last night at the grotto."

Liz's voice quavered. She pushed out one word, "How?"

"Yes, how?" Amanda wanted to know.

Natale hesitated and cast Hurtado a sidelong glance. He caught it and responded with a definite nod, adding, "Go ahead, Natale, you're allowed to tell six people the truth about it—I'm one—your mother and father will be two and three—your Aunt Elsa will be four—and telling Liz and Amanda can make it five and six. After that, no more."

Natale's eyes went from Liz to Amanda. Her countenance was solemn as she made her quiet announcement. "I saw the Virgin Mary last night. Everything was black before me, then a brightness of light, and an apparition of the Blessed Virgin stood above me. She restored my sight, and I could see Her, and everything else. The Virgin did it. She reappeared as She had promised Bernadette that She would, and She gave me back my eyesight."

Amanda reeled under the impact of the announcement. Her jaw was agape. She was shaking her head.

Liz was also thrown off balance, blinking more furiously than ever, scowling. "Wait a minute, wait a minute," she stammered. "You're sure this is true?"

Natale said simply, "Look at me."

Liz stared at her in silence, and tried to formulate words. "Natale, if this is true, and you'll support it, this is one of the biggest stories to come out of Lourdes in the century and a half since Bernadette. You— you've got to give me the details, every detail, at once."

Natale shook her head slowly. "Not if you're going to print it. I'm not allowed to have my miracle printed."

Hurtado stepped forward as if to protect Natale. "She's trying to tell you that this is one of the promises the Virgin Mary extracted from her last night. The Blessed Virgin told Natale, 'Your miracle and the way you came by it are for you, and six others whom you wish to tell about it. My reappearance before you, which had been intended as a secret in that earlier time, is meant to be a secret still. I trust you never to let the truth of your miracle ever to be known. Keep the trust, and I promise you happiness in this world, in Heaven thereafter.' "

Natale was listening to Hurtado, and nodding concurrence with every word he spoke. Natale faced Liz and Amanda. "I gave my vow to the Blessed Virgin that She could trust me."

"But—" Liz was too dumbfounded to continue.

"You both must pledge your word to me," said Natale. "You will not speak of this ever, or write of it, but keep it in your hearts. I told you as friends, meaning only to reveal to you that faith is worthwhile and miracles never cease happening. We have just been to the Basilica to give thankful prayers for our good fortune. We leave for Italy this afternoon. So this is good-bye, and good luck to both of you."

Their hands more tightly entwined than ever, Natale and Hurtado skirted around the speechless Liz and Amanda. The pair entered the elevator, and soon the two of them were gone.

Liz and Amanda stood rooted in their places, unable to speak or move for long seconds.

At last their eyes met.

Liz's voice caught in her throat until she could articulate words. "Amanda, maybe she—maybe she made it up?"

Amanda was shaking her head. "No, no, Liz. She *can* see."

Liz's head was going up and down. "Yeah, you're right." Then, almost to herself, "For Chrissakes, she *can* see. I—I don't know what to think anymore."

"Maybe we should both stop thinking. Maybe Shakespeare was right—"

"Yeah, yeah, I know that one. Hello, Horatio. 'There are more things in heaven and earth, Horatio, than are dreamt of in your philosophy.' "

"You better believe it, Liz. I—I'm beginning to."

"Yeah, maybe Bernadette did see Jesus and the Virgin Mary in Bartrès, and maybe Bernadette did see the Virgin eighteen times here in Lourdes, and maybe the Virgin did tell her that she would return to Lourdes in this week of this year, and maybe Natale did see her encore."

"Maybe," said Amanda.

"Something happened last night, that's for certain." She looked around her. "Do you see a wastebasket anywhere?"

"Wastebasket?"

Liz held up the manila envelope containing the portion of Bernadette's journal. "For this. I can't write it after what I just saw and heard. I'm not saying I've got religion all at once. But I've just graduated from atheist to born-again agnostic. For starters, anyway." She kissed the envelope. "Good-bye to this big story." She blew a kiss at the elevator. "And good-bye to that big story. Poor ol' Liz. I'm going out and get very, very drunk."

Inside the Centre Hôpitalier General, traversing the hallway to Ken's private room, Amanda slowed down.

She wanted to see her Ken as soon as possible, but she needed to clarify her muddled mind and take a definite stance about her fiancé's future. God knows, witnessing the results of Natale's miracle had rocked not only her but Liz beyond reason. Liz, a skeptic by nature and a perpetual cynic nurtured by journalism, had finally conceded her doubts (in her fashion) about Bernadette's visions, and Natale's as well. But Amanda, although more thoroughly shocked by the Virgin Mary's reappearance, more readily prepared to reassess all her rational beliefs, still clung to some last vestige of logic and reality. Her resistance to turnabout, she knew, came from her career-long conditioning as a psychologist.

Hell, a psychologist knows what is going on in the real world. There were always well-grounded explanations for every form of aberrant behavior. Sure, sometimes there were minor inexplicable mysteries, but certainly someday they too would be solved. Hadn't Goethe reminded us—"Mysteries aren't necessarily miracles"?

Yet, there had been no mysteries at all in 1858, or last night, if one had faith that puppet man and all humankind danced to the strings of a Master Worker. Of course, all formalized religions had been invented by man to make the miseries of life on earth and the terrors of death—with the promise (and carrot) of the hereafter—acceptable. Still, this knowledge did not negate the fact that human beings, placed on one spinning mudball planet, had not been an accident but had been arranged in an orderly fashion by Something that empowered life itself. If there were evidences of such arrangements and control, then events could happen to humans beyond the reach of human understanding.

What puny man wrote off as miracles could be logical interventions by an indefinable Higher Power.

This would explain Bernadette. This would explain the instantaneous cures at holy shrines. This would certainly explain the restoration of Natale Rinaldi to complete normality. It really came down to a belief in the effectiveness of unlimited faith and not in the restrictions of rationality. This was a new land where the feelings of a being knew a higher wisdom of the mind. Pascal had put it best: "It is the heart which perceives God and not the reason."

Ken had instinctively understood this, perhaps speeded toward his understanding by desperation. And she, in her mental arrogance, had tried to subvert his faith.

Amanda caught sight of a large container, beside a nurse's station. She supposed it was a trash basket. She walked over to it, removed the copy of Bernadette's journal from the manila envelope, with deliberation tore it into tiny pieces and dropped the pieces of paper and the envelope into the trash disposal. So much for dubbing all the mysteries with easy labels like hysteria. Until this moment she had fought Ken. Now she was ready to join him.

Turnabout. Conversion. Whatever it was, no matter. There was an energy force in total belief, and she would clasp hands with Ken in trying to attain it.

Coming away from the container to find Ken's room, she saw Esther, the nurse, thin and efficient-appearing in a long white starched uniform, crossing to the nurses' station. Esther saw her at the same moment.

"There you are," said Esther. "I wondered where you were. I was just going to phone you."

"I—I overslept," said Amanda. "I was positively worn out and didn't hear the alarm. How is he?"

"Mr. Clayton is, well, somewhat better. He's been up for several hours and his spirits seem improved. Dr. Kleinberg has been with him. Dr. Kleinberg is still there, waiting for you." Esther was guiding Amanda to Ken's room, opening the door. "You can go in now. They both want to see you."

Tentatively, Amanda went into the room. A white and antiseptic hospital room, with the smell of disinfectants and alcohol, like a thousand others. But with a difference. Ken was here, her Ken, her life. He was lying on the bed, gaunt but no less handsome, and unaccountably smiling. The older bespectacled man in the white jacket seated in a chair beside Ken came quickly to his feet. "Mrs. Clayton? I'm Paul Kleinberg. Glad to meet you."

"Hello, doctor," Amanda murmured, and then practically ignoring him, she ran to the bed, and bent over Ken, awkwardly trying to embrace him without doing him harm, kissing his face and his lips. "Oh, darling, darling, I've been so worried. But you're going to be all right. I know you will, I know it."

Ken weakly tried to return her embrace. "I expect to be better. Yes—"

Oblivious of the physician, Amanda had dropped to her knees beside the bed, holding Ken's hands. "Ken," she said urgently, "I want you to know I'm on your side, I'm with you all the way now. No more resistance from me. I beg your forgiveness for that. I'm going every inch of the way with you. We'll fight and win, and we'll do it together. I—I don't know how to explain it fully—but I'll try to, as soon as you want to hear. But something happened to me. I don't want to be corny, but—but somehow I—I saw the light, yes I saw the light. Soon as you can, I'll go to the grotto with you. We'll pray for your recovery together. We'll pray for a cure now, and you'll see, it will happen. I have faith now."

"Well, I don't," Ken said.

Having finished her outburst, her confessional, Amanda couldn't believe her ears. She was certain she had not heard him right. "You—you what?"

"I said I don't have faith anymore," Ken repeated. "I can't depend on faith to cure me. It might work, but it's too risky. I need more."

Astounded once again in this day of astonishments, Amanda stared at him in a daze. "What are you saying?" She wanted to speak of Natale Rinaldi, but remembered her pledge not to do so. She grasped for another proof of faith. "You—you saw for yourself. You were with Edith Moore several times. You saw her. You heard her. Edith suffered from what you have. But she was miraculously cured. She prayed to the Virgin, she believed, and her faith—it worked, it paid off."

"Edith Moore," Ken repeated from the pillow. "That's just it. That's exactly what's brought me to my senses. Amanda, maybe faith is good, maybe it can help some—but I want something surer." He looked past the bewildered Amanda toward the physician. "Dr. Kleinberg, you tell her. Go ahead, tell her."

Still dazed, Amanda came slowly to her feet and pivoted to confront Dr. Kleinberg.

"Doctor, what is this?"

Dr. Kleinberg's face was serious, but somehow relaxed. "I think I can explain, Mrs. Clayton. I'll do so briefly. Please sit down."

Confused, her newly ordered world topsy-turvy once more, Amanda took the chair with the stiffness of an automaton. Dr. Kleinberg pulled up a chair next to hers.

His tone was professional, devoid of emphasis, as he began to address Amanda. "When I was able to speak to Ken this morning, aware as I was of the gravity of his case, I urged him to undergo immediate surgery for his sarcoma condition."

"But I refused, as usual," Ken interrupted. "I told the doctor I didn't like the odds on surgery. But I did like the odds on faith healings, such as the one that Edith Moore enjoyed. That was good enough for me, I told the doctor, as I'd been telling you all along. If it could work for Edith Moore, it could work for me." He looked past Amanda. "Now go ahead and tell her, doctor."

Dr. Kleinberg gave an abbreviated Gallic shrug. "The fact is, Mrs. Clayton, it did not work for Edith Moore."

Once more, Amanda could not believe her ears. "It did not?" she echoed incredulously. "Are you saying it did not work, she wasn't miraculously cured? But all those doctors—"

Dr. Kleinberg agreed. "Yes, all those doctors examined her for three years, good doctors, too, and they testified that Edith had been instantaneously and inexplicably cured of a terminal sarcoma condition. I was brought down from Paris to confirm her miraculous cure, and I expected I would examine her, test her, X-ray her and certify her as cured. But I quickly found something was wrong. Just as her sarcoma condition had suddenly disappeared, without reason, I found it had returned, without reason. She had the tumor again. Apparently, faith alone had not offered a permanent cure. I could see that she would soon be in a serious condition, deteriorate rapidly, with her end inevitable."

"But she was a sure thing," said Amanda. "Her cure was on everyone's lips. And, even though I am a scientist by training myself, I've learned from experience there can be—well, inexplicable and miraculous cures that could be credited to faith."

"I won't deny the possibility," admitted Dr. Kleinberg. "Like Dr. Alexis Carrel, I don't know. It might be that some cures can be credited wholly to faith. Or maybe none can be. Mrs. Clayton, in the present state of science, we don't know. But as a man of science, I do know one thing for a certainty. Edith Moore, no matter what took place in the recent three years, is no longer a miracle woman. She is not cured. I told her so. Until last night, I had to keep this information confidential while Mrs. Moore considered what to do. Now I am permitted to speak about it. And so I spoke the truth to Ken this morning."

"But if faith can't cure a tumor—" Amanda said helplessly.

Dr. Kleinberg finished her sentence. "—then science, thanks to a recent medical advance, science can cure this tumor."

"It is the surgery you always wanted, Amanda, only newer, better."

"Better?" Amanda echoed.

"The one in Chicago offered a thirty percent chance of success," said Ken. "This one offers a seventy percent chance, right Dr. Kleinberg?"

"That is correct." Dr. Kleinberg turned to Amanda once more. "It is surgery combined with genetic engineering, which a colleague of mine, Dr. Maurice Duval, has been experimenting with for some years. He arrived in Lourdes from Paris last night. He will perform the operation on Edith Moore. Since he is here, he has agreed to operate on Ken also."

Amanda jerked toward Ken. "You've consented?"

Ken nodded. "It's our best chance, honey."

It was going too fast for Amanda. "When?" she wanted to know.

"Today," answered Dr. Kleinberg. "Dr. Duval must be back in Paris tomorrow. Therefore, he is undertaking the surgeries, both of them, in this hospital today. We cannot wait for morning. It must be done now. Shortly, in the afternoon." Dr. Kleinberg rose. "Mrs. Clayton, I assume you will wish to remain here in the hospital until the operation is over. We must prep Ken for surgery now. Let me show you to the waiting room."

Amanda came to her feet, and bent to kiss Ken. "Oh, darling, I—"

"It's what we both want, Amanda."

She shook her head as she went to the door. "I don't know what I should do anymore. Pray to Saint Bernadette or to Dr. Duval?"

"Do both," Kleinberg said with a smile.

In the main section of Madame Moore's Miracle Restaurant, all of the tables at this hour of the afternoon were empty save one. At the single occupied table, a woozy Liz Finch sat trying to interview Edith Moore.

Liz had tried to get drunk earlier, drown her sorrows in a series of Scotches, and had only succeeded in getting a mild buzz on and a headache. She had failed at everything else, and so she was not surprised that she had failed to earn a real hangover, the right of every veteran reporter. Then she had decided that it was just as well. She had this appointment with Edith Moore, and reluctant as she was to keep it, Liz knew that she must follow through. She had to file something from Lourdes and this dismal twice-told tale was the only bare-bones of a story left for her. Edith Moore, miraculously cured, the next-to-be-announced miracle woman of our time.

Arriving at the restaurant, Reggie Moore had served up dull Edith and some tea, and left them alone. And Liz had brought out her note book, peeled it open, and proceeded with the leaden interview.

In the last half hour they had covered all the familiar ground, Edith spouting her never-ending clichés, and Liz's cramped hand writing them down. Now it was almost over, the interview as well as Liz's future.

"All right, so you're fully cured by the wonder of Lourdes," Liz was saying wearily, "so soon you'll be announced as the latest miracle woman. How do you feel about that?"

There was no answer.

Liz, head bent over her tea and notepad, repeated her question. "Well, Edith, how does it feel—being a miracle woman?"

Still, no answer.

Liz looked up sharply, and to her surprise, the bland Englishwoman's cheeks were streaked with tears. She was crying, fumbling for a handkerchief, dabbing at her eyes.

Liz was startled. She'd never seen a show of emotion in this turnip, this pudgy brussels sprout, this vegetable of some sort, before. This was more than a show of emotion. It more closely resembled a nervous breakdown.

"Hey now," said Liz, trying to stop the torrent, "what's going on here?"

Edith's voice was a sad gargle. "I—I—I'm not a miracle woman. I'm a fraud. I'm a nothing. I can't go on with this talk. It's no use, I can't."

"Wait a minute, wait a sec," said Liz, suddenly interested. "What are you trying to tell me?"

"My—my sarcoma came—it came back. I'm not cured, not at all. The new doctor, he just found out. I'm sick again, and I'm going to die, but he can save me, he can save my life with a new surgery. But I don't want to live because I won't be the miracle woman anymore. I'll be nothing and so will Reggie."

"Ye Gods," said Liz, "at least you'll be saved, you'll stay alive. Are you crazy?"

"Can't you hear?" sobbed Edith, wiping at her eyes again. "I won't be a miracle woman anymore, and that's all Reggie and I wanted."

Liz had come fully alert again, pencil in hand. "Listen, Edith, that's a real story, now you've got a real one. It's something unusual, different, something I can really write. Give it all to me."

"No," said Edith, "not if you're going to write it. I'm a failure, and I don't want it written about."

"Listen, Edith, I've simply got to know what happened to you this week and what's going to happen."

"I'm not telling you if you're going to write it."

"Please, Edith."

"No."

"Goddammit," swore Liz, clapping her notepad shut with finality, "there goes another one. Three fat zeroes for today. *C'est la guerre.*" She considered Edith once more, poor bereft miracleless woman, and she felt a wave of compassion for her. "Okay, okay," Liz soothed her, "no story. I won't write it, I promise you, but I'd still like to know what happened."

Edith pulled herself together. "You won't write it? You promise?"

Liz put down her pencil, and put her hands in her lap below the tabletop. "See, no hands."

"What?"

"An American expression. Go ahead, Edith. I'm listening."

"Well, it all started after Dr. Paul Kleinberg came here to Lourdes from Paris to examine me—"

In a subdued wail of a voice, Edith Moore recounted the miserable saga of her downfall. She omitted nothing she could remember. She recounted the examinations by Dr. Kleinberg and his verdict given to Reggie and then herself. She spoke of the new surgery, the genetic engineering, that Dr. Kleinberg had told her about. It was all fine, the surgery that might save her life. But if she lost her miracle woman status, then all else was lost to Reggie and herself.

Edith went on and on, pouring it out to Liz. The effort to compromise Dr. Kleinberg by getting him to arrange for the surgical cure, but still validate her as miraculously cured. The refusal by Dr. Kleinberg to undertake the falsehood on his own, agreeing not to contradict her miracle cure story if someone high up in the church went along with it. And so, Edith continued, winding down her sad saga, in desperation she had revealed all to a priest, maybe Father Ruland himself, in the confessional, and asked him if he would collaborate with the doctor in the small deception concerning her cure. But the priest had refused to cooperate.

"He told me," Edith concluded, "that as long as I was cured by surgery, I could no longer be a miracle woman. The only way such a person could ever be declared a miracle woman was if she saw the appearance of the Virgin Mary at the grotto just like Bernadette. The priest said that person, too, would be a miracle woman, a real one."

Listening closely, Liz had wrinkled her brow, was blinking her eyes. "And—what did you say to that?"

"Why, what was there to say? I couldn't say a thing. I just left the confessional, and gave up, and, yes, said I'd have the surgery anyway. But it doesn't mean much to me, not much of anything. Because I won't be what I needed to be."

"Whoa there, wait a minute," said Liz again. "Let me get this straight. A priest told you that not just miraculously cured women were miracle women—but any woman who saw the return of the Virgin Mary, she'd be a miracle woman for life, also?"

"Yes, the biggest kind of miracle woman."

Dummy, Liz thought, you dummy. "Edith," she said softly, "suppose you were the one to see the Virgin Mary in the grotto today. Then you'd be a miracle woman again."

"Why, yes I would," Edith admitted haltingly. "But what good is all that? Suppose I don't see Her—I probably won't be the one to see the Virgin—and if I don't see Her . . ."

Liz leaned forward, closer to Edith, glaring at her, and she whispered fiercely, "Edith—"

"Yes?"

"—see Her."

Edith stared back at Liz, kept staring at her as she pushed herself to her feet.

She sought the restaurant door, cast Liz one last frightened glance, and then trying to run, limping and running, she plunged out the door and away.

Liz remained seated for many minutes in silence, in thought, and finally she ordered another Scotch, whether as a celebration or a suicide she did not know.

Twenty minutes later, Reggie came frantically into the room.

"Miss Finch, where's my wife? They're phoning from the hospital. She told you about the surgery—? I can see she told you. I suspected she would. Anyway, they need her at the hospital. They want to go ahead with the surgery now instead of tonight. Where's Edith?"

"She left here some time ago," said Liz. "Maybe she went to the hospital. But my guess is the grotto would be a better place to look. Come on, let's go down there together and see if we can find her."

The three of them were sitting, unrelaxed and nervous, in the special visitor's waiting cubicle on the same floor as the surgical room. To Liz Finch the cubicle had a unique smell, as if medically scrubbed and overly clean.

Liz sat hunched in a chair, chain-smoking, and from time to time fixing her attention on Amanda and Reggie propped more stiffly on the divan on the other side of the coffee table. Some hospital boy in a white jacket had served them all coffee a while ago. Except for one taste of her cup—French coffee, ugh—Liz had left her coffee untouched. Amanda drank distractedly, flipping the pages of a French fashion magazine, apparently paying them little heed yet trying to take her mind off what might be happening to Ken in the operating room. Reggie numbly drank his coffee, between puffs of his cigar, and appeared deeply distraught, fearful, constantly searching off through the doorway into the hall, waiting for some hopeful word, some good word on his Edith. It occurred to Liz as it had not before that this crude promoter, for all his bluff, might have a heart, might be hurting, and that he truly loved his old girl on the surgical table down the hall.

Liz squeezed her eyes to make out the hands on her wristwatch, the kind of watch that looks great but that you can rarely read. She was barely able to read the time now, but once she did, she calculated that they had already been watchfully waiting here exactly four hours and fourteen minutes, fast becoming an eternity.

Each of them, Liz realized, had so much at stake, so very much, on those cuttings and implantings down the hall. Reggie and Amanda, in this terrible holding pattern, had their mates and their own lives on the line. Maybe Liz had less at stake, but it was a considerable hope and by some means it was her life, too. Why Liz's life was at stake could not so easily be defined, but her hope involved what she and Reggie had found when they had hastened out of the restaurant to the grotto to learn if Reggie's ex-miracle woman was there.

Liz's memory spun backward to her arrival at the grotto with Reggie. There had been a mass of people, a great press of people, this being the last and eighth day of the time span the Virgin Mary had allocated for her reappearance. It had been difficult to find Edith in this crowd of religious fanatics. But after a few minutes they had found her, and Liz had been oddly relieved that Edith was there.

Liz had not been able to banish from her mind what had happened next. Edith had been found on her knees, rigid, not many yards from the edge of the grotto, gazing glassily upward at the statue of the Virgin in the niche. Reggie had tapped his wife on the shoulder, and started to speak to her, informing her that she was expected at the hospital and must leave now. But Edith had shown no reaction whatsoever. She had been as unresponsive as if carved out of stone. Reggie had continued to implore her to leave, but had received no acknowledgment that she heard him. When Reggie, in his desperation, had looked to Liz for help, she had pushed forward to assist him. But one glance told Liz that Edith was in some kind of catatonic state, in a trance at least, and would be difficult to move by ordinary means. Terrified by his wife's condition, Reggie had dashed off toward the bathhouses to seek help. In a few minutes he had returned with two sturdy older Frenchmen, both veteran brancardiers, one of them carrying a stretcher. They had lifted Edith off the ground like a baby, with some trouble had straightened her out on the stretcher, and had carried her to the domain ambulance which had sped her to the hospital.

Liz and Reggie had followed in a taxi, Liz wondering, Reggie worrying, all the way. In the hospital they had been shown to the waiting room, there to find Amanda already present.

After ten minutes, that angel in white uniform, Esther, had materialized to soothe Reggie.

"Is she all right? Can she be operated on now?" Reggie had begged to know.

Esther had reassured him. "Mrs. Moore was in a self-hypnotic state, but she came out of it when we brought her in. Dr. Duval examined her and found all her vital signs normal. He pronounced her quite ready for surgery, and she is being prepped this minute and will be wheeled into surgery the instant they are through with Mr. Clayton. Please sit down and try to keep calm. I should have word for you, Mr. Moore, and you, Mrs. Clayton in—well, I can't say exactly—perhaps in three or four hours. Just know your loved ones are in the best of hands."

That had been four hours or so ago, and by now four hours and fourteen minutes had passed, without a word from surgery.

They waited and they waited, the three of them, in the cramped room filled with the haze of smoke and the hanging suspense.

Suddenly, the attention of all three was drawn to the open doorway. For a fourth person was in the waiting room. It was that other white lady this Reappearance Time. It was Dr. Kleinberg's nurse, Esther, once more.

And there was a broad smile on the nurse's face.

"Dr. Kleinberg will be here any moment," she announced. "I'm sorry I could not leave his side earlier, but now that the surgeries are over, he did not want to lose a moment to have you informed—you Mrs. Clayton, you Mr. Moore—that the operations and implants by Dr. Duval are concluded and promise to be a wonderful success. No complications whatsoever. Both patients are resting comfortably. Dr. Duval foresees a complete recovery for each."

Amanda had lost her poise and was weeping as she staggered to her feet and ran across the room to throw her arms around Esther. Reggie was right behind, gripping the nurse's hand fervently and hoarsely voicing his thanks.

After Esther had settled them down, she peered back into the hall and added, "I can see Dr. Kleinberg on his way here. He'll have more to tell you."

Esther disappeared, only to be replaced by a weary Dr. Kleinberg, his surgical mask dangling from his neck.

He offered a tired smile, but a smile all the same, and he said to Amanda and Reggie, "You heard the news from Esther. The surgery on both patients looks like a complete success, and the gene-replacement implants were made with perfection." He directed himself to Amanda now. "Dr. Duval asked me to quote him as stating that you and Mr. Ken Clayton will be on that delayed honeymoon in no more than a month or two from now."

As Amanda once more wept tears of joy, Dr. Kleinberg faced Reggie, signaling for Liz to join him, and Liz sprang to her feet and was beside him immediately. "This is for both of you," Dr. Kleinberg said, "but for Reggie first. As I was able to tell Amanda that the operation and implant on Ken promised to be a success, I can tell you the very same about your Edith. She should be healthy, and able to return to normal activity in two months, perhaps less."

As Reggie, sniffling, began to thank him, Dr. Kleinberg held up his hand. "There is more about Edith, and this is for you, too, Miss Finch. After Edith's incision was sutured, and after she came out from under the anesthetic, an unexpected and really extraordinary thing happened. She opened her eyes and tried to speak to us—Dr. Duval and I were there together—and finally she did speak to us in whispers, but words that were clear and articulate—she said, 'Tell Reggie—tell him I saw the Virgin Mary in the grotto before I came here—I saw Her plainly, just as Bernadette had described Her—She reappeared above me and She spoke to me—She promised I would be healed and said that I should know that science is compatible with faith and, well—and—' When Dr. Duval begged Edith not to speak anymore, to rest, she visibly shook her head on the table, and said weakly but clearly, 'No, there is more. Tell Liz Finch—be sure to tell her, too, that the Blessed Virgin reappeared to me—tell her I'm a miracle woman again, and, Dr. Kleinberg, tell her all I've said, and yes, tell Liz thanks, many thanks.' " Dr. Kleinberg threw up his hands. "There you have Edith's entire message. Extraordinary, isn't it, her having seen the Virgin? And rather enigmatic, Miss Finch, the last of her message to you." Dr. Kleinberg gave Liz a quizzical look. "Now what on earth would she have to thank you for?"

But Liz knew.

"I'm the one who should thank her," Liz sang out happily. "Be sure to tell her that when she awakens again."

And Liz spun around and was running up the hospital hall as fast as her legs could carry her.

In Paris . . .

Bill Trask, in his glassed-in API managing editor's office above the Rue des Italiens, concentrating on the copy piled on one side of his desk, was distracted by the jangling of the telephone at his elbow and absently picked up the receiver.

The call was from Liz Finch in Lourdes.

"You've got a story?" Trask repeated. "Let me turn on the tape."

"A good one, Bill. I think the one you wanted."

"Hope so."

"The Virgin Mary kept her word to Bernadette. The Blessed Virgin, as the Church refers to her, materialized at the holy grotto, as an apparition, and one person saw her, a middle-aged British woman from London. A woman named Edith Moore, a married woman. The Virgin and Mrs. Moore even had a brief conversation."

"Authentic?"

"As much as any previous visions that have been accepted by the Church. This Mrs. Moore is no fruitcake. She's the solid-citizen type."

"And she saw the reappearance of the Virgin Mary? Great. Just what the doctor ordered."

"The doctor, yeah," said Liz. "But there's more, and that's what makes the story better."

"Go on."

"Three years ago this Mrs. Moore became very sick, and found out she had cancer, sarcoma of the hip. The medicos gave her up. She was an on-again, off-again Catholic, so clutching for a straw, she went to Lourdes for a cure. First time here—prayers at the grotto, drinking the spring water, taking curative baths, marching in the torchlight procession—nothing worked. So she came back here the next year, and on her last day after a bath she was instantly cured. She went through the medical routine, went the ecclesiastical route, and was coming nearer and nearer to being officially declared miraculously cured. A big honor, being on the roster, a miracle woman. Then something went wrong. Far as I can find out, it's never happened like this before."

Trask was becoming more interested. "What went wrong?"

"She was summoned to Lourdes this week to undergo one final examination by a Paris specialist in her disorder. He examined her and found that the tumor, the malignancy, was back again and beginning to spread. Awful blow for the woman. No more miracle woman. No more glory. Then she found out that there was another French surgeon who had been experimenting successfully in gene replacement or genetic engineering on test animals, and he was ready to try this treatment on Mrs. Moore."

"The French surgeon's name?"

"Can't use it, Bill. He ignored the medical chain of command to do this. He'd get in a lot of trouble if his name was publicized."

Trask, an opponent of anonymity, snorted. "You've got to be kidding. I'll make him the most famous French doctor since Louis Pasteur, for god's sake. They won't be able to touch him. Liz, you don't honestly think you can keep a lid on this, do you? Come on, give."

She held her breath for a moment, then said, "All right, but you didn't get it from me."

"Relax. You won't be the only source on this and you know it. Listen, Dr.—what's his name?"

"Duval. Maurice Duval from Paris."

"Dr. Duval will be the first to thank you when he gets back from Stockholm. Don't worry. Now, what else?"

"Just before her surgery in Lourdes, Mrs. Moore hobbled over to the grotto for one more prayer session, as usual invoking the good offices of the Virgin Mary. When the hospital wanted her in surgery, her husband and I set out to look for her. We found her on her knees at the grotto in a trance, almost catatonic, and she had to be carried away on a stretcher and taken to the hospital. There she came out of her trance, and was wheeled into surgery. I was in the waiting room while the surgery took place. After four and a half hours the word came out. The surgery on Mrs. Moore had been successful. She had gained her life but lost her miracle woman status. And then—hear this, boss—coming out of surgery, she blurted out that at the grotto the Virgin Mary had reappeared before her, promised that she would be cured, reassured her that science was compatible with faith—"

"Say, that's a new angle. This could be a super story. Does the entire press gang out your way have it?"

"Bill, I have it all alone for twenty-four hours. An exclusive beat."

"Wonderful, wonderful! Do you want us to work from these notes, because if you do we'll need a few more—"

"No, Bill, I've got the entire story in my mitt—everything from the Virgin Mary's latest fashion outfit to the name of the hospital, and so forth. I'm ready to read it to you. About a thousand words. You want me to go?"

"The machine's on. Go."

Liz's monotone read the story of the new miracle woman and Trask's recorder transcribed it.

When Liz concluded, she said, "Thirty. Okay, that's it."

"Congratulations, Liz. You've got a real winner there."

"I have more details, but that can wait for when I get back. I knew Mrs. Moore a little, you see, and I actually interviewed her before all this. I could do a follow-up color feature story once I'm in the office again." She paused. "If I *am* in the office?"

It was infrequent that evidence of pleasure ever marred Trask's constant scowl that came with his job. But now he sent the scowl off. "You have news for me, Liz, and I have news for you. I've been holding it back to see if you'd deliver. You delivered in spades, I assure you. Okay, my news. It was to be you or Marguerite, so spake the home office, and they left it to me to decide. Admittedly, Marguerite had the inside track, the juicier assignment. André Viron, possibly our next Stavisky, right? Well, Marguerite handed in her story yesterday. It read like a crummy publicity release. I knew she could do better, had done better, and wanted to know what happened. She's spent enough time with Viron, God knows. She played it close to the chest, until I backed her against the wall, roughed her up, so to speak. She finally confessed that there was more to the story. She'd gotten close to Viron—read that to mean bedded down with him—and got plenty of material. But she'd also fallen in love with the bastard, and didn't want to hurt him, wanted to go on having a relationship with him. So she couldn't give me the real thing, just wouldn't. I really chewed her out. I told her that was the pits of unprofessionalism. The story always came first. I told her if she held back she was fired. She held back. So I fired her. Sorry to. She had a nice ass, and a fair way with words. But she wasn't the reporter I wanted." Trask punctuated with a pause, then resumed. "But you are the reporter I want. You're a pro. You've got the job and you'll have a nice hike in salary. Oh, hell, you'd have had the job over her anyway, after cranking out the story you just did. Okay?"

He heard Liz crying on the other end of the line.

"Th—thanks, boss," she choked.

"Okay, miracle woman. Come home. Want to see you at your desk by nine tomorrow morning. Be on time and get right to work. No room for prima donnas round here."

In Moscow . . .

After the Aeroflot passenger jet from Paris to Moscow landed smoothly on the runway of Vnukovo airport, and taxied along till it reached the turnoff to the air terminal, the arrival in Moscow was announced over the loudspeaker. Unbuckling his seat belt, a clean-shaven Sergei Tikhanov took up his flight bag and was the first in the aisle for disembarkation.

Standing there, he reflected briefly once more on his flight from Lourdes. It had been a harrowing escape. After leaving behind the corpse of Gisele Dupree, he had worried that he might have been seen. Then he had worried, before checking out of the hotel in Lourdes, whether he would be able to get a place on the next flight to Paris. Luck was with him, Tikhanov learned. Everyone was coming to Lourdes, few people were leaving, and there was no trouble about a reservation. At the airport, early, he had worried that the police would get on to Samuel Talley before he was airborne.

But there had been no problem, and soon he was on Air Inter, and an hour and fifteen minutes later he had been put down at Orly. First thing, before going to the men's room, he had telephoned the Soviet Embassy, identified himself, and requested that a car be sent for him. Immediately after that, he had gone into the men's room of the airport, shut himself into a toilet, removed and discarded his hateful Lourdian mustache, then washed his worn face until Talley had been toweled away forever and the renowned Sergei Tikhanov had once more been restored.

In the Soviet Embassy, he had holed up for two days to establish a record of meetings and activity. The second day, he had learned two things. Reading *France-Soir*, he had come across a brief bit of reportage datelined Lourdes. A minor bit of violence during the holy week. The body of a well-known local, an agency tourist guide, Gisele Dupree, had been found in a friend's apartment, strangled. Plainly murder. No suspects. Ah, no suspects. How could there be? Samuel Talley no longer existed. Three hours later Tikhanov had learned a second piece of news. Premier Skryabin had died while in his coma. The Politburo was discussing a successor. Then followed a call from Moscow, from KGB chief, General Kossoff, advising him to wind up his affairs as quickly as possible and summoning him to Moscow no later than the following day.

And now Tikhanov was in Moscow's Vnukovo airport, the VIP airport.

And now he was disembarking from the plane with twinges of pain, not master of his muscular dystrophy and his mortality, but certainly arriving as master of the Union of Soviet Socialist Republics, and assured to be at his nation's helm and a world leader for at least two or three years.

Descending, he could see that his subordinates, soon to be his subordinates and do his bidding, had figuratively laid out the red carpet for his arrival. They were bunched together at the foot of the ladder waiting to welcome him.

He found himself surrounded by well-wishers, receiving kisses from that garlic-smelling brute, General Kossoff, from his old friend United Nations ambassador Alexei Izakov, and handshakes from several KGB officers.

Once through the bustling terminal, ordinary passengers making way and awed to have a glimpse of him, Tikhanov climbed into the luxurious rear seat of the black Chaika limousine. Within a minute they were off, preceded and followed by white police cars to Moscow and Tikhanov's seat of power, the Kremlin.

Throughout the half-hour drive, Kossoff kept pouring vodkas for the three of them from the backseat bar and telling coarse jokes about ballerinas. Tikhanov accommodated the KGB chief with restrained bursts of laughter, but he only wanted to know about the premiership and his immediate future. Once, he managed to wedge in a question about that. Kossoff, showing no mood for politics or business, simply said, "The Politburo has been meeting the entire afternoon. A verdict is promised by the evening. The verdict is a foregone conclusion."

Tikhanov had felt easier after that, and enjoyed another vodka as he endured yet another one of General Kossoff's interminable and boring stories. Tikhanov wondered if he would have to endure Kossoff's company after he had been made premier. Perhaps he would replace Kossoff. He would see about that.

Suddenly, he was aware that the limousine had slowed, and was stopping. Tikhanov thought that they had halted for a red light, and was surprised that the limousine had pulled up at the curb beside a white brick building, a building in a suburb of Moscow and unidentified.

Kossoff was pushing open the car door. "Come on with me, Ambassador Izakov, and you too, Sergei. Have a look around. The minister of internal affairs has something he wants me to do here, before going on to the Kremlin."

Dutifully, Tikhanov followed Kossoff inside the building, through a glass-paneled door. Going to the entrance, Tikhanov had caught a glimpse of a high whitewashed brick wall, topped by barbed wire, running around the side and back of the building. At the far end, he had seen an armed guard with an automatic weapon.

Inside the reception room—the barest he had been in for many years, a wooden bench, no tables, another door to the interior of the building—Tikhanov found three men on hand to greet them. Kossoff's introductions were hasty and slurred, and Tikhanov could only make out the titles of the three—one a director, one a lieutenant-colonel, one a major.

Tugging at General Kossoff's sleeve, Tikhanov was curious to know where they were. "What is this place?" Tikhanov wanted to know.

"Your home," said General Kossoff.

Carrying his briefcase, Kossoff stepped over to the bench, set it down, and opened it. Completely at sea, Tikhanov followed him.

"What did you say?" asked Tikhanov.

Ignoring him, Kossoff pulled a large envelope out of the briefcase, and removed a smaller envelope and several pages from it. Opening the smaller envelope, Kossoff took out what appeared to be a photograph.

He handed the snapshot to Tikhanov. "A souvenir for you of your holiday."

The instant he took the photograph in his hand, Tikhanov had a premonition of disaster. His eyes held on the photograph. It was a print of one of the snapshots of him taken near the grotto in Lourdes by that little French cunt Gisele. Tikhanov could feel his eyes burning in his skull and his dry mouth falling open. When he raised his head, Kossoff was out of focus, and the barren room was revolving, going round and round. To keep himself from fainting, he clutched the back of the bench.

"But how—?" he managed to gasp.

"Comrade Tikhanov, you deserve an explanation," the KGB head was saying. "Your young French victim was clever, more clever than you. She understood the danger of blackmail, and what you might have at stake. While she did possess a weapon to protect herself, she was too eager and naïve to have it ready. But she was not naïve in one respect. If you proved untrustworthy, she would have her revenge. The morning you met her, before your arrival, she had posted an extra copy of the snapshot she had taken of you at the Catholic shrine in Lourdes—that and a letter about one Samuel Talley—to an important Frenchman who had once employed her. She had posted all of this in a large sealed envelope, along with a cover letter, and sent it to the French ambassador to the United Nations, Charles Sarrat, who was in Paris. She had advised him that if he read in the Parisian press about any harm befalling her, he should then, and only then, turn over the envelope to the Soviet ambassador to France at the Soviet Embassy in Paris. As we all know, great harm did befall Miss Dupree. It appeared, the report of her murder did, as a short squib in most of the Paris papers. Naturally, Ambassador Sarrat read it, and following instructions, he turned the envelope over to our Soviet Embassy, which in turn promptly passed it on by courier to Moscow."

"But—"

General Kossoff would not listen. He was implacable. "Once the contents of the envelope sent by your young French lady were studied, the MVD convened a hearing at the Ministry of the Interior. You were heard, or tried, if you will, in absentia. A vote was taken, a decision reached, and I must tell you that it was unanimous. Because of your unthinkable escapade, your jurors determined you to be of unsound mind and too mentally unstable to any longer serve in any official capacity in the Soviet Union."

"I was ill, I was desperate—"

"We know about your illness, about the muscular dystrophy. We conducted a full investigation before the hearing. But any Soviet citizen of sound mind, especially one in high office, would have turned himself over to our medical specialists, physicians who are the envy of even our capitalist enemies. But only a man of defective mentality, deranged, unbalanced, even mad, would have considered doing and have actually done what it is now known that you did—travel to that sink of iniquity, Lourdes, that Christian shrine packed with idiots and drugged malcontents—there to grovel on your knees before a cave in a mountain, waiting for the appearance of a vaporous mother figure, a charlatan who allegedly performs cures and miracles. Therefore, you were sentenced to be confined to this place.

"What is this, you wanted to know? This is SPH 15—Special Psychiatric Hospital 15, at the outskirts of Moscow. You have been sentenced to spend the remainder of your life within these walls. These three gentlemen—the director of the facility, the colonel and chief psychiatrist, the major and head warder—will be in charge of your treatments and care for you for the rest of your days." General Kossoff snapped his briefcase shut. "Yet, out of respect for your long service to the State and the Party, you will be given a few advantages. While you will be confined to a cell, of course, a cell six meters square that normally holds two patients, you will be allowed to inhabit the cell by yourself. And for recreation, you will be permitted to read—thanks to the thoughtfulness of our UN ambassador—a new book that has been published in New York. You will find it on your bunk. The title is *Bernadette and Mary*. You will also find a rosary with which to while away the extra hours. Have a good long life, Comrade Tikhanov, and good-bye."

In Venice . . .

They had arrived in Venice just as the sun was dipping below the coast of the mainland, and their launch from Marco Polo Airfield had carried them skimming along the placid blue lagoon and up the short canal that led to the water entrance of the Hotel Danieli.

Mikel Hurtado had never been to Venice before and was dazzled and subdued by the beauty of the place, but Natale was animated as she had never been before by the opportunity to see this glorious city, this colorful carnival, once again.

After registering, they had rushed up to their second-floor room overlooking the blue lagoon and the Isle of San Giorgio shimmering with illumination in this early part of the evening.

There was a single telephone, and Hurtado wanted Natale to use it first. She had put through a long-distance call to her parents' shop in Rome, hoping to catch her mother and father before they had left for the day. But only Aunt Elsa had been there to close up the shop. The elder Rinaldis had gone off to dinner. And so, with difficulty in modulating her voice, in containing her thrill, Natale had spilled it all out to her dear Aunt Elsa—the miracle of seeing the apparition of the Virgin Mary at the grotto, of *seeing* Her—yes, Aunt Elsa, yes, yes, yes, I can *see* again, my sight is restored. An ophthalmologist in Milan had confirmed the inexplicable restoration of her sight two hours ago. There had been a high-pitched exchange in Italian back and forth, an uncontrollable torrent of words from both ends. At last Aunt Elsa was shutting the shop early, hastening out to locate Natale's parents at dinner, to inform them of the exquisite news. Natale had cautioned that no one must ever know, beyond her three relatives, exactly how Natale's cure had come about. Aunt Elsa had pledged her word. Natale had promised to telephone her parents at home later that evening and had promised to return to Rome—with a surprise guest—in two days.

Now it was Hurtado who was on the phone, speaking to Augustin Lopez in San Sebastián.

"I am glad you were not headstrong, young man," Lopez was saying. "I'm glad that you heeded my word and did the grotto no violence."

"I decided against it, after hearing from you."

"And a good thing, too, Mikel, you will agree. For the word is out everywhere in the city, on television, and radio, that the Virgin did make her appearance as she promised and she did perform some kind of wonder for a British woman pilgrim."

"Yes, I heard of that."

"Now, Mikel, you will be gratified to hear more, the results of our patience and trust. Not a half hour ago I had a call from Madrid. From old Minister Bueno himself. He was filled with the news, filled with religion, and absolutely euphoric about the miracle at Lourdes. He had made a promise, and he was ready to keep it. He wanted to arrange for a series of meetings in Madrid. He indicated that there would be an acceptable compromise, a compromise and settlement that every Basque would find agreeable. I believe we've won, Mikel. How's that?"

"That's great. Congratulations."

"When will you be coming home?"

"One day soon. I'll have someone with me. No questions. You will see for yourself. And tell my mother I'll be phoning her tomorrow. Good luck, Augustin. God go with you."

Descending the marble staircases to the Danieli lobby, Natale was pleased to note that Hurtado's limp had disappeared. "Faith," he explained cheerfully. Leaving the lobby, they made their plans for the balmy evening.

First to the Basilica of San Marco to offer up thanks for their resurrection.

Next to Quadri's café for camparis.

Then to Harry's Bar for *piccata di vitello*.

Then a gondola ride up the Grand Canal.

Then back to the Danieli to make love.

"And after that?" asked Natale.

"To Rome, to keep company with a young woman I know, and to write a play for a young actress I love."

"Who's this young actress?"

"Who do you think?"

"If you're speaking of Miss Rinaldi, she accepts the role even before you write it. You will write it, Mikel?"

"I'll write it."

"I'll star in it." She smiled at him. "And after that, Mikel?"

"I want to give you babies, a whole bunch of bambinos, our babies."

"Not unless you marry me, Mikel. Will you marry me?"

"Do you think I want children out of wedlock? You'll be the most married woman in history forever."

"And ever," she said.

Hand in hand, they walked on happily into the Piazza San Marco.

In Vatican City . . .

His Holiness, the Supreme Pontiff, Pope John Paul III, successor to the throne of St. Peter, still clad in the white-linen cassock, white skullcap, heavy gold pectoral cross dangling from the gold chain around his neck, slowly entered his bedroom, the favorite of the eighteen rooms of his private apartment, among the 10,000 rooms, chambers, halls of the Apostolic Palace.

Moving slowly across the Afghan rug toward the wooden shutters covering the two corner windows of this top floor, he meant to peer through the shutters down upon the vast St. Peter's Square below. His mind was on the news transmitted to him at dinner, and what had been transmitted to the world and its 740,000,000 Catholics, its one million nuns, its half million priests, its 4,000 bishops and cardinals. Surely tonight was the high moment of his entire pontificate.

Suddenly, in his profound joy, he was eager to commune with God.

He circled away from the window shutters, and shuffled toward his brass bed. Neatly folded on the bed covering was his white nightshirt. Above the bedposts was the touching painting of Christ in agony on the Cross.

On the bedstand were his electric clock with its Roman numerals and the worn Bible he had received at his first Holy Communion. By habit he checked the clock's alarm, was satisfied it was set for six-thirty in the morning, and then he sauntered, almost buoyantly, to the priedieu, his kneeling bench. Hanging over it, on the pastel linen wallpaper, were two objects, a simple crucifix and a delicate painting of the Virgin Mary in a thin gold frame.

The Pope stood silently gazing at the Virgin Mary, and gradually he lowered himself to his knees on the embroidered and padded priedieu.

Tired though he was, he felt renewed strength flowing through his aged body at the glad tidings that he had heard throughout the evening.

He placed the tips of his wrinkled fingers together in prayer and shut his eyes.

To begin with, a favorite passage from his beloved St. Mark. The Pope's lips moved as he recited the passage barely above a whisper.

"In My name shall they cast out devils; they shall speak with new tongues; they shall take up serpents; and if they drink any deadly thing, it shall not hurt them; they shall lay hands on the sick, and they shall recover."

His Holiness held his breath and resumed.

"O Lord in Heaven, hallowed be Thy name. As Thy vicar on earth and successor to St. Peter, I thank Thee for Thy goodness, for the return of the Immaculate Conception, and the reaffirmation that Thy miracles shall never cease. As long as Thee will permit it, there will be humanity on earth and belief, and there will remain goodness and hope —and there will continue to be miracles unto eternity, and we dedicate our grateful love to Thee Father, and to Thy Son, and to the Holy Ghost.

"Amen."

In Paris . . .

Late at night, not ten minutes before midnight, a weary and disheveled Liz Finch stepped out of the elevator at the API editorial rooms and dragged herself across the floor.

Liz could see that the night shift was already on, and the lone survivor of the day shift, Bill Trask, was still hunched over his desk inside his glassed-in cubicle.

She opened Trask's door, stepped inside, closed it, and leaned back against it. The sound brought Trask's head up, and he saw Liz Finch.

He swung his swivel chair in her direction. "Hello, Liz. When did you get in?"

"Just now. Air Inter from Lourdes."

"Why didn't you go straight home and get yourself some shut-eye?"

"Dunno, reporter's blood," said Liz. "Can't stay away. Actually, only wanted to look in for a minute to—to say in person thanks for the job, boss. Wanted to tell you again. Thanks."

Trask snorted. "You earned it, kid. I'm receiving reports. Your story is hitting big all over the world, getting top play everywhere."

"Super."

"I mean, what is it, after all? A terrific ghost story with a first-rate heroine and a happy ending. What more could anyone ask for?" Trask rattled some papers on his desk. "In fact this very minute, the minute you walked in, I was rereading the printout for maybe the tenth time. Helluva piece." He shook his head. "Imagine the Church sticking its neck out like that and coming up roses? Gutsy—or maybe unrealistic. Whatever. The Virgin Mary is going to reappear, and lo! she reappears, and Edith Moore of London sees her. Really, it's remarkable, an event without parallel in my time. But—" Trask hung out the word, and was momentarily lost in thought.

"But what, boss?" Liz prompted him.

"I was just thinking about something when you walked in."

"Thinking what, boss?"

"Wondering something. Liz, do you think—I keep wondering—did someone really see the Virgin Mary today?"

Liz gave a short shrug. "Did Bernadette?" she asked.

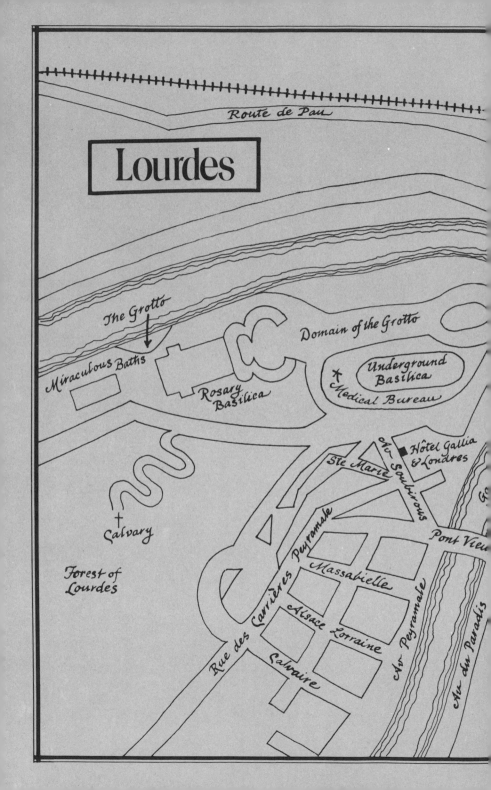